The screen door squeaked. ⌇d
body covered. The husband ⌇ ⌇d
wife's gold beaded purse clutched to his belly.

"It's the jinx," Sophie uttered in a low voice, her turquoise gauze skirt swishing as she turned, the summer colors and gently folded material so terribly out of place amidst the disaster. "God help us," she said. "We have another spirit."

"Stow it, Sophie," Police Chief Seabrook said with a fatherly chastisement, though the yoga instructor was two years his senior.

She stuck out her chin, undeterred. "I know what I'm talking about. I've lived here much longer than you, Mike. They visit me. Move my things. God help them all, but they're occupying my house!"

Sophie's metaphysical rants kept Edisto natives entertained most days, but on occasion, a hint of reality gave substance to her beliefs. Callie had adapted to Sophie's oddball view of humanity and her way of being right about human behavior in spite of her naiveté.

Callie frowned. "So your house is haunted?"

Sophie's long earrings brushed across her collarbone. "No, the beach. The deaths happened in several houses and along the water. All within a five-block radius of here." She rubbed the porch railing. "I keep telling you people that there's another world with a conduit to ours. Some spirit's pissed, and it rears its head every August, disrupting other souls with it."

Seabrook blew out hard. "We don't need your hoodoo right now, and neither does this crowd. Neither does the tourism of Edisto Beach, so collect your Tarot cards and keep your soothsaying to yourself, please. We'll interview you and let you go home earlier than the others. That suit you?"

She struck a pose. "I pay attention to the signs of the universe, and if you don't, you'll experience more of this," she said, swinging her other arm wide. "I'm a voice delivering the messages y'all can't hear."

Callie headed to the door. "We hear you."

Praise for *Edisto Jinx* and C. Hope Clark

Edisto Jinx has everything you want in a good island read: sand, food, drinks, people you care about, beautiful sunsets, secrets, murder, and page-turning suspense. C. Hope Clark took me to one of the most unspoiled South Carolina islands and gave me plenty of reasons to want to stay with Callie Morgan and a richly drawn cast of beach-town regulars. Pull up a beach chair, dip your toes in the gentle waves, and enjoy!
—Cathy Pickens, author of the *Southern Fried* mysteries and *Charleston Mysteries: Ghostly Haunts in the Holy City*

Edisto Jinx is a phenomenal read from beginning to end. The psychological twists are as intriguing as the vivid imagery of Ms. Clark's writing. From characters with just the right amount of flaws to make them realistic, to the eerie peek into a madman's mind, it is a gem of a story I didn't want to end.
—Sharon Sala, author of *Cold Hearts*, book two of the *Secrets and Lies* trilogy. August 2015 from Mira Books

Hope Clark has created another fascinating heroine in former Boston PD detective Callie Morgan. *Edisto Jinx* is a fast-paced mystery set against the backdrop of a tiny South Carolina island where murder never happens—or so the locals would like to believe. I'm happy to recommend it.
—Kathryn R. Wall, author, the *Bay Tanner* mysteries

A sparkling Edisto Island setting, a flawed heroine, a riveting mystery, and the hint of a paranormal twist makes *Edisto Jinx* THE book for your beach bag. Author C. Hope Clark brings to life the uniqueness that is Edisto, peppering the island with endearing and strong-minded characters that linger in your mind long after the last page is turned. Can't wait to revisit them in the next book in the Edisto Island Mystery series!
—Karen White, *New York Times* bestselling author

You can never go wrong with a book by C. Hope Clark. Honest, straightforward writing. Trust her ability to seamlessly take you wherever her story goes. This story's main character is perfectly flawed. You will be in Callie Jean Morgan's corner.

—G. M. Barlean, author of *Casting Stones* and *Recipes For Revenge*

Those who haven't read any of C. Hope Clark's books are short-changing themselves. You can't begin a . Hope Clark book and then put it down. Two-time Killer Nashville Silver Falchion Award nominee this year alone (for *Murder on Edisto* and *Palmetto Poison*).
—Clay Stafford, Killer Nashville Noir

The Novels of C. Hope Clark

The Carolina Slade Mysteries

Lowcountry Bribe

Tidewater Murder

Palmetto Poison

The Edisto Island Mysteries

Murder on Edisto

Edisto Jinx

Echoes of Edisto

Edisto Stranger
(Coming 2017)

Edisto Jinx

Book Two: The Edisto Island Mysteries

by

C. Hope Clark

Bell Bridge Books

Bell Bridge Books
PO BOX 300921
Memphis, TN 38130
Print ISBN: 978-1-61194-665-9

Bell Bridge Books is an Imprint of BelleBooks, Inc.

We at BelleBooks enjoy hearing from readers.
Visit our websites
BelleBooks.com
BellBridgeBooks.com
ImaJinnBooks.com

10 9 8 7 6 5 4 3 2 1

Cover design: Deborah Smith & Debra Dixon
Interior design: Hank Smith
Photo/Art credits:
Beach (manipulated) © Jon Bilous | Dreamstime.com

:Ljed:01:

Dedication

To Mayor Burley L. Lyons, a truly devoted son of Edisto Beach
who fought for our beach's character.
12/14/34 to 1/28/15

Chapter 1

CALLIE STUDIED ALL the tanned visitors with drinks in their hands. The last time she attended a beach house party she killed the host, earning somewhat of a reputation in the South Carolina community of Edisto Beach. Even two-years resigned from Boston PD, thank God, her instincts had served her well.

But instincts don't chase away nightmares.

This Saturday afternoon soiree served to capture the interest of both outgoing and incoming beach vacationers, per the leaflet in her mailbox. Typical of a South Carolina August, the sun blazed, the air-conditioning on high. Wainwright Realty's party aimed to keep the attendees indoors, fed, liquored, and appreciative enough to send business its way.

"Oh wow, you live here on Edisto? How lucky is that?" The late-thirties brunette stretched out her hand to Callie. "My name's Brea Jamison, by the way. I teach third grade in Raleigh. My husband and I are visiting my aunt for a week." She playfully scrunched her nose. "Hey, I could almost be your twin."

Callie accepted the light grip from the equally petite woman. "Callie Jean Morgan. Yeah, some might call it lucky." She shifted places in the beach house kitchen to let the woman fill her glass with ice. With their light build, dark shoulder-length hair, and tiny noses, they did appear eerily alike. She always hated her nose.

Brea splashed gin over the ice. "Thanks. This is a pretty rocking party."

Though close in age, Callie felt incredibly older than this teacher in a sandy-colored broom skirt and gold cotton tank, her tan smoother, probably enhanced with high-priced skin products Callie knew nothing about. Callie adjusted her periwinkle linen shirt covering a white tank, not exactly matching her khakis but not clashing either.

The teacher called her lucky. Funny. Luck had held no place in Callie's world for a long time. Her life seemed a combination of fate and what she scraped out of it.

After opening a bottle of tonic water, she topped the teacher's glass, then filled her own virgin version with a small sigh. She dropped in lime wedges and stirred both drinks, dodging temptation to lick the spoon. "Kids?"

The teacher's sparkle dimmed like a summer raincloud.

Callie recognized the emotional blow. "I'm sorry. Ignore that." Great, even polite social conversation felt like walking a minefield. Why did she come to this thing?

Brea smiled, her eyes still dulled with some hurt. "No, no, it's okay. It's just . . . we miscarried right before Christmas." She let herself frown a second, studying her glass. "You'd think I'd be over it by now."

"These things take time," Callie replied, using the phrase practiced so many times on her after the loss of six-month-old Bonnie. *God, I can't believe I said that.* Barely a day passed she didn't lift that baby blanket from its tissued home in her dresser drawer and inhale the memory.

The teacher ran a finger around the rim of her glass. "Grant and I hadn't planned to get pregnant at our ages, but we fell in love with the idea once it happened. Our baby girl came too early and lived two days." The ice cubes clinked as she swirled the glass's contents. She took a breath then seemed to flip a switch, regaining her former self. "But I'm being a wet blanket here. My apologies to you." She once again sparkled. "Do you have children?"

Callie's mind remained catatonic a moment with the image of Bonnie. "I . . . I have an eighteen-year-old son. He lives here on Edisto, too."

"Well, I'm jealous." She turned as more people poured into the kitchen. "I'm sure we'll chat later. Have fun!"

The crowd seemed to have doubled in the last half hour. Advertisements for the social had filled mailboxes in the blocks immediately around the host house, a rental managed by Wainwright Realty. An associate parked herself in the doorway, recording contact information with a death grip on her gold-covered guest book. The party was intended to bring strangers together to enjoy the ambiance of the community . . . and rebook their rental with Wainwright for the next year. Ten percent off.

Sophie, Callie's flamboyant New Age neighbor, had made it her mission to acclimate Callie into society and divorce her from a self-imposed seclusion after that last party fiasco. Right now, however, Sophie worked the room, seeking yoga clients as she bubbled with conversation near the rear door from the sound of her high-pitched voice.

Good, Sophie needed this. For the past ten days, Callie had listened to her neighbor's frequent frets about uneasy spirits. For a woman who claimed to be in tune with the spirit world, Sophie called every time she found an item in the wrong place or caught a whiff of an unidentified odor. Sophie's daddy had come to her in a dream two nights ago.

While Callie didn't mind being her new friend's sounding board, the middle-of-the-night phone calls were close to crossing the line. But Sophie had been unconditionally accepting of Callie since she'd arrived on Edisto two months ago with enough baggage to scare off a Catholic saint. Besides, Sophie apologized each and every time she called, assuring Callie the experiences peaked in August and eased off by Labor Day, taking life on the beach to Edi-slow time, when tenants and residents resumed their laid-back air.

Callie imagined lower temperatures and Sophie's kids returning to school did more to dim the craziness, but it didn't hurt to empathize with her friend's spiritual issues.

Callie scanned the crowd for anyone familiar. Folks always seemed prettier at a beach party, their fresh tans complementing the aquas, yellows, corals, and blues of their vacation clothing, sunglasses pushed on their heads or hanging in the front of their shirts. Coconut and banana scents drifted in the air, mingling with the smell of salt. Freed from old routines of home, folks pretended to be affluent, as if they lived this way instead of in an apartment in Detroit or the suburban ranch in Indianapolis.

Callie found a newly vacated spot on the end of a sofa and settled in. To wander through the clinging throng chatting with strangers held no pleasantry. She sipped her tonic once and rested it on her knee. She loved to people-watch, to read and play what-ifs about what folks really did with their lives.

Two boiled shrimp pinwheeled across the floor, slinging drops of cocktail sauce across Callie's toes. She wished she hadn't worn sandals in the slowed split seconds before a crash of glass and silverware jerked her around. Brea, the attractive little brunette she'd met not ten minutes earlier, lay sprawled amongst crab dip, melon balls, and Coke, clawing at her sunburned neck.

Callie dropped her glass on the coffee table and bolted toward the woman. Partiers already clustered tight around the convulsing body, frozen with helplessness.

"Give her space," Callie shouted, kneeling her capris-clad knees on the wooden floor. Dip slid off Brea's cheek as she fought for air. Callie tilted her head back and peered down her throat, searching for obstruction. Nothing. The girl's face, her neck, looked swollen. "Is there a doctor or nurse in here?"

"May I help?" An attractive fifty-ish man stooped beside her.

"Are you a doctor? Medic? Nurse?" Callie stroked the woman's cheek.

"No, I thought—"

Callie shook her head. "Then no. Please stand back." As she reached at the guy, emphasizing the need for him to move aside, her attention caught on a young man in an open shirt recording the incident on his phone. Fury flew through her. "You better be calling 911, you moron."

Callie's voice of authority served as a wave as the onlookers eased aside. The camera guy paled as Sophie appeared out of nowhere, snatched the phone, and punched in the numbers.

Brea's complexion took on a blue hue, her tiny body still writhing.

Doobie Brothers pulsed in the background. "Where's her husband? I think his name's Grant. And somebody turn off that damn music," Callie shouted over the throbbing beat of "China Grove." She turned to Sophie. "Get through?"

Sophie nodded.

"Put it on speaker." Callie raised Brea's eyelids, studying the empty gaze she didn't like. "Damn it." She reached to check for a pulse when someone knocked her off-balance to her butt.

"Brea!"

The music died. Silence draped across the room as Callie returned to her knees, a man in khaki shorts now blocking her way.

Callie gripped his shoulder and shook it once, recalling his name from the kitchen conversation. "Grant, is she allergic to anything? We've got 911 on the phone. Try to help us here."

Panic embedded so deeply in his face he seemed to age before her eyes. "Shellfish," he said urgently. "EpiPen's in her purse." He studied the floor, his glances darting. "Where is it?"

Oh crap. Seconds robbed this woman's chances. As she relayed information to the operator, Grant searched the floor around him then jumped to his feet. He panned the room, as if each guest sabotaged his wife. "Don't just stand there, hunt her purse!" He slung aside pillows on the sofa, shoved chairs. "It's gold with beads, small with a long chain."

Two women broke from the crowd to assist. Then the entire group awakened and scoured the place. Callie removed the speaker feature on the phone. "If they aren't quick, this woman won't make it."

"I understand," the operator replied. "Your name, please?"

Callie gave her the info and her address three blocks over. "I'm a former detective," she added, as if that made any difference in how fast help arrived. She once thought it did. The moniker felt impotent right now.

Returning the phone to its owner, Callie cursed her inability to open the woman's airways, angry no doctor was in the room. A doctor. She whirled and scrambled to the sofa. Digging out her own cell phone, she hit speed dial for Mike Seabrook, a former ER physician, currently the beach's acting police chief.

Voice mail. "Jesus, Mike, get over to the Wainwright party on Pompano. A woman needs medical help now! Seafood allergy. I called 911."

She hung up and returned to Brea, praying for improvement. She searched for a pulse once, twice. Barely a flutter. God Almighty. She brushed the hair from Brea's eyes.

Grant returned, red-faced and grief-stricken. "Can't find her purse. Nobody has a pen either." He stopped rambling and stared at Callie, waiting for an answer.

She threw her gaze around the room. "There's no damn EpiPen in here?" she shouted. People studied each other. A guy actually patted his pants pockets, as if searching for change. One couple slipped out the door.

Callie's anger flared, adrenaline pumping even as she stroked Brea's hair. Surely something could be done. Grant stooped down, frantic, whimpering. She asked, "You should have another pen at your rental house, right?"

"Yes, yes," Grant said, eager for an option. But he fixed on Brea, afraid to leave for a reason Callie clearly understood.

"Give me your keys," Callie ordered. "What house?"

He blindly fumbled in his pocket and gave her a lone key on a plastic tag. "The Rosewoods on Jungle Road."

Callie's eyes went wide. Sarah Rosewood was Brea's aunt? Callie knew them. They might even be home.

She grabbed the key but pulled out her phone, the Rosewood number already in her call list. The call went to voice mail. "Shit. I'll run and get it. I know the place."

Pained yet thankful, Grant nodded rapidly.

"Listen, an ambulance is coming." Callie felt the hollowness of her words, seeing he did as well. "Hold her. Talk to her. Tell her it'll be okay," she said in his ear, then bolted to the door. She yelled over her shoulder. "They'll be here any moment. I'll be right back."

He assumed Callie's place on the hardwood floor and cradled his wife's head in his lap. "I love you, I love you." His mantra continued into Brea's ear, half conversation to his bride, half prayer.

Feeling each second, Callie kicked off the sandals and made for the door. The lone gentleman who'd offered worthless help moments earlier teetered off balance as she bounced off him, but she had no time for apologies. The six-foot blonde woman held her arm in front of several others, offering a path. Callie bolted outside, down the stairs, and to the road. Two blocks over, one block down, she ran. Though she'd put in many a mile running along the water, she cursed at how slowly she covered the distance.

Taking two stairs at a time, she reached the residence. Hands shaking, she unlocked the front door, not caring if she startled anyone inside or not, and dashed inside. Nobody there. She raced to an empty guestroom, then down the hall to the other. There, on the dresser. She snatched the pen and headed outside, leaving the door wide open. The Rosewoods had been burgled a few weeks before, and they might freak over the gaping door, but so be it.

Callie ran like never before, ignoring the stones bruising her feet. She turned the final corner that put her in sight of the party house. Damn it. Still no ambulance. A police cruiser parked in front of the house, lights flashing, but as she reached the house, she ignored the familiar Officer Francis Dickens and shoved past him up the stairs.

Where was Seabrook?

Pushing through the crowd, which had dwindled by a dozen or more, she thrust the EpiPen at Grant. "Here!" she said, gulping for air.

But he didn't take the device from her. Instead, he remained crouched, cradling his wife, the unspoken being that Callie had taken too long.

"No," she protested and fell to the floor. She popped open the pen's case and jammed the needle end into Brea's thigh. "Wake up, Brea."

Grant sat unmoving, still holding his wife, as if Callie wasn't there.

Sophie kneeled at her side. "Callie."

Counting in her head, Callie made sure she held the pen, praying to whatever god would listen that she could make a difference. She'd lost way too many people in her life this summer already.

"Callie," Sophie repeated and took her friend's elbow.

Callie reached to pump the woman's chest and resuscitate her.

Officer Francis walked over and leaned down. "Ms. Morgan, it's not going to work."

Sophie stood, raised Callie to her feet, and moved her away. Then she looked back at Brea, and in a faint whisper of words, said, "Follow the light, sweetie."

Hot Atlantic breezes blew through the open doors, the surf pounding on the sand a block over. Except for Callie's hard, noisy breaths, the room hung quiet in respect for Grant, his mumblings to his wife the only voice.

Pain swelled in Callie's chest as she watched death settle on the woman. She reminded herself that her old panic attacks were in her past. She was safe now. Unlike the woman who'd formed a brief bond with her about beaches, luck . . . and dead babies.

She managed the breaths hammering her ribs as her doctor had taught her in Boston. Air entered more, then more. She raked her hair once, twice, again.

No damn way she would ever go to another beach party again. Never. Not ever.

Chapter 2

THE SECOND POLICE car arrived at a quarter after five, a few minutes before the ambulance, and the acting police chief took three steps at a time reaching the porch, then entered. Brea's body remained as it fell. Some of the beach house partiers hovered around the room's perimeter in a daze, while others made for the exits in spite of the arrival of the lone skinny officer asking everyone to stay.

Callie stood with Sophie on the porch, distanced from the drama as a slight breeze barely moved the hawthorns and palms. As Callie fought to regroup from the shock, she listened hard to the soft, smooth ebb and flow of the surf two hundred yards off. Drama in a place like Edisto should consist of councilmen getting drunk in public or a boat sinking while tied at the dock. That's how she remembered the beach. It had been anything but normal since she arrived.

Sophie glanced in a window, her bangles jingling against the glass. "Oh my God, hope I never have to rely on EMTs." Then her voice changed to a whisper, as if speaking to Brea's spirit. "You must move on, Brea honey. Please, move on."

"Sophie!" Callie wasn't in the mood to patronize her friend's spiritual convictions.

Sophie stood fast, not rebuffed in the least. "Spirits of the suddenly departed often hang trapped in the present." She peered inside again as if to catch a glimpse of the departing ghost.

An uneventful month of summer sun without a catastrophe had given Callie false comfort. To think she'd almost overcome the devastation of June with its death and bloodied visions forever seared on her brain.

She'd come to the Wainwright event to socialize, ease into local life, try to recall what regular living meant. Brea had given her a sweet taste of that normalcy for the barest of moments. The first woman Callie had met who experienced the sheer hell of losing a baby. She seemed so fresh and transparent. Callie would've enjoyed a quieter conversation to become acquainted with the woman.

Or maybe not.

Brea had been a third grade school teacher. A far cry from a burned-out detective. Who'd want to have tea with that?

The screen door opened, and a tall officer in a navy blue uniform appeared, scanning the porch as he put on his sunglasses. "Callie?"

"Over here, Seabrook," she said.

The Seabrook name boasted a long Edisto lineage. Callie had met the man after she called in a murder the first day she moved in. As they became friendly, the title of *Officer* Seabrook shortened to Seabrook. Somehow Mike never fit.

"I've only got Francis here at the moment," he said, referencing the first uniform on the scene. "Can you help me take a few statements? There are a lot of people, and you've done a lot of this."

She sighed heavily. Edisto only had six officers, and she doubted half them had experienced much more than drunk and disorderly. "I'm a witness," she said. "Sounds outside of protocol, and I'm not in the business anymore, Seabrook." Not that she ever wanted to be again.

A couple she'd seen earlier scooted across the road, and others jumped into cars. People wanted nothing to do with police or death during their vacation. "Seabrook, you ought to corral those tourists. It'll be a nightmare chasing them all down."

Seabrook spun around and hollered to his thin, young colleague. "Francis! Go down there and block those cars. Take down their tags. Stop those people from running off."

He turned to her. "And this is why I need your help. This ordeal is like herding cats." He keyed his mic and asked another officer to report. He disconnected and stepped close. "I know you aren't keen on the cop stuff anymore, but this is elementary. I'd really owe you, Callie."

Sweat already trickled down Seabrook's temple from another dog day in August. Bleached blond, easygoing, and forty-four, the man blended into the beach scene as if he'd been born behind one of the piers. The natives knew him as the ex-doctor from Charleston turned cop for reasons that remained rumor. When the former chief accepted a position in North Carolina, the town council slid Seabrook into the slot temporarily and advertised the job. So far no takers, leaving Seabrook as the department's reluctant leader. He had his plate full.

"All right," she said. "Give me a memo book."

He slid one from his pocket.

Callie took the pad and flipped it open, like she'd done so many times on the streets of Boston. "How's the husband?"

Seabrook shook his head. "Devastated."

"It's the jinx," Sophie uttered in a low voice, her turquoise gauze skirt swishing as she turned, the summer colors and gently folded material so terribly out of place amidst the disaster. "God help us," she said. "We have another spirit."

"Stow it, Sophie," Seabrook said with a fatherly chastisement, though the yoga instructor was two years his senior.

She stuck out her chin, undeterred. "I *know* what I'm talking about. I've lived here much longer than you, Mike. They visit me. Move my things. God help them all, but they're occupying my house!"

Sophie's metaphysical rants kept Edisto natives entertained most days, but on occasion, a hint of reality gave substance to her beliefs. Callie had adapted to Sophie's oddball view of humanity and her way of being right about human behavior in spite of her naiveté.

"Thought the spirits were only your father and aunt," Callie asked.

Sophie stuck up two fingers.

"Yes," Callie said. "Two. That's what you said."

Sophie waved a pointed finger. "No, honey. We have this same two-week period every August when somebody gets hurt . . . or dies. Always happens. Like the phases of the moon." Her aqua eyes stared hard as she gave a single determined nod.

Callie frowned. "So your house is haunted?"

Sophie's long earrings brushed across her collarbone. "No, the beach. The deaths happened in several houses and along the water. All within a five-block radius of here." She rubbed the porch railing. "I keep telling you people that there's another world with a conduit to ours. Some spirit's pissed, and it rears its head every August, disrupting other souls with it."

Seabrook blew out hard. "We don't need your hoodoo right now, and neither does this crowd. Neither does the tourism of Edisto Beach, so collect your Tarot cards and keep your soothsaying to yourself, please. We'll interview you and let you go home earlier than the others. That suit you?"

She struck a pose. "I pay attention to the signs of the universe, and if you don't, you'll experience more of *this*," she said, swinging her other arm wide. "I'm a voice delivering the messages y'all can't hear."

Callie headed to the door. "We hear you."

Sophie jerked her ringed thumb at the officer. "He doesn't."

The screen door squeaked. A gurney rolled out, Brea's face and body covered. The husband dragged his feet behind them, his dead wife's gold beaded purse clutched to his belly.

A lump filled Callie's throat, and she stepped closer to Seabrook. "Where'd they find her purse?"

Grant clutched the purse tighter and paused. "Someone found it under the sofa," he said to her. "Under the goddamn sofa."

Callie, Sophie, and Seabrook stared silently at the poor man.

Grant dragged himself around, each step falling tired on each step, and joined the EMTs at the bottom of the stairs.

"I'm sorry," Callie whispered. She fully understood how a split second or a cruel shift of fate could alter life forever. In the days following her husband's death, she'd wished she'd been with John to save his life, or died alongside him. Two hard years of self-doubt taught her that fate did whatever it damn well pleased.

Her chest hurt, and she instinctively rubbed between her breasts, easing the hint of panic. The last anxiety attack hit when she first arrived on Edisto. Gin used to be her medicine of choice. She'd emptied her house of the stuff to keep temptation at bay, but right now, the tension inside her called its name, and God help her, she knew exactly where it stood right now inside the party house. But she had too many eyes on her, damn it.

TWO HOURS AFTER the ambulance left, as evening descended, Callie and the police had canvassed almost three dozen witnesses, most of whom simply stated Brea "just fell over." The real estate lady with the sign-in book, however, had disappeared. But they knew where to find her.

"Such a shame," Seabrook said to Callie in the kitchen. Sophie remained outside, having discussed the event with almost every demoralized partygoer as they left. Seabrook's long arm reached around Callie's tiny shoulders and drew her to his side. "Don't let this undo you, honey."

She smiled weakly at the gentle gesture, glad he hadn't been able to read her mind about a drink. The vestiges of Seabrook's medical training appeared here and there even as he played cop, his respect for people's well-being ever present. She enjoyed the occasional dinner, walks on the beach, even a kiss or two, but they both fought a heavy history. Police work, tragic loss of their spouses—the similarities drew them together, but they remained apprehensive about taking their acquaintance very far.

"Uh oh, y'all," Sophie said in the doorway. "Janet Wainwright's invading."

Callie and Seabrook moved outside.

A gold Hummer crunched gravel and stopped. The signage on the side glinted bright red in the sunlight with gold swirls of waves that appeared to undulate in the heat as the driver opened her door.

An elderly woman in her late sixties stepped out and scanned the area through squinted eyes before she donned a pair of wire-rimmed aviator shades. After pushing sinewy arms into her yellow linen blazer, she strode to the stairs. The beach homes sat on stilts, thanks to South Carolina's predisposition to hurricanes, and access to front doors meant a climb of at least two dozen steps. In spite of her age, the agent tackled each step with purpose, as if subduing them would galvanize her mission.

The real estate agent sported a cropped head of gelled white hair and wore a red-stoned ring on her finger emboldened with USMC. She halted with almost a click of her heels. Callie resisted an urge to salute.

"Evening, Janet," Seabrook said. "One of your rentals, I assume. Your final summer hurrah to snag next year's customers."

"Damn straight. Report, please."

Janet Wainwright had retired from the Marines and stormed the beach of Edisto, claiming it as her territory twenty years ago. She bought a house, then two, and then decided retirement meant more than watching the tide rise and fall. The choice had no doubt hindered her aging as Callie observed the spark of fight in the narrow eyes. While half the island feared her, the rest swallowed their misgivings and begged for her to represent their deals.

The unsaid truth was that folk were confused as to her gender. She'd been a drill sergeant at Parris Island in nearby Beaufort, which only made her more formidable to anyone seated on the other side of the loan closing table.

"Accidental death," Seabrook said. "You don't happen to have your sign-in book with you?"

Wainwright's features hardened. "Well shit, Seabrook. Don't you dare let anyone blow this into something it's not. Don't make me spell it out for you."

Callie held out her hand and noted Wainwright's gloss over of Seabrook's question. "Callie Jean Morgan. Nice to finally meet you, Ms. Wainwright."

The agent jerked a quick shake, released her ironlike grip, and reared her head back like a turkey. "I see the resemblance to your mother. Fine woman."

"Thanks." Callie would contemplate Wainwright's connection to Beverly another time. She opened her notepad to another page. "We missed interviewing your associate. What's her name? She had a guest book that would've listed everyone. Some of the guests slipped off from us."

As if Callie hadn't spoken, Wainwright snapped at Seabrook. "Well?"

"Well what, Janet?" His impatience cracked around the edges of a usual genteel persona. "The poor woman had no idea she was dying in one of your properties. We do need to see that guest book, by the way."

The agent's exhale cut the air. "I need this upset to vanish fast, Seabrook. Can't afford to seed a rumor that stifles the market."

"Oh, I'll do my best," he said.

She nodded, ignoring his sarcasm. "Good. Got to do damage control, so if you'll excuse me." She marched into the house.

Callie closed her gaping mouth. "Wow."

"And she likes your mother," Sophie added. "That speaks volumes."

"Wait, shouldn't that room be treated like a crime scene?" Callie asked.

"No," Seabrook replied. "I'm not calling it a crime scene, but Thomas will stick around until Janet secures the place, won't you?"

"Yes, sir, Mike," he replied, and the squatty—and again very young—cop headed inside.

Wasn't long before Officer Francis' head peered out the door, eager for a reprieve. "Anything else you need me for, Mike?"

Seabrook shook his head and waved toward the drive. "No, we're done. Thomas can manage."

"Thank goodness." The skinny, one hundred-fifty-pound cop put his hat on and clomped down the first few steps. "I feared I'd get drafted in there. That woman's intense!" The young officer made a brisk escape.

The door slowly clicked shut on its own in Francis' wake. While Callie ached for Brea, and especially Grant, this death did her no favors. She'd hoped to avoid such incidents by moving to Edisto: useless death, human agony, stupid acts of misfortune that destroyed people's existence like it did her in Boston. She had barely begun to fit the pieces back together. Playing cop to other people's tragedies only served to scratch a scab off a wound, making it bleed all over again.

Francis settled into his cruiser, but he hesitated shifting into drive as a faded yellow Volkswagen Beetle pulled in behind him. Not a recent one with its flower holder on the dash, but an antique version from the '70s with rust on the fenders and a sun-bleached peace sticker on a side window. The officer looked in his mirror at the car and studied the driver. Not until the woman exited the vehicle did Callie recognize why.

"Alex Hanson." Sophie screwed up her face and let loose a reserved squeal. "Cute as a damn newborn kitten. I so wish Zeus would date her, but he says she's too old. Can you imagine ignoring that?"

The long-haired, mid-twenties girl bent over and spoke to the officer through his window. Her jeans fit like jeans ought to fit young girls, accenting nubile curves they would never appreciate until after they'd doubled their age and pants size. "Why would she come to a crime scene?" Callie asked. "She works for the paper?"

Sophie eyed the young lady, and Callie noted Seabrook's gaze didn't stray far either.

"No, our newspaper's a one-man show, and I mean *man*," Sophie said. "Alex's independent, one of those bloggers. Does that bird thing, too."

The corners of Seabrook's mouth slid up as he caught Sophie's meaning. "Twitter?"

Sophie swung around. "Yeah, that's it. I barely do email, so don't ask me to explain what a Twitter is. I heard it's all called *EdistoToday*."

"So she *is* seeking a story," Callie said.

Social media experts replaced the reporters of old, only instantaneous. Callie just never expected it to be all that active out here. Hit a button, and news went live. At her old crime scenes in Boston, she could never tell the difference between the paper reporters and the online ones. In her opinion, journalists were held to a higher standard, as ridiculously measured as that was. Bloggers operated in a no-holds-barred mentality.

Callie's opinion of the young lady tasted sour regardless of her adorability, because she bowed at the journalism altar. Like a hungry reporter, Alex took five pictures of Francis on her phone then the house and Callie, Seabrook, and Sophie watching her from the porch railing before she set foot on the bottom stair. There she paused, entered something into her phone, and then climbed the steps all bright and cheery.

Sophie rocked on her feet as the girl approached, overly excited with the brown-haired girl whose locks swept into a messy ponytail. She reached them with the phone in one hand, the other extended to Seabrook. "Hey, Officer Seabrook. What can you tell me?"

Sophie interrupted. "Zeus says hello."

Alex cocked her head. "Oh, Ms. Bianchi, I doubt that. But tell him hello for me."

Giggling, Sophie's grin widened. "Want to come over after . . . all this? You can tell him yourself."

"Thanks, but I'm on a deadline." Alex keyed in something again, a tight smile of satisfaction on her face. She turned to Seabrook. "Who died? Natural causes? Accident? Foul play?"

No microphone like the hordes of reporters at press releases or courthouse exits, but the pushiness rang true. Hoping for fame and a few bucks from others' losses. Funny how using a regular phone played down the obtrusiveness, but Callie's guard remained piqued.

"No comment," Seabrook said.

Alex snapped another picture of Seabrook. Then with a spin on her dainty sandals, she scooted inside.

Callie waved at the door. "Stop her, Seabrook! You don't want her in there, do you?"

"Thomas will catch her," he said, staring after the nymph.

Sure enough, Thomas appeared at the door, escorting the girl out by the elbow, and gently deposited her on the porch, gracing her with a wide smirk . . . and a wink. An unruffled Alex snapped three more pictures. "Come on, Officer Seabrook. What's your police chief take on all this?"

"Sorry," he replied. "This isn't Ground Zero. I'm not releasing information yet."

She pivoted toward Callie with the phone cradled just so. "How about you, Ms. Morgan? Heard you played the heroine. You seem to have a knack for that sort of thing."

Callie shook her head. "Nobody was a hero here today." The late afternoon's sun glinted harsh off a car window, and Callie slid on her sunglasses, a flutter in her chest warning dusk was nigh.

Alex leaned closer. "Didn't you kill the man responsible for those break-ins and attacks two months ago? You're always in the action."

Callie shook her head. "I'm not feeding your next edition, sorry."

Alex pushed a stray sun-lightened tress behind her ear. "There is no edition, ma'am."

Ma'am?

"News is live feed these days," the social media diva explained. "This is real time. Check your Twitter. Read it on my blog, EdistoToday.com. Care to comment, or do you want me to fill in the gaps?"

"I'll tell you, Alex," Sophie said. "I saw it all, and I'm not bound by any cop code or anything."

The phone spun toward Sophie. Two clicks for pics, then Alex waited, her twinkling eyes eager. "The stage is yours, Ms. Bianchi."

Callie moved away to the other end of the porch, not caring to be involved or to hear a rehash *a la* Sophie how Brea Jamison died. Seabrook followed. Alex peeked at them before honing in on her more cooperative citizen on the street.

"How come I've never seen her before?" Callie asked. "She seems pretty entrenched here."

"She hasn't been around full-time but a couple years," Seabrook said under his breath. "You're familiar with her grandmother. Ms. Hanson."

Callie almost tasted warm, gooey chocolate chip cookies as the connection registered. "Ms. Hanson's house was one of the ones that handyman burgled the week after I moved in. He took her necklace."

Seabrook relaxed against the railing. "Yeah, Alex lives with her, but she's been visiting parents in Atlanta. She hustled home when she saw Edisto becoming worthy of news releases after you dealt with Mason Howard. Surprised you haven't been accosted by her before now."

Callie had received numerous calls and emails from reporters from

Charleston, Columbia, Savannah, and more after the June episode, but she became numb to the ringing, never replying. They finally found other headlines. Callie clenched her jaw, not fond of one man who'd hounded her for three weeks after she'd killed the Russian mobster hiding out as playboy vacationer on the beach.

For a short while, she was the hottest story since BI-LO bought out the Edisto Piggly Wiggly and opened its door 24/7. Seabrook had kept most of the Russian's details secret from the press out of respect for Callie and Jeb, and she'd had no problem clamping her mouth shut to make the news go stale faster.

Alex didn't come back soon enough to surf the wave of that story, but she rode the crest of this one.

She finished with Sophie and approached behind Callie. "I'm covering the story, like it or not, Mr. Seabrook. This is the sixth year. Residents out here—"

The screen door slammed. "Do it, and you'll be the next casualty on that blog, Ms. Hanson." Janet strode out, shoulders braced. "I told you last year like I told you inside, news is fine until you start hurting people."

"Six times?" Callie mumbled to Seabrook.

The cop frowned and shook his head.

"Yes," Alex said, catching Callie's words. "Six years counting this one."

Callie recalled a call from Beverly about a drunk tourist falling down her stairs, the angle of the fall snapping a leg and breaking her neck in one fell swoop. She also recalled thinking that the woman shouldn't have been partying so hard. Someone else drowned another time, but what beach didn't have those events? She'd never considered that these little pieces of tragic gossip from Beverly were taking place in the same two weeks in the same month each year.

Janet reached for the reporter's phone. "Do *not* make this into something it's not, Lois Lane."

Alex deftly dodged the reach. "Neither this death nor the ones before it are classified secrets."

"You'll do damage."

"You don't have the right to decide the news."

The rigid old Marine and the young contemporary techie. Were these two women any more opposite?

But this history troubled Callie. Accidents happen. A death gives you pause. Six deaths, um, no.

Callie abhorred journalists and their desire to exaggerate the normal, but she also believed that public education made everyone vigilant, resulting in fewer victims. Her interest aroused as to where this new information fell.

"I tweeted on that drug overdose last year," Alex said. "On the twentieth. Today's the fourteenth, so we're in the ballpark for the two-week period. This *woman*, however," and she tilted her head at Wainwright, "went all over town confiscating the newspapers, trying to cover the incident." She scoffed. "I bet she'd even paid for advertising with them!" She laughed. "But you can't collect tweets and blogs, Ms. Wainwright. Nor silence them."

"I have business to tend to." On Janet's way down the stairs, she wheeled around on the landing. "I'll be watching, Ms. Hanson."

The girl *harrumphed* her. "You keep watching those empty newspaper stands, ma'am. You can't touch online journalism, but I'd love to sell you some ad space."

Seabrook held up his hand. "Heard all this before. I'm leaving. You coming, Callie?"

However, Callie's mind churned. Six years. Six deaths.

A tiny shiver coursed through her. The what if's and maybe's ran on a loop in her head. God, she felt ill at the fact a history even existed. She didn't need this. Surely Seabrook had files that explained it all.

She already struggled looking at the empty house next door where Papa Beach lived . . . and died. She hated walking past Water Spout where she'd killed Mason. Now she'd probably dodge driving by this poor place, too. If she wasn't careful, she'd be confined to her own house, listening to Neil Diamond every day on her porch, sipping gin to muddy the images, her cam-covered Chelsea Morning feeling the only safe spot on earth.

"Wait a second, Seabrook." Gracious and be damned, but she couldn't help it. She turned to Alex. "Were these casualties men, women, teens?"

"All women," Alex answered instead. "Late thirties, early forties. Sort of like you."

"All accidents," Seabrook said.

"The jinx," Sophie murmured.

Fantastic. How the hell was Callie supposed to blindly accept Brea's death as an accident now?

Chapter 3

THE SUN SET LOW over the marshland flanking Edisto Beach, South Carolina. Big Bay and Scott Creeks divided the scythe-shaped land from the much larger Edisto Island which provided the coastal residents with a sense of seclusion. Nature's evening magnificence performed its show across Jungle Shores Road behind Chelsea Morning, the Cantrell family beach home named after a Neil Diamond song that Callie's mother fell in love with many years ago.

Yet Callie drew the living room blinds.

While the average beach-goer dropped their jaw at the sparkling orange and yellow beauty of the melting sun, Callie preferred other vistas. Her heart fluttered in memory of her not-too-distant issues with dusk, when John was shot dead inside their house that burned to the ground. Something about the hour and the colors sometimes slammed her back to that dark time. Tonight was one of those nights.

Her husband's Russian murderer had followed her to Edisto, wooed her, then came close to killing her. Callie had harnessed some of her demons via a broken beer bottle to the hit man's carotid, but one or two of those demons managed to knock on her door from time to time, often when the view appeared most exquisite outside, the colors ever serving as a reminder of when John died.

She'd been doing so well until Brea.

The day before, Officer Seabrook had disappeared once the ambulance collected Brea. The schoolteacher's demise threw the tiny police department into a tailspin, detracting them from an already full agenda. This time of year the six-person office stayed strung-out with drunks, jellyfish stings, and seniors fainting in the heat. After seven straight days of twelve-hour shifts, however, Seabrook still managed to take the evening off. Seabrook continued to subtly court Callie, neither quite able to define their attraction. A similar history and a similar profession. Past that? They had no clue. But for two weeks they'd planned to visit Sophie's friend who'd recently returned to town, and both sensed an urgency to maintain that date. A craving for normalcy, a hunger for doing simple couple things.

Callie turned from the window toward the clean-shaven, long-legged man seated at her kitchen bar. "Why didn't you tell me about this death pattern before?"

"It never came up."

She hadn't delved into his past too deeply *yet*, but knew he'd lost his wife to a random act of violence, causing him to leave medicine for law enforcement. Rumor whispered his off-duty passion involved turning over stones to solve the eight-year-old case. She sensed he missed his prior life. He sensed her queasiness about sunsets. They'd become adept at recognizing moments of discomfort in each other.

"It wasn't about you," he said, almost fatherly.

She went into the kitchen, accepting his point. "Coke, tonic, or water? I might have some orange juice."

"Water, please."

Callie glanced at the row of lowball glasses on a shelf beside the refrigerator, behind which remained the remnants of her father's bourbon. Maker's Mark. Not his favorite, though. Not like the Jefferson Reserve Lawton Cantrell had kept at home in Middleton forty-five miles north of Edisto. At least before he died.

A note sat in the bottom of the closest glass, a note she'd read before, more than once, and chose to leave in place. *"Please don't. I love you, Jeb."*

God, she yearned for a drink. Stress exacerbated the need, but she'd promised her son she would abstain from what had become a less-than-pretty habit. The bourbon also represented her father, the once-mayor of Middleton. As long as that bottle remained where he left it, he seemed closer.

Her father and her son watching over her.

Shaking off the melancholy, Callie set the glass of water on the bar. "So, talk to me. These accidents go back six years. Doesn't that concern you? It does me, and I just moved here."

"It does and it doesn't." Seabrook propped his sun-brown legs into the beige leather bar stool. He looked smart but casual in khaki shorts, polo shirt, deck shoes, and no socks, the trademark of half the middle-aged men in the Lowcountry. It suited him.

"What exactly does that mean?" she asked, flummoxed why nobody considered the importance of these patterns. Admittedly, Brea's death rattled her. While no prominent, shady-looking character made her neck hairs stand at attention, a needling anxiety fermented in her gut, returning that familiar edginess she'd so hoped to shed by moving here.

Seabrook continued to gaze at her after a deep swallow from his glass. "The accidents aren't related, regardless of the time they occurred. And no, I don't have an open file on the coincidences."

Callie strolled around and placed her elbow on the counter beside him. "Pray tell, why not? I would."

"Pray tell why?" he said, with a mocking grin.

She returned to the kitchen for her own drink. Mike Seabrook's calm aura made her feel better. Always did. Her inaugural day living on Edisto had exploded into a cataclysmic disaster when she ran like a madwoman down the beach armed, fearful that her Boston career followed her to the beach. But Seabrook talked her down, even cleverly slipped her Glock from her shaking grip. They hadn't crossed the intimacy bridge, not that the thought hadn't crossed her mind. Not that she wasn't ready—or was she?

"I'd be curious about these so-called mishaps," she said, returning with her iced tea. "In Boston—"

"We're not Bean Town," he said with an engaging smile. "We don't have one percent of their resources. August is the height of our season, Detective. I'm lucky to be loose for dinner." He lifted a foot and rested it on a higher rung of the stool behind Callie, blocking her in. "In my five years of these infamous two-week summer periods, we've had a couple of drownings, a broken neck, a hot-tub accident, heart attack, and now anaphylactic shock. If you can connect those dots, I'll relinquish my badge and concede to your Bostonian prowess." He gave a slight mock bow of his head. "Madam."

She leaned on his propped knee, his warmth reassuring. "Alex said the victims, all female, similar in age, resembled each other."

"Yes, most were short with dark hair, and I imagine that's probably what's piqued your curiosity, but don't make it more than it is. It hasn't been that long since your whole mess at Water Spout," he said. "Don't let this accident ruin your progress . . . or make you paranoid."

Seabrook, still ever the doctor.

Mess. What a benign way to describe what happened. "I'm fine," she replied coyly, yet lying. Her insides still ached from when she saw Brea go cold on the floor. She didn't even want to think about what dreams this would conjure. Sophie would have some sort of New Age definition for all this.

With a gentle sweep, he shifted hair out of her eyes and behind her ear. She needed a cut, but Edisto time meant no schedule, and sometimes hair got shaggy.

"Did you know her?" he asked.

"We'd just met." She recalled the sparkle in the teacher's eyes. "I liked her, though."

"She was Sarah Rosewood's niece."

"Yeah, I realized that retrieving the EpiPen."

She hadn't told him the whole story about Sarah Rosewood and Callie's father, but word tended to spread. Maybe Seabrook had caught whispers about her father's longtime lover, maybe not. But that conversation felt best for another time.

Maybe because Callie still grappled with the concept that Lawton Cantrell once managed a mistress, Sarah Rosewood. Even worse, Callie learned about it from her own mother two weeks after her father's murder. Beverly even condoned the relationship, though Callie bet her inheritance that Sarah's husband had not been so understanding.

Seabrook draped both arms around her, his leg still boxing her in. Then he gave her the standard peck on the mouth they'd come to know.

"I don't believe in coincidences," she said, raising a brow.

"Good," he said, his breath cool and clean. "Because I totally mean to do this."

His muscled arms coiled around her as his lips pressed hard against hers. A tender rush coursed through her, an acceptable diversion from a dark topic that appeared to have no solution.

Callie reared and grinned. "Sophie and her friend expect us for dinner."

"Five minutes won't matter." He nuzzled her neck.

She held her head back, a thrill rippling across her shoulders at his move. "Nor will ten, Officer Seabrook."

WHEN CALLIE and Seabrook arrived at the Wyndham condo, laughter cascaded from inside, along with the divine aromas of garlic and curry. Jazz music drifted lazily in the background.

Seabrook knocked then tried the door, which swung open.

"I'll never get used to unlocked doors around here," Callie whispered. "You'd think after those June break-ins they'd learned a lesson."

Seabrook grinned. "You solved the crime. They feel safe again."

Sophie ran over and took their hands with unbridled zeal. "You made it!" Her bare feet flaunted red and blue braided anklets, the nails a matching red. Her ruby tunic flounced, embroidered in primary colors around the hem and deep neckline, the calf-length stretch pants showing off Sophie's assets defined by twenty-five years of holding poses and stretches. "I've been telling Rikki all about you and what you've been through and how cool a neighbor you are, and—"

"Damn, Sophie, let 'em in and pour 'em a drink," said the deep, slow drawl of the cook.

The tall, skinny woman juggled a skillet and two pans on the stove, her cutting board covered with what appeared to be basil. Chicken simmered in the skillet as the exhaust fan blew overhead. Callie caught a whiff of coconut.

Easily six-foot with an Uma Thurman resemblance, Sophie's friend came from behind the stove, spatula in one grip, and shared her other in a shake. Callie recognized the fifty-something gangly woman from the party who'd parted the crowd as Callie ran out for the EpiPen.

"Rikki Cavett," the woman said. "Glad you could come." She nodded to Seabrook. "How you doing, copper?"

"I call her Rikki Tiki," Sophie said from the open refrigerator. "You remember, from Rudyard Kipling?" The door slammed. "Admit it. She looks like a mongoose."

Rikki rolled her eyes and sighed. "You gotta love her, you know?"

She did resemble a mongoose. A quite tall mongoose. Her loose, flowing tank top would fashion a floor-length dress on Callie.

Callie smiled and glanced at Sophie after Rikki's subtle jest hinting of condescension, but her yoga friend didn't seem to mind. Instead, without asking what they wanted, Sophie presented Callie with a plain tonic and bent over to whisper, "Three different spirits showed last night." She raised a brow for effect and then delivered Seabrook his beer wrapped in a koozie from last month's Governor's Cup, the area's annual celebration of boats, fishing, and seafood.

As Sophie slid stools close together, distancing them a bit from the cooking activity, she winked conspiratorially at Callie.

Callie winked in return, appreciating Sophie, but having no clue why they winked. With Sophie, you went with the flow. She shifted her attention to the aromas of onion and clove. "Good lord, what's cooking?"

Sophie waved her spread hands through the air. "Frickin' awesome, don't you think? Rikki Tiki travels the globe, honey. She has recipes you can't even imagine." She turned toward the chef. "What's this one called?"

"Basil chicken in a coconut curry sauce," Rikki replied, watching her steaming pans. A long thick blonde braid hung down to her waist, and like Sophie, she stood tanned and barefoot, gold rings on three toes of what had to be size twelve feet.

Callie surveyed the lanky Amazon. "How often do you stay here?"

"I like to spend April through July abroad. Sometimes Christmas. Sometimes more," she replied. "The rest of the year I'm here. Moved to Edisto twenty years ago."

"Abroad?"

"German father. I have some of his looks and all his German real estate. The accent comes from my Edisto mother. The family can be traced to the Jenkins here on the main island, much like our Mr. Seabrook's heritage."

Seabrook raised his beer in acknowledgment.

Rikki heaped food on plates in healthy Southern portions. "Enough about me. Time to chow down, people."

Callie could almost eat the thick, spicy air around them, but when Rikki placed the entrée on the table, Callie opted for the mouth-watering chicken, a golden sauce running off the sides.

Silence surrounded the table save for the clutter of cutlery as everyone's bites turned into moans of enjoyment. When Rikki passed around the platter offering seconds, she hesitated in front of Callie. "I've heard you're the star of the beach. You killed the infamous Mason Howard, huh?"

Accepting another chicken thigh, Callie pushed it off her fork and cut into it. "Georgy Zubov. Howard was his alias." This wasn't a topic for dinner discussion. Even the very chatty Sophie knew that and remained silent. Some nights those memories snatched Callie out of her deepest sleep.

Rikki remained still, the platter hovering. "I met him once. Didn't like him."

"Ditto that," Seabrook said between chews.

Yeah, just what Callie needed to hear about the man she'd dated, then had to kill.

Rikki set down the platter. "So, Detective Morgan, you're practically trending today."

Callie paused over her chicken. "I'm not a detective anymore."

"What does trending mean?" Sophie asked, wiping sauce off the corner of her mouth.

Rikki's long arms reached over to a small accent table and lifted her phone. "On *EdistoToday*." She tapped one button, then another, then turned the phone around to Callie. "See?" The little online messages of 140 characters or less scrolled down the Twitter page.

@EdistoToday—Detective Callie Morgan interviews suspects outside
the scene of Brea Jamison's death on Edisto Beach #edistotoday

A photo of Callie staring off in the distance appeared below the text. And then another where she and Seabrook talked in the picture, probably about the time Alex finished interviewing Sophie. The ampersand sign denoted an identity, a handle of sorts. @EdistoToday was obviously Alex. The hashtag #edistotoday served as an identifier, to compile all messages containing this hashtag in one search. Alex wanted to make sure anyone found her posts.

The tweets went on, some with Callie's name and others without. Then another scrolled into the tiny screen:

@EdistoToday—New detective investigates an old jinx? Detective
Callie Morgan doesn't believe in coincidences & checks out
unexplained deaths #edistotoday

Callie took the phone. "Who told her that?" But she barely completed the sentence before she knew, and so did the rest of the diners at the table.

"She asked me what you thought," Sophie gushed. "I said what you always say."

"Not what I need, Sophie," Callie said, then studied the phone again.

@MyOuttake—Edisto detective tries to revive dying tourist
#edistotoday

Callie's heart almost stopped at the image of her whispering to Brea before the teacher died. "Alex didn't take this." She looked at Seabrook for support, trying not to express the fear in her chest.

Rikki turned the phone around. "No, that's from someone named MyOuttake. Obviously someone at the party. No surprise."

Callie recovered her own phone. Tapping the sender's moniker to reach his profile, she found nothing of value. Name: MyOuttake. Location: This World. No identifiers.

MyOuttake. An outtake meant a news bite, a buzzword, a quotation. Sounded like a rival reporter.

Racking her brain, Callie fought to recall who stood close enough to snap that shot, but she'd been too entrenched in the effort to save Brea. Surrounded by so many.

She really didn't like this, studying the phone as if to find clues she missed.

Rikki laughed. "Don't worry about it, Callie. This'll pass like everything else online. Here today and replaced with some other newsflash tomorrow. So," she said, taking her cell and turning it off, replacing it on the table. "What do you think about our jinx? You sure got a dose of it firsthand yesterday."

Callie put aside her own phone, trying to formulate an answer. This woman made her a tad uncomfortable with her manner of speaking so straightforward. Callie wanted to like that, wanted to like her.

Callie had agreed to dinner hoping to chill. Brea had been the fifth death for Callie in two months, a lot for anyone, even a former detective. A violent murder intrigued those not involved, and Rikki hadn't been on the island at the time. So she wouldn't see it as much more than a news story.

Sophie filled in the silence that had built. "Callie doesn't believe in hexes, and she thinks our unlocked doors are dangerous. She hasn't quite adapted to beach life."

Seabrook gave Sophie a stiff-faced look, tightening a grip on Callie's knee under the table. "Maybe that's enough, Sophie."

Leaving the partially eaten chicken, Callie eased her plate aside, eying Rikki's glass of wine. "So, Alex keeps a myth alive, and Janet tries to keep it hidden. That about it?"

"Pretty much," Rikki said as she got up to refill her glass. She held hers up as if asking everyone if they needed anything. All declined. "Alex has made the jinx look like that ghost legend at the Presbyterian Church. Nobody really takes that stuff seriously. If Janet would lighten up, she'd see Alex doing her a favor adding local flavor."

Papa Beach used to tell Callie the tale about Julia Legare's ghost. The daughter of a plantation owner died from diphtheria, sealed in the family mausoleum. Over a decade later, the family opened the tomb for another unfortunate member. Brittle, dry bones of the daughter fell out, her burial dress puddled around her. Seems she was interred while in a coma. Seeking the legendary claw marks, vacationers frequented the graveyard when the Edisto Historical Preservation Society held annual tours. Papa Beach once took her to see the tomb to teach her Edisto history, but Callie had refused to go near the site, much less enter like others did.

"In some ways I agree with Janet Wainwright," Seabrook said. "Don't embellish accidents into something they're not."

"Were the deaths all tourists?" Callie asked.

The women nodded. Seabrook sat still, fingering his water glass.

"All women?"

The ladies nodded again.

"Dark-headed?" she continued.

Rikki squinted. "The one who fell down the stairs and at least one drowning were dark-headed. I'm not sure about the others."

Callie turned to Seabrook. "You don't recall?"

"I can't be sure without pulling reports," he said tight-lipped.

Not likely. She remembered all the ones she had investigated, and her experiences sure outnumbered his.

"The hot tub case was weird," Sophie said. "A dyed brunette, if that counts." She turned toward Rikki. "Makes me glad I highlight mine."

"Can we stop this?" Seabrook said. "We're not looking for a killer."

"You never find what you don't look for," Callie said.

His jaw tightened, then he reached for his beer.

"Heaven forbid we have a serial killer in our midst." Rikki half-grinned. "But Wainwright would hunt the killer down and shoot him herself, so we're perfectly safe."

"I wish she'd shot Mason Howard," Callie added. "Instead, she rented him a house."

Sophie ventured forward over her plate. "I still wonder what's different this August. The spirits are driving me bat-shit crazy! Lights flickering, my ring moved from the kitchen to the bedroom, strange odors."

"So sage them the hell out of here," Rikki said, waving her monkey-length arms. "Order a truckload and set the beach on fire. There. That would solve all our ills."

"That's not funny," Sophie said with a pout.

No, it wasn't funny. Callie respected Sophie's spiritual beliefs. The woman had stood by her when they barely knew each other. Callie classified her as a solid friend, a pure soul who cared. Not as empty-headed as some thought and not as thick-skinned as she pretended.

Relaxing into her chair, Callie welcomed the lull in conversation . . . and marveled at the way intelligent people viewed the deaths. Seabrook reacted as any uniform would: simple facts and no sidetracks. Rikki felt it no more than comical gossip. Callie could say nobody contemplated thinking outside the box, but Sophie had never been in a box in her life.

Rikki twisted sideways in her chair and crossed her mile-long legs. "Sophie, tell us about your daddy." She winked at Seabrook. "You'll love this."

Ordinarily, Callie's New Age neighbor turned effervescent at the chance for the floor, but instead she flashed reticent and serious. Callie softened, worried Sophie had been joked about one time too many. "What's going on?"

Sophie set elbows on the table. "Three times in the last week, Zeus awoke chilly, his ceiling fan on high. My father used to swear by fans, having grown up in poor housing without air-conditioning. I also feel air at the kitchen sink, in the living room on the sofa, in my closet. My doors and windows are closed, but still, these currents sway my curtains. Daddy died in August ten years ago, but he's making way more appearances than usual. Ordinarily he leaves a subtle token message, but this time he's really active. It worries me."

Callie never tired of hearing the name of Sophie's son. *Zeus* fit him like a tailored tux with his tanned muscles and long, dark curly hair. *Sprite* fit the seventeen-year-old daughter, too.

As if waiting for a first-grader to tell her story from the playground, Rikki smiled patiently.

Sophie's head bobbled like a doll, animated now as she returned to her tale. "Of course I smudged my whole house as well as the porches. Someone's spirit bucked me several times putting out my sage stick, but I bested them. Or so I thought. Last week my bed creaked, and my bracelet fell on the floor. Today I can't even make my sage smoke!" She shivered.

Rikki picked her phone back up and scrolled.

Scowling at their host's inattentiveness to Sophie's feelings, Callie leaned in to her friend. "But you'll continue communicating with your spirits," she said, sympathetic, "because you feel they are there, causing trouble."

"Or in trouble." Sophie's brow furrowed. "Either way they aren't happy."

Callie's detective senses tingled, not unlike her friend's spiritual awareness. Truth was, if a cop didn't look for a homicide, he wouldn't find it. Bad guys capitalized on nonchalance and skepticism. Seabrook dismissed her axiom, but the concept was not hard to understand.

If it wasn't out there, it wasn't there. But what if it was?

What creeped out Callie more, however, was that time played the enemy if everything happened in the August two-week window. Brea's death happened a day ago, leaving Callie thirteen days at most to decide if she was paranoid or keenly aware of a new chapter in Edisto's head-in-the-sand, laid-back world.

Why the hell did everyone act so damn complacent about it?

Rikki shoved the phone under her nose, but Callie pivoted away. "I'd rather have a pleasant dinner with friends, Rikki."

Her mouth tight, Rikki replied, "I don't care. Read this."

@MyOuttake—Chelsea Morning. Home of Edisto's new detective Callie Morgan and her son Jeb. #edistotoday

Fear zinged through her. There was her home, her name and her son's name, plastered for all to see.

Chapter 4

THE CONVERSATION at Rikki's ventured well into the evening; the sun long set. Callie pumped the two ladies' memories and listed on a notepad all the partygoers they could recall, her appetite stirred to find some hint of a clue to connect Brea to the jinx. Maybe to identify MyOuttake. Though predominantly tourists, Rikki recalled some of the attendees from years past. Regulars. Some of those coincided with some of the faces Callie recalled.

Then after setting their phones for Twitter to follow @EdistoToday and @MyOuttake, the four of them had pondered the hidden identity of the rogue MyOuttake and if he, or she, represented a threat. Lubricated by alcohol, Sophie suspected twenty different people, and Rikki accepted or naysayed each one in laughter. But Callie had remained sober . . . quite sober. The potential reality of the situation felt too real.

"That's enough, don't you think?" Seabrook said, having been silent throughout the what-ifs. But between the food, the drink, and the hour, the energy had died anyway. They bid each other good night.

The night's brisk coastal breeze rattled the palmetto fronds near Callie's front porch as Seabrook walked her up the steps. His long, intimate kiss goodnight lingered sweet with the slightest hint of beer and coconut sauce, and she let the jinx mystery subside. She closed her eyes, arms wrapped around his neck, and her thoughts flitted from *too soon* to *why not.*

But then she recalled the online post of her house. Her eyes flew open to Seabrook's closed ones. Who might be watching them right now? Paranoia fed her temptation to ask him in . . . and maybe stay for the night.

Their kiss parted. He rested his forehead on hers. She hugged him close, his warmth, his sincerity, all so . . . welcomed. His heart pounded, and she felt guilty hers didn't match his speed.

With the sea nearing high tide, the roar of breakers adopted an ominous clarity even from several blocks away. A street lamp illuminated the waving branches of sagos and *pittosporum*, giving them the dynamic personality of distorted ghosts. Her long bangs repeatedly caught in her eyelashes.

She drew back from another brief soft kiss and smiled. "May I ask a favor?"

Tilting his head, he pulled away with one arm still looped behind her. He held up a finger. "Just a sec."

A string of cars shot by full of partiers obviously friendly with each other from the loud shouts thrown to and fro as they draped out the windows. Seabrook's hair blew wildly, his narrowed gaze seeming to weigh the need to address the raucous behavior.

A squad car tore by in the same direction with its blue lights flashing but without the siren.

Seabrook returned his other arm around her for a full embrace. "I'm glad Francis loves night duty. I couldn't function without that guy." He gazed at her and smiled. "So, what's the favor?"

"Think you might get me the files on those August deaths? I've got plenty of time, and . . ." She paused at his reaction. "What?"

He shook his head and frowned. "You're a civilian. Regardless of your qualifications."

Callie scowled. "You asked me to take statements yesterday."

"That's different, and you know it."

"Not really," she said.

His finger traced her chin. "If you came to work for me, you'd have access to whatever you wanted."

She should've seen this invitation coming. Seabrook had always seen her relocation as an opportunity for the department to acquire some much needed experience.

She recalled her old Boston PD boss and his words as he sat on her sofa right after her father's funeral, talking her through one of her panic attacks. "Stan told me eight weeks ago he wouldn't hire me, not in my state of mind."

Seabrook studied her with more seriousness, yet holding her hand. He gripped it tighter. "That was then. You neutralized that threat, Callie. Plus I'm not Stan, and this isn't Boston."

A swallow caught in her throat. He might be right, but too much had happened in her life. "Eight weeks, Seabrook. Nowhere long enough to put my head on straight. Not enough to carry a weapon."

"You underestimate yourself, and you carry a weapon."

"To defend me and mine, not the public."

"You haven't lost your skills. You won against Mason."

"I'm still embarrassed how it happened in the first place."

"Then take an auxiliary position."

Opening her mouth for another retort, she found herself stunned. Auxiliary was a volunteer position. Along the level of a doctor being asked to be a part-time school nurse.

What about her skills? BPD embedded those talents deep enough to take residence, and no doubt she'd react correctly to danger. But to be on guard all the time, to don the suit and defend citizens on the street . . . she wasn't sure of that part. Some days she craved the badge. Other days she wished she'd never worn it.

She let loose of his grip and propped herself on the porch railing, analyzing the breeze in the plants, suddenly missing her self-confidence. Seabrook moved to stand beside her.

All she wanted were those damn files, especially with someone tweeting about her being the resident detective. She existed in someone's nosy binoculars, probably harmless, but to her that could mean crosshairs, too. Her detective past had followed her home before—several times. The idea of wearing a badge, however, tightened her chest. Sooner or later badges exacted a huge cost, and she'd already paid dearly enough.

She should've gone to law school like her parents wanted. However, youth and a particular criminal justice student coaxed her to the other side, the side that better satisfied the naïve hunger for making a difference. She'd been raised as the only child of a political couple, and while the mayor of Middleton didn't make news on Fox or CNN, the dance was the same. Cops seemed so much more black and white than attorneys. More apt to bring justice to bear.

She shifted in front of him, palms against his cotton shirt. Then she peered into Seabrook's eyes. "Thanks for reminding me."

"Reminding you?"

She pecked him on the lips and reached for her house keys. "I've got no business returning to that job. Except for the Twitter stuff, I had a good time tonight. Thanks for the evening."

"No coffee?"

He'd ruined the moment, or she had, she wasn't sure. This whole cop thing kept squeezing in between them. Maybe because she was a cop at heart, and he wasn't. He wore the uniform, and she didn't. Whatever the deal, it created this painful little edge she couldn't seem to file smooth.

"It's late, Seabrook. You have to work, and I need my morning run." She smiled and kissed him lightly. "Maybe next time."

She turned to avoid seeing the hurt he tried to hide, and she let herself inside. After setting the alarm, she changed into her nightshirt and curled on the sofa with coffee, Neil Diamond playing on her mother's turntable.

She wasn't angry. Disappointed? Confused for sure. Between Seabrook limiting her investigative reach and Janet's stonewalling, why bother even worrying about Brea? Or Edisto's August reputation?

Or her abilities to be a cop.

Nobody but her seemed to care, so maybe she over-thought all this. Even the Twitter posts seemed trivial now. A lot of people were brunette. Every native knew her address.

She threw in a load of wash, unwilling to let Jeb's fishy-smelling socks and T-shirt ferment until morning. He texted he'd be in by 1:00 a.m. and wished her goodnight.

Then she slid a cotton throw across her on the sofa as the ceiling fan chilled her feet. If she kept one eye on the Tweets and laid low until the jinx period passed, the two weeks would pass in a snap. Maybe that's all she needed to focus on. Two weeks was nothing.

CALLIE AWOKE WITH a jerk, panting, wrapped in urgency, but her mind had emptied of the dream that implanted the rush. A buttery sunlight fell across her fern-green bedspread and slid off the edge onto a hooked rug, and she caught her breath. She fell back on her pillow with her palm outstretched to feel the warm rays.

Brea. The name had suited the third grade teacher.

Callie owed her condolences to Sarah Rosewood for the loss of her niece. Funny how her father's mistress gave off a sense of family. Something about the woman must have made Lawton Cantrell feel alive, though, and that made Callie want to hold a connection with her, however delicate, however frowned-upon.

Brea's husband Grant remained confined to Edisto, waiting for his wife's body. Callie held no desire to see his fresh, raw agony. Nobody said anything right during those hard first days of loss, and she'd rather not try.

Maybe Jeb could drop off some token gift from her?

She peered out her bedroom door for her son, but the house rang quiet. Her alarm clock read 8:00 a.m. He'd already be hosting day-trippers on a fishing boat in his joint business venture with Sophie's son Zeus, unless he gallivanted with the curvy, dark-haired Sprite. The trio had grown close these last few weeks. Sprite had one more year of high school, and the boys had opted for a year off from college to try and make a go of the business.

Not Callie's preferred path for her eighteen-year-old son, particularly since part of his justification included taking care of her in light of her old anxiety attacks and the occasional, maybe more than occasional, drink. His explanation for his choice, late one night on the screened porch, had not been a proud moment for her.

No. He didn't deserve this chore of visiting a mourning family. He took care of her enough already. She'd go herself.

She padded in bare feet to the kitchen for a glass of orange juice.

Per the slapping palmetto movement outside, a decent breeze kept bugs at bay and the humidity less oppressive. A run would help.

A half hour later, she pounded the Edisto sand, the tide out but working its way in, giving her lots of room to dodge SPF-coated sunbathers with all their brightly-colored beach paraphernalia. She ran in her long-sleeve, sweat-wicking shirt, not yet emotionally secure enough to display the ragged, wide, eight-inch scar on her forearm acquired from the fire.

She now coped with five-mile runs without the painful chest pressure of a few weeks ago. Crazy how she still sensed that goddamn Russian watching her from the upscale rental on the water's edge, the freak ever eager to catch up and match her stride. Not suspecting him as a murderer would stick in her craw forever. Testimony as to her rusty cop senses. Embarrassing that he took the upper hand in the blink of an eye.

Callie kicked her pace up a notch for the final half mile, to focus on something other than mistakes. Already people staked their claims on the exposed low-tide shoreline, and several yards to her right, a family of four dropped bags and coolers on blankets.

A few yards later, she recognized a bronze, fit, thirty-ish couple from the party and nodded. The woman appeared puzzled, but the man returned the gesture crisply, suddenly placing her identity.

The polite man who'd offered to help when Brea collapsed sat on a low-riding chaise with a book, a straw hat on his head. Singles on the beach made her wonder about their backstory. God knows she had one.

High on her second wind, she left the sand and jogged the side streets home to Chelsea Morning.

Moments later, she stepped fresh from the shower, threw on an extra stroke of mascara and a light coat of lip gloss, and before she changed her mind, drove to Lowcountry Hardware. The August heat had dwindled the plant selection, but she chose their fullest red geranium. At home she tied a yellow ribbon around the pot for some semblance of show.

In the midst of fluffing the bow, she stopped.

Sarah Rosewood felt awkward enough to be around without a death. And Callie'd have to face Grant and his pain.

She twisted the bow once more. None of this should be about her.

She cradled the plant, locked the door, and walked the two doors down. Twenty minutes seemed long enough of a visit. Thirty tops.

Callie's heart leaped when Ben Rosewood answered her knock.

His cocked brow heralded his mood. "Tell me why you felt the need to come by?"

Ben presented as a striking figure at six-foot-four, wiry-strong instead of paunchy or muscular, his wavy, well-groomed dark hair peppered with gray. His build easily captured a lady's eye, especially in creased khakis and a soft pastel polo. But every time Callie had met the man, he'd used his highbrow demeanor to do just that, demean.

She'd never crossed the guy, but Callie understood why he struggled with having a Cantrell under his roof. Her father had bedded the man's wife. Nothing PC about that.

Callie lifted the plant a few inches. "Wanted to check on Sarah and Grant. I tried to help when Brea—"

"Yeah." He stepped aside. "She's at the table."

He disappeared up the stairs.

I'm not the one who slept with your wife, dude.

Decorated in beige and golden hues, teak and vogue rattan, the home stood a far cry from anything considered a rental. The Rosewoods were natives, one of the reasons they got sucked into the serial theft spree in June when Callie first met them. Seated at the burl wood table, Sarah clung to a coffee cup while Grant played with an uneaten breakfast.

"Sorry to interrupt," Callie said from the doorway.

Sarah gestured her in. "Please, come sit. Want something to drink?"

"No, no." Callie set the plant on the table. "Wanted to tell you how sorry I am, to both of you. Brea seemed a sweet person."

Sarah appeared in her mid-sixties, not a beauty with small eyes and thin, middle-aged lips, but she carried a gentleness about her that served as its own charisma, even in mourning. That same charisma drew Callie to make acquaintance with her father's mistress a few times since the funeral, not alienate her as she thought she would. Sophie had commented a time or two about Lawton Cantrell's *other woman*, erroneously assuming Callie's mother had been forced to suffer the affair for years. Callie knew from Beverly that the situation wasn't like that. Beverly and Lawton each had a single separate lover via a string of happenstance events that somehow made it all acceptable.

While the term was still *cheating*, Callie saw why Lawton might need someone softer than his socialite, attention grabbing, hard-spoken wife to confide in. Beverly could make the devil doubt himself.

"So why did the damn cop question me?" Grant said, snapping Callie's attention.

She slid into a chair, recalling how devastated family members lashed out at cops. "It's routine."

"I didn't want her butchered in an autopsy," he said with less of an edge. "Damn obvious what she died of."

"Shhh." Sarah rubbed his arm as she spoke to Callie. "Brea knew better than to touch food at a party. She even ate here before she left. Pizza. Pepperoni and mushrooms," she added through fresh tears.

"Maybe she didn't think," Callie said, recalling how caught up she and Brea had been in conversation, and how simple it would've been to absentmindedly touch the wrong thing. The autopsy would show stomach contents. "Would you like me to check on how long they'll hold her? It's only been a day, but—"

"Would you?" Sarah peered at her nephew. "Callie used to be a detective, Grant. She solved crimes up north before moving here, then she solved a big case on Edisto. An amazing woman. She'll—"

"Detective?" He stiffened.

His reaction overshadowed the compliment from Sarah. Callie's senses bristled.

His tone rose, defensive. "Are you here to accuse me of killing Brea?"

"Oh no," she said, shaking her head. "I'm here as a friend."

Grant sank his head in his hands. "Good, because I can't stand anyone thinking I hurt her. She meant the world to me."

"Of course she did," Callie said.

Another knock sounded on the front door. Ben remained upstairs. Sarah seemed preoccupied with Grant's despondency. Callie stood. "I'll get it."

She trod gently across the yellow oak floors, then halted in the entryway, sinking into a deep white and beige oriental rug that she would've hated to keep clean. A slim gentleman waited on the other side of the glass. He peered nervously as she opened the door.

"May I help you?" she asked of the thick-haired professor type, the wire-rims of his glasses accenting bright sea-blue eyes.

She reached out. "I'm Callie Morgan from a couple doors down."

His button-up short-sleeved shirt had been precision ironed, and he wore it tucked in and belted. Even without the casserole, he obviously paid a formal visit.

"Dr. Ernest Maddington," he said with a nervous clip. "I've heard of you. Nice to finally meet." He paused to study his loafers, as if second-guessing whether to enter.

She took the casserole to put the man at ease. "I'm sure Sarah would love to see you. Follow me."

Callie led him to the table and set the dish on the counter.

Sarah warmed at the man's presence. "Ernest, how sweet of you." She escorted him to a chair. "Callie, Grant, this is Dr. Ernest Maddington. Brea and Ernest—"

"I know who he is." Grant's tone flew out from a dark place, seizing everyone's attention.

Maddington's face drained of color.

Sarah's smile vanished. "Grant!"

His fist struck the table. Everyone jumped, but not before Callie caught the grieving husband stealing a glance at her for a reaction.

"That's the creep who spent weeks alone with my wife last summer," he said with force.

Maddington's eyes widened, but he managed to speak, a quiver in his voice. "Brea volunteered for my loggerhead project, along with six others. She worked with me for three weeks and did a fine job."

Grant's face reddened.

Sarah spoke before Grant could. "Brea used the experience for her classroom and to work toward an advanced degree."

"Not the way I heard it," Grant said.

Sarah rested an elbow on the table and pointed angrily. "What is wrong with you! Honor Brea's memory under my roof."

Grant stood and slammed the chair against the table. "Like I'm the one at fault here?" he yelled.

Callie took a breath. "Nobody's saying anyone's at fault," she said. "Let's all settle down."

Sarah lightly touched Maddington's sleeve. "I'm so, so sorry, Ernest."

Maddington's grimace now morphed into a nervous smile. "I think I'll go now." Even taller and ten years older than Grant, the doctor didn't seem to hold much substance in comparison, and Callie had to admit leaving seemed a good choice.

But Grant pushed off the table and strode toward Maddington, blocking him from leaving. "You stupid son-of-a-bitch. You slept with my wife during those so-called research sessions."

Maddington pedaled his feet to stand.

Grant punched the man's shoulders, knocking him down in his chair.

Callie pushed her chair from the table. "Stop it. I'll call the police. This isn't the time—"

Grant turned and stared her down. "When *do you* confront the man who slept with your wife and got her pregnant?"

Maddington pushed Grant into the wall and escaped out the front door.

Chapter 5

CALLIE SPENT HALF an hour soothing Sarah Rosewood's nerves after Ernest Maddington flew out the door. Grant stormed to his room hurt, lost. Ben remained upstairs.

Not a soul had thanked Callie for trying to save Brea.

She finally excused herself politely, headed home, then, retrieving keys and cell phone, she rushed to her car. She pulled onto Jungle Road to head toward the police station, dialing Seabrook's number en route, pausing her Ford Escape at the stop sign before turning left. "Are you at your office?"

"No," he replied. "I'm just leaving the gas station."

The only gas location on Edisto stood in the opposite direction from where she headed, near the lone entrance to the island beach. "Can you meet me at McConkey's? It's important," she said. "Are they open yet?"

"Will be in thirty minutes. They'll at least pour us a tea. Why? What's wrong?"

She didn't care to risk Seabrook discounting on the phone her what-ifs about Grant and Maddington, especially with how she and the acting chief parted the night before. She also preferred an eye-to-eye so that she didn't miscommunicate any sort of readiness to join the force. "We'll talk there," she replied. "Outside on one of the porches to avoid ears."

"No problem. I'm practically there."

The Jungle Shack, McConkey's common name, looked just that . . . a rag-tag, almost lean-to type building that barely held eight tables inside, so it spilled several more onto two porches, one side for smokers. Overhead fans spiraled slowly, teamed with fast spinning portables along the plank and screen walls to keep the hot summer air moving. Strings of corks and Christmas lights draped from post to post. Multi-colored T-shirts hung along the one wall between the diners and the kitchen, some tie-dyed, flaunting a Tarzan-type character swinging on a vine.

Callie parked her car next to Seabrook's cruiser. As she stepped under the tarp-covered porch, he motioned her over to a picnic table. Two large Styrofoam cups sat waiting, but she studied him first, never tiring of resting her gaze on a well-filled out police uniform.

Fries, seafood, the aromas drifted outside to blend with the briny drift from the beach as the kitchen staff prepared for the onslaught. Already cars circled the place like sharks. Easing down on the opposite seat from the cop, she took a draw on the cold, almost syrupy, sweet tea. Her nerves still danced from the confrontation at the Rosewoods.

"So, do we need to order lunch, or can we make this quick?" he asked. Tourists trickled in. By eleven thirty the place would be elbow-to-elbow, with people waiting.

She couldn't read what his residual feeling was from last night, so she chose to take her time. "I need to eat." She glanced inside. "Will they serve us yet?"

Seabrook raised a hand. "The uniform. You ought to know that." A teenage boy hurried over with two menus.

"We know what we want," Seabrook said, and he ordered two pimento burgers and a shared basket of onion rings.

"Add jalapenos to mine," Callie said. The boy nodded and scurried to the kitchen not much bigger than Callie's largest bathroom. How McConkey's cooked so many meals, and darn good ones at that, escaped logic.

Ninety degrees was hot, the humidity making it hotter, no matter how you measured it. Though they sat under the tarp, she kept her sunglasses on her face. Even off the beach, the tinted blue shades made her world feel a degree or two cooler.

"So what's on your mind?" Seabrook seemed rather solemn, especially with his shades.

"First, are you mad?" she asked.

"I'm not particularly thrilled at how we ended last night . . . or rather how you ended it. Abruptly. But I tend to avoid drama."

She rested forearms on the picnic table to lessen the distance. "Listen, I like you, and—"

"Callie," he started, then stopped. He came forward too, and though she couldn't see his eyes, she felt their gaze. "I get the crap in your past," he said. "I understand why you left the force. So why bother trying to play cop? Or, if you still want to keep your toe in law enforcement, why do you let it come between us? One minute it's our attraction and the next it's our obstacle. I don't understand what to say for fear of pushing you away."

The words made sense, but hearing them so bluntly delivered made her straighten. He didn't say anything she hadn't thought, but his phrasing hinted at a more negative connotation, cloaking her in newfound guilt.

"Do you think I try to irritate you?" she asked, not happy with her tender reaction.

"No," he said, shaking his head. "I think you're afraid. You like law enforcement, but it backfired on you, robbing you of your grit. You don't want to experience all that again, but in spite of your reluctance you cannot help but see life through an investigator's eyes. It's instinctive, and whether you admit it or not, you're good at the job. Everyone gets drawn to what they do well."

Callie scratched at a cuticle. "I feel like I ought to be paying you by the hour," she said. "But I see what you mean."

"Not sure you do."

She scowled. "What does *that* mean?"

He pinched his sleeve near the Edisto PD patch. "This." Then he glanced over at her. "The uniform, or the guy in it, is not a threat to you, but you act like it is."

Callie fought not to mash her lips. She'd admired the damn uniform not seconds ago, as well as the guy in it. "You're wrong there."

His brows arched along with his shrug. "Could've fooled me. I commend you on your skills and try to flatter you with a job offer, and you run like I've tried to molest you. Sort of stomps on a man's ego a bit, Callie. I'm stymied what to say around you."

For a while they sat staring past each other.

Crime and death caught her attention, no doubting that. Without thinking, she picked information out of people, hunting for leads. She scratched where her wedding ring used to be. She wasn't pissed at him, but more at the fact that she hadn't recognized the mixed signals she gave off.

For almost three years now, she'd wandered around disconnected from what she used to be, a hardcore detective and a solid, logical woman. Time was fast stealing how both once felt to her.

She rubbed her fingertips along the table's wood grain. "It's like I'm in this foreign skin I'm trying to grow into. Sometimes someone pushes a button I didn't realize I had."

"Like when I offered the job with Edisto PD?"

A jolt raced through her, and she almost cursed. Geez, she hadn't recognized she had such a knee-jerk reaction to the possibility. "Exactly like that." She stretched one shoulder blade, then the other, as if the exercise shed the nerves.

"Well," he answered slowly, and Callie sensed a serious statement coming. "How about we forego the dating thing for a little while, not that we'd become anything serious. There's a wall between us that needs to come down, and I don't think it's happening overnight."

The hurt surprised her. She thought she caught a flash of pain on his face as well, but his sunglasses left her uncertain.

Maybe she did need more time to heal before dating. If he were just a man, it would be one thing. But his being a cop messed with her head. "Fine," she said.

"Okay," he replied.

She let a few seconds pass before speaking, wondering if she should regret anything, or change something, hell, she had no idea. "Still interested in what I learned this morning?" she asked.

A small smile appeared on his face. "Always open to your thoughts, Detective Morgan."

The old title melted over her until she recognized the way he'd shifted their relationship in those two words.

Callie glanced toward the dining room door for listeners. "Grant Jamison chewed out a Dr. Ernest Maddington for having an affair with his wife last summer. Not an hour ago. Apparently while he stayed home in Florida, she came here to participate in some sort of turtle research."

Seabrook looked over his glasses. "Ernest Maddington? Not sure I believe that. He's lived here for years, likes his single, uncomplicated life, has a soft spot for the turtles, and everybody loves him. Did the argument get physical?"

"Almost. Some shoving." She fingered her small loop earring, hindsight making her unhappy at how she handled the whole scuffle. Grant might have hit Maddington. She should've interceded, contained the anger, or at least separated the parties sooner. Something different than what went down. Was she that out of practice?

"Callie?"

"Yeah, well, the doc turned three shades of white when Grant accused him, and Maddington knocked over a chair on his rush out the door." Callie brushed grains of sand off the picnic table. "Grant and Brea lost a baby in December, and the dear hubby claims the doc was the father."

"Whoa," Seabrook said with a half laugh.

"Yeah," she said with a short nod. "Need to find out if Maddington came to the party, don't you think? I don't remember him there." She slid to the edge of the bench. "Both those men knew her allergy. See what I mean when I said you don't find homicide unless you look for it? This story is deeper than we thought."

Seabrook gnawed at the inside of his lip. "That does open things a bit, but I'm not ready to label it premeditated murder. We still have an autopsy pending."

"Brea knew better than to touch shellfish, and an autopsy won't tell you how she ingested it. Accidental or intentional, we need to know. You have one guy with motive. Don't understand enough about Maddington to judge whether to count him, too. Might be an insurance issue." She took another draw on her tea. "Clearly a rocky marriage situation."

"What were you doing over there anyway?" he asked.

"Offering condolences."

"Of course," he said drolly, his finger sliding through messages on his phone. "Changing the subject, seen this?" He turned the device around.

"Not sure I want to," she said, slowly taking the phone.

The online feed showed her and Seabrook on her porch, their bodies backlit by her door coach lamp. Most wouldn't recognize them in the mixture of dark and shadows, but she knew. Seabrook knew. Whoever took the photo knew.

The comment read *@MyOuttake—Det. Morgan and the Edisto Police Chief "collaborating." #edistotoday*

Her gut leaped at someone standing fifty feet from her door watching and eavesdropping.

Seabrook flipped through more messages. "And this one's from this morning I take it?"

@MyOuttake—Detective Morgan tearing up the beach instead of hunting the Edisto jinx. #edistotoday

She yanked out her own phone. There they were, the same tweets. Also a text from Jeb. *Why are we on Twitter?* Yeah, she'd like an answer to that as well.

"I'm not happy with all this," she mumbled, the old slithering feel of a stalker returning.

Callie opened her mouth to expound on her opinion of such mini-news blasts, but the burgers arrived, pimento cheese melting off the patties, the onion rings sizzling. Callie sat straight, her foot tapping the deck floor. The teenager refilled their teas and left.

She got closer. "Who the hell is MyOuttake? I'll be watching every person I see, including my friends."

Seabrook wiped some dripped cheese and licked if off his finger. "They may have camped outside your house, waiting for an opportune moment. I admit it has a rather sneaky feel, but think about it. This Tweeter started at the party comprised of predominantly tourists, right? Someone may have created a game with these posts, feeding off what Alex does. It's obvious he's using her hashtag #edistotoday to gain followers. My gut tells me amateur paparazzi."

Callie ripped off a bite of burger. "I need to talk to Alex," she said, mouth full.

"Doubt she can tell you anything. If it's a tourist, he'll be gone soon anyway."

"Yeah, like the Russian?"

He laid down his burger he'd been about to bite. "No, Callie. I really see this as a tourist. I don't envision a string of hit men pursuing you. Stan nixed that."

Stan had spoken to the Russian family who assured him they hadn't condoned the rogue family member. Stan believed them. All was supposed to be quiet on the Boston front.

Seabrook finally bit into his burger, then remembered something, struggling to speak. "I already tried getting that sign-in book from Janet. She won't cooperate, and I have no basis for a subpoena. I'm still inclined to write Brea's death off as an accident."

Callie lifted an onion ring, blew on it, then dropped it to suck on a blistered finger. "Want me to try getting it? I not only want to find who witnessed Brea's reaction, maybe seeing what prompted it, but I want to put eyes on who might be posting about me. All may be in that book."

Seabrook shrugged. "Do what you want, but I'm not expecting a murderer to sign some register. Or MyOuttake, for that matter."

"You're not quitting, are you?"

"I'm not completely incompetent, Detective."

She rolled her eyes. "Not what I meant."

"I'll talk to Grant in light of what you told me." He wiped more cheese off the dripping side of his burger. Then the finger pointed at Callie. "I'm only dealing with the Brea Jamison situation, though. I'm not questioning him or anyone from the party about the other deaths. Let's leave that history alone, okay?"

She dodged an answer. "Are you talking to Maddington, too?"

"Maybe after Grant. The husband possibly fabricated the whole affair accusation, so let me judge how to proceed with it. Maddington already sounds pretty upset, and he's proven himself a pretty solid citizen in these parts."

She tested the onion ring again. "Or Grant might be right about Maddington . . . assuming he isn't dusting over his own tracks. Watch him when you go over there. He's sensitive about cops."

He nodded with a mouthful of burger. "Hmph."

With the rings cool enough to eat, she tried to throw her interest into her meal, but the silence brought Seabrook's words from last night to mind.

You'd have access to anything you wanted.

She no longer saw sexual innuendo in his words. They'd *broken up* anyway, if she called it that.

But she had another thought, too. Seabrook held the acting chief of Edisto PD role, desperate for someone else to take the job off his shoulders. If she ever took him up on his offer, her experience would relieve some of the burden. Plus, he'd chosen to keep her in his cop circle rather than his social one, underlining his priority to identify her as a cop first and woman second.

Ketchup gone, she squirted more in her basket and trolled a small onion, then stopped. She stole a look at him.

Surely he didn't think she'd apply for the chief's position.

IF THE CARS WEREN'T packed so tight around Island Bike Rentals, Callie could've seen the Wainwright Realty office from McConkey's. After Seabrook paid the tab and walked her to her car, Callie drove behind him toward the police station, heat waves wafting from the asphalt.

She honked to say goodbye before peeling off to park outside Wainwright's office.

Janet Wainwright had owned two other offices before this one per the chatter at Rikki Tikki's condo the other night. The real estate broker would construct a house much like the others on the beach, around twenty-five hundred square feet. Then as prices peaked, she would change the zoning for it from commercial to residential via some town council arm-twisting, since sweet-talking had never been her *modus operandi*. She'd sell it as a beach house then build another home for the agency. The current address stood as close to the eateries, gas station, and state park as Wainwright Realty had ever been. Entrenched red roses and gold lantana bushes served as her brand across the front, giving a more permanent appearance. Maybe this office served as her last citadel. Edisto Beach was running out of lots.

The woman's gold Hummer sat in its spot around the side. Good. The drill sergeant was in.

Holding out her hand, Callie introduced herself to the thin blonde receptionist. A red cropped cardigan accented her yellow sundress. Was everything in this ex-Marine's life Corps color-coded?

Before the girl had a chance to respond, Wainwright's gravelly voice resonated from her office. "What can I do for you, Ms. Morgan?"

Callie turned. "Hey, Janet, I hoped—"

"Come on back. You're not shopping houses, so no need wasting my staff's time." The white-headed lady stood crisp in slacks and a red blazer, making the USMC ring pop on her veined hands. She turned to the girl who sat straight. "Check the water in the plants on the porch, copy those flyers I gave you, and see when the cleaning crew's getting here with my key for that house on Myrtle. That family's due in at four today. I want a progress report by the time I finish here."

Callie bet the poor girl never had time for lunch. "Thanks for seeing me unannounced, Ms. Wainwright. I hadn't planned—"

"Never give up ground, Ms. Morgan." She eased behind her desk and motioned for Callie to sit across from her. "You do look like your mother, girl."

Callie wasn't sure she wanted to resemble her mother in the eyes of this woman, or at any time, for that matter. She'd have to ask Beverly about Janet and why she'd never seen the real estate agent socializing at any of the Cantrell political soirees.

Elbows on her blotter, Janet faced her guest. "Now, what can I do for you?"

The old woman liked it straight, so Callie doled it out that way. "You can make me a copy of your sign-in book from the party."

"No."

"Ms. Wainwright, we have questions for those in attendance."

"I'm sure you do. The answer is still no."

"But we—"

"Who the hell is *we?*"

Though he might not enjoy being labeled her conspirator, Callie dropped his name. "Officer Seabrook and myself." But she already saw where this was going.

The weathered woman squinted. "Girl, you're no different than a tourist, and if any one of them asked me for a list of my clients, do you think I'd give it out?" Each word rose in tenor. "Hell no," she exclaimed like a preacher proclaiming from the pulpit. "I already turned down Seabrook's request. He had no warrant or subpoena; therefore, he held no authority to acquire personal information for a fishing excursion."

"But a woman died," Callie said.

"Unfortunately, yes. From an allergy, I heard."

Callie studied the Marine commendations on the wall, pondering another approach.

"Considering another tactical maneuver, Ms. Morgan?"

Indeed Callie was, but she wasn't sure Seabrook would be so keen on it. Ms. Jarhead, however, left her no choice. "The death might have been a murder."

"Shame, but the answer's still negative."

"Then tell me this," Callie said, standing, no longer patient enough to sit and joust. "You've been around here a while. You interact with almost everybody on the beach. You, of all people, should know most about what happened to all those who've died these last six years. How many of them were staying in your rentals?"

A white brow rose, but she grinned wryly.

"You ought to recall the beach's history," Callie said, "back when there weren't any deaths. You should sense what the deaths might have in common. We're trying to identify any trends."

The woman's other brow rose.

Well, hell. Inhaling, Callie piled it on thick. "Who's to say you aren't the one hiding something, Janet? You may have even housed the murderer."

Hands flat on the desk, Wainwright got to her feet, shoulders level, putting her body at attention . . . becoming a presence to be dealt with. Finally she allowed herself to make eye contact.

Callie gripped the front of the desk and braced for the onslaught, refusing to retreat.

"I've heard about you," Janet said clean and level, eyes locked. "You have your issues, but you possess a solid core of substance."

A compliment?

"But I'll tell you like I told Seabrook—"

"You might be aiding a killer."

Janet smiled. "Oh, so we have a killer amongst us now? I thought you rid the beach of our *killer* a few weeks ago."

Callie stiffened. "Didn't you rent Water Spout to that man? Aren't you the one who rented him a house so he could scour Edisto for targets? What does the owner think about the blood stains on the carpet and furniture?"

Janet's tanned, shoe-leather complexion took on a scarlet hue. "It took a small fortune to clean that house . . . out of my pocket."

"And it's still empty at the height of tourist season," Callie added.

"It's a hazmat issue thanks to you."

"You harbored a killer."

They faced each other across the polished oak desk. Callie's pulse quickened, but Janet appeared ready to eat entrails and ask for seconds.

"Listen, Ms. Wainwright. We'd like to see whom we didn't interview in case they saw something that clearly defines this case as either an accident or homicide."

"Show me your badge."

Callie cleared her throat. "We both know I don't have one."

"Then get the hell out of my office."

"Wait," Callie said. "Let's chill and see if we can meet in the middle. I can—"

"I told you about giving up ground, Ms. Morgan."

Craving to scratch her head, Callie didn't want to show weakness. "I'm trying to hold a civil conversation with you—someone who's supposed to have a solid head on her shoulders. However, she appears to be more concerned with *giving up ground* than solving a problem that might impact the entire beach and its future livelihood."

The rear of Callie's calves hit the chair as Janet came around the desk, arm raised, her arthritic finger aimed like a saber.

"I want this shit forgotten," she said, her finger an inch from Callie's face. "And I don't care for your questions, Ms. Morgan. You're playing cop, and I don't have time for the charade."

The real estate agent pressed forward, and Callie moved toward the door.

"You're worse than that damn nosey Alex Hanson," Janet said. "If I hear even a whisper of a rumor that you're stirring this shit, I'll make your life miserable."

Callie wiped her cheek, removing a drop of Janet's inadvertent spittle. Then she caught the sound of her own breath puffing. She'd stupidly allowed anger to sabotage the conversation. This pissing contest had to stop, and the broker didn't seem to be the type to lower her weapon first.

"I'm as dedicated as you," Callie replied in a calmer tone. "And I'm not scared of an ex-Marine who still thinks she's storming some hill."

"Get out." The order came through clear and sharp enough.

Though hesitant to turn her back to leave, Callie did.

Janet protected her business ventures. Callie got that. But what if this animosity tied to more than loss of rental income?

Callie rounded the corner of the reception area, her cheeks heated. The young blonde flushed and glanced down to chase her heels with her toes and retrieve the discarded shoes. Then she returned to study her copy machine that seemed to be operating fine without her attention.

Sure the girl had heard, but Callie expected the conversation to stay under this roof. Callie wasn't the first visitor the Marine had scalded and shown the door, and Janet probably put the weight of the entire Corps into threats to her employees, winning their silence.

Callie reached her car and let the air run a minute. The shimmering heat waves on Jungle Road asphalt had nothing on Janet Wainwright's blistering disposition. Callie adjusted her mirror, judging how beaten up she looked after that verbal boxing match. No doubt who won.

Janet Wainwright had been one of the Marine's finest teachers, per beach rumors. Exactly how many ways did they teach Marines to kill?

A shiver raced down her perspiring spine. From the air conditioner or the thought of Ms. Jarhead doing whatever she deemed necessary to protect her beach, regardless of the means, the message, or the casualties—to include putting a tail on her to post Callie's life online?

Chapter 6

CALLIE SAT IN HER drive, still hearing the clash of swords in Wainwright's office. She peered down the street to the Rosewoods. Two in the afternoon. Grant's car gone. With the air still cool in her car, Callie took a minute to gather her thoughts.

Sarah had lost her beloved niece, left tending the bereaved husband atop the daily dealings with a brooding husband. The woman probably struggled to get out of bed each morning.

Grant wallowed in misery, anger, maybe degrees of regret. Then there was Ben. Callie didn't want to pass judgment on a man whose wife cheated on him, but she guessed a story wedged in there somewhere, a reason Sarah sought Lawton Cantrell's attentions for so long. A reason Ben Rosewood didn't interfere. Unless he didn't know, but twenty years seemed a long time to be ignorant. A strange house full of tension with no relief valve.

How often had she wallowed in grief and taken it out on Jeb, her mother, even Stan? She and John groped for coping mechanisms after Bonnie died. Not a soul under the Rosewood roof would be expected to act normal. Empathy tugged at her being on the outside looking in for a change.

Callie liked to think Brea died of natural causes to expedite the Rosewood healing process, but questionable circumstances weren't completely ruled out yet. Brea's death wasn't her case, but Seabrook hadn't really made it his either. At least he agreed to interview Grant. If Maddington had bedded Brea, no telling how long before Grant would overcome that.

Maddington, too.

When did this island get so complicated? She almost felt she'd brought misfortune and adversity with her. This summer had to be the anomaly. Edisto epitomized placid serenity, or so she'd seen and heard since her childhood. Callie preferred the simpler Edisto lifestyle, the attitude adopted by almost everyone, including the police department. Assume everything happy-go-lucky, until you absolutely had to remove your head from the sand and see for certain. The unofficial mantra was that natives left the other life behind them and relocated to the beach to renew and live the simple life.

But she seemed drawn to Sarah. No simple live thrived under that roof. Her father's Sarah. Callie was the daughter of an adulterer, but with the adulterer being her cherished father, a crazy soup of emotions stirred inside her. Emotions that prohibited her from alienating the *other* woman. Lawton had never been less than noble in Callie's eyes, so she instinctively searched for a logical explanation.

She understood why Sarah loved the man. She just didn't understand what made her beloved father cross the line with a married woman. What made Lawton Cantrell sweep Sarah Rosewood off her feet? Or come to her aid? Or run from Beverly to such a serious degree?

Callie noted movement. Sarah exited and hung over her railing, head in her hands. Her shoulders quivered, bobbing to what appeared to be sobs.

Heartache swept through Callie. She left the car and trotted to Sarah's, praying Ben had left.

Callie approached, and Sarah lifted her head, trying to smile through tired eyes, her face blotchy, the skin dragged by gravity and sadness. "Come on in." Sarah wiped her face on a dishtowel she'd brought out with her. "I'm afraid Grant left."

"Are you okay?" Callie asked.

"Don't worry about me. I miss Brea. My sister died ten years ago, and she's the daughter I never had."

"All the more reason you need company. We're sort of tangled, in a way."

Sarah released a chuckle with a bit of a rattle. "Good word for it."

Callie grasped her wrist and led her toward a chair at the kitchen table where Sarah already had a cold cup of coffee. "Is Grant any better?" Callie asked.

"He went for a drive." Tears welled in Sarah's eyes. "He's in pain. Men handle grief differently, but he had no business carrying on like that." She wiped a stray tear with a trembling finger.

"Want me to have an officer stop him?"

Sarah shook her head. "That would only make him worse. He's not dangerous."

Callie chose her words, torn between helping and collecting information. "Sarah. There was an affair, wasn't there?"

Sarah shrugged, her fisted arms crisscrossed tight against her chest. "Who am I to judge?" She studied the dishtowel still in her grasp.

"Ain't that the truth," said a rough, deep voice from the stairway.

Callie peered around Sarah at Ben standing in the hall.

Sarah paled, appearing afraid to speak. Callie, however, wasn't. "So Brea told you about Maddington."

He pushed off the railing toward the kitchen. "No, but I read it on her face, heard it, saw it in how she behaved. It's not like I haven't had experience recognizing this type of thing." He made a show of retrieving a beer from the fridge and retreated without the first glance at his wife.

Callie waited for the door to shut. "Sarah, are you safe here?"

Sarah sighed. "He's a hard man, driven by his law practice upstairs when he's not flying to meet a corporate client. Not until Lawton died did Ben fully grasp my relationship with your father."

"For twenty years?" The words slipped out before Callie could catch them.

The women made eye contact, Sarah seeming to analyze the trust factor of her guest.

"I'm sorry," Callie said. "Didn't mean—"

"No, no, it's all right," Sarah replied and took Callie's hand. "I'm sure you have questions, and your father's not around to answer them."

While awkward, Callie couldn't deny her need to understand.

Sarah eased more forward and whispered, "Ben stayed gone a lot. He had . . . intimacy issues."

"Um, you don't have to explain," Callie said, rising.

"I feel I do, Callie, please."

Callie scooted against her chair.

Sarah took a breath. "When I revealed the truth about Lawton, Ben got furious. He stayed disgruntled and started traveling for months at a time, as if seeing me made matters worse. I used to wonder if he achieved his . . . desires . . . via some other manner, but I ultimately realized I could say or do nothing to make the situation better. I met your father, and things changed for me. Ben didn't find out until this past year." She took another deep breath with a hitch. "Now Ben can't place his anger anywhere with your father deceased."

Her tears fell steadily now, spilling freely over her lashes. "Now I'm so confused. Oh God, I feel like I owe you, owe Ben . . . your mother."

Callie shook her head with a slight scowl. "Mother's no saint, Sarah, and you don't owe her a thing. Let's leave it at that."

Beverly cheated first, Lawton next, then both agreed that the occasional tryst enhanced their marriage. Then Beverly's significant other died of cancer while Lawton's affair flourished anew. A pure page out of a hippie playbook Callie was so glad she wasn't made privy to until the trysts were no more. She just wished she hadn't had to lose her father for the truth to come out.

The agreement might have worked for her parents, but Sarah and Ben were perfect examples of the refuse left after the party.

"Ben isn't terribly wrong as a husband, Callie. Lawton just seemed more right."

Lips clenched at the impossible situation, Callie peered into Sarah's bowed face. "It's not my place to judge. But if you need a retreat to go to at any time, my place is open."

Then she caught herself. Sarah'd probably looked at her parents' bedroom ceiling more than Callie had. The bedroom Callie now stayed in.

"Thanks," Sarah said, the tears slowing. "But this is my penance to pay. He says he's trying to cope." She rose. "I can't talk about this anymore."

Excusing herself, Sarah passed the hall bath and disappeared into her bedroom.

Oh wow. Callie sucked in a breath down to her naval. The bathroom door clicked shut. She expected Sarah to take a few moments to wash her face and touch up makeup, maybe pop an aspirin, so Callie took the opportunity to text Seabrook. *I'm at Rosewoods,* she keyed. *Grant's gone if you plan to talk to him.*

Then she waited, studying the home, wondering how often Lawton sat at this table, slept in the . . . never mind.

Sarah returned composed, wearing fresh mascara and lipstick. She gripped the chair back and inhaled in a regrouping mode.

Callie's phone dinged with Seabrook's reply. *Then I'm headed to Maddington's. Text if Grant shows. Be my eyes there a few minutes?*

She gave Seabrook her reply in a simple thumbs-up emoticon, then flashed Sarah a sympathetic smile, uncertain how to fill in the time.

"You don't have to stay here." Sarah rubbed the woven placemat, her index finger following the sweet grass rows. "I've probably unnerved you."

"Don't worry about me," Callie replied. "But I did have a few questions to ask without Grant around." Callie wished for a notepad but would have to commit answers to memory and inform Seabrook later. "Do you mind?"

Sarah peered silently, reciprocating.

"How long did Grant suspect Brea and Maddington?" Grant's red face entered her mind's eye, the emphatic temper. "Was he violent with her?"

"He never hit her. She would've told me. Last summer they separated after eight years," Sarah said. "A trial situation. Their struggle to have children strained their relationship, but when she got pregnant, they decided to make it work. They were happier than I'd seen them in years."

Callie mentally cringed at the common misconception that a child's birth mended a marriage.

"Losing that child crushed both of them," Sarah said. "But my sweet Brea was too honest for her own good. She told Grant the baby was Maddington's."

"Told you," said Ben from the stairwell, and he finished coming down the steps in way-too-obvious plops of his feet.

With Ben wanting to eavesdrop so badly, Callie shifted attention to him. He strolled to the refrigerator for ice. Then he went for the bourbon, splashing it with the barest hint of water. He turned and settled his butt against the sink. "My wife doesn't see it, but I do. You're snooping for Seabrook."

Sarah glanced sideways at Callie.

"I saw Sarah outside, upset, and I came to check on her," Callie said, uncomfortable at Ben's astute, semi-accurate observation.

"Doesn't matter. She told you right." He waved his glass at Sarah. "Got to give her credit, she worked hard at fixing Grant and Brea each year, while she acted the hypocrite with your father."

The animosity in this house was intense, but vows had been broken. Trust gone.

Callie might as well jump into the deep end. Sarah had been in a mood to spill. Ben willing to converse. "Did you know any of the other women killed in August?" she asked.

"No, don't know and don't care," Ben answered.

"Why would we?" Sarah asked timidly. "They were tourists."

Callie had no idea where to start connecting dots, but it made the most sense to start with the most current death and work backwards.

Did Grant lash out at others in lieu of Brea during their rocky marriage, then target her when he learned of the baby? Did Brea fit a weird mold like the other women, continuing some sick ritual by Maddington? Had Maddington littered the coast with dead mistresses? Janet's potential still niggled at her.

One positive reared its head in all this mess, though. Maybe nobody else would be hurt this year. This year's deed might be done.

Her phone dinged. *Maddington not answering. Will try later. Grant returned yet? Not here*, she typed.

Thanks. Go home. Chat later.

"Guess I need to go," she said, standing.

Ben pushed off the sink and approached. "I have a question."

She slid her chair under the table and held the back. "Sure."

"How long is Seabrook going to let you play cop on this beach? You resigned from wherever you came from, right?"

Heat rose in her face. "I did," she said.

"I think you're intrusive, that's all." His nose rose, eyes shining down at her in passing, he headed to the stairs, stopped again, and turned. "Almost desperate, too. Can't let go of whatever it is you failed at."

Sarah covered her face and burst into silent tears.

Callie patted the poor woman's shoulder, tipped her chin at Ben, and then let herself out. She couldn't undo Sarah's embarrassment, and there was no answer to Ben's words. Callie knew she represented a substitute for Lawton. Fine.

Besides, Callie wasn't so sure Ben's analogy was all that wrong.

SOPHIE ROSE FROM her repose on Callie's blue-floral print settee as Callie climbed the last of twenty-four steps to her front porch. Beach house construction required the height, though Edisto hadn't seen a debilitating storm since Gracie in 1959. Her gypsy-esque friend stood, not a drop of sweat on her. *How did she do it?*

Sophie waved. "I would've had an iced tea poured for you if you'd left your door open, girlfriend, but no. You have to barricade your house."

"How long have you been sitting here?" Callie asked, hunting her keys.

"You're asking for trouble with the locks," Sophie warned. "You beckon bad luck by planning for it."

Cool air whooshed out, pushing against the nineties heat and humidity as the two women entered. Callie dropped her keys on the credenza where she normally kept her .38 when not on her person or beside her bed. Right now it stayed tucked in her purse. She meant to replace her stolen Glock, not caring that authorities kept it after the crime spree in June. She didn't want it anymore. Not after she and her son had once faced the business end of it.

"You have yoga today?" Callie asked, heading to the kitchen.

"Why?" Sophie pinched the material of her dry weave short-sleeved top away from her skin. "Do I look like I came from the gym?" She sniffed. "I don't smell. I never smell."

"No bangles." Callie placed two glasses of tea on the bar separating the kitchen and living room. "No earrings."

Sophie reached for her ears.

"Were you eavesdropping at the Rosewood place?" Callie perched on a barstool and took a long draw on the cool drink.

"What?"

Callie pointed at Sophie's head. "You didn't want to be heard. Your noisy bracelets and dangly ear bobs are gone."

"Shit."

"So what did you hear?"

A mild pout showed on Sophie's lip. "Y'all didn't talk loud enough to hear much."

"No, we held a confidential, personal conversation."

Sophie rolled her aqua contact eyes. "So, what's going on over there? Is the husband okay?"

Which one? Both were a mess.

"So, what did you hear, who did you see?" Had she spotted Maddington? Witnessed Sarah's meltdown? Sophie hinted, baited, and snooped with the best of them, using her wiles with that innocent pixie expression. Callie wouldn't fill in the blanks to satiate her curiosity and have snippets of gossip strewn around the island.

"Like who?" Sophie asked.

"Like anybody but the Rosewoods and Grant."

"No, not that I looked."

"You hid on the front porch, you sneaky heifer. Of course you were looking."

Sophie fanned her words away and toyed with her drink. "I needed the distraction. Today my rug moved two feet, after my bathroom light went out on its own."

"Two other people live in your house, Sophie, and maybe the bulb—"

Sophie's glass hit the bar hard. "Don't discount my spirits."

"Only ruling out possible explanations. Don't pop a blood vessel."

"I feel what I feel. These spirits aren't normal. Daddy and Aunt Mickie are expected, but all these others!"

Okay. Callie hadn't been friends with the yoga mistress for that long but thought the woman more grounded than this. She usually enjoyed the netherworld.

The microwave read three thirty. Callie wished she were in Seabrook's shoes heading to an interview. "So, why now?" she asked. "Why are your spirits so busy?"

"It's a death month. Daddy left ten years ago. Aunt Mickie four. But I . . . it appears they either brought others, or others followed them." She slurped as she rushed the sip to keep talking. "Or they channeled to me. Hell, I don't know. I can't feel alone in my own house anymore."

"Maybe they're headed somewhere else and stopped in to visit."

Sophie squinted. "Don't patronize me."

"Okay, okay."

They sat silent a moment. "Listen," Callie said. "Seabrook tried to get ahold of that address book that Wainwright's agent guarded at the party. Did you sign it? I did, and I wonder if I should have."

Sophie moved on the stool to assume a lotus-type pose, a balancing act that never failed to impress Callie. The woman rolled her head, stretched her vertebrae, and settled into a better attitude. "I avoided her, but she probably wrote my name down anyway. Janet likes to measure how many locals are sponging off her parties. She scolded me once, if you can believe that. I'm probably one of the most colorful people on the beach. I can talk anyone into buying or renting one of her houses. Heck, she ought to pay *me* to attend."

Callie frowned. "You told me locals were welcome."

"You met Janet. She wants locals to impress potential clients and spread the ambience but is too cheap to allow us to eat the food or drink her liquor."

"Hmmm," Callie said. "Well, the guy who's taking pictures of me is doing it again. Seabrook showed me more posts taken last night and today. At my house and on the beach."

"Ooh, I hadn't looked. That's creepy," Sophie said, reaching for her phone.

"Still wish I had that damn sign-in book, though. He had to be there, and if you're right, he signed in or the agent signed in for him." Callie retrieved the notepad sheet with scribbled cryptic scratchings, started at Rikki's, and read off the list of people. "Did you think of anybody else since last night? You'd try to sell yoga classes to the Pope."

Sophie didn't hesitate before she rattled off names. "The Martins, Hank Antonius, and—"

"Whoa!" Callie jumped off her stool and grabbed a notepad from the kitchen junk drawer. "Now, give me those again. Those aren't on last night's list."

"The Martins are from Ohio, staying in Sand Crab. Never been here before. Hank Antonius Something from New York, but he's originally from Italy. I doubt he'll return, though he might have more money than you can tell from his clothes. He might be a tacky dresser."

"Keep going." Scribbling, Callie wrote down ten names of couples and singles, their beach house rentals, and where they originated. "Gracious, Sophie. Your memory is awesome! Any more?"

Sophie repositioned her butt on the stool. "Bits and pieces. I paid more attention to the potential yoga people. I did miss that lesbian couple, but Rikki hit 'em up for me. They aren't interested. She also caught that hot guy and his wife with the hundred dollar frosting job. They prefer gyms, they said."

"Rikki noted a pudgy pair from New Jersey."

"Don't remember them." Sophie closed her eyes. "We can pick Rikki Tikki's head again, though. She's got down time since she got in from Europe."

"Who is Rikki really, Sophie? She's wealthy and travels, and the rest of the year she lollygags around the beach. Who does that?"

"More than you realize. You don't work. People have wondered about your money."

"I'm a friggin' widow and just lost my dad. Can you say insurance? Inheritance? Like it's any of their business."

Sophie sniggered. "You asked about Rikki, honey. Tit for tat. Same happens with me, but I have no problem telling everybody I have an NFL ex, and then they want to be me. But listen, I've known Rikki as long as I've lived on Edisto," she said. "Why do you ask?"

Callie's mouth twisted. "Hmm. She seems to pick on you. I'm not so ready to confide in her too much."

Scrunching her nose, Sophie waved off the thought. "She's fine."

Yeah, and you said the Russian was fine, too.

"Tell her I'll spring for a meal in exchange for conversation about who she recalls from the party, but before you call her, what about that dark-haired guy about fifty? The one who tried to help with Brea. You didn't mention him."

Sophie's eyes narrowed in an attempt to squeeze thoughts.

"No problem. Call Rikki," Callie said as her phone rang, caller ID indicating Sarah. Hopping off her stool, Callie went to refill their glasses. "Hello? You okay?"

The voice came across low, as if to avoid being heard. "Callie, I really didn't know who to call, but I'm worried about Ernest. Dr. Maddington? I feel so horrible about Grant embarrassing him this morning. I've been trying to phone and apologize."

Callie put new ice in the glasses. "Maybe he went to Charleston."

"No, that's the thing. His car's still at his house."

"Might be checking his turtle nests." Callie poured the tea. "Grant home yet?"

"No. He won't answer his phone either."

She gave Sophie her fresh glass with a smile, the neighbor's eyes studying her hard. "Want me to call Seabrook?" Callie asked.

"Would you?" Sarah almost whispered. "Ben would have a fit if I did."

She rounded the bar, Sophie following her movements like a dog watching a treat in his owner's hand. "Sure," Callie said. "Be glad to."

She started to hit speed dial for Seabrook then nonchalantly changed to a text. *Maddington? Sarah worried no answer at his house. Car in drive.*

"What's going on?" Sophie asked, trying to see the phone's face.

"Nothing," Callie replied, turning aside.

Pulling in drive now to check again.

Callie set the phone down.

"You're texting instead of calling in front of me. Mr. Seabrook is my guess."

"Guess all you like, but I can't talk too many more details on the case."

Tea spurted from Sophie's mouth. Coughing and sputtering, she reached for napkins from the starfish holder. Callie grabbed a dishtowel and dampened it under the faucet.

Sophie sniffled and swallowed. "You've got to be kidding me. Really? Like you still think you're a cop." She cleared her throat twice. "Hel-lo. You're unemployed, which means no privacy issues, and you can tell me anything. It's all gossip and ripe for the plucking, and I'm the basket you put it all into."

Scoffing, Callie finished cleaning the dribbled spots on the bar. "And you'll tell Alex, and she'll tell the world."

"No, I won't."

"Sophie! Have you forgotten what you said to her only two days ago? Your very words were broadcast online within hours . . . about me." Callie washed her hands. "I'd love to confide in you about all of it, but that *EdistoToday* girl wormed info right out of you. You never see the bad side of people, and sometimes that catches you with your pants down."

Sophie grinned. "Love it when you talk dirty."

Blowing out a laugh through her nose, Callie set down her drying towel. "Sometimes I don't know what to do with you." She draped the towel over the sink. "Seabrook asks me to help periodically because of my experience, so I need to honor his regulations. That's why I want to speak to people from that party. Might ask them about those online posts, too, since the first one came from the party. Dang that Marine. If she were more cooperative, this wouldn't be so hard."

Text came in again. Callie held off looking as she refilled glasses.

Her phone buzzed again. "Okay, okay." Punching the phone, Callie stiffened at Seabrook's message.

Get over here. Maddington's dead.

Chapter 7

"EASILY SELF-INFLICTED," Callie mumbled. This method of death had crossed her path several times: accidental mishaps during sexual experimentation, some suicide attempts. This case, however, was as neat as she'd ever seen. But then, the quiet ones usually surprised you the most.

Maddington's tongue didn't protrude from his mouth. As in life, his shirt tail remained tucked evenly in his belted khakis. No lamp overturned, no rug rumpled, no mussed hair. Ernest Maddington simply tilted forward with his eyes closed as though he tied a rope around the top hinge on the door, then his neck, and methodically levered his weight to strangle himself. No sign of resistance or regret. An aroma of feces gave a most distressing sensory stimulation, because he didn't appear dead. The air-conditioner kicked on. Cold air whooshed in, as if keyed to rid the house of the odor.

"Colleton County coroner and forensics are on their way," Seabrook said, standing off to the side of the bedroom.

Callie studied the body from the front, then bent over slowly, careful not to disturb as she walked to the side. Her analytical abilities kicked in, amping a calm focus. If the situation weren't so dire, she'd marvel at how Seabrook let her analyze a body but wouldn't let her sort through cold case *accident* files.

She rose and stepped back. "Did you find him?"

Seabrook rested fists on his waist. "I assume so. Car still in the drive. Door unlocked. I pushed it open and called. No answer, so I took the liberty of peeking around." He shook his head. "I never saw this coming."

"Then treat it as a suspicious death," she said.

He waved his arm out, sweeping the room. "Do you see any sign of foul play?"

"I'd let the coroner make the final determination, but if the man wasn't prone to such . . . behavior, I wouldn't label it suicide and close the book."

His fresh scowl lay heavy on her. "We're back to that, are we?"

She gave a half-shrug.

"You don't find homicide unless you look for it," he said, citing from their earlier conversation. "That's not normal thinking, Callie."

"I gave a lot of families closure with that line of thinking."

Seabrook had called. She came. But now that she worked the scene, he seemed . . . scorned. He couldn't have it both ways, and right now he needed to get over being out-policed.

Officer Francis poked his head in the door. "Getting a crowd out here on the porch, boss."

Seabrook spun on the skinny young officer. "Do your job, Francis. It's crowd control, no different than at the market festivals. Need me to call someone else?"

"No, no," he said, his words diminishing. "I got it."

Callie peered down the hall of the small house. Poor Francis. His youth meant he held little experience, and being from the Lowcountry, he hadn't worked on a large police force, either. Slowing down drivers, dismantling domestic disputes, seeing drunks home. Those were his forte. But he rolled without question to whatever Seabrook gave him. Good man. But he really should've closed the door.

Voices drifted inside—Sarah's mainly. Men and women talking, overlapping each other. Yep, a small circus in the making. Two Edisto police cars in someone's drive never failed to attract the inquisitive.

Perking at Grant's dialog in the mix, she peeked out a window and shook her head at the gathering, with more jogging over from across the street. Damn it. Alex Hanson stood rigid right in the midst of them, holding her phone steady as she took pictures for *EdistoToday*.

"We'll be on Twitter again," Callie mumbled, then returned to Seabrook. "Dang, the folks around here love a crime scene, don't they?"

"Maybe because it's so rare?"

"But this is August," she said, unable to help herself.

His brow furrowed. "You're turning into an irritating echo about that."

She gazed around the room again. "Suicide note?"

"Nope. A notepad by the computer, but it's clean."

Odd. She'd expect an educated man like Maddington to leave a missive of some sort.

Stepping gingerly, she went to the corner desk where every office supply seemed to own a designated place. An old-fashioned blotter, a clean notepad with only a few sheets ripped off and no imprint of a missing note on the blank page on top. A wooden business card holder contained about ten cards with a loggerhead logo. The pull-out drawer held trays of other people's business cards, paper clips of all sizes, stamps, and several unlabeled flash drives. As she slid the drawer shut, the desk shimmied, and the screensaver disappeared on the monitor that had appeared idle.

Callie read the first line. "Seabrook, come see this."

He covered the room in three long steps. "Good lord," he said after reading the first line.

I cannot live with killing Brea. I never thought anyone so phenomenal would grace my life like she did last summer. And to think I fathered a child, or almost did. That baby would've united us. Instead the loss ruined all the good between us. So I laced her drink with clam juice to end her pain, to end mine. I could not continue each August knowing I'd see her on the arm of another man she didn't love. Now she's mine and I'm hers. ~Dr. Ernest Renaldo Maddington, PhD

Articulate, romantic in a distorted way. Callie turned toward the body in an effort to envision the man alive, writing this note, then leaving this world as calm as a monk. She reanalyzed the details of the strangulation. If he did this himself, as all indicators expressed, he positioned himself properly, then leaned into the rope, letting his body weight do its thing. As a man engrossed in science, he'd probably done his research.

But no tears, no pain on his face. Maybe he took something first to settle his nerves?

He didn't design this death with any type of rescue mechanism like a breakaway or slip knot. He meant to do this. His ears would have buzzed first as oxygen fought to reach his brain. He'd have felt tingling, maybe experienced vertigo, then muscle weakness that would have only placed more pressure against his neck. She noticed his hands. Fisted as if in a personal battle to complete his mission . . . or an uncontrolled response to the life force leaving his body.

"Do you want me to interview Grant?" she asked and then caught herself. Not her call to make.

"You can sit in, but this is a different level of interview than at the party."

She acted aghast. "You think?"

He scowled.

"Sorry," she said, palms high. "You're right. No badge, no invitation to enter the clubhouse."

Seabrook shifted his weight. "I understand you want to be involved, but—"

She frowned. "You called me, remember? The way I see it, this is a consult. I can charge, if you want to make it legit. But however you deal with this, start with Grant. Use me or don't. Your call." She pointed toward the door as voices rose again. "He's out there. Pick his brain ASAP. Sarah hunted him for hours. Now the doc's dead, and Grant's watching this play out twenty feet from the body. How elementary do I have to get about that?"

"Francis," Seabrook hollered, his voice reverberating off the low ceiling.

"Sir?" he hollered back.

"Send Mr. Grant Jamison in here, please."

"That was subtle," Callie said.

Seabrook bent over and lessened the ten inches of height between them. "It doesn't matter whether I whisper, teletype, or sky-write his name now, does it? Everybody will see him come in." Seabrook headed toward the hallway. "I'll talk to him in the spare bedroom. The close vicinity to the body will throw him off."

Callie peered out front again. Another uniform trotted the stairs to relieve Officer Francis. Thomas, she believed. People hovered along the property line, and some across the street, as if Jungle Road made them more polite observers. She started to leave when a flash of recognition stopped her. Several of the faces were guests from the party. The guy who tried to assist her with Brea was there. The New Jersey couple. Maybe one or two others.

Grant's protests indicated he balked on the porch. The acting chief stepped forward to coax Grant inside. Any minute Callie expected to hear *I want a lawyer*.

"I'll be back." She squeezed around the uniforms and crowd and dashed out the front door, face turned from the tweeting journalist.

Humidity hung in the air, a strain to breathe. Combined with the ninety-degree heat, sweat popped on temples, faces, and armpits in seconds. Mosquitoes the size of small hummingbirds bit like bees as she crossed the street to the other side, having no trouble since cars crawled by to scan. A few people slid off as she approached. Ten, however, remained fast, eager to hear. All waited in the shade of a massive oak, Spanish moss dangling in the slight wafts of ocean air. They hadn't learned that shade identified them as dinner to gnats and mosquitoes.

She reached out, the other hand swiping at bugs. "I'm Callie Morgan. Didn't get your names at the party the other afternoon."

The pink New Jersey man in a floral, unbuttoned shirt flaunting an abundance of chest hair returned her shake. "Frank Weaver." He patted the shoulder of his even pinker partner, her bottle-blonde hair tied tight into a two-inch ponytail, an ample sundress hiding the ampleness beneath. "This here's Ava."

Callie remembered them.

Their arms and faces shone from suntan lotion, their vulnerable skin too fair for a Carolina sun. "Impressive how you handled yourself at the party," Frank said, "and now we see you here. You some kind of law enforcement?"

"Yes," she said, not caring to explain, her back kept toward Maddington's place as she sensed Alex's camera lens. "How did you guys get here so fast?"

Frank hunted to his right, then over his shoulder to his left. "Daniel saw Twitter, so we came to check it out. That *EdistoToday* person is on top of everything around here. We're not breaking any laws, are we?"

Callie shook her head. "Which one of you is Daniel?" she asked quizzically, innocently. She wiped her forehead, settling in with the group. "It's a hot one today, isn't it?"

"I'm Daniel Hahn." Peering over Frank's shoulder, a tanned man in his mid-thirties waved. Another memory from the party as well as during her jog on the beach. Callie recalled his wife's frosted hair.

"Y'all staying together?" Callie asked.

Daniel shook his head. "No, my wife and I are from Georgia. We met the others at the party. Our places happen to be two houses apart."

Callie rubbed sweat off her neck. "You have that cute wife, right?"

He beamed. "Tanya's making love to her tan right now, but yes, she's mine."

"So what happened?" Frank asked.

"Man was found dead in his home," she said.

Gasps traveled around the troop like a wave in a football stadium.

"Murder?"

"How?"

"Oh my gosh."

"Who did it?"

She widened her eyes, playing the part. "Whoa, nobody said anything about murder. I imagine it'll be a while before authorities release details."

Shoulders sagged, and furrowed foreheads softened as disappointment settled on the small audience. Callie had said enough but not enough to say anything, and this band thought they knew it all. "But I might use your help," she said.

They riveted their collective attention on her.

"Anyone here attend the party and not speak to the police?" she asked. "We wanted statements from everyone who saw Brea Jamison collapse, but some of y'all left fast." She smiled like she asked for a cigarette light.

A couple more hands rose. Callie's gaze roamed over the crowd. Two more people eased away. "We met, right?" she said to a dark-headed, slim, middle-aged man. Five foot nine, maybe. "You offered to help me when she went down," she said. "Sorry if I didn't thank you."

He nodded. "I felt so useless just standing there."

Callie grimaced. "Me, too. She seemed a sweet lady." She reached out. "Again, my name's Callie. Did you happen to see why Ms. Jamison collapsed?"

He reciprocated the gesture, his grip tight. "Terrance Mallory. And no. Sorry. Heard her go down, turned, and there she was."

"Did *EdistoToday* draw you over here, too?" she asked. Rikki identified him as one of the few deemed as a repeat visitor to the beach.

"No," Terrance replied. "Saw these folks hustling down the road this way. I'm staying at Paradise Lost. It's too hot to sit on the sand, and I got bored, so I followed." He shrugged. "Sounds juvenile, but blue lights mean there's something interesting to see."

Callie knew the dated, whitewashed clapboard-sided rental he referenced. Most of the homes, rental or primary residence, held creative monikers like Paradise Lost, not unlike her Chelsea Morning. His house resided on Pompano Drive, older than Callie had been alive.

"So everyone arrived after the police cars were already here?"

Again the unified affirmation.

"Well, thanks for talking to me."

She moved to leave then turned. "One more thing."

Their necks craned like birds.

"Anyone see who may have given Brea Jamison something to eat?"

"Why?" Frank asked. "Y'all suspect murder there, too?"

Ava punched him in the chest. "She didn't say it's murder, Frank."

"I saw her husband give her a glass of something," Terrance said. "But what husband doesn't bring his wife a drink?" He came in closer. Callie met him part way. "You were seen fixing her a drink, too," he whispered.

Callie almost grinned, but all eyes rested on her. They were sincere, and she didn't need to belittle their eagerness to assist.

"We heard about the jinx, too," said Frank.

Callie feigned surprise. "The jinx?"

"How the dead woman fit the model," Ava added to her husband's remark. "We dug into it after reading those tweets."

The tourists had formed a loose friendship anchored in the party's disaster and an island tale. A jaw-dropping incident bonded them, and now they were armchair detectives. This excitement beat anything they could hire a tour guide to experience. Two deaths in three days only fueled their vacation adventure.

"Whoa, look at this!" Frank exclaimed, holding out his phone. "We're *witnesses!*"

Phones came out of nowhere. Callie peered at Terrance's.

@EdistoToday—Detective Callie Morgan questions witnesses at residence of island death. #edistojinx #murdersuicide

There she was, right where she stood now, talking to Frank.

"She didn't get that right," Ava said. "The jinx is about women, not men."

"And it's not a murder/suicide," Daniel complained. "That person needs to get his facts straight."

"It's a her, not a him," Callie said, shading her eyes from the sun.

Perched on Maddington's stairs for height, Alex waved and took another picture, then typed.

"Oh my gosh," Ava exclaimed. "There we are again!"

@EdistoToday—Detective Morgan scouring the crowd for a suspect. #edistojinx

The pic showed Callie, shading her eyes, peering straight at Alex.

"Damn it," Callie whispered. "Listen, I need to go, folks. I'm sure I'll see you again."

These nice people were only late-to-the-dance bystanders today, but she took note to ask them later for a more detailed interview about Brea. Now was not the time. Not with Miss EdistoToday on guard.

Shaking each of their outstretched hands, she repeated names and etched them to memory. Then as she crossed the street, she caught the sweet rear end of Alex Hanson sliding into her VW.

Staring ahead, as if she had the right to be inside, she reentered Maddington's house past Officer Thomas to check on Seabrook and Grant. Her shell of a reputation still gained her access to a crime scene. At least until Seabrook tired of her assistance, interference, whatever he deemed it.

Frank and Ava walked toward the beach. Seemed Callie'd gained a ragtag band of groupies who had eyes and ears open on Edisto Beach. She wasn't yet sure if she ought to capitalize on that. Or how.

She also had no clue what to do about Alex Hanson, or if anything should be done. For the life of her she couldn't think of why the blow-by-blow Twitter feeds were wrong, but she darn sure felt like they should be. Fueling murder with fame would only go south, in her opinion.

Chapter 8

MEDICAL PERSONNEL worked in Maddington's bedroom, the coroner with them. They spoke little and moved at ease, urgency not an issue.

Seabrook and Grant sat in the guest bedroom of the deceased's home, Callie in the doorway. Francis stood guard in the corner, his uniform wilted from the damp beach heat. She'd never seen Seabrook so focused. She liked him this way.

"I drove around," Grant said under the scrutinizing eye of Officer Seabrook. "I never came over here. How many times do I have to tell you? If it wasn't true, I'd call a lawyer."

Officer Thomas kept the curious on the porch, but it wouldn't be long before they'd need to move this interview to the station. Callie liked Seabrook questioning Grant early, on site, as Maddington's body cooled only fifteen feet away. The in-your-face setting would make Grant think less about the formalities of an investigation and more likely to talk.

"Can anyone confirm your drive?" Seabrook asked.

Grant shook his head. "I wanted to be alone, to come to terms with losing my wife."

Callie spoke up. "How long have you and Brea been coming to Edisto?"

"Um," he said, raking his hair in jerky motions, which he'd done a dozen times now. "Six or seven years."

"You always stay with your in-laws?" she asked.

"Yeah. Not that I enjoy their company. Sarah spoiled Brea, and I always got stuck listening to Ben's rants, watching him drink himself stupid. Especially since last year when he learned about Sarah and the guy she—" His attention darted to Callie, then to Seabrook. "But why rent when you can stay at the beach for free? Brea would've come with or without me anyway." He froze for an instant at the sound of his words. "Look what happened the one time she came alone."

He fell silent, as if in remembrance of Brea. They gave him only a second or two.

"You've heard of the August jinx, right?" Callie asked.

Seabrook cut a disapproving stare at her.

"Sure," Grant said. "Sarah talks about it."

Callie calmly said, "Your wife fits the profile."

Grant tensed, and Seabrook started to protest. A glance from Callie hushed him, but she knew he'd only give her this one free pass.

"If I heard you right," Grant started slowly, "you not only accused me of killing my wife, but of possibly killing five other people just because I come to the beach?"

He made it sound far-fetched, but this was death number six in the same time period, and he'd had a difficult marriage. The others might've been practice before Brea, or a way to vent frustration.

They needed to question anyone who'd lived or visited here during that month, during each of those years. A tall, almost impossible order. Thus the desire for the guest book, to whittle down the number at least for this case. They had a ten-to twelve-day window before the guy disappeared for another year.

She cocked a brow at Seabrook, mentally thinking, *Push him.*

"We aren't accusing you of anything," Seabrook said quickly.

Not what she expected, but she followed his lead. "I didn't say you killed Brea or anybody else, Grant. I said she fit the profile."

Grant leaped to his feet, his arm stiffened, directed toward the other bedroom. "That man in there had a motive. Brea chose me over him after losing *their* baby. I'm the innocent party here."

"Spouses frequently do the deed," she replied.

"Oh, I forget." Tendons stood out on his neck. "You're this fancy detective. Of course you'd blame me instead of Maddington. He and your dead daddy walked the same walk around this beach. Guess you and me ought to share experiences over drinks, huh?"

Callie stood firm and gave him that one. She entered interrogations clad for battle. The accused always made it personal.

"Grant, that's enough. Sit down," Seabrook ordered.

The husband's arms rose out to his side. "Didn't he leave a note or anything?"

Seabrook feigned surprise. "A note?"

There you go, Seabrook.

Grant quickly hid his hands behind him, as if erasing his actions. "Stop trying to trick me. Most suicide victims leave a note. I'd assume our illustrious professor would be no different."

Callie shifted her position against the doorframe. "Too much television. Not everyone cares to enlighten the world why they killed themselves."

Grant frowned, his neck a different shade of pink than his blushing face. "Did he or didn't he kill himself?"

"Not sure yet," Seabrook said.

"How'd he die?" Grant asked.

"We can't say."

Grant wrapped arms around his body, head down, appearing to think hard. Seabrook patiently waited, Callie puzzled as to why the officer would play Grant with such a soft touch.

To heck with this. Callie pressed on while the time was choice. "What do you think happened in there, Grant?"

"Have no idea," he said, sarcasm dripping in the three short clipped words.

"Give it a guess," she prodded, poking at the animal in the cage. "Why is he dead?"

From his shoulder movements, Grant's breathing had accelerated, a slight twitching in the mix. His antsy movements, agitated and angry, broadcasted an inability to sort himself.

"Tell me what you're thinking, Grant," she asked louder. "Don't try to think of a good story, just tell us what happened."

"Callie, don't," Seabrook said, pressing the air with his palm. "Give him a second."

With Grant's back to her, she glared at the cop, trying to project her thoughts. *Squeeze him, damn it. Antagonize him. Bombard him with questions, make him slip and say what he doesn't want to say.*

Then as she expected, in those few seconds of leniency, Grant's muscles loosened, arms returned to his side while hands slid into his pockets. He regained a grip on his frayed emotions, and Callie wished Seabrook hadn't let him.

Seabrook had acted like a doctor instead of pressuring like a cop, and they'd lost their advantage.

"Brea got into kinky stuff last year. Now I see why," the husband said with candor, no longer nervous. "No doubt where she learned it." He shook his head and released a sad, soft chuckle. "To think I took credit for that, too. Shit."

This had gone on too long without a demand for counsel. Television serials schooled viewers weekly on how to act when cops hauled someone in for questioning. While they rarely got events procedurally correct, the series directors emphasized a suspect didn't have to talk if he didn't want to, and attorneys were usually the smart way to go. This bereaved husband enjoyed grandstanding.

Grant squinted at Callie. "You were there when Brea died."

"Yes," she replied calmly.

"So was Maddington," he said.

"I didn't see him."

"Well, I did. Who's to say he didn't slip her something?"

"How convenient would that be?" Callie asked, irritated at Seabrook allowing Grant to take control. "Don't you think he would've at least pretended to be concerned if he'd been in the room? Isn't that what any romantic interest would do, without worrying about what people thought? And if he wasn't romantically interested, wouldn't he have feigned it to disperse suspicion?"

Grant straightened, a hateful leer on his face.

"I didn't see him there, Grant," she repeated. "But I did see that type of behavior on someone else."

"How dare you," he whispered.

"How dare I what?" she asked.

His eyes fixated on her, intense under tight lids. "I've been trying to help you so I could take my wife home for a burial. Since you're either too stupid or plain callous to notice, I want my lawyer."

"There it is," she said.

Seabrook sighed and rose, aggravated. "Do what you like, Grant, but stay in town."

Grant strode to the door. Callie rolled her shoulder and hip to the side to make room for the man to pass. He leaned over and hissed, "I loved my wife," then exited the room.

He walked down the hall, not in a hurry but not taking his time, like a man on his way to work. Callie watched him leave, a puffy-eyed Sarah smothering him for information the moment his foot hit the porch.

Seabrook watched the drama as people stared, a few asking questions in paparazzi fashion. "Well, damn, Detective," he asked Callie. "What do you think?"

Callie glanced at Officer Francis. He caught the unspoken message and left her alone with Seabrook. Once Francis walked out of earshot, Callie turned on Seabrook. "What the hell was that?" She waved toward the door. "You let Grant off the hook."

"We haven't determined he's guilty."

"And you'll never find out interrogating him like that. Hell, Seabrook, you were ready to prescribe the guy two aspirin."

His mouth flatlined. "I asked you what you thought."

"And I'm trying to tell you. Did he kill Brea? I have no idea at this juncture. Motive's there, though. But you would've gotten a better read on him pushing his buttons. Trust me."

He ignored the jab. "What about Maddington?" he asked. "Suicide?"

"Who can say? Take a pill, suck an exhaust pipe, pull a trigger, but why erotic asphyxiation? Seems extreme to me, but I didn't know the guy."

"He wouldn't have killed himself if he didn't have the affair."

Callie kept staring toward the Rosewood house. "Who says he killed himself?"

"In the hospital, I saw people do things when they were distraught."

His reference to his past stunned her. The first time he'd spoken of his time as a doctor, a history nobody understood, but he cut himself off, his thought finished silently in his head.

"I've met all types, too," she said. "I want to see the sign-in book even more now."

"Why would he sign in if he planned to kill her?"

"Not signing would make him stand out more," she added.

"Well, if he did it, he didn't stand around and watch. He was too soft-hearted for that."

She let out a breath. "A soft-hearted killer. Imagine that. My guess is he'd want to watch Grant's reaction as Brea slid away. So if he were there at all, he'd have stuck around."

And here she went again, tumbling down that investigative rabbit hole. A question, a clue, maybe a red herring or two had her taking the bait. Two deaths now, with the players connected, and a slight link to past deaths. How does any cop ignore all that? Geez, it was like seeing all the straight edge pieces of a puzzle lying there on the table and nobody curious enough to play with them.

Maddington's note made Brea's death tentatively murder along with the affair, an unforeseen pregnancy, and loss of the same. A case in and of itself without any of the Edisto jinx attached to it.

"I'll start with our list from the other night," she said. Then she added, "Unless you object."

Seabrook shook his head. "No, I don't. As long as you don't run too far out there on your own without keeping me in the loop."

She scrunched her face as if he'd tried to tell her how to write her name.

He ignored her. "Why didn't Grant just kick Maddington out on his ass at the party?"

Her brows arched. "Now you're thinking." She gently tugged his shirt sleeve, seizing the moment. "Please give me access to your files. It's a long shot, but this case might overlap those others."

He sighed. "We don't need a serial killer."

Callie sighed back in challenge. "Nobody needs a serial killer. But wouldn't you hunt for one if you had the slightest hint?"

"Please don't go there," he said.

The hell I won't. "At least give me that list of license plates Francis wrote down the day of the party? I'll introduce myself to people and see if they'll let me borrow their cameras and cell phones to—"

"Nope."

This man was so close-minded. This middle ground, between investigator and convenient source of advice, grated on her nerves. "Damn it, why'd you even ask me here?"

"I value your opinion. However, opinions are one thing; relinquishing files and releasing info on open investigations are another."

"Thought they weren't open. They were accidents."

He ignored the comment. "Come work for me. It'd be good for you."

"Is that the police chief talking or the doctor?" she asked.

"Yes," he said.

"Told you I'm not cut out for that work full-time anymore."

Seabrook blew out long and hard then walked off to join the coroner.

Callie's gaze, however, shifted across the street where the number of observers had dwindled to Terrance Mallory and some older gentleman, the two engrossed in conversation. Callie turned and watched Grant and Sarah enter their home two houses down, but not before Grant searched for Callie, glaring at her before shutting his door so hard she heard it.

Callie didn't like him, suicide note or not. While an accidental death and a suicide didn't exactly warrant a suspect list, her gut had already started one. And she didn't need to wear a uniform to do it.

RIKKI STIRRED A spoon in figure eights through her shrimp and grits.

Blackened scallops stared at Callie, and a simple cup of clam chowder sat ignored before Sophie. She always ate like a bird, hated bread, and limited her meat to fish, a testimony to her lithe shape. The only one with a healthy appetite, Rikki scooped grits into her mouth, a woman in total agreement with the world.

Their table faced north, overlooking the beach running along the state park. Finn's Island Grill was a relatively new eatery, in name, anyway. Previously the Pavilion, Finn's represented the only restaurant on the waterfront, now the most upscale since Grovers unexpectedly closed its doors three weeks ago. Callie's mind drifted at the comparison. Grovers held memories of Stan, and if truth be known, Callie had no desire to revisit the place where she got drunk in front of her old boss. Her heart hurt thinking about how she tried to take advantage of him afterward. He had returned to his wife the next morning, leaving their twelve-year friendship torn and bruised. Six weeks ago. She used to talk to him at least once a week, sometimes more. He didn't phone even after she killed the Russian. That hurt the most.

Rikki tapped her bowl for attention. "Why are we here again? I could've eaten alone at the condo for a lot less." She aimed her spoon at her phone on the table. "By the way, nice new pic of you today, Detective. You came across all serious and important at the crime scene."

Her comment dragged Callie back to the present. "That Alex girl is becoming a nuisance."

"She's doing her job," Rikki said. "Hasn't seemed to hurt anyone yet."

"She increases the odds, though. I don't like people finding where I live. Or informing the public of half-truths."

Rikki tilted her head with a lackadaisical grin. "Miss Alex reports news. Throw your misplaced anger at MyOuttake; he's the amateur gossip slinger."

Callie had scrolled her phone a dozen times after going home yesterday evening and awoke scanning it again. Three more tweets, this time from MyOuttake, piggybacking on the *EdistoToday* reports. One showed Callie from a different angle outside at the party house, after Alex had left the scene. The covert exposure vexed her. She'd almost break one of her Neil Diamond albums to learn who this person was.

Callie felt it best to start sleuthing with these two ladies, people more willing to talk, then use the intel on others later who might not be so chatty. Like Seabrook, she might've considered Brea's death pure accident, until Maddingon too conveniently died. And even if they took Maddington's suicide note at face value, there was the history of the jinx.

She sighed. If only Brea had been blonde. Who knew whether Callie would've even heard about the jinx . . . until it happened again.

She squeezed lemon on her scallops. "Did either of you see anyone overly attentive to Brea at the party?"

Rikki laid another empty shrimp peel on her plate. "Just you and the husband."

"Y'all were familiar with Maddington, right?"

"I knew the little turtle meister," Rikki said. "Though I never knew *that* side of him. Can't believe y'all found him all trussed hanging from a doorknob."

Did Rikki take anything serious? This woman seemed awful rough around the edges for being so worldly. Too glib a personality to trust.

"Don't make it into something more than it is," she said to the Amazon. "Did y'all see Maddington at the party? Or were y'all aware he had a fling with Brea last summer?"

Rikki waved her spoon. "No, but love the juicy news. Didn't realize the guy had such tendencies."

The flippant response rubbed Callie wrong for the umpteenth time. No empathy, no sympathy, hell, no plain interest, for that matter. She appeared impervious to emotional connection. "Doesn't any of this bother you?" Callie asked with a frown.

"Actually no, it doesn't," Rikki replied, scowling down, flipping a crumb off her top. "Why should it?"

"Maybe because a death occurred right under your nose."

Rikki shrugged. "Sorry, but I didn't meet her. And I associated with Maddington, but wasn't drinking buddies with him, so no, he doesn't fire up my tear ducts either."

Tired of Rikki's irreverence, Callie suspected Sophie might be too, her ringed fingers mashing a packet of crackers into crumbs. Her chowder sat untouched, and she fidgeted as if she had another place to be.

Rikki laid a sprawling hand across both of Sophie's nervous ones. "Would you sit still! God, you're like a blur of energy."

Sophie tossed the cracker packet onto the table. "My house is full of spirits, and I'm lost what to do. More each night."

Rikki released her and returned attention to her dish. "Oh, that. Come on, Soph. We get the New Age mumbo-jumbo you're into, but don't overdo it. You'll chase people off from yoga class. We're here on Callie's nickel, so stay on topic."

Rikki's condescension toward Sophie the other night had slightly annoyed Callie. She assumed the two shared some understanding between them, a tit-for-tat volley of verbal jabs. This time, however, Sophie's mouth lines ran deeper.

"Tell me," Callie said and pushed her sneakered foot against Sophie's sandal in assurance. "How many spirits is too many? *One* ghost would make me have a cow."

Rikki's eyes twinkled, a mischievous smirk on her face.

"Who are the new ones?" Callie quickly added to stop Rikki from interjecting.

"I . . . can't tell." Sophie trailed into a mumble.

"What do you mean?"

Rikki wiped her mouth. "Don't feed her fantasies, Callie."

"They aren't fantasies," Sophie cried out.

Diners peered over shoulders.

Callie used to think Sophie the gossip-monger, but Rikki appeared to love it more, embellishing it to boot. "Stop it," Callie said under her breath.

Rikki licked the last of the grits off her spoon. "Stop what? Treating her like a child? She might be tiny, she might be cute, but damn this spiritual shit gets old."

Sophie's posture wilted.

Callie didn't trust Rikki. While nothing identified the woman's involvement in either death, Callie held no doubt Rikki could watch the final death leave a body and easily sleep through the night afterward. Not a friend she wanted in her camp.

The waitress arrived with their ticket. Callie took it from the girl. "I've got it."

Rikki reached for her purse. "Let me help."

"No." Callie slapped her credit card on the folder. "I'm sure you have commitments. Sophie and I want to stick around a few minutes."

The tall woman unfolded out of the booth. "This *is* childish."

Sophie stared into her cup of cold soup.

"Could you have killed Brea?" Callie asked as Rikki stood.

"I'm sure I could have," she said, as the question rolled off her like water. "Any of us is capable. But like I said, never met her, and I had no reason." She flipped her long braid off her shoulder and grinned at the challenge. "I was not here for two of the other August deaths. Rules me out as a suspect, right, Madam Detective?"

"Had to ask," Callie replied.

Flashing another cavalier smile, Rikki slightly tipped her head, then turned and left the restaurant.

Callie laid her elbow on the table. "Has she always been so rude?"

Sophie seemed shrunken by the experience in the oversized wooden booth. "She's strong-willed."

"So why socialize with her?" Call it a cop sense, or call it self-preservation from years of dangerous liaisons with the criminal element, but Callie slept easier when her friends were solid and loyal. Even if being selective limited her circle of trust to a few.

"There is a degree of good in her," Sophie replied. "Yoga isn't only exercise, Callie; it's a spiritual process, too. My soul thrives off a balanced, happy, unselfish life."

"Well, I didn't sense too many positive vibes coming from y'all's conversation. And you don't appear too *namaste* to me right now."

Sophie tossed her head, her curls prancing. "You are so right. I shouldn't let the negative take hold. My fault."

"Not what I meant. A patronizing snoot isn't welcome in my realm."

Sophie perked up. "Let me work with you. Come to my classes."

"Sorry, not feeling it." Callie moved from beside her friend to around the table until she faced her. "Let's talk about the party. Did you see Maddington there?"

"I stayed on the rear porch most of the time. Never saw him. Rikki would've said if she had. Did you invite us out to eat only to interrogate?"

"Of course not. Lunch with a friend is always worthwhile."

She'd hoped the two ladies to be more help. She didn't ask yesterday's rubberneckers at Maddington's if they saw the professor at the party. As quirky as the motley crew seemed, she seriously might question them next. At least they seemed eager to assist.

Thus far, the only person who placed Maddington at the party appeared to be Grant, the dead professor unable to speak for himself. Callie was eager to see if the medical examiner found clam juice in Brea's stomach. Even so, Maddington might've paid someone to lace the drink.

But what if someone killed the doctor after Brea and typed the note? With gloves on, of course. Such a scenario would scream hardest at Grant, but admittedly that seemed rather far out there. True conspiracy theory.

Again, God help her, she hoped Brea was the jinx target, and she hoped Maddington was the culprit. However, something needled at her that she couldn't be so lucky.

Sophie dabbed the last trace of tears from her cheek. Callie took the napkin from her friend and finished the job. "Oh, honey, what's so wrong?"

Sophie teared again. "You've got to solve these murders. Otherwise they'll keep coming, and I'll go insane."

"We aren't sure there *are* any murders, Sophie."

"Deaths, murders, whatever they are. I saw a dark-haired woman last night beside my bed."

Callie stopped. "Say what?"

Sophie rubbed a forefinger under her nose and sniffed again.

"Wait," Callie said. "Someone broke into your home? Why didn't you call the police? Call me?"

"No, no." Her friend's long silver earrings jangled as she vigorously shook her head. "A spirit."

Callie froze, pondering how to respond so she didn't come off sounding like Rikki.

"Don't you get it?" Sophie's fingers trembled. "She resembled you, which frightened me to kingdom come. She pointed right at your house."

"What does that even mean, Sophie?"

She scowled. "How the hell should I know? I've never *seen* a spirit before!"

Chapter 9

AS SOON AS SHE entered the door, Callie texted Jeb that she got home from lunch at Finn's. The routine started with Callie demanding Jeb keep her informed of his whereabouts, but it boomeranged with the son asking the same of his mother. One-and two-word texts were their specialty now.

Soon after, she rinsed off the last dish in her sink, phone on speaker on the counter, her mother's voice droning about the latest political mud-slinging in the town of Middleton.

Neil Diamond played on the turntable, her attempt to dispel the whole creepy vision of Sophie waking to a brunette ghost. Thinking about spirits led to thinking about the jinx. The jinx led to thinking about murder.

She shut off the faucet. Here at home, her mother in her ear, and her music in the air, she'd lost some of the eagerness to dog those old deaths. After all, Edistonians considered the cases already concluded.

Hell, even Brea's death had a confession.

She didn't like Rikki, though. Didn't like how she treated Sophie. The woman must have a deeply hidden insecure side behind the swagger. Regardless, the attitude remained unpleasant.

The phonograph needle reached "Sweet Caroline."

"Ooh, my song!" Beverly cooed across the phone.

Certain Diamond songs reminded her mother of an old flame *other* than Callie's father, this one leading the playlist. Callie dried her hands and scooted over to the turntable, gingerly lifting the needle as a stanza ended, and set it down on another song.

"What did you say about the county administrator, Mother?" she asked.

Callie held a fondness for all of Diamond's music, but so did Beverly, who connected hers to a fling with some guy years ago. *Too much information.* Returning to the sink to wipe the counter, Callie rocked to the beat of another tune from Diamond's *Hot August Night album* instead, rolling her spine and lifting her feet.

Her mother could talk and not come up for air for hours, Callie often housecleaning to kill the time. She once watched an entire movie while Beverly Cantrell ranted about Lawton's political adversary sporting an ill-dressed wife. Beverly intimidated every councilman, administrator, and cop in the town of Middleton, who'd ultimately conceded to the widow assuming the remainder of her husband's mayoral term. The role proved a blessing as it kept Beverly forty-five miles from Edisto.

In Callie's heart, however, she believed Beverly held onto Lawton by filling that seat. Much like Callie holding onto his bottle of bourbon.

"Do you think Sarah Rosewood taught her niece the kinky stuff?" her mother prattled on as Callie bebopped around the kitchen. "They call it erotic asphyxiation on the Internet."

Callie stopped dancing, snatched the phone off speaker mode, and returned it to her ear, forgetting nobody else lived in the house to hear. "Oh my God, Mother, I seriously doubt that. Where did you hear how Maddington died?"

Beverly Cantrell *harrumphed* from her end of the line. "One would think a daughter would update her mother, but I have my ways. You forget your beach house used to be mine, dear. I'm familiar with everybody. Ernest seemed a sweet man, but his image is rather ruined now."

Dear. Her mother delivered the endearment with an aristocratic poignancy. Hypersensitive to the word, Callie shrugged off goose bumps when her mother used it.

"You're the last person to question Ernest Maddington's love life," Callie chided. "He had an affair. He loved Brea. No telling how much of the gossip spinning off of that is true."

"Your father never did erotic stuff with me." Beverly seemed more interested in the sexual connotations than murder. "I wouldn't know how." She gasped, sounding more curious than hurt. "Do you think Sarah enticed him with those . . . antics? Where does a person learn such things?"

"Books? Movies? Swinger parties?" Callie smiled at her jabs.

A stranger listening would gasp at a mother's gall for such conversation, but Callie'd long grown used to Beverly's shock-and-awe moments.

"Swap meets?" her mother asked.

"Not quite, Mother, but your description works." Tea poured, Callie moved to the sofa. At ninety-five degrees outside, the porch in the daytime would be off limits until Labor Day. The fan whirred overhead. "Mother, I thought you didn't hold Daddy's affair against him."

"I said *him*, dear. Nobody said I had to like *her*."

Callie avoided defending her father to her mother, not sure she wanted to hear the details of their bizarre marriage. She wondered if Lawton strayed because of Beverly's lover. How hurt he might have been when she'd broken their vows with an ex-fiancé. Did Lawton meet him? Maybe steal her from the first beau, thus reaping what he sowed? Her father had carried a suave air about him, urbane comportment, and she wanted her memories preserved as such. Callie shifted the phone to her other ear. All these details of the past were just too . . . weird.

"Do you see her much?" Beverly asked. "Sarah, I mean."

"Why? What difference does it make—" Callie omitted *now Daddy's dead.* "You sure act more interested in his girlfriend now than before."

A pause hung on the other end before Beverly answered, "I can't really explain it."

"Well, I feel sorry for her," Callie replied, feet tucked under her. "She has a crappy marriage, plus she misses Daddy."

"A rather bold statement to say to the grieving widow."

"Hey, you're the one who said y'all's extracurricular relationships were consensual. How I shouldn't be such a prude. Frankly, after your confession, I started seeing Sarah in a whole new light."

Her gaze strayed to the turntable as the last song on the album reach its end, and she felt silly now about their old argument over Neil Diamond albums. Two months ago, Lawton's death brought the mother-and-daughter-war to a veiled truce over the turntable and record collection and a strange level of open conversation. "You saying Daddy had bad taste?"

"Your father had marvelous taste."

"All right then. Let Sarah be. She's not a threat."

"Hmm."

The vintage record player shut off with a familiar click.

Then an idea struck. "Mother, how much info have you heard about the deaths out here?"

"Dear, I only met Sarah's niece a couple of times. Never liked her husband, but—"

"No, no, I mean the death last August and the August before."

Beverly laughed. "They're jabbering about the August accidents again, are they? Let me guess . . . Sophie?"

"So, nothing to it?" Callie didn't want to stir her mother into an hour extension to an already lengthy call, but she'd be foolish to disregard this source. Like Beverly said, she'd owned the beach house for decades. "They weren't related to anyone like Brea was to the Rosewoods?" Callie asked. "Any of the deaths considered murders? The families didn't demand deeper investigations?"

She almost asked if Beverly envisioned Grant as a murderer, but the question would generate a gossip thread from Middleton to Edisto and back ten times over.

"Heavens no, Callie. They were only tourists," she said, as if stepping on ants. "Oh my goodness, who says they were murders?"

Nobody but me. "People talk."

Beverly *harrumphed* again. Callie pictured the well-practiced eye rolling accompanied by a swoop of her mother's bejeweled fingers.

"They all looked alike, did you hear that?" Callie asked.

"No, I didn't. Does it matter?"

"Never mind. Oh, I ran into a friend of yours who said I resembled you," Callie said.

"Who might that be?"

"Janet Wainwright."

Beverly blew an air of disgust. "She's not a friend. She's an acquaintance and one not very high on *my* list. The old biddy is why we used Rhonda Benson to rent out our house."

"How come?"

"The Marine relic kept telling us what to do, when to do it, and how to do it. I finally told her she worked for us, not the other way around. Then we signed with Rhonda."

Callie laughed out loud. "I would've paid good money to be there, Mother. She seems to still respect you."

"Well, of course she would, dear. Your father and I hold a commendable degree of business savvy and a solid reputation."

"It's getting deep."

"She'll do anything for her highfalutin company," Beverly said, ignoring the remark. "I can't see red and yellow without thinking of her stupid wardrobe."

The door opened, the inside vacuum temporarily broken as Jeb stormed in. With a slam, he stomped into the kitchen.

"Jeb's home." Callie watched as her tanned, blond-headed son poured a glass of water and chugged it, his brow creased with anger. He'd come home early. "Let me go, Mother."

"Oh, let me talk to my grandbaby," the senior woman clucked.

Jeb refilled, drank, set the glass hard in the sink, and marched his lanky, six-foot frame to his room.

"Not a good time," Callie said. "I'll update you when I have something new."

"No, you won't, but I need to get to town hall anyway. I have a teleconference at four."

Callie hung up. She went to Jeb's room and knocked. "What's going on, son?"

In spite of his age, she considered him a child. However, the boy rose ten inches over his mother, his height and color inherited from his father, along with a cockeyed half grin that never failed to send Callie back to her days with John. Right now the smile was nowhere to be seen.

Jeb stopped pacing, stood rigid, and growled.

Her brows rose at the emotion. "What's so bad? Wait. Did you have a fight with Sprite?"

Callie had been waiting for such a moment. Still in high school, Sophie's daughter held the sexual energy of her mother with the stamina of youth and all its intense beauty. Boys gravitated to her. Sprite seemed to adore Jeb, for now.

"Damn them, we lost our right to do fishing charters."

"Who's *them*?" she asked.

"The town of Edisto Beach. Somebody in their ivory tower claimed our papers were out of order and incomplete. And we weren't twenty-one. Yeah, that's about it."

Callie would've laughed aloud at Jeb's ivory tower reference if he weren't so exasperated. The beach's tiny administrative office resembled more of a bureaucratic closet. "How have you and Zeus been chartering until now? What prompted the sudden shift?"

His eyes widened, and he threw out his arms in an exaggerated shrug.

"Who the hell knows? Zeus has been doing this for two years. He called his dad."

Sophie's ex-husband had played NFL ball for enough years to amass a decent bank account and recognizable name before he blew out his knee. He'd given Zeus the boat. Amazing how many people swooned at his notoriety, and per Sophie, his clout came in handy at times.

She lifted a worn T-shirt off the foot of Jeb's bed, a pair of shorts from a chair. "Well, no point in you going nuts over it. Sounds like Mr. Bianchi will take care of the mistake."

Jeb stared at his mother like an annoyed senior studying an ignorant freshman on the first day of school. "We were booked through August, Mom. What're we supposed to do about our customers? They'll go elsewhere and never return." He slammed his dresser with a fist. "It's not fair. We've had a great season."

A revelation settled over Callie. One she wouldn't share with Jeb.

Janet Wainwright was making good on her threat to irritate Callie. Nobody else had the town council connection Janet did, at least nobody mad at Callie. She doubted there were such rules to be broken. Kids fished from the time they walked on the coast, and too many boys graduated high school and went straight into the business. There had to be more to this.

"Well, don't let it keep you awake, son. Give it a day or two. Relax for a change." She eased his door closed.

She marched to her desk for her laptop. "All you've done is intrigue me, you old warhorse," she said under her breath, suspecting Janet had made good on her threat. "What're you so afraid I'll find?" She opened a blank document and began listing potentials to interview in one column. She tried to remember the deaths of the past victims, but couldn't recall who drowned when or fell down what stairs. And Seabrook wouldn't give her the old files.

But Callie knew one person who might have the intel. Two, actually, and they lived under the same roof.

Ms. Hanson answered on the fourth ring. "Oh, honey, how have you been?" she asked once Callie introduced herself.

The sixty-ish neighbor across the street and several doors down from Chelsea Morning met Callie in June when a handyman burgled her home. The only interview in Callie's history where the subject greeted her with warm, out-of-the-oven chocolate chip cookies.

After a few minutes of chitchat, Callie said, "I hear your granddaughter stays with you. Cute girl. I met her a couple days ago."

The squeal told Callie she'd hit a sweet spot.

"Ooooh, that baby is a joy. With my husband on the road, she gives me such pleasure."

"Is she there now?" Callie asked. "We haven't been able to talk much, and I wanted to ask about her blog. I hear she's pretty successful."

"Wait a minute." The phone muffled, probably against the woman's ample bosom. Unintelligible voices exchanged words before Ms. Hanson returned. "Sure. Come on over. I'll whip up something sweet, or maybe even dinner, so plan to stay."

Callie slid the phone in her purse. "I'm headed to Ms. Hanson's place," she hollered to Jeb. "You want to come? She has a granddaughter about twenty-five. If you don't, you're on your own for dinner."

He came out of his room. "I've been meaning to ask you about Alex."

Really? Her son mentioning a cute girl other than Sprite commanded a hundred percent of Callie's attention. Ms. Hanson might need to wait a minute or two. "You know her?"

"Mom," he replied in a tone of teenage indignation. "How do you live on this beach and not meet Alex? She reports on everything and everybody. Look at how much more talk stirred up since she got back from Atlanta."

Thank goodness the blogger had been gone in June. "So, have you met her?" Callie asked. "I mean, seen her?"

"The word is dated, or hooked up, and no, Mom. You do remember Sprite, right?"

Callie flashed him some indignation of her own. "I didn't mean *date*."

He grinned. "Sure you didn't." But then Jeb's face took on a pensive expression, and for a moment she saw John. "Are you working again?" he asked.

"As in . . .?"

"As in I'm still seeing the name *Detective* Morgan a ridiculous number of times in the pictures on Twitter. At places where people have died. You know . . . with cops?"

The only person in the universe who hated the concept of a badge worse than herself was Jeb Morgan. She could thank Alex Hanson for keeping Jeb informed of Callie's whereabouts.

"Don't worry. I turned down the job offer," she said.

Surprise stretched his eyes wide. "*What* job offer? Wait a minute. I thought we agreed to stay on Edisto." He rapidly wagged his head. "No, we're not doing this again. We're not moving." His accusatory finger made her step back. "And you're not becoming a cop again. Geez, Mom. What were you thinking? What *are* you thinking?"

Her heart beat bongos in her chest at his reaction. She gripped both his arms. "Breathe. They came to me, not the other way around. And the offer came from Edisto, nowhere else."

He would've blown out every candle on his eighteenth birthday cake with the rate he huffed. "You're not drinking anymore," he said, ironically trying to assure her. "You're safe now. You have nothing to prove by becoming a cop again."

Callie closed her eyes to collect the right words to say. She'd do anything to remove Jeb's fears. While she had nightmares about the fire, he slept restless because of her. She hadn't touched alcohol in weeks, not that she had a problem. Plus her last anxiety attack had been, God help her, two months ago. Jeb's kidnapping.

She opened her eyes to see his staring, analyzing.

He checked on her before he went fishing in the morning. He peered in at night. Until she convinced him of her stability, he'd continue to postpone college and charter with Zeus off the coast of Edisto Beach. Her weakness was his weakness, and she wasn't sure how to change that.

"Edisto PD offered me an auxiliary position, nothing more."

"What's *auxiliary*?"

"Unpaid, volunteer. One or two days a week." She stroked his arms. "I turned them down."

"But the pictures online . . ."

She nodded. "They learned who I was and like to use the title for effect. It's nothing. Officer Seabrook likes to ask my read on crime problems. People just keep catching me in the act. This is a small place. I was good at what I did. They want my advice."

He stared, as if seeking the truth in her words.

"Honest," she said.

"Well, tell Alex to quit calling you detective," he ordered. "It creeps me out."

"I'll try." She went for her purse. Ms. Hanson would begin to wonder.

"Mom? Why are you going over there anyway?"

She didn't turn around. "For coffee, and I'll speak to Alex if I see her."

"Okay, I might be with Sprite when you get back."

If she glanced back, her guilt would show. But this coffee chat was for him. Janet Wainwright fired the first shot of intimidation over Callie's bow by sabotaging Zeus and Jeb's fishing business. She felt it. Now, more than ever, Callie wanted to unearth what Janet feared when it came to the jinx.

Alex was a journalist. Ms. Hanson knew Edisto. Either could shed light on why everybody worked so hard to ignore six dead women.

Chapter 10

CALLIE HEADED OUT her door to meet with Ms. Hanson, only to stop at the doormat. A cadre of people climbed her twenty-four steps like a horde of overaged trick-or-treaters, huffing from exertion. She dropped her purse inside on the credenza. When would she learn that Edisto time meant *Edislow* time, and appointments were never set in stone, assuming you made them at all?

The six visitors looked up from their feet plodding on each step. She recognized all but two.

Frank Weaver led the bunch, his wife Ava at his side in a multicolored muumuu. Terrance Mallory, the man who offered assistance at the party, hung in close behind Frank's bulky mass. Then Daniel Hahn. Callie didn't recognize the other two women except having seen them chatting with Rikki at the party.

"Um, hello," Callie said, watching Frank conquer the final step.

"Whew," he blew out, sweat dripping down his temples. "Guess . . . guess you're wondering how we found you, huh?" Frank's beefy hand pressed her porch post.

Why was more like it.

Callie caught a whiff of his sandalwood cologne and body odor it failed to mask.

Ava panted, her cheeks moist and rosy, tendrils of blonde hair stuck to her neck. The turquoise ribbons of her muumuu dug into her sunburnt shoulders. Both husband and wife removed shades to reveal white raccoon eyes.

They rented houses about five blocks from Callie, not far with a cool breeze. However, the distance might prove a struggle for out-of-shape vacationers on a hundred-degree day. Frank's complexion screamed heat stroke.

"Do I need to get y'all some water?" she asked. The sooner they cooled off and delivered their message, the sooner she headed to Ms. Hanson's.

"We'd really appreciate it," Terrance said. "We didn't expect the heat to be so oppressive."

Each plopped on her rattan furniture, four to her left and two to her right, the creaks and pops taking a moment to settle.

Callie returned inside to the fridge. The coldness numbed her skin as she piled bottled waters in the crook of her arm. What the hell were these people doing here? While her friendly approach yesterday opened a necessary dialogue, she hadn't intended for them to become buddies.

On the porch she passed out bottles. Then she flipped the ceiling fans on high, dragged over a chair, and sat in front of her doorway to best hear her guests on both sides. For a second she felt bad about not inviting them in, but she wasn't keen on their sweat on her sofa or interested in enticing them to stay longer than necessary. "So," she said, settling in her seat, "what brings you to my porch?"

"Let me explain," said Daniel, the voice of authority.

She always profiled, regardless what the PC police thought. For instance, Daniel might easily be a small firm attorney, if not one with his own shingle.

He held out his card: *Hahn Law Firm, Tifton, Georgia.* "Don't let it upset you that we found where you live, Ms. Morgan."

She read the card and tipped forward to slide it into her back pants pocket. "It's hard to hide an address on an island this small." She turned to the two unidentified ladies. "I'm sorry. I didn't catch your names."

"Kris and Cynthia," Kris said, motioning to herself then her friend. "We'll keep our last names to ourselves, if that's okay."

"Um, sure," Callie replied, amused at the secrecy. One call to Sophie, and she'd have all the intel she needed, but she'd play their game for now. She glanced around, connecting with each one. She'd never had groupies before.

"We want to discuss that woman's death," Frank said, a couple of the others nodding. "I'm an insurance agent."

Big surprise.

Frank's smile faded. "We wondered whether there might be some insurance goal. Like maybe she committed suicide, or the husband committed a homicide." He wiped his temple off on his shoulder. "We're assuming you didn't meet her until that day, right? I mean, since you were seen talking with her."

Interesting.

Callie traced her jawline. "Insurance is a good angle. And no, I didn't know Brea before that afternoon, but I understand. Cover all bases, right?"

Their heads moved in unison in the affirmative.

"Why come to me and not the police?" she asked.

"It's only theory for now, and you're the conduit to the police chief," Terrance replied. "We'd be perceived as nosey amateurs."

The impact of Seabrook's kiss on Twitter. *Thank you, Alex Hanson.*

Terrance rested elbows on his knees to see better around Frank. "But we've got time to kill, and since we have all this experience amongst us, why not use it?"

Callie fought not to smirk at the word *experience.* They had enthusiasm, though. They'd witnessed Brea's death and seemed more open-minded about the jinx than the entire Edisto PD. "Maybe y'all can help me."

"Sure," Terrance said. Daniel echoed behind him.

She chewed her lip, deliberating. "How long have you been coming to Edisto? Do you stay in the same houses each year? Most people do."

Ava rolled the cold water bottle across her neck. "What does that have to do with that poor lady dying?" She glanced over to the other women. Kris shrugged, Cynthia's skeptical expression telling Callie she might be reluctant support.

Frank's wheezy bass of a laugh turned everyone's head. "I get it. They hope to connect those other deaths . . . those that always happen in August."

There you go, Frank. Just don't get crazy with it.

"We don't *hope* to connect anything," Callie said. "We study options and sift out the parts that don't fit. Right now we haven't culled or concluded anything."

Terrance scratched his neck. "If the husband didn't kill her, or she didn't kill herself"—he jerked around to Frank—"which seemed stupid to me when you suggested it"—he turned back—"then did that guy who died yesterday do it?"

Daniel snapped his fingers. "Got it. Maybe the husband killed all those other jinxed women, the wife found out, and he had to kill her. But she was banging that other guy, so the husband took care of both problems."

"Or wait . . ." Ava sucked in, mouth open. "Try this! Maybe the boyfriend killed the others and then took out his girlfriend and committed suicide, like Romeo and Juliet. The husband didn't do anything."

Kris crab-walked her butt to the edge of her seat. "Listen. I have another one—"

Cynthia nudged her. "Stop it, Kris. I promised to come, but we're not getting sucked into this. It's not a dinner play you leave after dessert." She stood with a searing glance across her shoulder. "These are people's lives. See you at the house."

Cynthia took the stairs in a fast hip-hop, drawing Kris to rise, her glances darting everywhere except at Callie. "She's right. She usually is. I better go. Y'all have fun."

Kris hurried to join her partner, and Callie turned to the remaining four. Edisto Beach gave tourists a liberal leash in most activities and behavior, for the obvious financial reasons. These people might actually have fun with a mystery. They might even unearth something. Goodness knows the police weren't helping. "So," she said to the awkward emptiness. "Any of you been coming here for the last six years?"

"Whoa, we're not suspects." Daniel jumped up, ready to bolt on the heels of the departed Kris Whoever and Cynthia No-Last-Name-Please.

Callie straightened, too. She needed to meet Alex, and these groupies would project plots until dark if she let them. "Mr. Hahn. If I'm not a suspect, you're not a suspect."

The lawyer relaxed, but less eager to spin more what-ifs.

Frankly, if Seabrook thought anyone but the boyfriend or husband murdered Brea, Callie and all these people melting on her porch should be suspects. Seabrook, however, remained convinced that Maddington's suicide note sealed the deal. He was probably right. Didn't matter. Victim and probable murderer were deceased. Nobody to pursue. Though she held no love for Grant, nothing connected him to the deeds. The deceased, yes. Their deaths, no.

"However," she continued. "It's important to learn how long you've been coming to Edisto. You have inherent knowledge. You might be able to tell me who else, neighbor or fellow renter, has also been here. I've not lived here long, making you more experienced. I'm interested in the five block area around the other deaths."

"Cool, a grid." Daniel's wide grin flashed white against his tan.

"A what?" Ava asked.

"Babe." Frank shushed his wife. "I'll explain later."

"Oh," she replied, a hand over her mouth, embarrassed.

Frank patted his wife's knee. "We'll walk you through it."

"But I don't know anyone," Terrance said, shoulders hunched in puzzlement. "Who were the old deaths? Where do we start?"

"Who says we can't find out?" Frank puffed his chest and thrust out his hand. "Ms. Morgan, we are at your service." His grip vibrated Callie's arm to her shoulder. "Ava and I have come here for three years. We do stay in the same beach house. I think Terrance has a year or two on us."

"That's right," Terrance said.

The team turned toward Daniel.

"My first year," he said. "And damn, has it been a doozy."

The tension release gave everyone a reason to laugh and shuffle toward the steps.

"Text or call what you find." Callie stood and relocated her rocker to lock the door and keep her appointment across the street.

"Six years, right?" Terrance asked.

Callie nodded. "More or less. Preferably a renter."

Frank touched a two-fingered salute to one eyebrow, gripping the railing to leave. "Will do!" Glancing over his shoulder, he said, "Right, guys?"

"Oh, we got this," Daniel said. Terrance nodded like a bobble-head.

The heat hadn't let up a single degree since the team had arrived. If anything, the temperature had climbed. Callie watched the crew wait for traffic before they crossed the road on their return trek. They had their mission, though she couldn't see them doing much with it. They'd head home soon anyway.

Seabrook would be irritated at her involving civilians in ancient history, but tough. Edisto was her island, too. These visitors had the right to ask questions about the place they paid good money to occupy for a week or two each year. They were bored. She felt frustrated at the lack of cooperation from the powers-that-be. What could it hurt?

Terrance trailed the troop, the last to round the corner home.

She hoped all her Dr. Watsons made it back without fainting.

CALLIE SMELLED warm cookies before she knocked on Ms. Hanson's door. Chocolate chip, maybe? How the heck had she whipped up a batch so quickly? She glanced at her phone for the time. *Oh.* Her surprise guests took longer than she thought.

Ms. Hanson opened the door. "Come on in, neighbor!"

"My apologies for the delay." Callie sniffed. "You weren't kidding about the cookies."

She set her purse on the floor. The kitchen resembled any place other than the beach, with roosters on wallpaper borders and curtains, plastic fruit in a wire basket on the counter. A white, flour-dusted mixer sat tilted, beaters still spackled with batter. Not a seashell or branch of driftwood in sight. The kitchen could've relocated to any twenty-acre mini-farm, with chickens and goats in the yard and the farmer's wife buxom and full-bodied behind a bibbed apron.

Ms. Hanson held the refrigerator handle. "Milk? Or coffee?"

"Milk." Callie glanced around the house's open design living room. "Where's Alex?"

Treats set before her guest, Ms. Hanson plopped across from Callie at a small four-person dinette, her own mug dotted with thumb prints from a child, *Alexandra* written in crayon fashion around the sides.

"When you called, she figured she needed a shower," Ms. Hanson said. "She'll be out any moment. Probably got distracted by that phone she keeps glued to." The baker pinched off half a cookie. "What brings you here?"

"Your niece and her *EdistoToday* activity. She's quite the journalist. She might be able to help me with local history. You, too."

Ms. Hanson set down her coffee cup to use her hands to talk. "The baby's been coming here since she was, well, a baby, so she might. You're right. What she doesn't recall, I probably do." Her voice lowered, and she gave a sideways glance. "Is this about Ernest?"

Callie wiped chocolate off the corner of her mouth with a finger. "No, ma'am. It's more about Edisto's August jinx."

A voice came from the hallway. "I wondered when you'd come to me."

"And I expected more direct contact from you," Callie replied, glancing around. "Other than Twitter."

Alex entered fresh and young, the shower adding a crispness to her appearance in contrast to the crushing outdoor heat. Phone in her grip, she pushed a clip one-handed through her hair, then poured her own milk and snatched a cookie, balancing it on the glass after taking a bite. "Dang, Grandma. I've been dying for one of these ever since you cranked the mixer. Mmmm."

Though Callie wore a size four, the spry fitness of this girl gave her skin a saggy feel. Alex oozed energy that Callie'd forgotten about. "Thanks for meeting me," she said. "But wait. I've got to have another cookie before we talk."

For a moment everyone cleaned crumbs and chocolate smears. Then Alex broke the ice. "Anyone mention the tweets?"

"You think?" Callie laughed with an edge to it. The tweets followed her like a shadow. The tweets spurred someone named MyOuttake to spin gossip. The tweets educated the Frank and Ava club. "How would anyone miss them?"

No reaction. Only a girl eating a cookie. "Ms. Morgan, I'm judging how viral I am. Edisto isn't big, but I'd like to saturate it with *EdistoToday*'s presence and send it home with all the tourists. I have a blog, too, and Facebook, but I'm hoping the Twitter posts take both to a new level."

Callie moved her glass aside, her cookies gone. "I think everyone under sixty follows you, and half of those over."

Alex smiled.

"Not that all of us are happy about it."

The smile dimmed.

As the island's only paparazzi, Alex potentially ran unchecked until someone took issue. Callie didn't mind being that person.

"I understand news. I don't appreciate drama. Back off posting my face, please." Callie used her hardened stare practiced in the old job. "And I'm no longer a detective."

"Yeah," Alex replied, flippant. "But you gotta admit it sounds good. *Detective, investigation, jinx, clue.* Key words snag attention. It's like using mayor or senator after the person's no longer in office."

Callie did miss the title, but that wasn't the point.

Alex waved with her cookie. "At least I don't try to dig into your past. Be grateful for that."

Callie tensed. "Or else?"

The girl wrinkled her forehead. "Or else nothing. I'm saying I don't smear people."

A journalist with ethical limits? Or a lazy one who preferred to skim across the surface of news, spitting out short snippets of current events while they're hot, ignoring them once they'd slightly cooled.

Or she simply lied.

"Thank goodness for small favors, huh?" Callie replied.

Alex slid into a retort. "You appear at crime scenes, Ms. Morgan. What do you expect? If I didn't report, anybody with a smartphone would spread the story. I give it shape and validity."

Callie's jaw tightened. "But you represent the media, so out here you carry more credibility than the average Joe with a phone. I have a son to consider, something you wouldn't understand."

The reporter's eyes narrowed. "I understand more than you think."

"I doubt that," Callie said. "Some pretty nefarious players riddle my past. One already followed me here. Don't bait anymore."

Alex didn't need details of the Russian. She'd absorb the info as more material for her tweets.

Ms. Hanson clutched her cup hard. "Alex, honey, she makes sense. I already worry about you taking pictures without people's permission." The older lady might not understand Twitter, but she understood privacy.

Alex left her seat and stole another cookie from the pile on the counter, facing the window. She'd yet to set her phone down, and a thought crossed Callie's mind that pictures may have been taken in the last few moments for later distribution.

Alex flipped around. "Grandma, I told you. When people are in clear view in public, I'm allowed." She aimed the cookie at Callie. "You get that, Ms.

Morgan."

Callie did. She could also recite Alex's spiel. Once on a first-name basis with every key reporter and TV anchor in Boston, Callie had endured those journalistic, freedom-of-speech arguments, most often and more ardently during the violent, more viewer-attractive cases. Journalists cared little about the repercussions of flashing someone's face on a screen. They deemed the universe fair game.

The quickest thumbs on a keyboard won the race these days, and with that speed came missteps and half-truths. But the world grew callous to those mistakes, willing to accept a degree of error for expediency in hearing the latest first.

"You mentioned the August deaths," Alex said, pushing off the counter and returning to her seat. She clicked on her phone and studied it. "Why do you care?" she said, her face still stuck in the phone.

"Someone compared Brea Jamison to those incidents, but nobody seems to take them seriously. As an investigative journalist, why haven't you delved into them?"

Ms. Hanson spoke first. "Because it's a myth, honey. People don't get murdered on Edisto. We only have accidents."

Like Papa Beach and Pauley Beechum two months ago. *Accidental* bullets to the head and chest, respectively. The Russian she'd killed. No, murder didn't happen on this side of the bridge. Not at all.

Alex's tanned arms rested on the rooster placemat, fingers typing at light speed, sliding through apps. "Why do you care?" she asked, glancing up once.

"None of this conversation goes online, by the way." Then Callie weighed the question. Why *did* she care? Professional radar? Maybe. But who would want an annual murderer vacationing down the street? Then there was Janet. If that Marine feared the myth so much, there had to be some foundation to it. "Simple concern for me and mine," she summarized.

"I'm sure," Alex scoffed.

"Alex," chided Ms. Hanson.

The girl didn't seem too bad a sort, just young and daring, possibly excited to earn a name for herself.

"Let me put it into clearer terms," Callie said. "How would it look if the myth became reality, and someone else reported that *you* ignored it? For six whole years. I've barely moved here, yet I see the connection. Edisto heads would roll from the top down, including the town council. All those rental owners pissed. Certainly the police force would be held to task. Charleston press would have a rally day."

Alex's brows rose in a shrug, but she didn't glance away from her screen. "Might improve business. People love scandals."

What was Callie missing here? "Why not solve it? That would attract tourists, too."

The girl remained fixated on her phone.

What the heck? At any other time, reporters would stand in her way and in her face. Now that she needed one, she was stuck with a reluctant type. "I've had some experience unraveling cold cases," Callie added. "Don't let someone scoop you."

Sarcasm tinged Alex's laughter. "I'm the *only* current source of news on Edisto."

"Think NBC, ABC, CNN, or whatever their equivalents are for blogs. Their Charleston affiliates. They'd roll over you. Maybe name you as the journalist living ignorant and naïve in the thick of a story that strangers had to break. Might damage that burgeoning career you have in mind."

Alex didn't respond. Ms. Hanson watched the two of them patiently.

Finally the girl raised her chin and laid down her phone, irritation in the lines around her mouth. "Janet Wainwright would whip your ass for stirring crap out here, attracting big media like that about crime on her beloved island."

"I'd be the last of her problems with FOX camped out at her office."

Ms. Hanson's eyes widened.

Yep, Wainwright would fuss and fume, but Callie had no intention of taking it to the press. She found herself loving this beach more and more. Was it too much to ask to want to understand who died within blocks of her house? If she stumbled on a connection, she'd pass it to Seabrook. And if nothing came about from the sleuthing, no harm, no foul.

She needed either Alex or Ms. Hanson to educate her on the particulars of those dead women. Anywhere else on earth everybody would be able to recite the story of each woman inside and out. Why did everyone act as if speaking aloud about them would split open the gateway to Hell or make it rain locusts?

"Brea Jamison might be attached to the string of deaths," Callie said, baiting.

"What happened to the love triangle?" Alex's mouth quirked on one end, reminding Callie of Jeb in one of his craftier moments.

"Aren't bloggers journalists, or are they just wannabes?" Callie asked. "You claimed to be covering Brea's death, but you don't want to cover the whole story. That's called half-assed where I come from."

Alex's smooth, toned shoulders drew back. "My journalism degree comes from the University of South Carolina, Ms. Morgan. I worked in Atlanta for the *Constitution.*"

Callie kept at her. "So why not dog this case to a conclusion?"

Unless mistaken, Callie caught a flash of trepidation. The tweeter's spine appeared not so stiff. But since Callie couldn't retrieve the police files on these women, her next best source would be a journalist. Alex was it.

"So, what do you think?" Callie asked. "Do you want to scoop the biggest story of your professional life? Be the face on CNN?"

Alex's laugh came across half-hearted. "Fine. What do you need?"

This was better. Typical reporter. Typical detective.

Seabrook would not be happy.

"Get me details," Callie replied. "I can't find anything online."

"That's because the articles aren't online," Alex said. "The local paper covered them, as infrequent as it is, but the paper isn't on internet speed, much less social media level. But I can locate the archives. Give me a sec." She stood and left the room, exiting to the porch with her phone to her ear.

Ms. Hanson collected napkins and dishes. Callie drained her glass and followed her to the sink.

"She's not as tough as she appears," the older woman said under her breath.

Callie rinsed her glass and set it on a dishtowel. "She seems pretty tenacious to me."

The aproned maternal figure turned to face Callie. "And you appear the same to her. I'm simple and old but wise enough to see two peas in a pod. There's a crack in your armor, too, Callie, like there's one in Alex's."

"What do you remember about these women?" Callie asked, avoiding the discomfort of analysis. "Did you meet any of them?"

"I don't know much more than Alex. Never met a one of them, but feel free to return and have another cookie. I'd like to learn what you find. I don't like August and would love it if I didn't have to feel that way anymore."

"So you believe—"

"Got it," Alex said, bouncing back into the room.

"Got what, baby?" Ms. Hanson said, her voice shifting to a softer, higher pitch.

"Access to the newspaper office. Told the editor I wanted information on old fall festivals to prepare for the next one in October. He's the *unofficial historian* of the beach," Alex said, drawing air quotes with her fingers. "He's a sweet man. Wants old Edisto to remain just that, old Edisto."

"Why would he mind us reading through his archives?" Callie asked, puzzled.

"You have to ask?"

Callie tipped her head. "Is he related to Janet Wainwright?"

Alex scoffed once. "In some ways. Let me get my purse."

Good. With Alex leashed like a bloodhound on the scent, Callie might uncover something without Seabrook. Following Alex down the stairs, Callie even let the girl drive with the hope this new camaraderie might also dampen the tweets about Callie's personal life.

The girl eased out of her grandmother's drive. They soon parked at the newspaper office in the Station Court complex a mile out of town on Highway 174. Four businesses lined in symmetric Lowcountry design of neutral siding and colored metal roofs, each building no bigger than a large beach house. Low key, elementary, with none of the ostentatiousness of the other Carolina beaches. The surrounding hundred-year-old live oaks draped with Spanish moss enhanced the ambiance.

"So what's our deal?" Alex asked, the car lurching to a stop outside the office on the end. "I want to hear it plain and clear."

"You show me the details of these deaths. If there's nothing to it? Fine. If there is, it's your story to do with as you please. Bury it or blow it all the way to Mars, but let's put this mess to rest."

Still, Callie wondered if Alex had it in her to expose anything nasty. And if she'd lead Callie to the worst of it if there was.

Chapter 11

THE MIDAFTERNOON sun shone harshly on the little VW as Alex got out of the car. The tiny newspaper office seemed to hang on the end of a long, small office building, like an afterthought. Alex walked right in the door. Edisto people trusted the universe.

A picture of a middle-aged man accepting a framed certificate from a smiling woman in capris graced the wall to their immediate left. Straight-laced in appearance, the recipient stood too starched for the beach, too polite to be a news-hungry journalist in his button-down collar encircling his neck too tightly. Maybe a little lonely.

Callie scanned the plain two-room office measuring maybe fifteen feet wide, the front door and the door to another room lined along the left side. The rear wall seen through its tight doorway went equally that far back. Cramped. "Is that the editor?"

"Mr. Jenkins. Yeah, like I said, he's all right," Alex said, dropping her purse on a desktop devoid of papers or computer. "We stay out of each other's way with him doing the paper thing and me managing the web."

Callie performed an exaggerated side-to-side glance. The desk's purpose seemed only to take space. Either the editor formerly used hired help or he hoped to grow into some, but for now the bi-weekly *Island Tribune* appeared to be a one-man show. Callie dropped into the chair behind the desk. "We have permission to be here?"

"Sure."

No file cabinet. No business tools. No sign of life. "Is there a computer in the other room, or are we talking microfiche?"

Alex walked toward the rear office. "We're talking hard copies, baby. Let me hunt a bit. Keep talking. I can hear you back here."

"I can help," Callie said, rising to follow.

Alex held up a palm. "Um, you better not. He's awful protective of his archives. Probably take me less time to do it on my own anyway. I'll be right out." She disappeared.

Odd. Callie sat. "So why have the office?" she mumbled.

"What?" Alex asked.

Callie rose and walked to the framed copies of past newspapers on the soft green walls. "Why does he even rent this place?"

"He doesn't. He owns the building complex. And a half dozen beach houses."

Oh. Callie moseyed from one framed headline to another: hurricanes to grand openings, elections to fishing tournaments, flood control to lawn watering deadlines. *New Editor at the Island Tribune* said the headline of an edition dated ten years ago, with mention of retirement from another paper and a need to feel part of the community he moved to.

Next to it, *Blogger Returns to Her Roots* ran across another eighteen-month-old front page. Callie studied it closer.

Alexandra Joy Hanson, previous reporter and blogger of the Atlanta Constitution newspaper, arrived this week to install social media on Edisto Island. "I don't wish to compete with the newspaper. Instead I hope to bring new ideas and become an inherent part of the Edisto community," Hanson said. When asked about what made her leave the big city and relocate to the beach, she simply replied, "To let the public learn that reporters have a heart and care about the people they write for."

Even as young as Alex was, she'd arrived like the other full-time residents on the sand. She left one life behind her to begin anew. The editor retired. Alex quit and relocated. Callie wondered what secret made her leave her job so young.

Alex returned and opened a newspaper across the desk.

"Why'd you leave Atlanta?" Callie asked, stepping over.

Alex turned a page. "Let's say I possess a better grip of privacy and people's feelings now than I used to." She reached over, grabbed her purse, and rummaged through it. Extracting a tiny notepad with sunflowers on the outside, she clicked a pen and wrote. Pen returned to her bag, she ripped off the paper and put it in front of Callie, a finger over her lips.

He's in the back room.

Callie tilted her head and mouthed, *Jenkins?*

Alex nodded.

"I never met a reporter that didn't want to make a mountain out of a molehill in time for the morning paper," Callie continued, uncertain how to behave, maybe baiting him a little. Why didn't the man just come out and greet her?

"We're not all the same," Alex said with a wink.

Callie piled on the charade, asking what she'd ask anyway. "Brea Jamison ranked as the sixth dark-headed woman to die in six years. That would be a story to every journalist I've ever known. Wonder why he let it go by?"

Grimacing, Alex rolled her eyes at the ceiling.

Callie pressed on. "And you aren't as fretful about this story as much as I thought you'd be, either. You had Janet believing you were chasing a Pulitzer scoop."

"I think she's more worried about you, but you're right about one thing," Alex said. "She doesn't trust me." She flipped the paper to the front page. "Here's last August's edition. You can read it while I hunt for the others. Those drawers are full of all sorts of junk."

Callie bent over the paper, eager to gather details. She'd push Miss EdistoToday in the corner later about the ruse, but for now, she needed information. Nothing on the front page other than a consignment store closing and changes in federal flood insurance. She flipped inside until she found the story on page four. "I feel more like a reporter than a detective doing this."

Alex grinned mischievously in the doorway, cute with her hair pulled away from her face. "Thought you weren't a detective anymore."

Callie ignored the sarcasm and held the paper, waving it once and speaking loud enough for Jenkins to hear. "This poor woman's death earned no more coverage than three inches of one column on page four. Unbelieveable."

With a furtive glance behind her, Alex shook her head. "The *Tribune* isn't most papers. Exposés are managed with care, not indignity. Pissing off people means the paper never makes it into gift baskets for the rentals. The Janet-types steal them from the racks. My grandma gets phone calls." She retreated again.

Still no Jenkins.

Cable news would dub Edisto news coverage prehistoric. "Any chance you can find the statistics for deaths on the beach? Maybe he has research notes. Would sure keep me from making a trip into Walterboro to the coroner's office."

"Don't see anything like that in here."

"Look harder. Journalists usually keep decent records . . . unless they're hiding something."

"I'm telling you, I don't see—"

Callie'd had enough of this flip-flop game. "Don't you remember some of those numbers off the top of your head?" She stepped quietly to the other room and poked her head around the door.

The same genteel man from the picture on the wall posed at a file cabinet, sifting material. Alex appeared stunned from his right, her hand out, waiting for him to approve which papers she could have.

Editor Abe Jenkins cleared his throat, barely affected. Alex, however, paled.

"For instance," Callie continued, as if expecting to find the man there. "What are the annual death and accident statistics for August? I'm trying to find commonalities, contrasts, something to define a norm."

"I'm not the census bureau," Alex said, one eye on Jenkins.

"And if I asked the editor, what would he say?"

Jenkins quit flipping files. "The town council puts out a newsletter with monthly statistics, but it only goes back three years." He returned to his task and lifted out one of the newsletters, passing it to Alex, who turned it hesitantly over to Callie.

After a slack-jawed expression moment, Alex returned to her normal self. "It's entertaining to see how everyone justifies their existence down to the number of golf cart violations and DUIs issued. Did you realize cops travel five thousand miles a month on this five-mile beach? And warning tickets doubled since last year?"

She knew warning ticket statistics but nothing about deaths?

Screw the play acting. Callie held out her hand to the man. "I'm Callie Jean Morgan, Mr. Jenkins. How are you?"

Jenkins gave Alex another paper, rolled the drawer shut, and locked the cabinet. "Those don't leave the office." Then to Callie, he added, "I'm not here. You didn't see me." He eased around her, avoiding contact as if she were wet paint. His footsteps tapped through the outer office and out the door.

Callie lowered her hand. As a native, if she'd learned anything in her few short weeks at the beach, it was that quirkiness thrived here, but what the hell?

Why the cloak-and-dagger? Why even let her in to see the papers in the first place if he pretended she wasn't there? She almost felt suckered, as if they led her down a wrong path. What if the papers weren't real? What weren't they showing her?

Okay, that sounded stupid. Of course the documents were real. Alex didn't have enough advanced notice to fix a hoax. But why blow Callie off?

Alex moved past Callie to the desk. "Go online to read the other council reports."

Callie scowled and nodded at the archive room. "The man stood right there. He gave me one newsletter. Why not give me the others? What's his problem?"

"I went out of my way to get you this much," Alex snapped.

"Why?" Callie asked.

Alex reacted puzzled. "Why?"

"Yeah. You act like this story is a hot potato. Jenkins is totally weirded out about it. Yet you sorta, kinda pull me here." Callie leered sideways at her. "What are y'all up to?" She shook the papers. "This stuff is authentic, right?"

Alex tried to snatch the papers, but Callie jerked them against her body. "Oh no, you don't."

The young girl's teeth clenched. "Seabrook's shop provides many of the statistics. Why don't you ask him for confirmation since y'all are so tight?"

Callie returned to the desk. "We're not tight."

"He won't cooperate with you either, huh?" The young girl laughed once. "He's no different than Wainwright, you know."

Callie spread out all the papers.

Alex re-sorted them in order. "This one is from two years ago. These others are the three years before it." She set the one off to the side of the other spread open. "And I didn't stalk you. Someone took a cool picture of you swapping spit with Seabrook, and who says it's a guy? You probably make a lot of women jealous since he's a pretty hot bachelor in these parts."

Callie slid the papers to her liking. She tried to accept her life being under a microscope in a town that specialized in who used to do what, who does what now, and who might be the person to do it next. She had more privacy in Boston surrounded by millions.

"I remember that story there," Alex said and pointed to the words Callie still hadn't read. "A senior stroked two years ago. The year before, a man shot himself in his kitchen, by mistake. Those occurred in June in two different years. I lived here during one of them, and Grandma told me about the other."

Alex's words echoed, barely noticed in Callie's head.

The editor, the police chief, and the lead real estate agent turning a blind eye to dead people. She'd blown the last two off to being hypervigilant, but after meeting Jenkins with his Stepford-wife personality, she dared to ponder a conspiracy theory. Geez, she didn't want to suspect Seabrook again. Not like before.

"Callie?" Alex asked.

Callie inhaled. "Why didn't the families of these people raise hell for answers?" she asked, refolding the first paper and reaching for the next.

"All the families accepted the deaths as mishaps. Maybe because they were."

"Et tu, Brute?"

Alex laughed. "Or you can accept the theory of this whack-job detective running around Edisto—that murders were made to seem like accidents."

Finally, a side of the girl Callie enjoyed.

And admittedly, the girl had helped her more than anyone else, even more than Seabrook, and Callie needed to keep that avenue open.

For the life of her, Callie did not understand Edistonians. A huge difference divided those visiting the beach and living there.

Callie skimmed the header on loggerhead turtle rules and moved on. Alex sat across from her reading. "Remember, I want an exclusive if you break anything."

With a smile, Callie brightened. "There's the reporter Walter Cronkite would love."

But Alex didn't respond in kind. Instead, her voice turned guarded. "No, you don't understand. It means I cover this story my way. Damage control."

An odd reaction.

Callie's instincts kicked in, unable to tell if they stemmed from her mother or detective side. Alex left Atlanta and didn't want to talk about whatever she left behind. The girl pounced on Edisto's current events for social media but stopped short of burrowing into the story for details. If she wasn't wrong, Callie smelled a story behind this girl, too.

Both cops and reporters dove into trenches and climbed out dirtier and damaged. Anyone who'd ever championed a cause ran the risk of getting caught in the crossfire and losing. Wrongs might not be righted, or a victim lost. The bad guy might have won. Which had tainted Alex?

"Something happen in Atlanta?" Callie asked softly.

"Suicide," Alex said, as if she'd answered the question so many times its edges had smoothed. "I blogged on a situation without all the facts. The fourteen-year-old daughter of the subject hanged herself. That's all I'll say, if you don't mind."

Of course Callie didn't mind. A reporter with feelings deserved a plaque in the Smithsonian. "I appreciate you helping me. Mind if I take notes since I can't take these?" Callie hadn't seen a copier.

Alex opened a drawer. "Of course. This isn't Watergate." She extracted a full-size lined notebook. "Here. Scribble on this. It'd take you forever to snap pictures with your phone."

The stories were pure copy anyway, no pictures unfortunately. Not surprised. A house picture potentially hurt the property owner, and the community wouldn't recognize the deceased tourists. Seems Jenkins followed Alex's mantra: *let the public learn that reporters have a heart.*

Or maybe Alex had recuperated under Jenkins' tutelage, learning along the way to represent Edisto only in its best light. Keeping it Mayberry-esque.

Callie drew columns on her legal pad, labeled them, and started with the oldest case first, a simple drowning. Though a good swimmer, Margaret swam out to fifteen-foot deep water past the breakers. Thirty-four and described in the paper as an athletic brunette, she had recently married and had no children. They found her body two hours after she went missing. No foul play suspected. Date August tenth.

Refolding the old paper along its creases, Callie pushed it to her right and moved on to the next case, Lee Anne. Dead on August twelfth. Age forty-one. No mention of her hair color, so she peered at Alex and lifted one of her own chin-length locks.

"Dark, like the others," Alex answered. "Grandma can go on and on about that one since she came here with a real sad story. Lee Anne was single, no parents, with pancreatic cancer. Her friends brought her to enjoy a week of normalcy. As a nurse, she knew her odds and wanted to enjoy the moments while able. Again, a drowning. They didn't find her until she washed up that night. We don't do life guards."

"You'd have thought her friends would've been watching her," Callie grumbled.

"That's part of what made it so sad," Alex said.

"No blogging or tweeting then, huh?"

"I was in college when those happened."

Yet the journalist almost quoted the column verbatim, except for one thing. The paper omitted mention of the cancer.

Alex already knew these cases.

Why had they bothered coming here? Then as quickly as Callie thought the question, she answered it. Callie's firsthand review of the reference material enabled Alex to stand outside the loop, and any junk stirred in the community fell on the new detective.

Whatever.

The next year's death proved more morose and received slightly more coverage. Thirty-five-year-old Carolyn fell down twenty steps leading off her rental house, her leg catching between balusters, snapping her neck as it whiplashed over the edge of a step riser. She'd gone outside for a breath of air during a party. Callie recalled Beverly mentioning that one.

"She was drunk," Alex added. "So was everyone else in the house. They didn't find her for almost an hour after she went outside.

The column omitted those facts but gave the date as August thirteenth.

Three down, two to go. Alex strolled to one of the framed newspapers. Callie sensed this slow analysis wearing on the girl. The fourth paper dated the next incident August tenth.

"Heart attack?" she exclaimed after reading the opening paragraph. "At thirty-five!"

"Yeah," Alex said. "Everyone got out of the hot tub but Angelina and went downstairs. An hour later, they found her dead. Alcohol and hot tubs do not mix as well as tourists think they do. I'd never put one of those things in a rental."

One case left. Last year's. Reese. A pretty one-syllable name like Brea. Drug overdose. The briefest article of any of them. Age thirty-nine. August seventeenth.

"Happy now?" Alex asked.

"Not sure happy is the right word, but I like having the facts," Callie said. "Are there any notes? The parts that don't make the newspaper?"

"You have all you're going to get."

Callie frowned.

"His words, not mine," Alex added.

Never mind. The details probably resided more in Jenkins' head than on old notes in a manila folder. "Anything else you can think of?" Callie asked, flipping through the papers. Then she slowed. She put the cases side by side in date order. "Wonder why the deaths quit being drownings?" She glanced over the neighboring articles, hunting for other commonalities. "And these latter three happened at parties, like Brea."

A stretch of a hypothesis, but someone might have found drownings too easy or worried the trend would be noticed. He maybe escalated, using social opportune moments. More cover in a crowd maybe?

Callie wanted to confirm the locations. "What were the addresses for each of these cases? I know you know them. That includes where along the beach the first two drowned and where each of these ladies rented."

Alex came around her side and wrote the party addresses on Callie's pad. "Don't share those."

"Where did they rent?"

Alex shook her head. "I'm not sure."

"What about family?" Callie prodded. "Especially those who had kin with them at the beach."

Alex shook her head. "No idea. You'd have to go to Seabrook for that."

"Or the rental agent," Callie added.

"Yeah, there's that."

This investigation seemed so loose, but most investigations started untethered with no clear logic. This part of a case captured Callie's attention most. A smart detective dogged such scattered pieces until finding two that fit, then three, then more. The newspapers, aka Alex's knowledge, were a healthy start.

Four days had passed since Brea died on the seventh. If Brea was the target, and a killer had accomplished his token kill, the culprit had achieved his deed for the year. But he wouldn't pack and run home for fear of being noticed. He would remain, lurking. Especially with Maddington's death on the heels of Brea's and Alex's coverage online. The newspaper hadn't even come out! Too much drama to walk away from this early. Killers, pyromaniacs, burglars . . . they loved watching how their schemes played out.

Unintentional injury represented the number one killer of people in their thirties, and like doctors playing the odds in making diagnoses, law enforcement went with accidental injury as the causes of the deaths. She didn't blame them. Young women were more likely to die of cancer, heart disease, and suicide than homicide.

Even Callie wasn't confident of foul play, not yet. But the last four died at parties. All six in their thirties and dark-headed. Enough parallels to keep her going.

"I say odds are less that a native killed them," she said. "Assuming these *were* planned."

"Oh, I agree," Alex said. "Owners try to rent their places in June, July, and August for the high income, so they'd be out of town."

Callie ran another option through her head, not trusting the girl to keep it to herself. The option that a real estate agent set up tenants to become victims. How hard could it be to learn which realties managed the properties?

Assuming it wasn't one realty.

Assuming it wasn't a particular real estate agent.

"What are you thinking?" Alex asked.

"Nothing," Callie said, erring on the side of caution. "A visitor makes the most sense. Comes once a year to claim a prize."

Alex smoothed her lip gloss. "I can't imagine someone doing that. This whole thing makes me nervous."

A thought popped into her head. "Are you babysitting me? Overseeing my moves? You and Jenkins spoon-feeding me minimal information?"

"No, I'm not. Like you, I don't enjoy thinking anyone would go all Ted Bundy on us," she replied.

"You've already weighed accident versus murder. You spout off details from memory too easily not to have studied these cases."

Alex's eyes widened a micro-second at Callie's spoken revelation.

"It isn't that you don't believe there's a killer," Callie continued. "You and Jenkins just can't figure what to do about it," Callie said.

The girl played too busily with a pen, no longer able to feign nonchalance.

"Okay," Callie said, relieved on some bizarre level that somebody other than her might see the string of deaths as possibly malicious. "We've got about a week before he's gone for sure, assuming he hasn't been here for a week already."

"I don't like this."

"Remember, it's your exclusive if there's anything to it," Callie said, brows raised.

"Yeah," Alex said, "but what if I don't want it?"

"Oh, you want it. You want it to control it. Remember CNN."

"Let's go," she said rapidly and gathered the papers.

Callie watched Alex return the papers to the cabinet, uncertain how to interpret her. Was she an ally or someone keeping track of the too-curious detective? The damage control girl. But for whom? Jenkins?

If Callie didn't know these people better, she'd wonder if they harbored a secret, even the murderer's identity . . . keeping his face secret for a reason.

But then she didn't know them well either, did she?

Chapter 12

ALEX AND CALLIE exited the newspaper office, leaving it unlocked as usual. Callie had a mental chuckle at the concept of the tiny two-room office, then sobered at the deception. Jenkins hiding in the *archive* room. Alex pretending he wasn't there.

The more Callie thought about the day, the less she trusted this girl.

Once in the VW, Callie flipped through her notes as Alex waited in silence for three cars to pass, all with out-of-state tags. Then they turned home toward the beach. A slight shiver raced across Callie's shoulders as the air-conditioner chilled the car. "What the heck was that with Jenkins?"

"Be glad I got the info for you. I'm your gracious connection, thank you very much."

"Sure. Right." Callie's frustration hung thick in the air. Not that she feared Alex or Jenkins, but she hated being lied to, especially when the lie seemed so unnecessary. Unless she didn't fully understand what had happened. Callie scowled at the ridiculousness of it all. "So why bring me period?"

"To read it firsthand. Mr. Jenkins protects his material." Alex shrugged. "I think he likes you, though."

Callie laughed with disdain. "How could you tell?"

Alex started to wave to emphasize when the VW swayed toward the center line. She regripped the wheel with white knuckles, and the car righted itself. "You have a reputation. Your family's been around for decades. Maybe Seabrook spoke of you. Who cares why? Be grateful."

"He sounds paranoid."

"Maybe."

"So do you."

"Not really."

"Yes, really. How does that man even run a paper?"

"Everyone feeds him stories. The *Tribune* isn't published often enough to feature earth-shattering news, and everyone's patient enough to wait until he publishes the details."

"That they provide to him, on *Edislow* time," Callie said. "Meaning whenever they feel like it."

Alex nodded. "*Edislow* time."

Hmm, that system sounded a bit incestuous. "And that gives you all the scoops," Callie added.

The girl painted swirls in the air as she dipped her head in a pretend bow. "So be it."

A young opportunist still inside the girl. Callie liked that better than someone skitterish and secretive. "Well, ease off the online remarks that Seabrook and I are an item. Stalking me at my house is not cool on anybody's scale."

"Hey," Alex replied, her eyes darting from the road to her passenger. "That's MyOuttake doing all that, not me. Kinda eerie how he's latched ahold of you online, but don't blame me."

"MyOuttake. Do you know him?"

Alex gripped the wheel tighter, her jaw working. "Of course not."

"Have you tried to identify him?"

Alex exhaled in indignation. "I gave it barely five minutes of my time, but he doesn't list who he is or where he's from."

Callie questioned again why a journalist would fall so short in her efforts. "He feeds off you. He walks in your shadow."

"I said I looked for him." Her shrug seemed stiff, forced. "But he'll freelance regardless, so don't sling your insecurities at me. He is who he is and has every right to be."

"Unless he's the killer."

Alex flinched as her eyes glanced at Callie and quickly returned toward the road. She waved at someone who beeped from a passing pickup truck. "Why would you say that?"

"It's a theory, and only a fool would discard it."

The young girl studied her rearview mirror. Callie checked her side mirror. Nobody there, and Callie recognized the girl's struggle to be smooth.

"Thought you said you understood journalism," Alex said.

Irritation began to coil in Callie's gut at this pony-tailed Barbara Walters. "I do. I've dealt with enough of you to recognize the drills."

"Social media is a trillion times more dynamic than regular reporting," Alex explained, tossing in a sprinkle of condescension. "Bite on anything, and the bloggers and tweeters go all shivery orgasmic at the opportunity to unleash more tripe. As long as he's on Edisto, he'll mess with you. Fight him, and he'll mess with you more. Let him be."

They both silenced.

Callie had thought MyOuttake might be an online version of Frank Weaver and his crew, a tourist enjoying his holiday in his own way. MyOuttake's Twitter and Instagram histories were nil until he arrived on Edisto, as if using online as a journal log of his trip. A few pictures of sea oats, gulls, Botany Bay and its dead skeleton oaks on the beach, then bam . . . Brea. Then Callie and Seabrook. A one-man paparazzi. At least she sensed it to be a man.

Which reminded her . . . Callie grabbed her phone and logged in to her social media in hope MyOuttake took a hiatus. "Aw, damn," she said, scrolling.

"What?" They'd crossed the marsh, and Alex turned right onto Jungle Road.

Callie showed her the phone and a picture taken of Jungle Road . . . from her front porch. No people, no activity. "He was at my place," Callie said.

"So?"

"What do you mean, *So?*"

"At least it's not from inside your house. I'm telling you, he's just messing with you. Don't fall for it."

Easily said when it wasn't her house, plus Callie felt Alex equally capable of dangling a few worms of her own. MyOuttake, however, made Callie's pulse spike. She registered the throb in her neck right now. Rubbing her eyes, she fought the notion of another pervert on her tail, as well as some of the Edistonians in plain view.

ALEX LEFT CHELSEA Morning's drive, and Callie glanced at her corner cameras out of habit. The previous home invasions drove her to go full bore and install cams around her home's exterior. While Sophie considered it overkill, and Seabrook hinted the same, Callie slept easier. The feeds ran to her laptop, and as she drank her morning coffee, she often watched their time-lapse recordings from the night before in lieu of *Good Morning America*. She had missed this morning, yesterday, too, so she'd spend supper in front of her laptop tonight.

Callie took her long line of steps to the front door, slowing as she reached the top. Three pieces of pink paper fluttered, taped to the glass.

She ripped off the first, the Town of Edisto Beach letterhead across the top.

We unfortunately feel the need to notify you of recent town ordinance violations . . .

What the crap?

She skipped the printed formality to read the handwritten transgression. *Did not take in trash can same day of pickup.* The small print explained that a pink notice represented a warning. Yellow indicated a $25 fine, and red merited an appearance before Town Council.

She ran to the end of her porch and peered. Sure enough, the can sat on the street's edge. What? Pickup was two days ago, and she certainly . . . Wait. Where did all that green trash come from?

Dead palmetto fronds, prunings from lantana bushes, and hawthorn twigs lay strewn across her rear drive and lawn. Yet along the side of her driveway her bushes remained straggly, in sore need of trimming she hoped to take care of once the heat lessened. Her palmettos still screamed for attention, their dead dangling limbs intact twenty feet off the ground. None of the dead branches on the ground were hers.

Hurrying to the door again, she snatched off the second pink notice. *Unsightly debris in yard. Horticultural cuttings should be piled and properly placed at base of driveway for Monday pickup.* Chelsea Morning faced Jungle Road. She resided in an area that allowed her driveway to come off one road, run under her house, and out the other side, namely onto Jungle Shores Road. Most traffic ran along the asphalted Jungle Road, and she enjoyed the latitude of using either side to come and go. In this situation, however, someone *conveniently* took advantage of the less-traveled road to wreak havoc at her expense.

Warily, she lifted the third pink slip.

Per Section 70-71 of the Town of Edisto Beach Code of Ordinances, each occupied dwelling is required to post its designed address number of no less than three and a half inches high near the property's entrance. If the property sits over fifty feet back from the road, the number shall also be placed near the walk, driveway, common entrance, fence, gatepost or other appropriate place so as to be clearly visible from the road. Failure to comply within thirty days grants the town authority to install the numbers, resulting in a $75 charge to the property owner.

The heat in her face had nothing to do with the summer temps. She eyed the street, mentally ticking off the distance. She guestimated the distance around fifty feet, depending on whether the powers-that-be measured from the asphalt or the right-of-way. Or stopped at the stairs or the house itself. In one of those measurements, however, somebody found their loophole.

Until the end of May, Chelsea Morning had belonged to Lawton and Beverly Cantrell, revered and respected from Edisto to Middleton and back for most of Callie's life. Not three months after Callie took ownership from her parents, the beach sanctioned her. The house had never posted numbers near the road. Callie peered up to judge if the familiar brass numbers over her door were three and a half inches.

Son of a—! They were missing, their faint outline evident in the light dust and faded paint.

She spun and trotted down her steps, crossing the grassy span beside her house. Hatha Heaven, the beach name to Sophie's home, stood barely fifty feet to the side of Chelsea Morning, assuming Callie remembered how to count to fifty anymore.

She knocked then opened the unlocked door. "Sophie?" she hollered. "You home?"

Her friend yelled from the living room. "Come on in. Rikki and I are having a wine since it's past five."

Rikki? Callie shut the door and followed the voice to where Sophie sat curled on her white sofa in leotards and baggy tank. "Wine's in the kitchen. Whoops, sorry," she said and smacked her cheek in retribution. "My bad. Juice, water, and Cokes in the fridge. Get what you want. You can find the glasses."

Across from Sophie, stretched out in the recliner, Rikki's legs hung a foot over the end, shoes tossed on the floor. She lifted her wineglass in salute, her alto voice slow and aristocratic. "Callie."

For more than one reason Callie wished she could snatch that drink out of her hand.

In the kitchen she grabbed stemware and lifted the wine bottle—to study the label. A moment to pretend, to seize a second of how calming and indulging the feeling to swallow any kind of alcohol would be. To feel that buzz, to loosen muscles, to melt into sofa cushions, and let the evening slip into night as girlfriend laughter stole her cares.

Instead, she slammed the bottle on the counter and reached in the fridge for a Diet Coke. Out of pure spite, she threw an ice cube in her wineglass and filled it with the soda.

"What's wrong?" Sophie asked when Callie reentered the room. She assumed her place on the opposite end of the sofa, leaning against the arm.

Amazing how Rikki had cut into Sophie's heart only hours ago, yet here she sat holding no grudge, a stance Sophie had tried to explain to Callie several times. Something to do with the practice of yoga. The forgiveness appeared admirable in theory but ridiculous in practice when the culprit repeated her behavior. Someone like that held ulterior motives or relished games or didn't respect people.

Thoughts she began to have about Alex, too.

She sank half her soda then bit on the piece of ice. Her mood gnawed at her insides. "Hey."

Callie blinked and faced her friend. "What?"

Sophie's feet were flat on the floor now. "You seem like you could chew rock. What's wrong?"

Callie dragged the pink tickets out of her jeans pocket and slapped them on the glass coffee table. "Either of you ever get these on your door?"

Sophie lifted them, reading. "What the *fairy dust* are these?"

"Let me see," Rikki said, folding down the footrest in her chair. She studied the infractions then eyed Callie. "Well, you sure pissed someone off."

"Ya think?" Callie replied.

Rikki dropped the warning notices on the table. "Edisto doesn't crack down on people like this. That's not this beach's nature. It takes a lot of complaints to force council to enforce these rules. They might be sticklers when it comes to construction and business licenses, but they don't harass the owners. Did you do these things?"

Jumping to her feet, Callie went to the kitchen, added more ice, and retrieved the opened bottle of soda. "Somebody else moved my trash can. Then that somebody or another somebody threw branches all over my back yard."

"What about the house numbers?" Sophie asked. "Your house is older than mine, and we probably sit the same distance off the pavement. I don't have a number at the road."

"I have no numbers at all! They've been ripped off my house! I'd love to wring that somebody's neck."

Sophie reached over and flicked Rikki's knee. "You're an attorney. Can't you do something?"

Why had she assumed the woman merely a trust fund baby? "You practice law?"

Rikki laughed. "Yeah, I'm more capable than you probably think I am, Detective. Contract law," she said. "But I don't think you need me for this."

"No," Callie said, "I don't. The obvious move is to rectify everything and move on. I know one thing, though—" and she stopped before she mentioned her motion sensors and cams. Not that Rikki hadn't seen the devices, but she might not have, and she hadn't proven herself as trustworthy. Frankly, being a lawyer only made Callie trust the Amazon less. Heck, breathing made Callie trust anyone less these days.

Sophie tucked her leg under and sat. "What?"

"I'm not letting it get to me," Callie said.

The hell she wasn't. But coming undone would be what they wanted, whoever *they* were. She would check the cam recordings tonight, then regularly from now on. No way she'd permit paranoia to slip into her life and take root. No way she'd let some bureaucratic baloney cause her to awaken every hour listening for intruders again.

Not that she didn't approach that bus stop already.

She had what she came for, confirmation someone directed this harassment at her. Though she might be wrong, the approach reeked of a certain Marine putting an arm-twisting maneuver on the council.

Then she had a distressful thought. Someone had posted the notes on her door in her absence just like someone had snapped that online picture . . . standing in the same spot.

The same person? Janet didn't seem the social media type, but still . . .

But Janet wasn't at the party to take the picture of Brea.

Callie caught Sophie staring at her.

"So," Callie said, determined to lighten up on the hatred for Sophie's sake. "How're the ghosts behaving today?"

Rikki popped her feet and reclined again. "They haven't appeared since I've been here."

Sighing, Sophie returned attention to her white wine, taking a sip for reinforcement. "I had to turn the kitchen faucet off once, but other than that, it's been okay. They tend to stir at night."

"Sure they do," Rikki chuckled.

"Do Zeus and Sprite notice changes?" Callie asked.

"Some. They don't discount me, but they don't understand, either," Sophie said, her voice turning childlike.

"They're patronizing you," Rikki said. "Keep saying this stuff, though, and you'll give them ammunition to put you in a home."

Callie's lips tightened. "Rikki, hush—"

The soft voice said, "I'm almost out of sage, Callie. You wouldn't have any, would you?"

The discrete warning told Callie not to rip into an argument, not under Hatha Heaven's roof. But this was the third time Callie'd met the Amazon and the third time she disapproved of the woman's treatment of Sophie. Rikki fed off their mutual friend somehow, and for the life of her, Callie didn't see the relationship being all that symbiotic.

CALLIE RETURNED home two hours later still tense. She'd been unable to fully speak her mind to Rikki and unable to get MyOuttake out of her head. The sun began to sink behind the trees, her heartbeat rising a pinch at the sign of dusk. *You're good. Don't let the evening mess with you.*

She locked the door behind her, set the alarm, and listened for Jeb. Though Zeus's dad, Mr. NFL Bianchi, would likely rectify matters with the town about the lost business license, Callie hoped that her son had taken this down time from fishing charters to enjoy being a normal teenager. She loved his devotion to Zeus and the business, but a piece of her wished Jeb would tire of the job. Too late to enroll in the fall college semester, he might still enter for spring.

"Jeb?" she yelled as she made her way to her desk. She booted the laptop and went to her bedroom to change into looser clothes, her jeans, tank, and linen shirt sticky with the day's moisture.

One day she'd build the nerve to go sleeveless and not care who saw her left arm's ragged scar from the fire. Beverly suggested she have it cosmetically corrected and of course knew a good doctor . . . but Callie didn't want to forget. The scar served as a reminder of how precious life was and how quickly it could be snatched away.

Cooled down and more comfortable, she parked herself in front of the computer with an ice water and an egg sandwich. Click, click, there.

First she wanted to see who'd come and gone on her porch. She rolled past Frank Weaver, Terrance, and the others, because they came and went in her presence. She watched herself leave for Ms. Hanson's. A town pickup parked in her drive, a man with a name embroidered over his shirt pocket going to her door. He taped the papers and left, the cam unable to show both his hands the whole time. He didn't dawdle, but how long does it take to snap a pic?

She pondered marching down to town hall and demanding to meet the guy, but they might consider her too wacky and disgruntled. She'd think about that later. His identity wouldn't be difficult to nail.

She didn't recall him at the Brea party, though. Had he taken the picture from her porch for someone else?

She rewound the recording to two days ago, no, better go to three. That's when she took out the trash that morning and brought the can in that evening. She took a huge bite of the sandwich, the smell reminding her how hungry she'd been.

The recording ran slow, so she fast forwarded. Why had she not noticed the rear of her house sooner? The people traipsing Jungle Shores must think her a slob.

There, stop, two days ago. A hooded person at sundown rolled her trash can to the curb. A man from his size. No shrub debris, though. The yard remained neat, or at least not ravished. Darkness fell across the screen as she continued. She didn't leave her outside lights on at night, making details hard to make out. Night lights were frowned upon so that the loggerheads didn't mistake spotlights for moonlight over the water and not make it to sea. Though she lived four blocks from the sand, she felt like many others that there was something garish about ruining the gentle calm of the island with LEDs.

But as the recording reached 5:00 a.m., limbs, clippings, and leaves appeared across her yard. She reversed the recording, scanning for taillights of a vehicle or at least moonlight glinting off a fender as someone drove without lights. Nothing. A shadow walked into view about 3:00 a.m., dragging two large, dark bags. He distributed the mess quickly and headed west toward the Rosewoods, but she couldn't tell how far he went past Sophie's drive. Shadows and a hoodie hid his face. The same guy who moved the trash can. She'd bet money on it.

Callie jumped up. *Crap.* She better bring the can in or risk another pink notice, maybe even yellow. Closing the laptop, she ran to throw on her sneakers. Her phone rang . . . Seabrook.

"Hey," she answered, the phone resting on her shoulder as she tied her shoes.

"Listen, it might be last minute, but you want to grab dinner? I'm off work, and it's been a helluva weekend, so I thought we'd—"

"I just ate a sandwich," she said and switched on her lights.

"Then I'll bring dessert. Maybe I'm the one who needs an ear. What do you say?"

No doubt she'd be awake a while, especially with the issues of the day spinning in her head. But she sure hoped he didn't ride her case again about what she should and should not be investigating. "Fine, but I might be out back."

Popping on her spotlights, she went for the trash can, rolling it toward the house, making a mental note to buy a bicycle chain to anchor it to one of her house pilings. She blew off the idea of fingerprints on the handle. Too many people had touched it plus Seabrook probably wouldn't bother.

The can caught on one of the branches, and she turned to alter her grip and snatch the receptacle loose. Her shoe caught on another strewn branch. Her angle and the weight of the can threw her off balance, and before she regained her bearing, the can knocked into her.

Arms outstretched, she sprawled across gravel and shells in her drive. Several of the rogue branches slid and snapped beneath her. But while Callie skidded to a halt, the can's momentum continued. The handle on the thirty-pound container came down sharp on her lower lumbar area, the hinged top flipping open to smack the back of her head.

Her heartbeat galloped as her five-foot-two body lay sprawled across the broken limbs and crushed clippings. A stinging started in her elbows and palms as she lifted her head. Her knees felt bruised. She studied the darkness around her in embarrassing fear of seeing a neighbor or a tourist out for a late stroll. Her yard seemed so much bigger from ground level, her door so far up the stairs.

A gust of evening salt air blew across the ground, lifting papers from inside the can. They danced like happy butterflies across her yard, headed for the street and whatever other yards they could reach.

"Mom?"

She rolled over, kicking off the can. "I'm fine, Jeb."

"What the hell happened? You all right?" he asked, setting the can upright with one motion and reaching for his mother with another, his fitness evident from days hauling coolers on his fishing excursions.

Standing, anger shot through her at the asinine antics being played at her expense. She jerked a little as she sought for the muscle trying to cramp in her back. She took out her frustration on the massage, kneading, wishing she had a place to dump her temper.

The squad car eased in and parked alongside Jungle Shores. Seabrook got out and rushed over. "What's wrong?"

"I fell dragging the dang trash can," Callie grumbled. "Some crazy person played a trick and set it on the street. Did all this, too," she said, waving before returning to her stiff pose. "I tripped, and the can came down on me. Didn't you notice any of this?" she asked Jeb, scolding him in place of herself.

Jeb gave her his best *seriously?* look.

"Hurt yourself?" Seabrook scanned her front, walking behind to scan again.

"I'm good," she said. "Just . . . not happy."

"Wait, there's blood here." He raised her shirt, hunting for wounds. Finding nothing, he ordered, "Show me your hands."

She spread them open. A cut creased the butt of her palm, seeping blood. "Jeb, would you collect those papers before I get another notice?"

"What kind of notice?" he asked.

She flicked toward the scattering debris. "I'll explain later."

He sprinted after the furthest piece, collecting the loose paper into wads against his body. He gathered papers under and around Callie's Escape. As he stood, he noticed one under the windshield wiper. "Um, Mom," he said as he read the words on it. "I don't think this one came from the trash can."

Callie straightened. "Please tell me it's not another notice from the town."

He walked over. "It's a notice, but I hope not from the town."

She took it from him.

Asking questions will get you hurt, Detective.

Chapter 13

SEABROOK SET THE first aid kit on the coffee table. "Let me see your hand."

For the first time Callie witnessed Seabrook's medical skills, not that cleaning and bandaging a minor wound would demonstrate much. He took his time picking out the gravel and dirt with her eyebrow tweezers he'd dipped in alcohol. His touch . . . felt nice.

Jeb sat at the kitchen bar, watching.

"I'm about ready to rip into somebody," Callie said, wincing.

"Be still," Seabrook said. "And who would that somebody be?"

"Have no idea. At least not yet, but I'll find them. Ouch!"

The cop peered skeptically. "That didn't hurt."

Busted, Callie shifted gears, chagrined she snapped at allies. She glanced around, not remembering Seabrook bringing in a bag or container. "What happened to the dessert you promised?"

"Sorry," Seabrook said. "Don't think you want it now. That reminds me . . . Jeb, you mind retrieving the bag off the seat of my car before it melts into the leather?"

"Don't tell me," her son said.

"Yeah, ice cream."

Shaking his head, Jeb started toward the porch. "I haven't forgotten about that note, Mom. I want an explanation."

Seabrook waited until the door shut before he turned to Callie. "Good kid, and I'm with him," he said. "What have you been up to?"

Callie's gut clenched at the onset of another lecture. "Who says I've been *up to* anything?"

"Can't you talk and sit still at the same time?" he asked, teasing another piece of gravel from her palm. He irrigated the wound again over Callie's salad bowl, then studied the cuts. "I think it's clean now." He patted the cut and surrounding abrasions with a towel and reached for the antibiotic cream and bandages. "Keep this dry for a day or two. And don't be surprised if you have a bruise on your back tomorrow."

"Thanks, Dr. Seabrook."

He smiled, and she suspected he hadn't heard that title in a while, even tinged with sarcasm. Once a doctor, always a doctor. He probably felt somewhat naked without the status at times.

Sort of like an ex-cop unable to flash the badge.

Eight years had passed since the tragedy took his wife, his fanaticism in hunting her murderer costing him his position at a Charleston hospital. Or so she'd heard. Their parallel universes were freakishly coincidental, but they'd never discussed his in detail. Not that she'd spilled all the intricacies of hers.

"Hey," she said, touching his sleeve when he stood and gathered the medical materials. "You have history on me, some items I'm not particularly proud of. You owe me your story, Dr. Seabrook. I'm tired of only getting the gossip about your medical life."

With only the slightest movement in the corner of his mouth, he watched her. "Not until we discuss this note." He left for the kitchen, tossing a cloth atop her washer, bandage wrappers in the trash.

She flexed her fingers and examined his finished work. "Thanks, by the way."

"Never had a patient hit by a trash can before. One for the medical journals."

Jeb returned empty-handed. "I dumped it in the grass. Some raccoon will enjoy mint chocolate chip tonight."

Her attention moved from Jeb toward Seabrook. The man had soothed her yet again when she hadn't seen it coming. "How'd you know?" she asked.

"How'd I know what?" he replied.

"That my favorite was mint chocolate chip?"

"You're the detective. You figure it out," Seabrook said, soaping his hand at the sink, smiling so smoothly. "Maybe it's my favorite, too."

Jeb plopped onto the sofa beside her. Seabrook came around the bar to join them, settling in the arm chair. Both men crossed a leg and waited.

Seems she had no choice but to relay her activities, or they'd be staring at her all night. "I visited Janet Wainwright yesterday," she began, "about the sign-in book from the party. She kicked me out. Pushing her buttons probably got Jeb's license revoked, which I never could've foreseen. And then someone trashed my yard, and town hall sanctioned me with pink slips." Her lips tightened as she turned to face her son. "Sorry, sweetheart."

He shrugged, trying to appear unbothered. However, she suspected he disliked this situation from two fronts: losing his fishing license . . . and hearing that his mother continued to sleuth around when she'd promised otherwise.

Avoiding his censure, she hurriedly spoke to Seabrook. "Then I visited Alex Hanson, and she took me to the newspaper office outside town." Jenkins had been deadpan-serious about keeping his presence secret, and Callie decided she'd honor his wishes. She also didn't see the need to mention him yet. *Need to know* had always served her well. "Journalists possess a lot of intel about a community. She found me details you won't tell me."

"About what?" Jeb asked.

"I can guess," Seabrook said with derision.

In anticipation of Jeb's response, she reached over to pat his leg. "About the August deaths."

Jeb sat rigid. "Deaths? Somebody else died? This place is worse than a zombie movie."

"No, no," she said. "These happened last year, and the year before, and every August for the last six years." She left out the women's kinship to her own looks.

His eyes narrowed. "And you feel the need to check it out."

She'd already forecasted his disapproval, but he sounded so like her father. "It's okay," she said. Since when did turning eighteen make him her keeper?

Jeb snatched the car note off the coffee table. "It's not okay. Not if you get threats on your life." He let the paper flutter to the floor.

"It's frivolous," she said, though she wasn't so sure.

"Don't start," he replied. "*You will get hurt* is not frivolous. It's pretty damn straight forward, if you ask me. Now I've got to watch as this stuff winds you so tight you—"

"It won't. It's not," she said, soothing, assuring him in those few words that she wouldn't touch alcohol. Since losing his father, he'd seen his mother abuse the stuff enough nights to generate his doubt.

Yet right now she'd almost gnaw her foot off for a gin and tonic, light on the ice.

But what was she supposed to do, ignore the harassment? She knew Jeb's most vivid recollections of her life as a detective were from the months after John's death, when she'd rabidly pursued his killer, mentally collapsing by the end of a year when she resigned. Jeb didn't remember her prowess as an investigator, only the flaws. Damn it, she'd been good at her job.

But Jeb's face darkened, and Callie jerked as he jumped to his feet. "Will you speak to her?" he said to Seabrook, a stiff finger directed at his mother. "She won't listen. Instead, she chokes on her own misery, play-acting all is well in the world as if I'm six years old. I have to find her on the porch drunk or hear her crying at night." He reached down and snared the note from the floor. "I don't even want to know what this means. I probably do, but I don't. I mean . . . hell, I don't even know what I mean." He shook it at her. "You're not a cop anymore, Mom!"

Tears welled in Callie's eyes.

"I'll take care of her, Jeb," Seabrook said. "But this isn't Boston."

"Seriously?" her son replied, lines tight in a face too young. "You're saying that to the person a Russian mobster kidnapped a couple months ago right here in this house? It doesn't have to be in Boston."

"And your mother saved you, son. She was good at what she did. Still is."

"Was," Jeb spit in return. Standing at the foot of the sofa, he sucked air like he'd run a race. "The key word is and should remain *was*. She doesn't do it anymore. Why can't she get over this law enforcement crap? Hasn't it cost us enough already?"

She hated being discussed as if she weren't in the room. Unable to hold the buildup in her throat, she released a soft sob.

Jeb's plea reminded her of his adolescent years, when he didn't understand one of her stakeouts or his father's retrieval of an escaped felon as a Deputy US Marshal. If she understood anything about Jeb, it was that he'd never wear a badge. And he'd never respect her for talent she spent fifteen years sharpening to a fine skill.

Callie cleared her throat. "You're taking this over the top. I visited a real estate agent, she got mad, and then I got a note on my car."

"You didn't even get a note last time, Mom. He just waltzed in and tried to kill us."

When would their roles reverse back to normal, where she became the parent and he the child? At eighteen he needed to laugh, miss curfew, slip a beer or two onto the beach. "Stop it, Jeb."

"Stop what? I'm not dealing the crap around here, Mom! You are! I'd sleep perfectly fine if you would let other people make the headlines. You don't have to fix everything!"

Callie rubbed her face. Since leaving Boston, she'd fallen into a bad habit of second-guessing her people skills, to include her parenting. When she moved to Edisto she meant to start over, but for each step forward, she fell back five. She couldn't fix everything, but Jeb was wrong. She did have to try, because whatever she did, she did it for the two of them. All her decisions held him in mind, and their new home. Just not always how he liked.

"I can't sit in my chair on the porch and rot," she exclaimed, her fingers fisting. "If you want to see me drink then leave me here locked up all day with nothing to do. Is that what you want?"

"No, of course not." He blew out long and intentional. "Promise you won't do stupid stuff."

Seabrook leaned forward. "Whoa, Jeb. That's uncalled for."

"I promise," Callie spoke almost in a whisper, hurt that her son would consider anything she did stupid. If only he understood who she was.

But as she waited for his acceptance of her promise, he denied it from her and walked to his bedroom. He closed the door, the choke in his last words not fooling her.

Callie turned her head and swiftly wiped the errant tear from her cheek, changing to her left hand to avoid staining her bandage. Seabrook's empathetic gaze served her a dose of pity she really didn't need at the moment.

"Who do you think wrote the note?" she asked and wiped her nose again. "Or typed it, rather."

He let her change the subject, though his stare remained hard. "Maybe Janet, whom you already suspect. Any of the real estate agencies. I would sure like to think this note way over the top for town council. Childish."

"Agreed."

"But they have a lot at stake." Seabrook lounged deeper into the chair, moving the small pillow from behind him to the floor. "Alex may not be the patriot you think she is, and let's not forget our friend Grant. But doesn't this tell you to let it be? Nothing you uncovered shouted serial murder, did it? These people out here aren't criminals."

He said serial murder like a menu item, with no distress behind it. His stance hadn't changed, and he still seemed bent on changing hers. If she weren't already tired from the evening, she'd get mad all over again.

Instead, she gave Seabrook a five-minute rundown of the past six years as conveyed in the *Island Tribune's* archives in hope he'd confirm or deny some of the information. He did neither. Instead, he showed minimal concern about her discoveries, which stung. To disappoint her even more, he changed topics. "Well," he said. "I had a call from the town administrator today. Who is Frank Weaver?"

Weaver's image appeared sunburned and nonsensical in her mind. "A big guy from New Jersey. Insurance salesman. He's a renter from the Wainwright party, there when Brea died." She tucked her feet under her on the sofa, her exhaustion sinking into the fabric. "He stood across the street outside Maddington's that day."

Seabrook raised his brow. "And?"

"He and a few others from the party visited me. They think they're gumshoe detectives."

He nodded. "Well, your protégés—"

"They aren't my protégés." What had the motley crew done? She only asked them to query their neighbors about how long they'd been coming to Edisto. More to give them something to do than to collect anything serious.

"Whatever you call them, they're slinging your name around like you're the attorney general. They knocked on doors and interrupted people's vacations with their questions. Three individuals called town hall today leaving threats they might not return to the island," Seabrook said. "They weren't thrilled to be interrogated about their vacationing habits."

Callie sank deeper into her cushion. So the ice cream was a guise. One minute it's business with this man and the next it's social.

Still, she appreciated the official message from him instead of the town, wishing they'd handled the sanctions in the same manner.

"I'll settle Frank down," she said, thinking she'd find out what they knew as well. "Tomorrow morning. He probably saw this case as excitement for a boring vacation, reading way too much into our conversation. Still, I'll see what he found out."

Seabrook slapped his thighs, and his head dropped forward with emphasis. "When are you going to learn there is no case, Callie? And what'll I tell my riled town administrator?"

Callie raised her voice in turn. "Tell him you spoke to me, and I'll speak to Frank. What's so hard about that?"

His fist sprang open, splaying his fingers in animated frustration. "You're dancing all around the words *I won't investigate anymore.*"

"Who says I have to?"

"But you promised Jeb—"

She unwrapped herself into a seated, fighting position. "I promised not to be stupid with it."

He lightly laughed, shooting his own displeasure in return. "I highly doubt he sees it that way."

"Well, somebody has to do something. You discount a threat left on my car."

Stick in the knife, girl. Draw blood. Everybody's forgotten you have a brain.

"You caused the threat!" he said, and his mouth flattened. "Callie, I'm not discounting it, but you keep poking a stick in cages around here. I'll mention the threatening note to town hall when I go in in the morning." Pointing at the laptop still on the coffee table, he said, "Check your cameras and see if you can at least save me the trouble of talking to the wrong people."

She showed him the images and lack of evidence of who performed the trash can stunt. A few moments later, they witnessed a hooded individual in the dark, slipping into her parking area, then coming out. Nothing but grays and blacks, shadows and gloom.

"Nothing," he said, discouraged. "Do you want me to file a report?"

"Suit yourself." She reared into the sofa, sorting through her animosity for logic. "Maybe it's that Twitter guy. You saw his post from where he visited my front porch today?"

"No." He sighed, pulling out his phone. After he'd seen the picture, he said, "Well, you have shifted the axis of this town. Somebody's out of sorts."

"Well, tell me this, doc. Why would anyone feel threatened in the first place unless there's substance to my theories?"

"This might be no more than a lone owner who relies so heavily on rental income he wants to scare you into silence. Possibly any of two dozen real estate agents. A renter having fun."

She shut the laptop. "Try spreading your warnings to Janet Wainwright and her ilk, if that's not too much bother."

He rose to his feet. "I have to balance personalities on this patch of sand, but I'll try."

She stood to face him. "Janet had the town screw with Jeb and Zeus. And when I didn't crumble and cry, she stepped it up a notch." Some silence passed between them. "Aren't you even worried about another death?"

"We had our calamity," he said. "That means your jinx is over for this year."

"If Maddington killed Brea, your August killing hasn't even happened yet, and it's a damn shame I'm the only person who sees that." Tired of their conversation going nowhere, she turned to go to the kitchen in hopes he'd take the hint and leave.

But Seabrook's stride cut short the distance, and he spun her around. "Do you not hear yourself? Nobody believes there's a serial killer. Your problem is you need something to keep you occupied."

"Is this where you beg me to come work for you again?" she asked, adjusting her shirt.

"Not begging," he replied with a softer tone. "Listen, it's almost midnight. I need to go. At least consider being auxiliary for us. You'd be more credible when you spoke to people."

"Why would I talk to people with nothing to investigate?" she asked.

He mashed his lips. "I mean if and when you want to talk to people." He raised a brow. "Now that you mention it, though, I'd let you see the old files on those women. To appease your curiosity. Plus Janet may leave you alone."

"A badge won't intimidate that old piece of jerky, plus Jeb would have a cow. And you want me occupied, under your nose."

He shook his head in disbelief.

Auxiliary. A far cry from the level she'd achieved in her career. An unpaid position she could quit any time she wanted. She already met the standards. At most, she might have to range qualify again. "You'd let me see your files? Any one I wanted?"

"Absolutely," he said.

"What else would I have to do?"

"At least one day a week you're mine. That means traffic, golf cart accidents, domestic, you name it."

Like Jeb's temporary fishing charter interest, maybe an auxiliary position suited her needs for the time being. Open new doors. Wrangle Janet from a different angle, this time from behind a badge. Intimidate the power of the beach into leaving her home alone.

"Well? What do you think?" he asked.

What else *did* she have to do? No wonder her mind leaped head-first into this case. At night she dreamed reruns of the Russian. His mouth on her. His blood on her. She needed mission in her life.

She couldn't even call her old boss Stan for his take on things. She'd so screwed that relationship.

Rikki's return had consumed most of Sophie's attention.

"Let me think about it," she said.

Good Lord, she needed a drink.

Chapter 14

CALLIE ROLLED OVER, and her sore back jerked her awake. Not as bad as she thought it would be, but she'd definitely forego the jog. Per her clock it was 9:00 a.m. anyway, the sun out strong. Tuesday, August eleventh.

None of the other women died on this date. Hopefully a good thing.

She liked having the dates, the death information, the names of the women. Intelligence meant empowerment, the start of a logical path to solving a mystery.

Which made her remember Seabrook's offer. In the aftermath of pink slips and a threat, an injury, and her son's scolding, the auxiliary police role had held major attraction in the middle of the night. A life preserver thrown at a vulnerable moment. Now, in the light of day, she held doubts.

She didn't know which was worse: having too little to do, or getting sucked into the job again. Which seemed more important: fixing herself and appeasing Jeb, or serving the inhabitants of Edisto Beach? Lying in bed, the sun melting across the spread, the former made so much more sense.

But one day a week wouldn't hurt, would it? Auxiliary. A pretend officer on a tiny police force.

She grabbed her phone and texted Seabrook her declination of the offer before she changed her mind, then laid the cell on her nightstand. Big exhale. There. Easier than delivering the message while staring into those blue-gray eyes.

Snatching the phone again, she hunted for more tweets. No new pictures. She dropped the phone on the spread. Good.

This day got better and better.

By nine thirty, she barefooted to the bathroom and let the shower run until hot. Pushing against the stall, she let spray beat her back until sure the skin shone lobster red. Finally, the muscles loosened.

Donning baggy shorts and a button-up cotton tunic, she greeted the day, her first move to locate Frank Weaver's business card. Frank and his crew needed to ease off the gumshoe business. Their antics, not Janet's, may have very well instigated the pink slips from town hall.

"Can we talk?" she asked after the appropriate salutations.

"By all means," Frank said, assuming they were on first name basis now that they collaborated. "Our little band of detectives has been knocking on doors and taking names."

"So I heard. Y'all moved fast."

She pictured his belly jerking as he gave a deep, smoky laugh.

"Hope that's good news, my friend," he said. "And while I'd love to call us efficient, fact is most of us leave in a week, so we hustled. Kris and Cynthia depart Thursday. Besides, rousting the good folks of Edisto into vigilance might be what this place needs."

Good grief. Seabrook was right. This had to stop.

"Meet at your place?" Callie asked, afraid to make this crew climb her stairs again. Her reputation was already as bruised as her back. Orchestrating a posse embarrassed her.

"Absolutely. Why waste this gorgeous view of the Atlantic?" Frank exclaimed. "We paid dearly for it, and not to be derogatory, but you don't really see much from your place."

A stated truth, but facing the water brought traffic, noise, people crossing your yard, and exorbitant property taxes atop crazy insurance rates. She could stroll to see waves whenever she liked and avoid the direct hit of a hurricane. Natives and visitors saw the beach through different eyes, using it for diverse needs. "Be over after I grab a bite to eat," she said.

"Callie, Callie, come on now. Ava has bagels and fruit, and you have your choice of screwdriver or mimosa to drink. Got to keep things healthy, right?" He chuckled again. "Ava's calling the rest of the bunch as we speak. An absolutely beautiful day for sleuthing, don't you think?"

"As good as any," she replied with a sigh. "Be there in ten minutes."

"Oh," he said. "While chasing a few drinks last night, we created a name for us."

"A name?"

"Yeah. The Edisto Sleuth Society. It's official. Every time we come here, we'll ask the police if they have something going on we can assist with. If not, we'll create our own mystery and plant clues around the island. I'm telling you, beats the hell out of sitting bored getting sunburned, wouldn't you say?"

She lightly laughed with the man then hung up and pounded her forehead with a fist. Good gracious. She had half a mind to tell *them* Seabrook needed auxiliary assistance on the force.

SHE PARKED BEHIND what she assumed to be Frank and Ava's Cadillac Escalade. The insurance business apparently paid well in Morristown, New Jersey.

The beach view rental ranked average on Palmetto Boulevard, one of the largest homes. Once a person lived around Edisto a while, they learned to recognize a house not only by its common name, but its rental capacity. Lost Horizons slept eight, ten tops counting cots stashed in the closets, but Callie bet its amenities jacked its value an extra thousand a week.

An uncovered deck stretched across the entire front of the place, for the sun lovers. A massive screened porch stretched behind that. A small pool filled the tiny backyard, always a nicety after a day of sticky salt. The glassed sunroom beckoned from atop the roof with views to the Atlantic horizon, enabling the tenant to see unobstructed over the top of houses across the street that hugged the water's edge.

Of course this group ignored the best of the house's assets and sat inside the screened porch, ceiling fans on full speed, some sort of portable air-conditioner blowing across their feet from the corner. Yeah, Lost Horizon's owner would pay a hefty power bill this month.

Callie climbed the stairs and reached out. "Thanks for inviting me over."

For a stocky man, Frank gave her a gingerly grip once seeing her bandaged hand. "What happened?"

She scrunched her nose. "Fell in my own yard," she said, not wanting to stir a conspiracy theory angle with the ESS. If they thought their snooping caused her harm, their excitement would rise to new levels.

Daniel and Tanya had finished eating earlier, with only crumbs on their plates. They lounged loose and easy, savoring drinks. Terrance chowed down on a bagel slathered blue with jelly. Kris waved for Callie to sit on her side of the rattan table while Cynthia sat at the end of the table and sipped a wine cooler in a koozie, picking at a bunch of grapes. All greeted her with nods and smiles, except Cynthia whom Callie read as one who held her emotions in check regardless. Two glass pitchers beckoned, both with orange juice. Frank held a glass. "Which is your poison?"

"Just plain, please," Callie said.

Frank selected one and poured. Ava pushed the bowls in Callie's direction. "Go ahead. Eat up."

Frank plopped the glass in front of Callie as she buttered a bagel. "So, we made an impact, huh?" He turned to the others. "You hear that? We *can* make this an annual thing."

The silliness slayed her. She crammed the bread in her mouth and chewed, thinking. Shame that these were the only people who believed in the jinx and were willing to do something about it. But then they had the option to go home and leave the danger behind. Callie, Seabrook, whomever, would get stuck with the aftermath.

But they *were* nice.

Callie mused at the bizarre membership of the society, an assemblage of sorts glued together by a single event. No way these people would socialize in the real world, and if she threw a wet blanket on their nosiness, especially with two naysayers in their ranks, they might dissolve the union. Best for all parties concerned, especially the town administrator.

"We haven't met," Tanya said, the Georgia drawl defining her origin, her deep tan indicative of her vacation purpose. At least three shades darker than when Callie saw her at the party. "I'm Daniel's wife, and I'm not sure I like what you've asked these people to do. Can't they get in trouble?"

"I'm not all that keen on the idea either," Cynthia replied dryly.

Callie tried to swallow a bite fast. "I didn't really—"

"Honey, we've been over this," Daniel said to his wife, ignoring Cynthia.

"I'm an attorney; I appreciate where the line is."

Frank flopped into a wicker chair challenged by his weight from the creak and pop. "Can you update us?"

"Oh, Frank, let the girl eat," Ava said, her own chair complaining as she rocked.

Callie bit the bagel again, then reached for her glass to wash it down. The mimosa slid into her throat before her nose registered the alcohol.

"Good, huh?" Ava asked.

Chafed at the misstep, Callie almost pushed the glass aside to leave. But in light of the fact she delivered bad news from Seabrook and the town, Callie accepted the drink with the manners Beverly taught her. After all, it was only one, this was business, and the damn thing was oh so friggin' good.

"So you're done with this case, right?" she asked, sucking the last drops from her glass.

"Yes," Cynthia said, no doubt in her tone.

"Unless you tell us something else we can do," Terrance inserted quickly.

Ava looked eagerly at her.

Dang it.

"So, what exactly did you learn?" she asked, not quite able to drop the hammer yet.

A half hour and two mimosas later, Callie had learned that no tourist had heard of the jinx, only two of the two dozen they spoke with had previously stayed in Edisto, and nobody knew Brea died.

The time seemed right to drop the news. "The town received three complaints yesterday about your inquiries. They want you to butt out, their words, not mine. The acting police chief delivered the message to me and asked me to convey it to you."

"I knew it," Cynthia said, on her fourth screwdriver. "I'm glad we're leaving in two days."

"Wait." Daniel inclined forward, elbows to his knees. "Thought you were dating the chief?"

Callie shrugged.

Frank snapped his fingers. "Can't beat *EdistoToday* and Twitter for Edisto news."

"We learned you can ask a native. Better yet, ask a real estate agent," Terrance said. "They hear everything around here and are very willing to share if you even hint at throwing them your business."

"Still," Callie said, eying the empty mimosa pitcher, considering the screwdriver. The familiar lightness in her head only made her yearn for more. "You might back off."

"Awww," Ava said.

"I know, I know," Callie said in faux sympathy. Sad enough that the only allies she had about the Edisto cold case were overzealous tourists, but she should've thought twice about inviting them. They had no filters and ran at one speed. Assuming the Edisto jinx cold case held substance, they might've even knocked on the killer's door.

"I'll have to find another way of learning who's been around here for six years," she said, winking at Terrance. "Maybe I'll use your trick and ask a real estate agent. Appreciate y'all's effort. The authorities believe they've solved Brea Jamison's death, though."

"Insurance fraud?" Frank asked.

Can you spell one-track mind, Frank?

"They'll consider that, but more than likely an affair gone badly. That's all I can say."

Kris reached over and fished the last of the melon off the platter. "What about the jinx? Same hair color and all."

"Same time period," Daniel added.

Wow. While she dug info out of Alex Hanson, the ESS had milked the natives and done equally as well. "You *have* been busy."

"You learn a lot at the restaurants," Frank replied. "We split up and worked the place last night after we canvassed the five-block area."

Cynthia lifted her drink. "Very productive, especially if you tally doors slammed in our face."

"And the strange looks," Tanya said.

Ava raised a finger. "The threat to call the cops."

Terrance raised his glass. "A guy promised to shoot me if I didn't leave."

Callie stared at him, surprised. "Shooting sounds a little harsh."

He laughed. "Yeah, but we had fun, didn't we, guys?"

Frank slapped Daniel on the shoulder as chortles and joking one-liners made the rounds, the ESS rehashing their adventure with gusto.

Callie caught herself hee-hawing with them as Cynthia finished off the pitcher of screwdrivers. She wished she'd moved faster to snag a refill.

Then Frank went inside and brought out another pitcher.

IT WAS AFTER ONE before Callie left Frank and Ava's. She ran inside Chelsea Morning, straight to the bathroom, and brushed her teeth. Gargling twice, she swallowed part of the blue minty mouthwash for good measure.

Crap and darn it all. She had only planned to settle the ESS down, dismantling it from detective agency to acquaintances talking over drinks. How had such a quirky pod of people kept her occupied so long?

She'd delivered the message as promised to Seabrook, unsure the ESS heard it. Mainly because she wasn't quite sure she'd made it clear, thanks to the best mimosas she'd ever drank in her life.

"Mom?"

Damn. Guilt poured over her like a waterfall. She'd sleuthed, she'd drank, and Jeb wouldn't understand no matter what she said. Callie breathed into her good hand and sniffed. She seemed okay.

Jeb appeared in her bedroom. "You okay?" He sounded down, even nervous.

"Yeah," she said, washing her hands quickly and grabbing a towel. She walked toward her son, but stopped short, just in case. "Anything new about the fishing license?"

He rubbed the doorframe and studied her a second before he answered. "No, but it's a little early, I think."

"Okay," she said, trying hard to behave normally, at the same time pondering what Jeb would interpret as abnormal behavior. *Stupid.* Perps or victims, she'd always been able to spot a front, and her son wasn't dumb. He stood in the doorway unsettled, as if sorting what to say. She waited to be shot.

Damn it, she could've demanded plain juice or coffee or water, for Christ's sake, but no. She drank the friggin' mimosas for an idiot reason that escaped her now, and the slip might cost her the trust of her son. Then she sighed. "Just spill it."

Jeb seemed jittery. "Would you talk to Sprite's mom?"

"Um, what? Why?"

A whimper came from somewhere in her bedroom. Jeb gazed over at the sound, hurt on his face.

Callie walked past him and peered toward the entrance. Sprite Bianchi leaned against the door, wrapped in a wide-weave crocheted sweater over a spaghetti strap tank top. Callie bet the tiny shorts rose almost to her butt cheeks. While the seductive dress would've ordinarily given Callie pause, as if she had the right to say anything about how her son's girlfriend barely clad herself, the tears on the sweet child's face stole her attention.

Callie's mothering instincts swept in. She rushed to the girl and pushed the lush black spiral curls out of her face. "What's wrong, honey?"

"You . . . you know how my mother gets sometimes, right?" she asked, hitches in her timid voice. "Jeb said you'd understand better than anyone."

"What specifically are you talking about?" Callie continued to stroke the curls. How did anyone have that much hair? Like a raven's feathers, the black almost reflected blue.

"Her spirit communications," the child added.

Callie grounded her *understanding* more out of courtesy and respect, not of knowledge. She didn't discount Sophie and her otherworld beliefs, like Sophie accepted Callie's inordinate distaste about locks and alarms. Unlike Rikki Cavett, who never passed a chance to ding their mutual friend as silly. For Jeb to suggest Sprite come to Callie, and for Sprite to agree, gave Callie a sense of pride, almost replacing the guilt needling her for sneaking mimosas. "Is she experiencing more spirits?"

"Yes, ma'am. She can't sleep because of her ghosts. She barely eats, and she's too tiny to lose weight. They startle her so much that she fights to stay awake. Would you talk to her?"

This child appeared genuinely distraught about her mother. But what the hell could Callie do about it?

However, doing nothing was not an option. Callie stretched to reach the girl's shoulders and hugged the curvy tall brunette to her. Rubbing Sprite's back, she whispered in an ear buried somewhere beneath those corkscrew curls. "Sure. I'll take care of your mother."

Jeb beamed from behind his worry for his girlfriend.

What mother didn't yearn to be the savior of her child's world?

Chapter 15

AN HOUR LATER, Callie found Sophie next door on her porch, the yoga lady wadded in a chair, head tucked between her knees, far from in commune with the universe. Retrieving Sophie's favorite carrot juice from the fridge, Callie joined her under the fan despite the heat and humidity, her friend obviously needing nature to work through the thoughts in her head.

"I don't understand," Sophie kept saying. With nervous twitches in her face, she relayed her night terrors. "Why me?"

"Why not you?" Callie said. "Who else out here is nutty enough to recognize spirits?"

Sophie caved to a tentative smile. "You're sweet."

Callie took her friend's hand. "I may regret this, but . . . do you want to stay with me a few days until you sort this out?"

Sophie sprang out of her chair, practically in Callie's lap, and hugged her tight. "Yes, yes, oh yes. Thank you so much. I think if I can get through August, I'll be okay." She bounced to her feet and darted to the door. "Let me throw some things together."

As the squeal dissipated into the bedroom, Callie rose to help. Who said anything about the *end* of August?

Her foot slid on a folded piece of paper. She bent over, retrieved it, and then entered the house and set it on the table. As she closed the door, the paper fluttered to the floor again, open. *Keep your neighbor out of trouble or I will.*

Typed. Like the one on her car. How long had Sophie hidden it from her?

Ignorance was Sophie's answer to life's negatives. Face it, and it will come. Pretend it didn't happen, and it evaporates. One day this mentality would bite her in the butt. With Sophie at Callie's, she'd find an opportune moment to interrogate her friend because Callie didn't care who said what under her roof. Karma, luck, fate, or whatever else you called it, found you regardless of whose walls you lived in.

She tucked the paper in her pocket.

Barely five minutes later, they left Hatha Heaven, Callie somewhat suspicious that Sophie had packed in advance.

"Need help carrying your bags upstairs?" Callie asked as they rounded the inside stairs in Chelsea Morning.

Sophie hoisted her second bag's strap higher on her shoulder. "I got it. This ought to be fun."

Three weeks seemed a long time cohabitating with such a high-strung soul, but Callie'd promised to help the Bianchi household. Besides, the distraction might be nice. The company would be nice. Callie'd alienated most everyone else.

She pondered how to broach the subject of the note. Then she wondered if the note carried more weight than the ghosts in Sophie's decision to move in.

"You sure the spirits won't follow you here?" Callie followed her up the stairs, worried the friend would trip on her ribbon skirt. Sophie wore flare well. She had to own at least five sets of colored contact lenses.

"It's less likely they'll come here." Sophie tossed her belongings on the bed. The large room encompassed the whole top floor and held two double beds and a queen, designed for the days when the Cantrells rented the place to vacationers. Callie had dusted and vacuumed quickly, thankful for clean sheets in the closet.

She sat on the opposite bed as Sophie unpacked, unsure why Sophie brought much more than a toothbrush and change of clothes with her wardrobe only next door.

Sophie pointed at the dresser, and Callie nodded. Tanks and yoga pants went in the drawers while Sophie chatted like a chipmunk, relief evident in her voice. "The less I disturb the atmosphere in my house, the better."

"But you're leaving the kids in a ghost-infested place by themselves."

Sophie shrugged. "They don't see the spirits. Plus they would prefer the house to themselves."

"Sprite seems pretty worried. She's your baby." And for a second she rued the remark as Bonnie oozed into her thoughts. She'd never have a daughter.

Sophie pooed the remark with a wave. "She has Zeus, and she can walk over here anytime she likes." She giggled. "I'm sure Jeb won't protest."

The clock on the nightstand read almost five. "What do you want to do about dinner? Order pizza from Bucks? Throw some shrimp on the grill?"

"Oh, honey," Sophie said, sliding the drawer closed and collapsing on the bed. "Dinner's on me. Let's go to Whaley's. We can ask the kids if they want to tag along, but with a whole house to themselves, why would they eat with their moms?"

The unchaperoned house next door gave Callie images she wasn't quite ready to see. "We need to set some ground rules for that *empty house*, my friend."

"Zeus is there."

Callie pulled her new roommate from the bed. "Like that makes me feel better. Don't know about you, but I'm not prepared to be a grandmother yet."

SOPHIE DROVE THEM in her vintage powder blue, early nineties model Mercedes convertible, top down, two girls on the town, as small as town was.

However, cold fingers walked down Callie's spine. The last time she'd visited Whaley's had been on a date with Mason, before she learned of his Russian heritage and his ties to her husband's murder.

The dinner had been sublime, the conversation engaging, the entire restaurant noticing Callie had accepted an invitation from the hottest guy on the beach. But then the sun set, the sky lit with the peach and blue highlights of dusk, and Callie fell apart with one of her anxiety attacks.

Same restaurant, same time of day, in a convertible. Why hadn't she driven the Escape?

You're so over this. A shiver rippled through her.

The two women grabbed a bistro table in the center of the floor where Sophie could greet the regulars as they came in.

"The kids were awful glad to get rid of us," Callie said. For a fleeting moment she wondered if Jeb and Sprite had set her up to claim the Bianchi house for their own for a while. However, she bet they knew nothing of the warning note. Sophie wouldn't have shared that.

"I shouldn't have to explain that those kids can find privacy at way more places than my house, right?" Sophie schooled.

"Yeah, I know." Callie much preferred pondering murders than second-guessing her son's sexual activities.

They shared an appetizer of boiled peanuts, Sophie sensitive enough to Callie's limitations not to imbibe on anything stronger than iced tea. When the crab legs arrived, they dove in, Callie's new roomie leading the conversation with who divorced whom and how many times different houses were turning over.

"Why do you keep glancing out the window?" Sophie asked as they opened miniature wipes and cleaned their fingers.

"Old habit," Callie answered, checking the time on her phone again.

Sophie took the device from her and set it across the table. "Enjoy just being here. Breathe." The yoga instructor turned her hands backside down on the table, palms open. "Relax."

Someone dropped a glass behind the bar. Callie jumped. A sunburned family of six argued over who would grab the biggest bed when they returned to the rental. Sunbleached elders guffawed drunk from the bar.

Callie waited until a wave of laughter subsided. "How do you relax in this racket?"

"Reflect inward. Like I said, breathe."

"I need a drink," Callie said and motioned for the waiter.

Sophie slapped Callie's hand down. "What are you doing?" Her aquamarine eyes honed in on her dinner partner. "Oh my gosh, you've had a drink lately, haven't you? I thought—"

"May I help you?" A different waiter. Callie'd seen him at BI-LO and around town. Jeb's age. Maybe older, more like Zeus. He wore a T-shirt stamped with Whaley's logo.

"She needs dessert," Sophie interjected. "What about the triple chocolate cake, Callie?"

Callie released a short frustrated sigh. "I'd rather have the bourbon pecan pie."

Sophie squinted. "Sure you would." She eyed the young man. "The chocolate cake, please."

As the waiter left earshot, Sophie practically crawled onto the table as she whispered, "What did you do?"

"Seabrook asked me to talk to some tourists who were at the party. They had mimosas."

"And you couldn't say no?"

"They made me!"

Sophie laughed. "Sure they did."

Hindsight remarkably clear, in her opinion, Callie struggled seeing anything wrong with the morning's activities with the ESS. "I did okay, Sophie," she said. "Didn't get drunk. I managed myself."

"Well, I won't be party to you falling off the wagon," Sophie said with a nasty pout. "Does this mean you're kicking me out?"

"I never got on a wagon," Callie replied. "And no, I wouldn't kick you out for caring."

"Good, because I'm keeping my eye on you." Sophie pointed from her eyes to Callie's.

"So now you're babysitting me?"

"If I have to," Sophie said.

"Was that your goal all along?"

Sophie wilted. "No. I really am going nuts in my own house. I need a break. Please, only until August is over."

Callie reached across and squeezed her friend's arm. Sophie owned a good soul. And she'd see that Callie didn't drink, that's for sure. She made a note to show her Lawton's partial bottle of Maker's Mark and label it off limits. She didn't want Sophie accidentally or otherwise throwing out her father's memory.

Yes, Callie'd self-medicated with gin after losing her husband. Moving in with her parents for a year engraved a deeper habit, parallel to her mother's. But she'd relinquished alcohol after her daddy died. Had today at Frank's been all that bad? She saw no damage done whatsoever.

The cake arrived, not that either of them wanted it. Callie swiped off a layer of icing with her fork and ate it, letting it dissolve on her tongue as she stole another glance out the window. It faced east which meant the sky behind Whaley's held the more vivid colors.

With half the cake done, she waved to the waiter for the check. "How about let's go home?"

"Did I set you off?" Sophie asked then quickly pasted a wide, sparkling smile on her face as the fire chief came in with a couple of other guys, all three making eye contact with her.

"No, you didn't." *Yes you did.* "Hey, has your ex done anything about the boys' business?"

"Hey you!" Sophie shouted to someone else new coming in before turning to Callie. "He says somebody's got their ass on their shoulders. Said maybe the boys stepped on somebody's toes, but he'll take care of it. Give him a few days to donate to a campaign or pay for something the town needs."

Somebody's toes got stepped on, all right, but the boys didn't do it.

They'd been at Whaley's for over an hour, and the dinner crowd began a line outside. The ladies' plates were clean, their glasses empty on the table, the cake half eaten now ignored, but Sophie remained planted in her seat.

"Sophie?" Callie asked.

"Hmm?"

"Are you stalling going home because of the spirits? Maybe you're worried about the note you dropped on the floor at your house?" Callie laid it on the table.

The sparkle faded as Sophie's gaze came down from the crowd and settled on the note, then on Callie.

"Keep your neighbor out of trouble or I will."

Sophie blushed even under her olive skin and summer tan.

"Aren't we a pair?" Callie stood and grabbed her purse. "Come on. Let's go back to the house and face our demons." She lightly pinched her friend on the arm. "And I can take care of myself, Sophie."

Suddenly several tables of people stood at once. The women glanced right to left at the coincidence. The fire chief waved off the waitress and dashed to the door, his dinner partners with him. Callie wedged between tables to let them through.

"Somebody's grill's on fire again!" said an old guy bellied to the bar, sending a raucous round of chortles around the room.

"Whose is it?" Sophie asked.

"How do you tell this time of year?" The laughter rolled around the room again.

Callie pushed her chair under the table. "Come on, Sophie. I'd rather be curled on my sofa and out of the noise."

Sophie sighed and collected her drawstring bag. With a deep, settling breath, Callie led them outside into the dimming light. Two minutes later, they headed home, her shoulders tensed and her jaw knotted. One day a hot, melting sunset wouldn't throw her back to Boston.

Sophie turned the Mercedes onto Myrtle Street, shifted gears, and gunned it. Wind whipped their short hair helter-skelter as she tried to gain some speed in spite of the short distance to Lybrand Street. She laughed as she passed someone's house, educating Callie on how much money they made, where they were from, and what famous person they were cousin to.

Callie's phone rang. Seabrook. She wanted to wait until she could hear better. Between Sophie and the wind, she'd never understand what he said. Voice mail would catch the call. They'd be home in five minutes.

Before she could tuck the phone into her purse, it rang, once again Seabrook.

"Hey," she answered as Sophie cornered the Mercedes onto Lybrand where in a hundred yards they'd turn onto the straight shot home.

"Callie? Where are you?" he yelled, and she wondered why he'd holler when she had all the wind noise.

"On the way home from Whaley's," she said. "I can barely hear you."

Sophie turned onto Jungle Road.

"Pull off the road," Seabrook yelled.

"What? Why?" Callie hollered, covering her other ear to hear.

"Just do it!" he yelled.

Holding the phone to her chest, Callie turned to relay the message to Sophie but froze as the distant light caught her eye.

"Oh dear lord," Sophie uttered.

Fire lit up the sky.

Chapter 16

THE FLAMES SHONE bright against the darkening navy sky of late evening, rising from the direction of Callie's and Sophie's homes. Both women stared stunned for the briefest of moments. Then adrenaline kicked in.

Callie slapped the dash and yelled, "Go, Sophie!"

Sophie's foot stomped the gas to the floor, her fist hard on the horn, Callie thrown against the seat. The Mercedes raced the mile down Jungle Road, three cars jerking aside, none challenging the pale blue blur.

Callie gripped the handle, staring, trying to identify which house. The glow grew, her galloping heartbeat recalling a moment like this before. Please don't let it be Chelsea Morning.

Oh my God. The kids are at Sophie's.

"Is it my house?" Sophie cried, hugging her steering wheel.

"Just drive," Callie yelled.

Sliding on the gravel drive, the convertible tapped the rear of a parked police cruiser as Sophie skidded to stop.

Callie screamed as she leaped from her seat. "Jeb!"

Sophie's house was clearly untouched, yet the fire felt so close, the smoke choking, the melee too confusing to tell where flames started or where they stopped at Chelsea Morning. Callie raced toward the onslaught of waves of heat. She coughed from the familiar stench of wood and insulation, the melted shingles.

Behind her Sophie shouted her children's names. "Zeus, Sprite!"

Callie reached her home, pulse ripping. She made it to the first landing of her stairs before Seabrook grabbed her around the waist.

Like the cop who'd caught her before she dove into the fire that consumed John. The similarity rocketed to explode her fears to a new level.

"Jeb!"

"You can't go in there, Callie," Seabrook yelled over the chaos of water, siren, and the eerie personified roar of fire as she heard part of Papa Beach's roof collapse.

"Jeb!" His name ripped from inside her. Her heart pummeled her ribs, shoving so much pressure into her throat she couldn't repeat her son's name again. Angry, unable to shout, she released a guttural scream.

Not again. Not again. Dear God, don't do this to me again.

"Jeb's not in the house," Seabrook shouted as he strong-armed her, easily lifting her down the stairs as she fought in his grasp. "He's fine."

Tears streamed down her cheeks. Seabrook had her arms constrained, preventing her from wiping her eyes to see. He said Jeb was fine, so where the hell was he? How was he? God, someone show her he wasn't hurt. And where were the other kids?

The smoke burned her throat. She swallowed, only to gag. Then with all her being she shrieked, "Jeb!" Long and hard until she thought her throat would bleed. But the name fell short in the cacophony of the shouts, fire growling and popping, water gushing. *He can't hear me.* She bucked only for Seabrook to rewrap his arms tighter.

"Stop it, Callie!" he yelled in a tone foreign to the gentle man. "Jeb is safe. And it's not your house on fire. Slow down and look."

She lifted her head.

The inferno ravaged Papa Beach's house thirty yards to the side of Chelsea Morning. Five firefighters struggled to contain the flames, one additional fire truck wetting her home down, the closest dwelling to the active flames.

Blazes darted in and out of Papa's front windows, the roof fallen in behind the porch. Along the property line, fronds on her palmettos lit like matchsticks. Her lantana bushes lay black and crinkled into the ground with spits of tiny flame bragging about the damage. Black soot coated the siding on the northeast side of her home, with some of the timbers smoldering from the heat. Water showered her house, soaking her porches and shingle roof.

Sophie ran over with Sprite, both drawing up short, gaping at the inferno, then at Seabrook's grip on Callie.

"Find Jeb," Callie pleaded with them. "Sprite, weren't you with him?"

Sprite pointed. "He's over there, Ms. Morgan. He moved your cars and started hosing your house before the trucks got here."

Sophie nudged her daughter. "Go get him, sweetheart. His mama needs him."

Callie quit bucking and strained to see. Seabrook's grip lessened.

When Sprite reached Jeb with the message, he jerked around and bolted past his girlfriend, crossing the road. Though smoky and smudged, a rag wrapped around his hand, Callie embraced her son, and he her, much as they had that night almost three years ago, clinging as if they held onto sanity by a thread.

He rubbed her back. "Mom, it's fine." He reared and waited for eye contact, then pulled her to him. "Don't shake, Mom. Don't shake."

Yet her son trembled as well.

"I left you," she mumbled into his reeking, wet T-shirt. "I almost did it again. I'm so sorry, Jeb. So, so sorry."

"Don't, Mom. Don't. It's okay."

Her son lived, saved by God's own hand, but the possibility of what might have happened continued to ransack her mind. Memories mushroomed, growing, overstepping each other. She fought to clench her chattering teeth by gripping Jeb tighter. If she let go, she'd fall apart. This wasn't John, this was Jeb. This wasn't Boston, this was . . . was Edisto.

She talked to herself, fighting to differentiate the here and now versus the hell of back then.

There were so many people in the street. Dozens of neighbors, tourists. Terrance, Frank, even Kris and Cynthia. Alex would be there. Faces everywhere, staring.

"You two sit down," Seabrook said and assisted them.

Callie squeezed Jeb again, as if to remind him she stood there. This tiny spot on the ground seemed all she needed at the moment as the two of them collected themselves. As she compartmentalized. As she fought the past to focus on the present.

People touched her. She shrugged them off.

"Give them a moment," Sophie said.

The whoosh of fire rising and the sizzle of water pounding it down came and went distantly in Callie's ears. She tried not to rock her child, or was he rocking her?

"There's a medic here, Callie," Seabrook said after a time. "He'd like to check out Jeb. Why don't you let him give you something to settle you down?"

She released her embrace and reluctantly stood as they reached to take her son. She kept a grip on Jeb's arm. "Check him out, but don't think about touching me."

Seabrook eased her from Jeb as a medic took the young man aside. Callie peered around Seabrook to note where they took her son. Jeb made the same effort to maintain visual of her, Sprite at his side. Then Zeus appeared, equally as smudged.

Someone gave out bottled water, and Seabrook put one in Callie's hand. She downed a third of it, suddenly thirsty, yet feeling like she swallowed smoke with it. The taste stuck in her mouth.

The crackle and spit seemed not as enraged, as if someone slowly turned down the volume. Edisto firemen brought the fire under control quickly, safely contained to Papa's place. Their faces dripping wet and red from the confusion of summer heat and flames, they sprayed and expertly worked the ruined house, leaving nothing to chance.

An hour passed. Callie remained watching, making sure no sparks leaped the short distance to Chelsea Morning.

Authorities had shut down the street, but the gawking crowd still grew. Seabrook left a couple times as his officers kept the walk-ins at a reasonable distance, but he always returned to her. A quarter of the beach population had to be crammed on Jungle Road. Callie studied it with intensity as their interest gravitated from firemen to cops to the dwindling fire.

Another hour later, the medics packed to leave. The throng remained.

"Are you okay, sweetie?" Sophie asked, stroking her friend's back.

Callie sighed. "Yeah. You don't have to stay with me."

"Come in my house," Sophie pleaded. "You don't have to watch."

Arms crossed, Callie couldn't explain it, but she did have to watch. Though the remaining flames were but tiny flares in miniature hot spots, she couldn't leave. Not yet. Her house had come so close to the same demise as before, her child much closer to being harmed. Standing guard seemed the right thing to do.

"Go on in, Sophie. I'll be there in a little bit," she said. "Wait," she remembered. "You're staying with me!"

Sophie shook her head. "Not tonight. That smell is too much. We'll all stay at my house. We need each other. No argument." Sophie hugged her briefly and left to join her children, then diverted. Unable to help herself, she skirted toward neighbors waving her over, eager to hear what happened; the yoga teacher all too eager to tell.

With fear gone, Callie's emotion slid to anger as these people found this catastrophe so entertaining.

"Callie," Seabrook said. "I'm worried about you."

"Well, don't," she said as an aftershock rippled through her. So many tourists ogling, natives she hadn't met yet. She suspected an arsonist in their ranks and had spent the last half hour trying to commit each face to memory.

Vacant houses didn't catch on fire.

In light of the prank in her yard, the note, she found it too darn convenient that this fire appeared next door.

"You're still trembling," Seabrook said, arm sliding around her shoulders.

"Adrenaline," she said.

Jeb left a covey of teens and started toward her, a better bandage on his hand. Now they could joke about matching wounds.

"You don't have to sit with me," she told him after her son hugged her again. "Go be with Sprite."

"You sure?" he asked, puzzled, his movements slow as if uncertain whether to take her at her word.

Callie patted Seabrook's hand, still draped across her collar. "I'm good."

As soon as Jeb left hearing range, she glared at the tall cop. "I want that auxiliary badge."

He removed his arm from around her. "There's a reason they take cops off cases that get personal. Their focus gets myopic." He hesitated. "You of all people understand how that works against you."

"Aren't you still short-staffed?"

"You don't have to ask," he said.

"Did you fib when you promised me access to the police files if I came on board?" she asked.

His eyes darted then he caught himself, as if retaining his position. "I meant it then, but—"

"But what?" she pushed.

"Not sure I want to hire you now. Not with your frame of mind."

She'd heard that before. Boston PD understood when she gave notice after a six-month sabbatical, and that had been after she'd spent a year chasing leads to her husband's murder. Obsessive. A description her old boss Stan had called her many times. He'd labeled her that with earlier cases and meant the term as a compliment. The last time, however, he'd mentioned it like a disease.

Like Seabrook now.

"Two deaths and one possible arson, and you don't need me?" she said. "The most experienced person on this island. What, I'm supposed to jump when you ask for assistance, but I'm not good enough for the force?"

Officer Francis appeared. "Mike, want me to send these people home?"

Seabrook nodded. "Yeah. It's late. They've seen enough."

Callie didn't expect him to respond after the interruption, but Seabrook rubbed her shoulder once Francis left. "Let me think about the auxiliary offer," he said.

Think about it all you want, she thought as she left his side to see how much the fire had touched her home. The roof seemed fine, but the gutters appeared scorched. The siding needed a scrubbing to tell soot from damage.

She took this fire personal.

Sophie waved from her front porch. "Callie," she hollered. "Come over here when you're done out there. I mean it when I say I want you to sleep at my place."

Great. A hundred people knew she wouldn't be in her house tonight. Sophie probably had some mystic explanation for not staying at Chelsea Morning, but Callie suspected Sophie preferred her family around her. Jeb probably wanted to be with Sprite. Callie's body dragged with too much residual fatigue to argue, and being one extra house removed from the wet, black slaggy mess at Papa's house might help her sleep easier.

She hugged Seabrook goodnight and climbed her steps to retrieve a change of clothes, taking a moment to say a prayer that her house and belongings were still intact. After one more glance around to ensure no damage, she locked her place and went next door, Sophie waiting on the porch.

God, she dragged. So much so that she bet even Sophie's spirits wouldn't rattle chains loud enough to wake her.

SHE DREAMED about Stan.

Even in her fuzzy-around-the-edges vision, her old boss stood out in his gruff yet marshmallow way, his hair freshly buzzed, buff still in his fifties. Still chewing cinnamon gum. The man she thought she could love only to realize he was just a connection to better times.

You're using Jeb as a crutch.

You said that before, Stan.

I wouldn't hire you if you applied.

You said that before, too, Stan.

So why haven't you listened?

Callie moved slowly, aching. She opened her eyes.

Sophie's bedroom.

On television, heroines awoke after a traumatic event with allies and friends bending over, worried, ready to embolden her with accolades and moral support.

But this wasn't television. She was a far cry from a heroine and thanked the world that nobody hovered when she finally stared up at the ceiling.

Oh crap. She'd only meant to lie down for a second before showering. Her nightgown remained draped over the foot of the bed, unused. Callie hadn't even bothered to crawl under the spread.

Still wearing the clothes from the night before, she stank, the acrid, stale smoke embedded now in the threads. Her fingers traced stitching over the off-white comforter and sighed. She'd have to send that beautiful spread to the cleaners.

With a heavier sigh she fell on the bed, her arms crossed over her face. Snapshots of the night flickered in her head along with short action moments that scared her to death even now, safe on a luxurious comforter with gentle sunshine lightening the room. Tears leaked from behind closed eyelids, trailing down her temple to the ruined cover. Was she this damn fragile?

She feared losing Jeb, her home, and something else, though she couldn't name it. Crawling into a hole scared her as much as running down leads.

So many leads for too many different cases. Brea's death, the August deaths, Jeb and Zeus's fishing license, the pranks in her yard, now this fire. Controversy from all directions. Why didn't people leave her alone?

A bolus of grief, fear, a convoluted entanglement of feelings tried to rise in her throat and force out a sob, but she swallowed and pushed against it. Her breath caught as the pressure built again. She wouldn't cave like this.

But better to fall apart behind closed doors than on the street. On the street ... Crap. She didn't even want to face social media this morning. Alex probably reported so hot and heavy last night she had cramps in her thumbs.

Unfolding her arms, Callie rose. No way she'd walked out looking like this ... feeling like this. What time was it? From the sun streaming in the room, she guessed nine or so.

She stumbled once walking into the bathroom, the minor aftereffects of the evening toying with her balance. She brushed her teeth with her finger, then crawled into the shower, tossing her stinky clothes in Sophie's garden tub so they didn't contaminate anything else. Clean and feeling more alive, she blew her hair dry and changed into her T-shirt. Short sleeves. Forget hiding her scar. Her life belonged to Twitter now plus it was too damn hot and muggy.

In old jeans and sneakers, she moved to the bedroom door and dared to reenter whatever world waited on the other side.

Holding the knob, she hesitated, hearing Sophie's voice.

"Yeah, I think she's awake, Mike." A pause. Callie figured Sophie must be on the phone when she didn't hear Seabrook's voice. "Okay, I'll tell her."

Callie opened the door. "Tell me what?"

Sophie's face brightened, her arms thrown out wide. "Hey, honey! How are you feeling?"

"Tell me what?" Callie repeated, her voice ragged from smoke, from screaming. "And where's Jeb?"

Sophie rushed over. "Don't get upset. He said he'd be next door trying to spruce things up for you."

Callie exhaled at the fretting over her. She'd scared a few people last night, including herself. Sophie'd felt some of the same until she located her children. That fire . . . She inhaled deeply and walked to the kitchen, trying to level herself out. "My house is still standing, right?" She went to pour the orange juice and remembered the mimosas. Returning the pitcher, she grabbed a diet soda. "Why don't you keep tea in here?"

Sophie appeared at her side and drew out a chair from the kitchen table. "Callie. Slow down and sit."

The soda seemed a poor substitute for her morning sweet tea. "Sophie. If I slowed down any more I'd be in a coma." But she allowed herself to be seated.

Sophie flitted around, touching one item in the kitchen, then another, accomplishing little. She appeared antsy, her nerves not in sync, spiritual or otherwise. Finally she settled on chai tea and sat across from Callie.

Callie rubbed her face. "What time is it?"

"Quarter to nine."

Callie took a sip. "Why aren't you in yoga class?"

"Dang, Callie, do you not remember last night?" Sophie's eyes were wide with green contacts today. "I was so scared. You were scared. I was scared for you. The kids halfway freaked, but they seem fine today."

"Where are they?" Callie asked.

"Jeb next door. Sprite at the grocery store. Zeus working on his boat. I think each needed their space."

At Sophie's mention of being scared, the night rushed at her . . . of her gripping Jeb, shaking, almost unable to control herself. The sirens, the people, the gut-wrenching smell. A smell she would inhale the minute she opened the door. "Tell me what?" Callie asked again.

Sophie tilted her pixie shag. "Huh?"

"What did Seabrook want you to tell me?"

Sophie raised her chin in acknowledgment. "Oh. He said stay in bed today and rest. And if you didn't, he'd get you something that would make you sleep, but that you—"

"Gracious, Sophie, I'm fine, and I have to see to my house. File insurance. At least for the water damage if nothing else." The whole Brea-August death situation paled in relation to her personal life now. Someone waged a vendetta against her, and until someone proved her wrong, she returned to watching over her shoulder. "How bad's the damage now that we can see it?"

"Your house is fine. My house is fine. You can stay at your place or stay here again, totally up to you," she said and rose from the table. "Let me fix you some eggs."

Sophie had sacrificed her fear of the spirits for Callie's well-being for one night by returning to Hatha Heaven. However, no reason for her to do it again. "My place then," Callie said, studying the kitchen, then over the bar into the living room. Sunshine poured in those windows, too, tinted like lemonade this time of day, and she figured no haunt in its right mind would fight that cheery environment.

"Um, I'll stay here," Sophie said.

"Why? Thought your spiritual guests were too rowdy."

Sophie dropped the spatula on the stove top and whirled around. "Do you see how close you came to losing your house?"

"Why, no, Sophie," Callie replied, her sarcasm caustic. "I missed that."

"Make fun. Go ahead." Sophie jerked around to her cooking, the skillet popping. She lowered the temperature and leaned on the counter, her back to her friend.

Callie jumped from her seat and reached around Sophie for a hug. "What did I miss last night? What's wrong?" Fear slithered into her chest. "Nobody's hurt?"

"Nobody's hurt."

Relieved, Callie gently shook her friend's shoulder. "That's what's important. So what's upsetting you?"

Sophie stared at the oil sizzling in the skillet, as if it spelled out her words for her. "Here they keep me awake. There"—she nodded toward Chelsea Morning—"they tried to kill us."

Callie stepped aside in amazement. "Are you kidding?"

Her friend's gaze turned cold. "So now you're Rikki?"

"No, no, sweetie. I'm sure that fire had nothing to do with ghosts. There's a logical explanation for how it happened. Even if the fire was deliberate, a human did it. That's one thing I want to check into."

"Well, I overheard one firefighter last night say this fire might be set. And the only thing different yesterday was me moving into your place. The negativity followed *me*." Her finger aimed at the floor. "Here they play games." She thrust her finger toward next door. "There they get even."

"Oh, Soph."

"I'm staying here," Sophie said with an unmistakable period on the end.

Callie sat, letting Sophie serve breakfast and hopefully calm down. Somebody did have motive, just not how Sophie envisioned. And Seabrook had an open investigation whether he wanted one or not.

Could Grant be that angry? Maybe.

Was this a new step for MyOuttake?

Could this be the killer striking at her for being nosy?

Had the Edisto Sleuth Society unknowingly shaken a hornet's nest and pissed off a serious suspect? They certainly slung her name around like a lasso.

While Janet Wainwright had thousands of dollars to lose, surely she wouldn't go this far. The town council wouldn't dare. Both had too much to lose, plus they weren't criminal in nature.

Her mind jerked back to the Russian . . . Damn it! She never saw him coming. Fingers scrubbed through her damp hair. Who did this, and who wouldn't dare? She hesitated now, too afraid to whittle down the suspect list for fear of overlooking someone. She second-guessed herself . . . like before. Afraid to investigate. Afraid not to.

This limbo mentality had the potential of freezing her decision making and shutting her down to where she couldn't read people.

She smiled at Sophie as she placed the plate of eggs on the table. Then her friend left, as if her feelings were scorched, too.

Elbows on the table, Callie took a bite and stared out the window facing the street. Was the fire a warning to her? Acting on the note from her car? Why not just burn Chelsea Morning?

How could deaths and a fire not be connected in a place as small as Edisto Beach? For the life of her, the only connection to all of this she saw was her.

Chapter 17

"HOW BAD?" CALLIE asked as she approached Jeb tossing yet another soggy cushion from her porch into a pile near the road. People gawked as they drove, walked, and rode their bikes along Jungle Road. Eleven in the morning, and Edisto seemed almost normal, just not at her house. Her piece of the neighborhood served as the day's attraction after last evening's misadventure.

Rivulets of sweat, exacerbated by humidity and the wetness of everything on the porch, ran down Jeb's head, chest, and back. He'd stripped to his shorts, which were soaked as well. He grabbed a damp kitchen towel from his waistband and rubbed it over his face. "We lost all the cushions, and hopefully the wicker stuff isn't shot. The Adirondack chairs are fine but need scrubbing. We have to pressure wash the porches and the side of the house; they're covered in soot. I'll get on that later then I'll plug in whatever additional fans I can find to dry things out. Haven't tried the overheads yet to see if the water shorted them."

"The inside is fine?" she asked, staring at the outside as if she could see into the rooms.

He tossed his head with a faint smile. "Yeah, it's good, Mom. We were lucky."

Curled remnants of screen hung either loose and flapping or melted against itself. So odd against the noises of gulls calling overhead, the sound of high tide rumbling in four blocks over. A hot breeze blew through, and though laced with a dank, acrid whiff of the damage, it felt good on Callie's face.

She closed her eyes, thankful for the disaster they'd avoided. The stench only grew worse. When she opened her eyes, Jeb studied her.

"How do *you* feel?" he asked.

She noted his mouth so like his father's, avoiding his eyes, still surprisingly ashamed at how the night had played out. "Okay, I guess. For a second I got trapped in a loop. The fire, dusk . . . it reminds me of . . . you know."

He listened very still.

"How are you?" she asked, tossing a small pillow on the pile.

"Couldn't sleep," he said. "Kept seeing the flicker, plus Ms. Bianchi's sofa isn't all that comfortable." He sniffled and rubbed his nose. "I'll never get rid of this smell."

She nodded.

Callie craved to coddle him but recognized her boy being the man. His overt effort to take over cleanup told her his sweat served as substitute for anxiety. Goodness knows she understood that feeling, too.

"I wish I could do something, Mom."

Callie wilted, then stroked his face. "Aww, sweetheart. You are. I see a difference in the place already."

"No, I mean it's hard watching you when you react like last night. It scares me."

The term stung, and she flinched. The last thing she wanted was for him to feel bound to her indefinitely. An eighteen-year-old ought to be itching to see the world. She hated the pity in his eyes.

His mouth went tight. "Not how I meant that to sound, but you get it, right?"

"Jeb," she said and held out her arms. "Look. No shakes. I'm fine." *And eager to find out who did all this.*

He dipped his head in acknowledgment. "Good. Want to see what I've done?"

Following him up the front stairs then around to the side porch, she noted all he showed her, so satisfied at him tackling the job. He'd changed since moving to Edisto, beginning a freelance job, and above all, weathering a kidnapping. She loved this kid with immeasurable passion. John would've been over-the-moon proud.

"Don't face Papa Beach's house until you're ready, Mom. It's sad."

But with those words, like any other curious soul, she had to look. She left her house and ventured next door.

Yellow tape crisscrossed the destroyed house all which-a-ways. The front porch no longer existed, the floor caved in, and while she wanted to sift through the debris, she feared climbing to do so. A shell of the living room remained where as a child she counted Papa's silver dollar collection, same as the kitchen where they shared peanut butter cookies and hot chocolate, making up stories using porcelain chicken salt and pepper shakers. All lay exposed to the world. Dead like Papa. Like a corpse, the place held no life anymore.

A silver BMW Z-4 pulled into Chelsea Morning's drive.

Callie cocked her head toward the BMW. "That's Rhonda Benson. Let me go talk to her." She left Jeb to his scrubbing and approached the real estate agent who managed the shell of a property.

Rhonda once managed Chelsea Morning as a rental for the Cantrells and remembered Callie as a teen. Callie liked the flamboyant lady with silver sandals to match her nail polish. She wore a simple, sleeveless shift due to the heat, but the leopard design ensured people remembered her as anything but simple. Now, however, the woman stood motionless, awestruck with the devastation.

Stuck in probate, the house remained the responsibility of Rhonda's real estate agency management. Both Papa and his son had been killed by the Russian. If the house had been an albatross before, it was ten times that now.

"Hey," Callie said, approaching the agent.

"Hey yourself," Rhonda groused. "What am I supposed to do with this mess?"

Callie gave her a moment. Then the woman turned to her. "I heard the fire sort of overwhelmed you last night. You okay?"

News sure traveled fast. "How many times should I plan to hear that?" Callie asked.

"A lot," she said. "You're news . . . again. The best source of gossip we've heard in years."

Lucky me. "Sorry for your loss."

"August, our month of accidents," the agent sighed. "Think it's the heat that draws the crazies out?"

August. Suddenly Callie recalled the newspaper office, the archived stories, the dead women, and wondered if they were somehow related to the fire. But a fire represented a different MO.

The why in all this eluded her. Motive. What was the friggin' motive?

As if answering her thoughts, the famous gold Hummer stopped behind the BMW.

With Papa Beach's burned timbers as backdrop, Callie held her ground as Janet Wainwright exited wearing khaki slacks and a red tailored, short-sleeved button down shirt, her thick gold cuff bracelet flashing in the sun. Black sunglasses make her white cropped hair stark.

"Can I help you?" Callie asked as the Marine stopped a pace short of her.

The old woman's posture remained ramrod, poised for confrontation. "Why would anybody want your help? Seems everything you touch goes to hell, young lady."

Callie instinctively straightened to match what was still a six-inch difference. "Or at least that's what somebody would like us to think, Ms. Wainwright."

Janet's thin wrinkled lips curled as she walked off toward Rhonda.

A thud caught both their attentions. Jeb moved furniture down the stairs into the yard to clean. The revoked business license hacked Callie all over again, and she turned toward the Marine. Then she caught herself. She had nothing on the woman, and right now emotions ruled the day.

Damp hair stuck to Callie's cheek, and she slid it behind her ear. This woman didn't storm beaches as everyone imagined. She preferred more sneaky, underhanded tactics.

Janet and Rhonda discussed and toured the mess, and as hard as Callie thought, she could not find reason to confront Wainwright. She needed more. She'd get more.

Movement caught her eye across the street. Terrance raised his phone and wagged it side to side, Frank beside him. At first she thought he took pictures, but then he waved at her to join them.

The humidity stuck Callie's shirt to her skin, the heat amplified by the evaporating moisture coming off the wetness from the night before. Shrugging her shirt loose for a whiff of air, she joined the men and motioned them to the shade of some Carolina jasmine growing wild around palmettos at the edge of the road. They'd already demonstrated their inability to handle midday temperatures.

"What's the covert behavior about?" she asked.

"We don't know those ladies to trust them. But hey, are you all right?" Frank asked, like a doting father.

"Just a scare," she replied. "I'm fine."

"You sure?" he asked again. "We saw what happened last night."

She tried not to appear impatient. "Yes, I'm sure." They meant well.

Terrance held up the phone. "Then maybe you won't get too disturbed seeing these."

Callie patted her pocket, but her phone was at Sophie's. She took Terrance's, showing his Twitter account. She scrolled through the posts from, surprise, Alex, reporting for *Edisto Today*.

There was Callie's house, fire hoses wide out open to dowse it. There was Callie in Seabrook's bear hug. Another of her sitting on the ground clinging to Jeb. Jeb spraying water on the house. Sprite wrapped in a towel. Firemen going this way and that. Fire served as the emotional embellishment in each and every shot.

@EdistoToday—Detective Callie Morgan overcome by the fire at her home.

Callie shook her head. "She makes it almost sound like I got caught in the house."

"Keep going," Frank said, wiping sweat off his forehead with an already moist handkerchief.

@EdistoToday—Arson suspected at Jungle Road home as firefighters save neighboring houses.

That one was tolerable. But her breath caught as the familiar MyOuttake spread Alex's messages, then elaborated on a few of his own.

@MyOuttake—Revenge? Malice? Unknown person sets fire to Edisto home. #edistojinx

@MyOuttake—Big city detective and small town police ignorant to causes of arson and deaths on #Edisto. #edistojinx

@MyOuttake—Anger and mayhem on Edisto as someone gets even with detective. #edistojinx

"Who is this guy?" she exclaimed. The posts were bad enough, but others were retweeting them, redistributing them to their readers as an avalanche of interested parties who'd ever heard of Edisto, visited Edisto, or lived on Edisto, did their best to make Callie's calamity a trending topic. She kept glancing up, comparing the pictures with the reality. A few of them were taken about where they stood now.

Over and over comments and pictures spread across the ether. MyOuttake had been at the fire. Photos more dramatic than Alex's, as if he tried to show her up and make the world realize that *EdistoToday* fell short with her reporting. He, however, enjoyed the retelling with zeal.

She scrolled through them twice, then three times. A dozen posts that rapidly became a hundred or more. *EdistoToday*'s followers had tripled.

"Did you gentlemen see who took these?" she asked, raking fingers through her hair to push it from her face. *Dang, it was hot.*

Both men shook their heads in the negative.

"It was chaos," Frank said. "Everyone watched you and the fire, taking pictures, comparing notes."

"Wonderful," she mumbled, returning the phone.

"What do you want us to do?" Terrance asked.

"Yeah," Frank echoed. "Want us to ask people if they were here? Ask if they can identify this guy? We'd be glad to talk to the police chief, too. We want to help."

While the red-faced, perspiring men in cliché tropical shirts might be considered welcome support, a contrast to so many others in her circle, they couldn't remain involved. She'd been remiss not hammering her message the other day over mimosas. Without question, they still needed to ease off the sleuthing. This situation had risen past amateur range.

"No thanks," Callie said in an exhale. "I appreciate the offer, but go enjoy the rest of your vacation. This is not for you to get involved in." She turned and waited for two cars to pass. Jeb would work himself to death if she didn't help him out.

Terrance took her arm, returning her to the shade. "Do you realize how much of our personal time we've invested into your case? The police obviously don't care, and you can't go it alone."

Frank closed in as well. "Let me put it this way: Have you considered this fire a threat due to you investigating those August deaths?"

Being boxed in unsettled her, though she saw them as harmless. Still, she took a half step back. "Yes, I have, Frank. That's one of the reasons I don't want you involved."

"You're blowing us off after what we've done for you. Not sure I appreciate that," Terrance said.

"Tell me this." Callie gently removed his loose grip on her arm. "How do the other ESS members feel about you being here?"

Frank's eye movement gave it away.

"I see," she said. "They've moved on already, haven't they?"

"Ava's all right," he said, "but the others got scared. Kris and Cynthia left this morning."

"Listen," she said. "I really appreciate what you guys did already. What you found out in such a short time is amazing. However, the town and business folk aren't happy with me for involving you." Callie waved at her home. "And I have no idea who did this, but if it's deliberate, the person's dangerous. Too dangerous for the ESS."

The guys weren't happy, but they weren't arguing either. Callie felt sort of sorry for them. She finished with a gentle firmness in her voice. "Unfortunately, the Edisto Sleuth Society needs to step down and let the authorities take over."

Sweat rolled down Frank's temple again, and his cheeks reddened. "We sure read you wrong."

"Guys, seriously?" Pressure built behind Callie's eyes, pushing a headache with it. "Let it go. Problems are escalating, and the town administrator already thinks I'm Frankenstein creating you."

But a mixture of insult and anger filled their eyes. "Ava will be crushed," Frank said.

Callie's headache continued to build. "Listen—"

"We're not as dimwitted as you think, Detective Morgan," Terrance said, giving his side to her, along with a jerking finger. "We get it, all right."

Frank spun and marched in the direction of his rental, Terrance taking a second to scowl at her before he did the same.

"Guys, I'm sorry," she called after them.

"Mom," Jeb yelled from the porch. "Sophie wants you to come in for lunch."

She turned and watched Terrance reach Frank and take a right at the corner. She felt badly about the ESS. However, safety was foremost, for their own good. They ought to be enjoying the beach.

She hurried to Sophie's, calling for Jeb to come in and take a break as well. He said he'd change and come right over.

Inside Sophie's, Callie located her phone in her purse, relishing the air conditioning as she sat on the bed and retrieved messages. The cell held a dozen voicemails and two texts. Seabrook had called three times, no mention of the auxiliary job yet. She wanted the job this time. With that shiny authority on her chest and access to files, she might put the jinx story to rest. Nail the parties riding her. Settle down the parties harassing her son and Zeus.

Alex had left two texts, one asking if she was okay, the other needing an interview. *The Island Tribune* editor Abe Jenkins asked for an exclusive, as if he weren't the only press in town.

Her mother's message asked about Jeb, then the house, then Callie. Callie smirked. In her own way, Beverly worried. Callie would return that call after lunch and listen to Beverly prattle on as Callie made a list of damaged items.

The next six messages took her by surprise. Back to back media. The Charleston paper, two freelance reporters, and three Lowcountry television stations wanted her take on the fire and the jinx. Apparently the tweets had connected with people and spread roots. The myth nobody knew about had escaped the confines of Edisto Beach and crossed the bridge. No wonder Jenkins wanted an exclusive.

She'd have to think about this swell of media interest. Should she fuel reporters or ignore them? Her first instinct was to run it by Seabrook for advice, but she guessed his response. Keep controversy on the other side of the island bridge. Don't bring it here. Besides, an auxiliary badge wouldn't be allowed to talk to the press.

"Callie?" Sophie called from her kitchen.

"I'm coming," she hollered, then checked the last message.

"Call me, Chicklet. I'm worried about you."

She froze, gobsmacked at Seabrook's exact words coming from a voice she hadn't heard in two months. Not since Stan kissed the top of her head goodbye after breakfast at the Seacow eatery. She'd have bedded him but for the call from his wife. Instead, they talked through the night, watching dawn rise over coffee from her front porch as they agreed to part ways and not add sex to their relationship.

The only person with the power of comfort and familiarity, Stan all but read her mind. Or rather, he used to.

But she'd ruined that coming onto him, seeking his comfort to avoid falling apart after her father's funeral. Calling him would accomplish . . . what? She cringed imagining the awkwardness.

His voice made her feel naked all over again.

Chapter 18

SOPHIE HAD LUNCH waiting in the kitchen, chatting from the muted voices. However, Callie, still sticky hot from inspecting her house, continued staring at her phone as if the voice mail from Stan would explain itself.

Once upon a time, hearing her boss put her soul back to right. The voice of firm reason and compassionate understanding. A man who covered her ass when she screwed up and praised the heavens when she did good.

When John was alive, Stan served as her boss and mentor. When John died, Stan kept her sane. But when Callie moved to Edisto, and Stan ran down for moral support, Callie had blurred the lines.

Still, she wanted to talk to him so damn bad.

Voices wafted louder, and Callie decided against the call. She no longer sported an appetite, but Sophie was too gracious a host to refuse. Together they'd almost lost their houses and children, a new sisterhood of sorts.

"Callie!" Sophie yelled again, like calling a farmer from the field. "Let's eat."

Phone tucked in her pocket, Callie exited Sophie's bedroom and halted at the unexpected guests around the table. Rikki didn't surprise her, but the Amazon chatted with . . . Beverly.

Callie's radar flicked on but offered nothing definitive . . . yet.

Seated on a tucked leg, Sophie nibbled a carrot because God forbid she eat anything as big as a sandwich. Jeb and Sprite shared a bench on the far side hunched over their phones sharing discoveries, oblivious to old lady talk.

Sophie waved rapidly. "Come eat before they devour it all. I saved you a turkey sandwich."

Callie sat next to Sophie and across from her mother. "Who scheduled a luncheon?"

Conversation ceased, all eyes on her. She studied her shirt. "Is something unbuttoned?"

In navy capris and a nautical tunic, her mother's crisp, ready-for-a-soiree appearance clashed with the *laissez-faire* T-shirt and shorts crew that gathered with her. She reached across the table and beckoned with a palm, her charm bracelet hitting the table like a chain. Callie cautiously gave her hand to her, and Beverly covered it with her other. "How are you feeling, dear?"

Callie tsked and withdrew to eat. "Rikki showed you the Twitter pictures of the fire, didn't she?"

"I thought you were better," her mother continued.

Callie glanced to Jeb for support only to see him scrunch his mouth and sit silent. The boy never could cross his grandmother.

Callie lifted her turkey and bread. "Mother, quit the theatrics. I'm fine."

Or she would be if people got off her case. It was a damn fire! Fires scared anybody.

Rikki nudged Beverly. "I was there. She was frantic."

"Until I found Jeb, of course I was," Callie said. "I would hope my mother would feel the same about me." Some days she had doubts.

"Dear, all this happening on the heels of what you've been through? A mother has to worry." Beverly released a timed sigh. Rikki nodded.

"Good gracious," Callie mumbled, biting into a sandwich she now didn't want, washing it down with carrot juice she didn't like.

Beverly took the floor, speaking to the gatherers like a town council. "I believe we all agree that my daughter has endured more than any person should. I—"

Callie dropped the sandwich loudly on the plate, flustered she didn't see this coming. "I don't believe you're doing this."

"I'm here to bring you home," Beverly said, dipping her chin once for emphasis.

The others sat against their chairs, as if extra inches from the table buffered them from blowback.

"You need to get away from Edisto Beach," the older woman said with aplomb. "You keep thinking there's some kind of crime that merits your attention."

Callie gaped at her mother. "You've got to be kidding me. An intervention?" She faced her friend. "Sophie?"

"I'm sort of worried but didn't want to say anything."

"No, but I bet you mentioned *your* note, didn't you?"

Sophie stared down.

Callie pivoted to Jeb. He cleared his throat. "You never shook like that in Boston, Mom. But I didn't start this. Promise."

"Good grief, you drank your grandmother's Kool-Aid." She ran fingers through her hair then stood. Her circle of so-called supporters stiffened as she slid her chair from the table.

"Beverly," she started, purposely calling her mother by name for emotional distance. "If you want some time with Jeb, if you want to hear your Neil Diamond albums, or if you want to inspect the fire damage, knock yourself out."

"Dear—"

"No," Callie interrupted. "You've had your say. We've had this conversation before. I'm a trained police officer."

"Not anymore," Beverly said. "It's like you can't let go of that work you used to do."

"Besides, we police ourselves around here," Rikki said.

Callie dropped her head back in frustration. "You ignore it, Rikki! Women died on this beach, for God's sake, and you all brushed them under the rug."

"There's still no jinx," Rikki replied.

"On that we agree. There is no jinx," she said, tossing her crumpled napkin in the middle of her plate. "I'm done. I'll sage your house later, Sophie."

She stormed out the front door. Her sneakered feet pounded asphalt as she sought saltwater. While she craved to visit Botany Bay and its flat, almost prehistoric beach where dead oaks reached to the sky with gnarled fingers, it held memories of Stan. She wanted her Adirondack chair on the porch, Neil Diamond music in her head, but the humidity and stench from Papa's wet, scorched house might be too much. Plus Beverly might come over.

Callie shoved her sunglasses on. *Un-friggin-believable.*

They needed her when *they* had problems, but *her* problems were mythical? Was she supposed to live on a constant even keel so they all felt better?

She owned feelings, and she had a right to fret about her son. Hell, she had every damn right in the world to cringe when anyone's house caught on fire, but especially one that close to hers. The second fire in her life. None of them could relate to that.

An intervention? Seriously?

Screw them all.

Digging her feet into the sand with each step, Callie trudged to the water's edge, turned right, and struck out in a fast walk. It wasn't far to the end of the beach, three to four miles, but she'd conquer the damn waterfront two, three, four times if necessary to clear her head and decide . . .

Decide what?

Weeks ago, she clashed with her son, begging him to leave. Before that, her parents dropped her here against her will, her father confident his daughter would regroup from the tragedies in her life and find happiness again. How could she mar his memory with such a juvenile decision to tuck tail and run? She lived on Edisto now, and as ironic as it sounded, she fought to remain here.

Edisto was supposed to be where she stopped running . . . and planted her flag.

She fingered a large busted cockle shell and hurled it into the surf. A gull flew over the water, checking out the small splash. Callie watched it return to its mission, hunting for bait fish.

She appreciated that sort of focus.

The breeze moved hot but briskly. Sweat evaporated quickly. Her trek took her to the mouth of Big Bay Creek where she reversed and headed north, covering the same ground again, weighing the same thoughts. Her calves held a steady burn now, so she slowed the pace and strolled, which allowed her to put a name to her frustration. Disappointment.

Disappointment that so many people were ignorant, naïve, or just blind to who she was. Disappointment that her brokenness now defined her.

Impenetrable as a detective, she'd fallen from grace when John's death dismantled her fearlessness. Like a broken bone, she had mended but could no longer be what she was before. The break didn't make her stronger like all the lyrics said. It made her face the reality that she could be broken again, just in other places.

Beverly triggered her self-doubt, a finger constantly pushing the button. Callie had no problem blowing off her mother in years past, but with her father gone, she had no other family left but Jeb . . . and her mother.

The little trust Callie'd leaked out to so few, mainly Sophie and Seabrook, served only to let them see her faults. She realized that now. Even Jeb . . .

Her anger gone, her frustration now numb, she'd reached a level beyond tears. However, she still hung in limbo between doing nothing about what she suspected was a killer on this island or burning bridges hunting for him until she couldn't bear to live here.

She could not live out her life watching the tide come and go. She held one absolute, though. Hell would freeze over before she moved in with her mother.

"Mom!"

Haltingly she studied the crowd of beachcombers, seeking the familiar voice. She didn't respond, though. He would have to come to her.

Jeb jogged to her, healthy-looking even sweaty. Callie's gaze moved across the bodies around her son. Six clusters of sunbathers, a fisherman, and a few sand castle architects. No sign of Sprite. At least he had the decency to come alone.

"I've been calling you," he said, huffing.

She kept walking. "I turned off my phone," she said, glad she wore sunglasses, not wanting him to see her hurt eyes.

His long legs easily kept pace. "Listen, I'm sorry about all that."

"Not *completely* your fault."

He hesitated at her response. "Listen, I can't do fishing charters with Zeus, and I have Dad's old Jeep to carry me between Middleton and here."

Reading the lead-in, Callie's lips tightened, her steps faster. "What are you trying to say?"

"What's wrong with spending time at Grandma's?" he asked. "Her house is big enough for privacy. I thought her offer was—"

"Ludicrous and insulting," Callie finished.

"She used the term Don Quixote about you," he said softly.

Callie braked and faced Jeb. "Was your kidnapper a windmill?"

"I never studied Don Quixote, Mom."

With a sideways glance at the beachcombers around her, she moved closer, her jaw already rock hard at what she finally had the nerve to say. "I think like a cop. Face it. Live with it. Accept it. If you can't, then go live with your grandmother." One hand fisted and the other pointing at the sand, she continued. "I will not be disrespected. I will not be discounted, and most of all, I will not be addressed like a half-wit. Is that clear?"

His eyes widened as he shifted his sight off her solid fix on him. His mouth hung slightly agape as if unsure what was safe to say.

Callie returned to her march. Jeb caught up and took her arm to make her stop. "Why don't I go stay with Grandma a while?"

"Be my guest," she replied firmly, to hide the hurt. They'd never parted this aggravated with each other. She dodged his stare, paying attention to a child's squeal at the water's edge.

But Jeb maintained his focus on her. "Mom, I think you need space. My only concern is what you do when I'm gone. You piss off more people than you make friends with."

"It is what it is." She shook loose from his grip and returned to her walk. "I can whip most anyone on this beach."

"Nice image there of my mom picking fights along the streets of Edisto."

"I'm not the antagonist, son."

"Do you mind if I return with Grandma?"

"Not at all," Callie answered over her shoulder, speaking atop the hot breeze pushed in by the tide. "Like you said, I need my space."

"Will you drink?"

She wheeled on him. "Don't!" Then returned to her march.

A large crowd dominated the beach before her with towels, assorted kids digging in the sand under a canopy tent, so she moved toward the water to avoid them, wading ankle deep and saturating her sneakers. Twenty yards later, she shifted again to the packed sand and hunted for Jeb. He was gone.

Her chest tightened. *Fine.*

At one of the protective beach groins, she gave her temper a rest and sat on a timber, ten feet from the foam left from rolling waves. A tern tippy-toe ran in spurts along the water's edge, capitalizing on what small morsels the current forced on the shore. Watching the horizon, Callie pulled her phone out of her pocket and hit speed dial, the soothing ebb and flow of background noise enabling her to make the call.

"Hey, it's me," she said without salutation or pause. "Did you call Stan Waltham and ask him about me?"

"Yes, I did," Seabrook replied.

"For a reference?"

"In a way, yes."

She searched the hypnotizing water for porpoise fins, the sun's glare on the undulating water making the scan a challenge. "So what did you ask him? It's a non-paying, part-time position, Seabrook."

The sigh came through despite the wind in Callie's ear. "I wanted his opinion on you in this type of job," Seabrook said.

"My stability, you mean?"

"No," he interjected quickly. "Dropping from detective to temporary beat cop on a two-bit police force doesn't work for some people."

"Hmm," she mumbled.

"Hey, if things check out, do you want the position or not? Tell me if you don't, and I'll quit wasting my time."

Two tern buddies joined the original tiny bird, and they darted, one then the other competing for snacks.

When she didn't immediately answer, he asked, "What's under your skin?"

She needed a conversation with someone, but that someone had to come without conditions. Seabrook ... wasn't quite there yet. "Nothing," she said.

"Just tell me what you decide. I'm ready to take the job."

"Callie, something wrong? This might happen pretty quickly."

"Nothing's wrong. I appreciate you considering me," and she hung up.

She shifted, and the terns skittered in the opposite direction, leaving her more alone than she'd felt in a long time. A wave rushed in, not coming as far. An outgoing tide. A huge vessel hugged the horizon.

She ran a finger across the face of her phone, hitting the button for her favorites. Stan was third down, under Jeb and her father. Daddy died, Jeb on his way off the island.

She tapped Stan's cell number. She feared calling him at home or the office, like the mistress she almost became. On the third ring, she reminded herself they hadn't done the deed, and Stan had been separated, planning for divorce at the time. But his sudden return to his wife had soiled his and Callie's Edisto experience, putting her too uncomfortably close to her mother's image.

Yet she still let the phone ring.

"Hello?" he answered gently. "Callie?"

She rose from the pier and walked again, only in the direction of town this time. "Yeah, it's me." Her legs were taut from the sand, but she would not go home. Not yet.

"How are you, Chicklet? I hear the beach."

Starring down at her soggy shoes, she smiled, recalling that day he visited. Took her all day to make him say *beach* instead of *shore*.

"Bad day, Stan. I'm sorry to call, but . . . anyway, how are you?" She sidestepped an eroded sandcastle. "How's Misty?"

"She's fine," he said and let the silence build between them. "I'm . . . fine."

Callie wished she could read his eyes. "You called and left a message?"

He cleared his throat. "I did. Mike Seabrook's call surprised me."

"How so?" she asked, knowing full well that Seabrook mentioned to him about her stability, the auxiliary position, maybe the fire. She wavered on how Stan would respond about any of it.

She heard his breathing, no gum sounds. She hoped he wasn't smoking again.

"Listen," he started. "I should've called before now."

"No," she interrupted. "I get it. You don't need me wedged between you and Misty."

"I owed you a call after Zubov," he said.

She was grateful he didn't say *Zubov's death*, or *after you killed Zubov*. He, of all people, would appreciate how such courtesy worked.

"How are you?" He groaned. "God, I should've asked you this weeks ago."

She let him feel bad.

"Officer Seabrook sounded concerned, which means I'm concerned," he said. "Talk to me. About the Russian, about whatever is going on now, your father's death, the job offer . . . the fire."

She shifted the phone to the other ear as someone called Stan by title. He ordered them to leave and shut the door, with a few louder words about not interrupting until he came out.

Thank goodness he was at work.

"I'm all ears," he said. "All yours."

It was as if water poured through her, washing her worries loose.

As she strolled, they discussed Lawton first. They shifted to Jeb as she neared Finn's. There she detoured and crossed the street, heading into BI-LO where, as she picked out eggs and bananas and checked out, they chatted about Beverly.

She exited BI-LO, entered a tiny shop next door and made her purchase, but not until she wandered down Jungle Road did she open up about the Russian.

Stan knew the Zubovs, their roots being in Boston, their patriarch's arrest having instigated John's murder. Walking along the edge of the road, she let some tears fall, unleashing thoughts about that bloody, fateful night that saved Jeb and redefined her. Stan understood. He knew John. He knew her. He'd trained her. He'd almost loved her.

Across from Chelsea Morning, she sat on the ground under the shade of a young, more sprawled palmetto, not ready to enter her house.

"What are you doing now?" Stan asked.

The BI-LO bag was cool, so she laid it in her lap. She set the other one beside her. "I'm sitting on the ground. Looking at my house. At Papa's burned house."

Jeb's Jeep was gone. Also Beverly's white BMW. Sophie's car next door. Everyone had scattered. So why so afraid to go inside?

"Nightmares back?" he asked.

"They were better until this."

"I guess so," he replied.

She bent her knees and wiped grass off the back of her legs. "So what did Seabrook fret about?"

"Callie, you can understand how he'd be skeptical of you asking to be auxiliary, right? It's quite a step down for someone like you."

An ant crawled across a dead palmetto frond two feet away. "Of course he didn't tell you that he actually suggested the position only three days ago. Saying I needed to stay busy so I didn't chase shadows."

"*Au contraire*, Chicklet. He admitted it. But after the fire, he wondered whether you were solid enough for the job. Then he reversed himself and talked about how strong you were. He sounded more unsure of himself than you. If I weren't so fond of you, I'd say the man had designs on Callie Jean Morgan. Sensed a bit of guilt in the mix, too."

"Good," she spat. "I'm sick of being patronized." A lump rose in her throat, and she sat straight. "God help me, Stan, but now I understand those guys who do time, get out, yet can't find work because of their past." She tossed the bag off her lap, forgetting about the eggs until they rattled.

In a swell of awareness, she realized she needed this position. Needed it badly. Not only for the files, but to prove herself . . . to all the others.

"My own son, my mother, and a few neighbors just tried to move me off the island, all because of the fire. An intervention, they called it. No, I called it that, but still, it's what it was." She hit her chest. "I'm entitled, Stan. I'm entitled to see a fire at my house and scream for my son. I still bear the scars of the last time, dammit!"

A couple walked by on the other side of the road, taking furtive glances at Callie's animated conversation with herself.

"Honey, go inside," he said calmly. "Find some air conditioning."

She stood and dusted off her butt, then retrieved her bags. "Tell me you understand, Stan."

"I know you better than anyone," he said. "I was there. Yes, I understand."

She crossed the street and climbed the stairs to Chelsea Morning, the smoky stench not so bold anymore. Inside, she locked the door behind her, the phone tucked on her shoulder.

"Fix yourself a cool drink and sit on the couch," he said.

"Fine," she said, putting away the eggs and bananas, emptying the other bag on the counter. "But I'm sitting on the side porch instead." The sofa prompted a memory of Stan she didn't need to relive.

"Good. I'll wait."

She put ice in her glass and filled it.

A knock sounded at the door. "Callie? It's Terrance. I want to apologize."

Heavens, she wasn't letting that character in. He probably remained the last vestige of the ESS left on Edisto, and loneliness had set in.

"Who is it?" Stan asked.

"Nobody I need to see," she replied. "You're my only guest at the moment."

The old familiar *he-he-he* came across the line deep and bass-rich, making her smile.

She stole a sip from the drink and then slid a Neil Diamond album from its sleeve and set the needle to play. As she stepped out to the porch, she flinched a little at the view of Papa's charred house and some of her screen melted in corners, but she sure appreciated the cleanup Jeb did. Her wooden Adirondack chair sat in its regular place, damp yet scrubbed, ready for her retreat. "Song Sung Blue" floated from the living room.

She'd been talking to Stan for two hours, and he seemed willing to stay as long as necessary. That's the kind of friend she preferred. Everyone needed such a bellwether.

She started to ask more about Misty but changed her mind, afraid to hear the answer. Right now she owned Stan in voice and spirit.

Finally, he broached the last unspoken subject. "Can you do the job?"

"Surely I can be a part-time beat cop," she said, her left leg crossed over the right, swaying to the tune coming out the door.

"You know what I mean." His next words were more firm. "Can you hold it together?"

She sighed, a little stung. "Of course, I can." She'd handled Brea. She handled Grant. She saved Edisto from the Russian, for God's sake. "The fire, Stan. What were the chances? Put yourself in my shoes."

"The greater the love, the greater the fear, Chicklet. You were a good wife, are a good mom, and yes, a good cop—all because of the love, and the fear."

He nailed it about the fear. It ruled her of late. "In any other situation, I'd have been 10-8. What if you'd lost Misty like I lost John?"

"Let's not discuss Misty."

She set her near empty glass on the wide arm of her chair. "I miss you, Stan."

"Well . . . I better go, Chicklet."

"You calling Seabrook back?" she asked quickly, holding on another minute. "With a positive reply?"

"Sure thing."

"I said I miss you, Stan."

The sigh was barely audible. "Miss you, too, Callie."

She lowered the phone to the other arm of her chair, glad Stan hung up before their words got personal.

Refilling her glass and flipping the album, she returned to her chair. "Play Me" was one of her favorite Diamond tunes. She closed her eyes, letting it settle over her.

No worry about Jeb coming in. Beverly escorted him to Middleton. Sophie would give her space out of courtesy and in fear of vindictive ghosts under her roof. Callie enjoyed the chance to be off guard, her mind free to brainstorm about the beach's current events, their meaning, their connections. The intervention had served her well by pushing people out of her way and out of her business.

She did the right thing sending Jeb off, too. His presence stifled her ability to think as crystal as she needed to. Notes on her car, pink slips on her door. Abe Jenkins and Alex Hanson treating her oddly. Some Twitter person teasing her. She seemed to be irritating somebody by simply being here. A fishing license was one thing. Backyard vandalism quite another. But burning a house down elevated this situation to level red.

If Seabrook didn't call her by noon tomorrow, she'd go to him. Time to put on the uniform, throw some weight around, and pursue her curiosity with earnest. Auxiliary might be the Boy Scout level of law enforcement, but she'd own it a hundred percent and work it to its max.

Bottom line, this was who she was. It was all she was, this mission to solve the unanswered, especially when it hurt people. If she ignored her instincts, she'd have nothing left. Then she'd be good for nobody.

She'd already knocked on that door.

Yet the ground didn't quake under her feet at her decision. Actually, her choice felt rather anticlimactic as in nothing had really changed.

She refilled her tea glass for the third time, taking another long draw as her butt returned to the Adirondack chair. Alone. Evening noises coming alive from the shrubbery and marsh across the street behind her house.

Tucking a leg, she closed her eyes and thought only of Brea. Then the ladies that died before her. The details. A cricket began to chirp, hidden somewhere under the porch.

Condensation ran down the sides of her glass, and she rubbed it across her neck, the ceiling fan evaporating it with a brief chill.

Marvelous. Nobody pestering her. This was the most relaxed she'd felt in days.

An ice cube escaped into her mouth, and she sucked it a moment before spitting it back into the glass. She had all night to ponder all this crap, and without interference she could.

She finished off her third gin.

God, she deserved this.

Chapter 19

THE BANGING ON her front door rolled through her head like deep, echoing peals of thunder. Callie forced her scratchy eyelids open, each weighing a pound each, as she checked her phone for the time. Through a dim haze, she read eight twenty and fell back on the bed.

"Go away," she grumbled.

The knocking ceased. Phone still tucked to her chest, she dug under her coverlet to fade to black again.

The phone played "I'm a Believer." "Hello!" she answered, coughed once, then repeated, "Hello."

"Answer the door," Sophie said, the pitch penetrating. "I see your car out here, and your porch lights are still on. We need to talk."

Callie wadded herself under her covers again. "No, we don't."

"I'll bang until you let me in."

Dressed in one of John's old T-shirts, Callie slid from the high mattress onto the floor, giving the room a moment to right itself before she shuffled to the hallway. Phone still gripped, squinting at the sun's glare magnified by the cut glass accenting the door, she let her neighbor in.

"Oh dear Lord in heaven," Sophie said, pushing closer to analyze Callie's eyes. "Did we do that to you?"

Bending from the light, Callie scuffed to the kitchen for water and aspirin. Sophie shut the door. "You did nothing," Callie said over her shoulder, amazed she could speak, much less respond with a double entendre.

Sophie threw a newspaper on the kitchen table and began flitting around the room, hunting through cabinets. "Sit down," she ordered.

Gladly, Callie did as told, then reached for the newspaper. "What's this?"

"The reason I came over, knucklehead." Sophie placed a cup of tea, a glass of water, and four aspirin on the beige quilted placemat. "They put out a new paper because of you."

"What?" Callie ate the aspirin and chased them with water, then unfolded the paper and attempted to read the headline.

"Fire Almost Consumes Detective's Home" jumped off the front page. Callie blinked hard at the picture of her standing beside Seabrook, her hand over her mouth, like she held it now.

#New resident Callista Jean Morgan, ex-Boston detective, almost lost her home Tuesday night to a fire set in an empty house next door. Thanks to the quick response of Edisto firefighters, her residence was saved. The empty house, however, was a total loss.

Better known as Callie Morgan, the detective has been assisting the local Edisto PD in seeking closure to both the Brea Jamison and Dr. Ernest Maddington deaths. Based upon a recent interview with Ms. Morgan, this paper learned that she also has been investigating earlier Edisto Beach deaths that some label as the Edisto jinx. This paper questions whether she thinks the current and past deaths are related.

When asked if Ms. Morgan's investigation triggered someone to set the fire, neither the Edisto Fire or Police Departments would comment.

The article covered half the front page.

"He never prints two papers in one month," Sophie said. "You are news!"

Callie closed her eyes, laid her forehead against the heel of her palm, and dropped the paper. "How exciting."

Her phone chimed "Hello Again," her Neil Diamond ringtone for unknown callers. Not recognizing the Lowcountry number, Callie sent the call to voice mail. Another call came on the heels of it: "Heartlight." She'd have to change his ringtone fast . . . Seabrook. She sent that one to voice mail, too.

"Sooner or later you have to answer," Sophie said, sitting across from Callie, fingering her teacup. "You realize I'm on your side about the deaths, right?"

Wearily, Callie's arms dropped across the table. "What's this? You're on my side? I've never had gin mess with my hearing like this before."

"Seriously, I am," Sophie said. "I had no idea yesterday would turn out like it did." She shrugged, trying to appear cute. "Rikki called your mother, and there you go . . . the snowball started down the hill. Did we make you fall into the booze again?"

Callie sipped her tea to help push her headache aside, then reached for more sweetener to aid the effort. Her stomach held a tinge of uncertainty, her eyelids feeling twice their size. "I enjoyed my evening, thank you very much. Without y'all hanging around I finally had a night to myself. You don't make me drink. I decide to drink. Last night, I had a drink. It's that simple."

Another knock sounded on the door.

She bet her house would turn into Grand Central Station thanks to that headline.

"See?" Sophie's aquamarine contacts widened. "You better get your act together. Everyone knows where you live thanks to this article. Want me to get it?" She started to the hallway.

"Everyone already knows where I live thanks to Twitter." Callie stood. "Let me get rid of them. I'm in that kind of mood." But as she approached the door, she recognized the uniform. "Good grief," she mumbled, reaching for the knob.

Seabrook stood crisp and ready to serve the citizens of Edisto, dangling a cloth bag from some law enforcement conference. "Morning. I came by because . . . aren't you bright-eyed and chipper?" He sidled past her and entered. "I chased off some people taking pictures, by the way." He set the bag on the sofa and nodded at Sophie.

Sophie dipped her head toward Callie.

"I wouldn't be here if I didn't need you, Callie," he began. "Though I'm having a few doubts now that I see the shape you're in."

Callie glanced down and remembered John's T-shirt. "Sophie got me out of bed too early."

He shook his head, not humored by her deflection. "What did I tell you? Call me before you binge."

"I didn't binge."

His eyes narrowed a bit. "You're hung over. Don't even try to deny it."

"I choose to drink. Drink doesn't choose me."

"Don't double-talk me. I see the signs." He started to reach into his pocket.

Callie almost retreated a step then stood her ground. "Don't even think about giving me an AA card."

He bent down into her space, to avoid Sophie's ear. "I mean it. Call me." Then he straightened, reached into the bag, and drew out a badge and an Edisto PD uniform shirt. "I'm three officers down today. Two with family issues and one I'm on the brink of firing if he doesn't get his love life straight. That's half the force. If you're interested in this auxiliary business, we do this now. I need you on traffic control by one, noon if possible. There's a craft market thing going on plus it's Friday."

Almost gripping the bookcase at the news, Callie stood stymied, not sure if the room seemed unsteady from the drink or Seabrook's request. After a day and night of soul-searching, after Stan's counsel, after a half-bottle of Tanqueray, she went to bed positive she needed the job. Here was her moment, at a time she physically felt anything but ready.

Sophie stood motionless in the kitchen entryway. Seabrook studied Callie as if he were reading her mind, her body language, maybe define a reason to leave with his offer.

Callie walked over, took the bag, and peered in. A utility belt, a vest labeled POLICE, and paperwork.

Then she saw it, her old Glock the police kept as evidence when she killed the Russian. She touched it, lifting it gently like an old friend.

Callie peered up at the tall man, grinning wide. "How do I know the shirt will fit?"

AFTER A QUICK whirlwind of paperwork, Callie stood on Highway 174 decked out in an oversized Edisto PD uniform top, the black vest, an almost oversized gun belt, and her old firearm, waving traffic one way or another. She still grinned from behind her shades. The badge lifted a weight she didn't realize she bore. Her breaths came easier, despite the exhaust of the passing cars. The hangover pushed aside, almost.

She fondly recalled the nervous first time she managed traffic, not a year out of college, her shoes fresh and unscuffed. A learning curve she hadn't expected almost resulted in a Lexus greeting a utility van head on, one of the bumpers stopping a foot short of her knees.

An hour into her new job, she marveled at the quantity of cars arriving on and leaving Edisto. She didn't recall the drivers' stares being this intense, but then she hadn't performed traffic control in over a decade. Maybe Edisto never saw a woman in uniform before. Through her headache, she made eye contact with each driver to get their attention and avoid a gridlock. As sweat soaked her shirt under the vest, cars lined twenty deep, snaked across the marsh fed by Scott Creek, with as many fighting to get off the beach. The craft market, the state park, and the comings and goings of tenants on a Friday congested the roads worse than she ever remembered. If the day ended without an accident, she'd count herself lucky.

"Hey, Callie!" came a voice from the BI-LO parking lot. "Looking good!"

With a split-second glance, she recognized Sophie with Rikki and a few others, eyes shielded from the sun, watching. A few thumbs up drew a chuckle from her in spite of Callie's dry mouth. Someone held his phone out to take pictures, which made everyone else do the same.

Sweat had long ago disposed of her makeup, maybe even her deodorant.

Forward came the infamous VW. "Well, hello Detective Morgan," Alex said with a smirk, her phone clicking as she passed.

That picture would appear on Twitter any second.

A few more cars later, a twenty-something kid without a shirt eased by, likewise capturing her image.

A television van from Charleston, its logo huge and gawdy on the side, advanced. The driver held out a mike. "Solved the jinx yet, Ms. Morgan?"

What the hell?

"Move along, ma'am," Callie ordered, keeping her attention on the encroaching vehicles, questions building in the recesses of her mind.

Window rolling down, an F-150 truck approached, the driver pushing a newspaper under her nose, a pen under his thumb. "Can I get your autograph, Detective?"

Stunned for a moment, Callie quickly regained her wits. "Keep it moving, sir." These people weren't locals. How did they know her name?

"Ms. Morgan?" hollered someone from beside Sophie and Rikki. "We need to talk."

What the ever-lovin' hell was going on?

A short middle-aged man with a slight spread to his khaki-clad rear end waved at her at the curb, a straw hat overshadowing his sunglasses.

"I'm busy, sir," Callie replied, with no idea who the man was.

"Then I'm calling Officer Seabrook," came the reply, as he marched toward McConkey's, phone to his ear. *Whatever.* Callie figured she'd learn in due time what somebody thought she did.

Her radio clicked. "Callie?"

She responded. "Officer Morgan here."

Seabrook's voice came in clear. "Callie's good enough. Take a break. Come meet me in my cruiser behind McConkey's."

"I'm still good here," she replied, pointing and waving extra hard at a family paying more attention to their argument than her directions. "Traffic's a bear! Is there another problem?"

"Yes. Meet me in ten minutes."

"Morgan out."

She redirected about ten more cars then made one vehicle stop short, allowing her to exit the road. As she trotted off, a cheer arose from Sophie's crowd, almost lost amidst the growing throng. The market fair consumed the parking lot behind BI-LO and McConkeys, pockets of people running into each other, but Callie caught a glimpse of Frank, Ava, and Terrance when Ava waved like a high-strung cheerleader. "Callie! You really did good out there!"

Good grief, it was only traffic control, but she nodded and smiled as she pushed through the herd of groupies. Seabrook's ten-minute deadline expired five minutes ago.

Frank reached for Callie's arm on her strong side. Instinctively, she stiffened to protect her weapon, her old ways snapping into place about someone in a crowd touching a cop.

"Oh, sorry," he said, jerking in retreat. "We want to say we're sorry about walking off the other day."

"I went to your home, but nobody answered," Terrance added.

Callie nodded, continuing to walk. Seabrook would be waiting. "It's all good, guys. Listen, I've got to go. We'll talk later, like maybe tomorrow." Then she turned and left, jogging to McConkeys, thoroughly enjoying the bounce of her new leather belt.

Seabrook's car idled in the parking lot, the unidentified straw-hat man at his window. As Callie approached, the gentleman shook his head at Seabrook and left, his short choppy steps taking him quickly away.

Callie opened the passenger door. "Hey," she said, sliding into the front seat, taking her sunglasses off to feel the full brunt of the air-conditioning. "That was actually fun. What's up?"

"That might be enough for today," he said, his eyes noncommittal.

Callie's face fell. "Why? Thought you said a day a week? Or more? It's only been three hours."

"It's almost supper time, but that's not the issue."

The happiness of the day slid off her like melted butter. She sighed. "What's the issue with that guy?"

"That," he said with a tilt of his head to where the man walked, "was the town administrator. He says traffic *is* the issue."

Not one mishap. Callie managed the exceptionally large influx like a pro. The hairs rose on her arms. "What's his beef?" She thumbed toward the road from whence she came. "My work was textbook, sir."

He raised his hands in a truce. "Yes, and I thank you for that. Your first taste of Edisto policing, but did you notice anything unique out there?"

She laughed at the memory. "Yeah, somebody asked for my autograph."

"Exactly," he said. "A good chunk of that traffic is probably because of you. The town honcho has been fielding phone calls asking about the jinx, the fire, Ernest Maddington, and especially you. Everybody wants an interview.

We're headed into the weekend, and people saw the news and suddenly decided that Edisto deserved their attention."

"I had no idea," she said, stunned.

He gave her a puzzled look. "Your phone hasn't driven you crazy?"

Her phone rang so much today that she put it on silent mode, letting everything go to voice mail. She pulled it out of her pocket. *Holy crap!* Twenty-seven voice mails.

Holding the phone for Seabrook to see, at first she drew a blank what to say. "All because of the *Island Tribune* publishing an extra edition?"

Then she got it. She opened Twitter. Using the Edisto jinx hashtag, Alex tweeted like a fiend yesterday while Callie dealt with the intervention debacle. But MyOuttake kicked those tweets into overdrive, embellishing with dynamic vigor.

@MyOuttake—Detective Morgan on the trail of the #edistojinx

@MyOuttake—Detective Morgan thinks a reward is in order for the #edistojinx

@MyOuttake—Detective Morgan turns myth into reality #edistojinx

@MyOuttake—How close is Detective Morgan to the truth? #edistojinx

@MyOuttake—Does Edisto's Detective Morgan chase clues or ghosts? #edistojinx

@MyOuttake—Why did Detective Morgan leave Boston for Edisto? #edistojinx

@MyOuttake—What is the real story behind Detective Morgan? #edistojinx

Then anyone ever connected with Edisto noted the messages, adding their own spin, some of them adding a hashtag to DetectiveMorgan—#*detectivemorgan*. On top of that, she noted that MyOuttake no longer gave credit to *EdistoToday* like they once did. This person had gained enough momentum to surpass the public's interest in Alex and ran rampant with his own.

As a matter of fact, he was trending.

Not that she held a serious attraction to the social media venue, but she knew enough to gasp at the quantity of messages scrolling ten times faster than normal across her screen, the activity scaring her. Who read this? What crazy might take these remarks seriously and stalk her? God, she didn't need to go down that road again.

The Edisto Sleuth Society's cheerleading might've been because new jinx groupies entered the island. Amateur gumshoe competition.

"I didn't do this, Mike," she said, slipping into his first name, eager for support. "This guy." She shook her phone. "This guy is probably here, and close." What she didn't say, however, was that he could be the killer, excited about attention . . . or manipulative enough with his new tool to shift everyone's focus to the past deaths, so he could plan his next.

Or toy with Callie.

Maybe set another house on fire.

Her pulse started doing double-time, reminding her of the headache.

"Let me talk to the town administrator," she said.

"I'll deal with him," Seabrook replied, his tone level as always, an attribute that Callie read as poised one moment and naively ignorant of danger the next. He hadn't put clues together about the Russian until Callie sat amidst busted furniture, broken bottles, and blood. He beat himself silly for days afterwards, maybe still did for all she knew.

A methodical doc confronted with a differential diagnosis. She liked the man. She really did. But he was not a natural cop.

"I take it you missed the news last night," he said.

"I haven't watched the news since I moved here," she replied, annoyed.

"Well, one of the Charleston stations did a quick piece on Edisto last night, thanks to someone feeding them details about you and your activities. Not long, a minute, maybe two, but it condensed the fire, the August incidents, and Edisto ghost stories into an overblown story at the end of the broadcast. Guess enough people saw it on a Thursday night to decide that they wanted to spend their weekend on Edisto. Or meet you."

Alex Hanson, seizing an opportunity. "All the more reason to corner that Barbie doll," Callie said, her jaw tense. "To think I liked her."

Seabrook draped an arm over the steering wheel and faced her. "Stop and think about what might happen if you confront her."

He didn't need to elaborate. She understood a conversation with Alex would only fuel the flames. Callie almost groaned at the analogy.

"How about you go to the station if you don't want to go home," Seabrook said, reaching over to take her hand.

Straightening in her seat, she glimpsed down at his grasp, then into his eyes. Her heart thudded heavy, pushing her ribs. "I'm a liability to the force after my first day on the job?"

"No. You're a liability to the beach."

The words smacked her, and she retracted, reaching instead to push the vent aside. "Damn."

He blew out hard. "You get what I mean, and you're smart enough to understand why."

"The real estate agents ought to be happy," she said, conceding to common sense. "I'll go to the station." She opened the door, then peered back. "I can research the old files, right? Remember the deal."

He made a face.

"Part of the deal, if I recall," she said then shrugged, a smile tugging at the corner of her lip. "I can always direct traffic again. Or chase down speeders. Which is it? On the street or reading those files?"

"Go read your darn files," he said, waving her off. "Still say you're wasting your energy. I'll be by in a couple of hours. One of my guys returned to duty, but I'm still short. Go home if you get bored. Log in your hours like I showed you."

Callie closed the door and saluted. Seabrook drove off smirking. As Callie made for her car, a man called her name. "Ms. Morgan?"

She walked faster.

"Officer Morgan! Mayor Talbot here. May I have a word?"

Crap, why did Seabrook have to leave so quickly? She pasted on a smile, understanding full well how to play this game, turned, and reached out. "Why hello, Mayor. I don't believe we've met."

A woman dressed way too upscale for sand and surf did a fast trot toward them, a cameraman behind her.

Callie threw on her sunglasses with her left hand, the mayor still gripping her right. "Nice to meet you, sir. If you don't mind—"

"Hold on, Officer Morgan. This lovely lady here wants an interview," he said, motioning at the reporter. The camera rolled, and the reporter had found her spot.

"Thank you, Mayor." The journalist's dark hair hung below her shoulders, the waves styled just so as if coifed in the van before stepping onto the pavement. Lipstick carefully coated full lips in a matte dark rose. Her eyelashes were thick, black, and fake, her eyes held wide as if she worried her lashes would tangle.

The mayor continued to grip Callie, his smile stuck in place.

The reporter donned her professional face like flipping a switch. "Mayor Talbot." She swooped her manicured nails around her, drawing attention to the mass of people enjoying the craft market. "What has stirred this secluded paradise of yours?"

The mayor shook Callie's hand, placing his other on her shoulder. "We have this lady right here to thank," he said. "Callie Morgan, our first female officer. She's made everyone feel safer."

Where the hell was Seabrook?

"Officer Morgan," the reporter said, pivoting with microphone outstretched. "I understand you used to be a detective. Edisto has a few ghost stories that attract tourists, but never this one—the Edisto jinx. What in your professional opinion made you unearth this myth and dust it off?" The woman flashed a Hollywood smile.

"I'm new to Edisto, and I found it curious," Callie replied. "Like any other Edisto visitor."

A perfectly lined eyebrow rose. "Oh, but you aren't a visitor. You're a native. A native with serious credentials earned in Boston, no less. Gives you a special skill, wouldn't you say?"

"That's why we hired her," the mayor exclaimed with lots of pride behind his words, giving Callie a firm shake. "Edisto Beach believes in a safe environment for residents and visitors alike, and Officer Morgan brings exceptional experience to our town. She's visited Edisto since a child. Her father was the late Lawton Cantrell, mayor of Middleton. She's a package we could not ignore." He nodded to the crowd gathering. "Her presence has given this craft fair its largest turnout in its history."

Oh good grief. Callie's hand turned clammy in the man's unrelinquishing grasp. As she fought not to roll her eyes, she caught Janet Wainwright's spiked white hair, the agent bent over in conversation with the irritated town administrator, both watching the mayor's grandstanding on camera.

Good Lord. The town administrator hated Callie, and the mayor wanted to ride on some sort of popularity swell. What was she supposed to do with this?

"Everyone on Edisto brings their own talent of some sort. It's a great place," Callie stated and feigned attention toward a distant corner of the parking lot. "Excuse me, but I'm on duty, and I see I'm needed." She slipped loose from the mayor's hold, tipped her head in thanks, and left.

Without checking back, she pretended to wave at someone, anyone, then jumped in her car and drove off, giving them her taillights.

Stupid press.

Irritated at Alex, incensed at the person behind MyOuttake, Callie fingered her phone. She wanted so damn much to sling comments at the two online, but Seabrook's words rang in her head again. She'd only make matters worse.

She approached Chelsea Morning, thinking she'd drop in and make a sandwich to carry her into the evening at the station as she studied the files. Five cars parked in her drive.

Son of a gun! A dozen people sat in her porch chairs, leaned on her railing, and sprawled along her stairs. One peered in her windows. The others probably already had.

The reason we have locks, Sophie.

Gunning the gas, she drove toward the station. Maybe Officer Francis or Seabrook could clear her drive when she headed home.

Alex and MyOuttake watching her seemed bad enough, but this circus made everything worse.

Chapter 20

THE RECEPTIONIST AT the police station aimed a pen toward a file cabinet then retreated to her desk, a slight whiff of aloofness catching Callie's attention. She let the minor chill go unrequited, eager to lay hands on those even colder case files.

Then her stomach growled. "Is there a drink or candy machine here?"

"There's water and Cokes in the refrigerator," the receptionist replied, attention still on her computer screen.

The station barely held the three desks, file cabinets, and chairs, much less house a fridge. "Um, where's the refrigerator?"

"Over at the fire station next door. In their kitchen."

Made sense.

"Marie, right? You live on the beach?" If Callie had to work here, part-time or not, she needed to befriend the lady who would make or break the station's efficiency. The administrative side of the house made a difference.

"Name's right, and no, my pay grade isn't high enough to afford the beach. I live eight miles out on the main island."

Marie appeared a plain woman, two or three years older than Callie. Short finger nails, though polished. No wedding ring. Short dark hair, maybe a few grays. Callie'd heard Seabrook rely on her numerous times by phone and radio, and supposedly she'd worked at the PD since high school.

The one and only time Callie had seen Marie had been when she met Seabrook in his office. Marie seemed nicer then. She hoped like heck Marie didn't harbor feelings for Seabrook.

She strode to Marie's desk and reached out. "Call me Callie. I look forward to working with you."

The drawl defined Marie as Lowcountry, and accordingly, owned enough manners to return the shake. "We'll see," she said, then dropped Callie's hand, attention back on the screen.

"Have I done something?" Callie asked. "Or maybe it's what I haven't done, to annoy the power behind the Edisto PD?"

The woman's lips pursed. "Stirring useless shit, that's what you've been doing since you moved here, only now you get to do it from behind a uniform. This whole station is different since you arrived."

Wow, okay. Callie still appreciated the directness, though. At least now she knew where she stood. "Only doing my job, Marie."

"Oh," Marie laughed callously, "four hours wearing your shiny new badge, and you're on a mission?" The woman shook her head. "I leave in thirty minutes, so I suggest you get your drink and get back here. The phones are *your* job once I'm gone. The natives tend to call us direct and go around 9-1-1."

Yes, ma'am. As the freshman on the team, Callie knew better than to argue. She needed such a personality, assuming some *woman* thing for Seabrook didn't interfere.

Callie quickly rifled through the files first, feeling Marie's glances on her back, and found the five she needed. Brea's file must be on someone's desk, or totally in the computer. She knew that case well enough anyway, having witnessed the whole ordeal.

Then she ran to the fire department next door, the place small enough to make finding the fridge easy. Two guys recognized her from the Papa Beach fire, asked how she felt, one whistling at the uniform. Laughing, she threw one-liners at them, like she used to do. Guys could be jerks, but she didn't hold it against them.

Marie waited with purse over her shoulder, one arm on the counter, fingers tapping. "You got a key?" she asked.

Callie patted her pockets by habit. "Um, not yet."

"Well, I'm not leaving the place wide open."

"Is there a rear door?"

"It's locked, too."

So stupid to let something so simple as a key get in the way of her need to read those files. "Lock me in. Seabrook will come in later, I imagine. I'll leave when he does."

Marie smirked. "I bet you will." She left, key securing the door.

Callie watched the woman get in her car. When Marie glanced, Callie smiled and waved, receiving nothing in kind. She had to work on her rapport with the office manager. No doubt the island rumors ran amuck about Callie thanks to Twitter, *EdistoToday*, and now Jenkins in his special edition paper. Words didn't quell doubts, but her steady dedication to Edisto Beach and its police department might melt some of that ice with time. She hoped so.

With the place to herself, Callie opened the files, hungry to read.

Margaret and Lee Anne drowned. Carolyn fell down stairs. Angelina died of a heart attack in a hot tub, and Reese overdosed. In that order. The first two were alone. The last three were at parties, similar to Brea. Why the shift in method, from water to a party environment?

Then she answered her own question. To shed attention. She couldn't knock his logic; it had worked. If she hadn't come to Edisto, he'd still be on the loose, with zero worry about getting caught.

August 10th the earliest date. August 17th the latest. Brea died on the 7th, putting her outside the normal range. Frankly, it appeared that the deaths took place within a week, not two weeks like everyone professed. Did that make Brea an anomaly? Maybe not. Callie still made a note.

She flipped through the interviews. Who were with the women when they died, or at least were the last to see each woman alive? That question pressed her the most as she yearned to study the histories.

She scattered the files across six feet of counter, in chronological order. With her question in mind, she read each case, stepping down to read the next, then the next. A notepad slid with her. She'd make a spreadsheet when she got home, to seek discrepancies, similarities, and trends.

Son of a gun. Nobody had been with the five dead women when they died. None of them! Brea died in the middle of people. Everybody saw her collapse. Callie scribbled another note.

Okay, who were the closest friends, family members, or acquaintances present? Pen in her teeth, gnaw marks on the end, Callie reread each report and the statements from the next of kin. Friend, friend, fiancé, girlfriend, boyfriend.

None of the women were married. Brea, however, had been married to Grant for almost a decade. Another note on her list.

What else? Once again, she pilfered through each file, placing similar pages on top for each case, walking down the counter, reading the same material each time, hunting for likenesses and differences. Nothing that time. She turned to another form, another page, another interview.

All in their thirties. All brunette. They came from several states, big cities and small towns. Two knew Edisto from years before. The other three were new visitors.

As she winnowed out details and took note of others, excitement swelled in her stomach. This helped define who she was in Boston. God help her, but the pain of others seemed to feed her love of law enforcement, encourage her desire for truth. Glancing down at her uniform shirt, gaze straying across the badge, she wondered if abstaining from them threw her off balance solving the June mystery, almost getting her killed. Fingers rubbing her shirt in appreciation, she allowed herself a grin. She hadn't felt this alive since she left Massachusetts.

One more thing. Suicide. Did any of the women suffer from depression? Lee Anne had cancer. Carolyn planned a fall wedding. Reese battled alcoholism, but her boyfriend said she had been doing well. No thread there.

Returning to an empty desk, taking a seat, Callie draped back and closed her eyes in hope for a different perspective. What else?

The facts swirled in her mind. Single, hair color, no witnesses, within the same one-week period though two weeks wasn't that dissimilar. Where was she wrong? How was she wrong? She sipped her Diet Coke, then rolled the cold bottle across her forehead.

Wait, time of day. She ran to the counter. Yes! All five women died at sundown or after. Brea died in broad daylight.

While Seabrook would express his doubts, Callie's instinct screamed otherwise.

Brea didn't belong in the Edisto jinx profile. Whether Maddington or Grant killed her, Brea didn't match the serial killer's target. Way too many differences.

To Seabrook, Marie, Janet, and the rest of those wishing to look the other way, this would be considered good news. But that also meant the August killer was probably not Grant or Maddington and still ran loose. No sixth kill had taken place—not yet. Today was Friday, August thirteenth. Well within the window of time for it to occur.

A sharp tingle ran through her. With all this attention on Edisto Beach, with all this media frenzy, she envisioned the guy thrilled about the opportunity to find another victim. No, she didn't have a suspect. No, she felt clueless where to turn. But she felt ninety percent sure of one thing: Brea wasn't a piece in this puzzle.

And Callie saw this guy thoroughly enjoying the show on Edisto this weekend.

And her gut told her MyOuttake would capitalize on the whole damn mess.

She straightened the papers and flipped through the cases one at a time, seated, from a different angle. As she read the last page of Lee Anne's file, the phone rang.

Callie hesitated, wondering if the line redirected to 9-1-1 or if a recording came on. After the fifth ring, she answered. "Edisto Police Department. Detect . . . um, Officer Morgan speaking. May I help you?"

"Callie, oh Callie. It's Sarah Rosewood. I hoped you'd be there. Sophie told me you were working again." Her voice breathed with rasps and hitches, fear wrapping her words.

Straightening in her chair, Callie reached for her notepad and flipped a page. "What is it, Sarah?"

"Grant's been shot," she said. "Ben's out of town. What do I do?"

Callie jumped up, closing files. She threw them in a drawer. "Call 9-1-1. I'm on my way."

Banging through the swinging counter entrance, she yanked the front door and jarred her upper body at the lack of response. Locked.

Son of a bitch!

She didn't have to control every emergency and wouldn't be expected to handle this one, but the caller was Sarah, the victim Grant. They were involved in the very cases she had spread out in front of her. How could she not be a first responder on this situation?

Seabrook and his two, maybe three, officers remained overwhelmed with traffic, tourists, and crazy paparazzi wannabes while she guarded paper.

She ran out the back, unable to enable the alarm, with no time to fret over it.

"Hey, you," she said to a passing fireman. Suddenly she recognized him as the fire chief.

He frowned at the missing courtesy. "Is there a problem?"

"I received an emergency call. Don't have a key. Keep an eye on the place, would you?"

"The door locks when you pull it shut."

But Callie already ran, her fingers keying her mic for Seabrook, praying she got there first.

"IN HERE," SARAH said, her expression pained.

Grant lay sprawled on the Rosewood living room floor, blood staining a Persian rug under his head. He hadn't hit anything on his way down, the closest piece of furniture a coffee table, too distant. The smell of gunpowder remained in the air. She feared touching the man to study the damage inflicted, but refusing to sit and watch him bleed out, she ran to the bathroom for a towel. Gingerly, she placed it against his wound, her brief contact not feeling a hardcore point of entry.

He lay slumped, right arm under him, legs bent to his left, his left arm out to his side. The position gave no hint of what happened other than he probably fell from the tufted chair behind him. His eyes closed, his expression seemed . . . benign. Even from three feet away she'd smelled alcohol. A lot. The glass on the floor five feet from his hand lay empty, but the blended whiskey bottle on the table beside the chair looked two-thirds gone.

"9-1-1 on its way?" Callie asked, kneeling.

Sarah moved in and spoke over Callie's shoulder. "Yes."

Callie hovered over the recent widower. "Any sign of a break-in?"

"No." Sarah's voice quivered. "Do you think he did it . . . to himself?"

Grant opened his eyes. Sarah exclaimed and jumped.

"Grant, don't move," Callie ordered. "Don't move a single inch, you hear?"

"I did it," he whispered. "Just lost it."

His meaning escaped her unless he tried to kill himself.

The room showed no sign of struggle, but no obvious sign of a suicide attempt. This situation seemed more happenstance . . . a moment of opportunity.

She needed to record the scene, especially if Grant seemed eager to talk.

Sarah released a soft sob.

Callie didn't need an emotional bystander hovering. "Go outside and wait for the ambulance and Seabrook, okay?"

With quick, jerky nods, Brea's aunt stumbled two steps then left for the exit.

The door shut, and Callie set her phone to video and began recording. She knew better than to touch Grant and risk exacerbating his injuries. Not with medics en route. Where was Seabrook?

Grant whispered again. Callie bowed lower to hear.

"I loved her."

"I know you did. Who did this to you, Grant?"

His eyes shut again. She waited, hoping. He lifted his lids. "Didn't see. He surprised me."

"A he? The shooter was a he?" she asked.

He winced, which she interpreted as he didn't know—probably didn't see a thing. "You said you lost it," she repeated.

He nodded once then stopped, as if recalling.

"What did you do, Grant?" she asked gently. "There might be a bullet in your head. You and I both understand what that might mean. You said you lost it. How?"

His eyes widened then closed for a moment. When he opened them, he stared at Callie with a sense of acceptance.

She'd never liked Grant's explanation about his innocence. Call it old school gut feeling, but she'd never trusted Brea's husband. This whole time, Callie'd harbored two questions about the man. First, what did he hide, and second, could he be the August killer?

His mouth moved, but nothing came out.

"What is it, Grant?" she asked softly. "What's on your conscience?" Seabrook would kill her for doing this.

"I killed Brea."

She nodded, empathetic as if his murderous act didn't matter. "Okay. I'm so sorry," she said, keeping him talking. Inside, she screamed, envisioning her fist in his face.

"Saw him at the party . . . the way he stared at her . . . she tried to pretend."

"And you killed him later," Callie added.

"No." He swallowed and tried to clear his throat. "Wainwright. I wanted . . . proof. Proof he was there. To show the police. The agent confirmed his name was in some book. I could put it on him."

The fact Wainwright knew Maddington attended the party flew through Callie. The bitch! Assuming Grant told the truth.

"I went to his house and found him . . . already dead. So I typed the suicide note."

"And destroyed his, I take it?" She held her anger. "Maddington left a note of his own, didn't he?" A man like that would.

"Burned it," Grant managed to say.

"Well, it's all over," she whispered. "Rest. Medical help is on its way."

Feet clamored up the stairs and across the wooden porch. EMTs rushed inside, Seabrook holding the door for them and their gurney.

Callie hid her phone in her palm, against her body, and leaped aside to get out of their way. Seabrook nudged her over to the kitchen and murmured with a twinge of disgruntlement, "Aren't you having a fine first day?"

"You have no idea," she said. "Grant's a first-rate bastard."

Seabrook raised his brows. "What—"

"By the way, don't be surprised if I'm on television tonight."

He shifted to a scowl. "What?"

"Tell you later. Blame the mayor."

Sarah stood barely five feet from them, so the two moved to the other side of the room. "Did he try to kill himself?" Seabrook asked.

Shaking her head, Callie closed the gap until they touched. "No, I honestly think someone shot him. Who, we don't know." The medics took vitals and then carefully applied a cervical spine brace.

Seabrook scrutinized the EMTs' efforts, mumbling once and nodding, wincing one time. He probably itched to jump into the medics' business. "Are you allowed to help them?" she asked, understanding the yearning to do what she'd been trained to do without thinking.

Without taking his gaze off the medical activity, he answered, "Not licensed, plus they're managing all right. All they can do is stabilize him and get him to a hospital with the right equipment."

"Well, I got a confession out of him," she said and turned on her phone.

Seabrook whipped around. "What?" His whisper came out loud, and he glanced around, making sure nobody listened near. "You made him confess on video while he bled out on the floor?"

Callie shrugged tight. "He's not bleeding out, and he wanted to talk. I listened. And the way nobody ever finds me credible, I figured I needed proof."

Her new boss threw fists on his waist and then stooped to get in her face. "I can't believe you did that."

"Well, I did," she said.

"Is he dying?" he asked, peering at the medics. "What did the wound seem like to you?"

"I'm not a doc, Doc," she said. "You could tell better than I, but if I had to guess, he'll have a concussion and a huge headache for a few days, then realize that he was damn lucky that's the weapon the attacker used. I think there's a bullet lodged in the room somewhere, and the attacker wasn't very confident. Whoever shot him got sidetracked or couldn't shoot close and personal. Regardless, Grant can't identify him."

Officer Francis came through the front entrance. "Mike?" he asked.

"Yeah, over here." Seabrook beckoned with a wave.

Francis approached. "You won't believe this." He held out his phone. MyOuttake had posted a comment.

@MyOuttake—What goes around comes around. #murderonEdisto

"Damn," Callie breathed as she recognized the picture of Sarah's living room and Grant slumped across the Persian rug. A .22 lay to the side, a weapon that hadn't been there when Callie arrived.

Chapter 21

PALE, SARAH HELD her arms tightly crossed over her chest, shaking her head in disbelief every time she answered one of Callie's questions. Officer Francis placed a glass of Coke in front of her, and the woman mumbled, "Thanks" as he left the room.

Callie watched him imperceptibly disappear. Always there, always prepared, never in the limelight. She liked this cop.

The Rosewoods' ornate ten-seat mahogany dining room table dwarfed Sarah's huddled form, the huge piece of furniture making the pricey teak one in the breakfast area look cheap.

"Let's go over this again," Callie said, Seabrook seated beside her. "Your husband Ben is where?"

"He's in Atlanta. He left yesterday morning. I spoke to him by phone this afternoon around four."

Callie believed her father's former mistress, but Seabrook had to as well. While she yearned to wrap her arms around Sarah, ease her through the interview with coos and pats of affirmation, she couldn't. Sarah had to tell her side.

The afternoon's traffic control in ninety-five degree heat atop the morning's hangover made for a draining day, but Grant's attack would make for a longer night. Callie wasn't on the payroll exactly, but Sarah had no one to trust, and Callie wanted this interview done right.

Also, the more consistent and solid the story, the easier Seabrook would feel about the facts, and the sooner they moved on and got proactive. She tired of teaching Edisto PD the meaning of the word. She craved a glass of sweet tea . . . or a swallow of gin. "You weren't home?"

"No."

"And what time did you find Grant?"

"When I called you," Sarah said. "My phone says six thirty-two so a few minutes before that."

The facts already written in her notes, Callie went to the next question, satisfied yet disappointed that Seabrook let her run with the show. "Did you see anyone suspicious or unexpected outside? Anyone visit recently?"

"I already *told* you nobody's been here." Sarah finally lifted her glass, a ripple in the liquid as she shook.

"Which door did you come in, and was it locked?"

"Front and no. Grant was here."

Having worn-out her warning to the Edisto residents to keep their doors locked, Callie reserved judgment for the habit to another time and place. They'd done this interview twice already, and Sarah's nerves only worsened.

The next repeated question. "Why weren't you here?"

Sarah smacked her glass down on the table with a sharp crack. "Don't you think I wish I had been here? I told you, I ran to Charleston." She burst into tears and covered her face. "I didn't have a dress to wear to Brea's funeral."

Unable to restrain herself, Callie put her pen down and covered Sarah's hands with her own. "We're establishing a timeline, honey. I'm sorry, but this is necessary."

After allowing a moment, she went ahead and closed her notebook. "Thanks, Sarah."

Callie reached for the woman to pat her arm, but Sarah moved out of reach, face blotchy and aged. Of course Sarah felt stepped on and abused with the questions. Callie would try to make nice with her later, once the necessity of the experience had a chance to sink in. "You've been through an awful lot," she said, "and we appreciate you talking to us like this. Is Ben coming home tonight?"

Sarah shook her head. "He said there was nothing for him to do." The simple fact hung in the air that her husband wasn't one to run to his wife's side.

Unbelieveable. Callie stole a sideways glance at Seabrook whose expression said he'd like to shoot the man, too. "You aren't sleeping here alone, are you?" he asked.

"I'm going to stay with Ms. Hanson until he gets home." She peered toward the entryway, even though the crime scene wasn't visible from where she sat. "I'm throwing out that rug; I don't give a *damn* what Ben says it cost."

Good for her. And staying with Ms. Hanson worked. Alex's grandmother had appeared flighty when Callie first met her, but several conversations with the gray-haired woman told Callie she had substance behind that flour-sack apron.

Everyone left the house, Callie and Seabrook watching as Sarah locked the door and walked across the street to the Hanson place. Approaching dark, close to nine, the tide echoed a few blocks over, pushing a briny aroma through the air. The day had been a cloudless Friday, perfect for the craft market event and the beachcombers and freelance reporters inundating Edisto for sun, souvenirs, and breaking news stories. No clouds made for a less picturesque dusk, but still colorful in its subtle blend of pinks, oranges, and blues. Her discomfort fluttered across the nape of her neck for a split-second then dissipated quickly, the Rosewoods' crime fresh and commanding her attention.

Two gulls squawked, one crossing the other's path not far over their heads. Seabrook peered at them a second then moved toward his squad car. Callie snared his shirt. "Wait a minute. Where are you going? What do you want me to do?"

He twisted around. "We need to start canvassing the neighbors, asking if anyone heard a shot, saw a parked car, saw anyone run out of the house. Nobody would hold it against you if you went home until tomorrow. Won't turn down your help, though."

She moved around him to stand with her back to the road, ever cognizant of passersby, and now social media fanatics with their ever-loving camera phones. Plus, Miss EdistoToday lived across the street. "It's about time to get proactive, don't you think?" she asked under her breath yet firm enough to illustrate. "Try getting in front of this guy instead of chasing his shadow?"

"This guy? What's with *this guy*?" he said, squinting hard as his shoulders rose in a cynical shrug. "This incident is nothing like any other, including your jinx."

She rested thumbs on her belt, appreciating the old habit creeping in. "It's *our* jinx. You are acting chief of police, Mike Seabrook." She nudged her fist lightly against his stomach. "It's time you acted like it."

"What?" he asked with a touch of aggravation.

Callie matched his expression. "Meaning that damn post online could be from a killer, and I say it might connect the jinx to Grant's shooting. Too much is happening for events not to be connected. You see that, so don't play stupid to keep me contained, settled, or . . . *sane*."

His brow creased deep. "I do see that."

"Sometimes I wonder, Seabrook."

He relaxed his posture, ready to return to his car. "We don't have time for this."

She poked him harder. "No, we sure as hell don't. What we need is your spine in negotiating cooperation. Not from the neighbors, not from the other cops, but from the community. Especially the power base." She inhaled the thick evening humidity. "Instead of sucking up to them, we need them on our side, with us in the lead. You have authority. Get these people to recognize that authority. Think like a cop instead of a cat-in-the-tree saver."

He studied her, mouth flatlining. "Then what's the plan, big city hotshot?"

Indeed, what *was* the plan?

Today was the thirteenth, a stupid cliché yet in the exact middle of the time period in which the August deaths occurred. Callie, then Alex and Jenkins, then Charleston's oblivious news anchor, had raised awareness of the jinx, resulting in the day's record influx of visitors which might fuel this guy to act.

If MyOuttake hadn't taken the picture of Grant bleeding on Sarah's floor, Callie would think a kook got swept in with the weekend crowd, or the shooting resulted from a robbery gone bad. Not now though. Unfortunately, the sea of people swarming over Edisto supplied more possible targets and definitely more confusion. Edisto PD didn't have the manpower to oversee this many people.

They needed to lure the guy to them.

Seabrook scratched his ear then waved off a mosquito. "Still waiting for this brilliant plan."

Her gaze rose to meet his. "You wouldn't have Janet Wainwright on speed dial, would you?"

SEABROOK WASN'T FOND of Callie's brainstorm, but he conceded as she piled one thought on another, then demanded that he accompany her . . . him driving his cruiser.

Callie hated the pomp and circumstance of the police car because everyone noted which uniform went where, and whose house merited the Edisto PD's presence. They drove along Palmetto Road, spotting the address from three blocks from the forty-foot flagpole hoisting an American flag on top, the USMC flag below. They parked at Wainwright's residence on the beach a little after 9:00 p.m., Janet's red and yellow color combination represented on the carved wooden sign bearing her home's name, Beach Head.

Seabrook twisted toward Callie, his left arm still holding the door handle. "Let me do the talking, okay? You're lack of tact might—"

"Like Janet Wainwright understands the word. There's a place for tact, and Janet Wainwright hasn't the patience for it." But this was Seabrook's turf, and Callie hadn't exactly melded well with the lady Marine. "But go ahead. Pave the way. I'll speak as needed."

"Somehow I think *as needed* holds different meanings for us."

The scolding meant little to her. She'd function as she deemed necessary. However, the acting police chief appeared too gentle as far as she was concerned. Sweet and caring, the two traits matched with Seabrook's tanned, blond looks and drew smiles from the opposite sex, to include her. But the package clashed with his job.

Sometimes she thought he recognized that mismatch as well. Better for him to police on tiny Edisto Beach anyway, where he felt at home. He'd have been shot a long time ago in Boston.

The Marine answered the door after Seabrook knocked once. She still wore her day clothes. "I rise early, Officer Seabrook. This better be important." The woman didn't acknowledge Callie's existence. As Janet pushed the door, Callie slid in and gently let it latch.

They moved to the living room, Janet assuming a place behind a small oak desk. She waved her guests to the sofa facing her, no refreshments offered.

Who put a desk in the living room?

The smell of leather tainted the air, along with something tomatoey from dinner. While most of the coastal homes flaunted pastels, blues, maybe beiges accented with beachy colors, Janet's residence stood at parade rest in deep brown overstuffed leather sofa and chairs. Hardwood floor and plush rugs reflected oriental and European designs. Naval brass lighting overhead and on the table. No dust in sight, the room carried pine paneled walls with tapestries, carvings, sconces, and art from around the world hung in sync and leveled perfectly. Scented candles on the mantel.

But the wall behind the desk captured Callie's attention most. Photographs, certificates of commendation, plaques, and shadowboxes of rank and medals would intimidate anybody. An Expert Firearms medal and a Bronze Star. Two triangular oak shadowboxes contained folded American flags, almost identical except for one with darker wood, its brass plate reading Douglas Wainwright, 1920–1945. The other box read Janet Elaine Wainwright, Service 1964–1993. Quick math said Janet was born right before or right after her father died, most likely in World War II service.

This room became where Janet Wainwright sank back into time and identified with who she was. During those active duty years, no telling what she endured to rise to Sergeant Major, the rank noted on her retirement certificate to the right of her flag.

"We need your help," Seabrook began as soon as he sat. "Grant Jamison, Brea Jamison's husband, has been shot."

"Dead or injured?" Janet asked.

"Seriously injured."

"So what does this have to do with me?" she replied stiffly, bordering surly.

Seabrook still held keys but stopped rubbing them when Janet stared. "We'd like you to host another one of your parties," he asked. "It's short notice, but—"

"Why?" she interrupted, eyes narrowed.

"To possibly attract whoever shot Mr. Jamison."

"Sounds like a long shot, Chief. Why would he appear at a party? And what do you call such an event so nobody catches on: Bait the Bad Guy Soiree?"

Callie had avoided crossing her arms to now, but they fell into place as she bit her tongue.

"What do you call your other parties?" Seabrook asked. "Simple as that."

"I advertise those well in advance. When would you want to do this?"

"Tomorrow night? Time is short. The guy just struck, and—"

Callie tired of the verbal volley. "When you withheld the fact Maddington signed in at the party, you possibly obstructed a homicide investigation. Then when you gave that information to Grant, he used it to construct an alibi for murdering his wife, and he diverted attention to someone else." She rolled forward on the sofa. "He had most of us believing Maddington killed his wife, thanks to you."

Janet rolled a pencil on the desk but held her attention on Callie, the first time they'd spoken since walking in the door. "How does all this merit a party?" Janet's white brows arched.

Callie met the gaze hard, sensing a small open door of possibility. Janet hadn't said no. "The same person who's been tweeting about the jinx, about me, about Brea, managed to enter the crime scene before anyone else and snap a picture, then post it online. He did something similar with Brea. He loves to be at a scene, which means he could be a killer. Or if the killer took the picture, MyOuttake at least knows who the killer is since he sent it across the Web. If he's only an attention-seeker, he's crossing a line inflaming people. Regardless, he's thrilled to be wrapped up in Edisto business, history, the personalities. He's playing us. From all we've pieced together, he'll be attracted to a party. Wait too long, and he'll be gone."

"I smell jinx again," Janet said.

Seabrook slid forward in his seat. "Maybe not exactly, but we might as well—"

"Yes, you do smell the jinx," Callie replied. "Out of six events, four took place at parties. Even if he didn't kill Brea, he attended the party and got off on taking a picture of her dying. Today he made his appearance at an attempted murder scene."

What Callie didn't understand was why he'd go after Grant. They were groping in the dark on all of this, but six years represented nothing to sneeze at, and two deaths and a shooting during the annual time frame shouldn't be lightly dismissed as unaffiliated. Better to throw a ball and nothing happen, than not throw one and have something happen at a private gathering. What did they have to lose?

Seabrook gently touched Callie's shoulder, reminding her of her promise to let him sway Janet. "We're asking you to help. As Callie so wisely instructed me, we need the beach's assistance. This isn't a police department issue, or a tourist issue, it's everyone's issue. We need you."

"Yet Little Miss Detective seems to be taking over the beach, Chief. A lot of us aren't too excited about that."

Irritation roiled in Callie's chest. "Are you talking about the television interview? The mayor blindsided me, I don't care. It's what mayors do, Janet!" Callie planted both palms on her thighs, gripping as she rested forward on them. "I only wanted to help out a shorthanded police department and got caught in this whirlwind of press." Callie whipped a wrist, as if shooing words away. "I don't care about anything other than catching whoever is killing people on this island. Can't you see that?"

Janet's chin rested in her hand; humor laced the edge of her mouth. Seabrook settled deeper into the sofa, and Callie took her cue.

"There's no such thing as a jinx," Callie said slowly. "This isn't the Legare ghost story where a restless spirit knocks down a tomb door. This isn't the lost lover at sea or the bride killed on her wedding day. I believe this is a person on some sort of mission, for a sick reason. Whether he or she's the Twitter poster, is another story. Either person is dangerous, and a party will bring one or both of them out."

Then Callie stood and walked around the coffee table toward the desk. She had to win this woman over. "You reminded me I had no badge and that you pushed Seabrook out the door, not accommodating his request for the sign-in book. Well, we're both back, this time pleading for your help." She left arms-length distance between them and avoided penetrating Janet's space. "A killer has staked out your rental population as a feeding ground. Why doesn't that blister you? Someone invaded your beach. Why are you letting him infiltrate without the least bit of offense, much less a defense?"

"Hmph," the Marine replied. "Isn't this a bit obvious? Desperate even."

Callie almost high-fived the woman for showing promise.

"We are desperate. But we call it a celebration for the success of Edisto,"

Seabrook explained. "Let's capitalize on this herd of people who appeared for the craft market and the people who want to see Callie."

"All my places are rented," Janet replied. "The restaurants are filled to capacity. We can't party on the beach. And I sure as hell can't pull off a party in twenty-four hours and make it appear legit."

Callie smiled. This is what she wanted. "Hold it at Chelsea Morning." She had cameras inside and out. The fire had given her place notoriety, and if a few reporters showed, the party would be all the more of a magnet. "If not Saturday, then how about Sunday evening? Can you do that?"

"How's your fire damage?" Janet asked.

"A piece or two of siding on the northeast side facing the Beechum house. The screen melted on part of the side porch. Nobody'll see it."

"A lot of the weekend people go home Sunday afternoon," Janet bantered, the spark in her eye accepting the challenge.

"This guy stays for at least two weeks," Callie replied. "Besides, the online person is already here."

"Sunday would give me time to grab a couple deputies from Colleton County," Seabrook said.

"And I'll spend tomorrow spreading the word around the craft fair, posting at the venues," Janet added.

Callie leaned on the desk. "So you're on board with this?"

Janet smiled for the first time since they'd met. "Why not?"

Callie's snicker escaped. "You're awesome, Marine."

"That's still not long to organize," Seabrook said.

"Non-issue," the real estate agent replied, standing. "I'll get the word out and order the wine and beer. I can also convince the BI-LO to set aside the food before this avalanche of people cleans it out. One of my contractors will replace your screen."

Finally, Callie had a quasi-team to pursue the jinx. Between Sophie, and possibly Rikki, maybe Ms. Hanson, they'd turn Chelsea Morning into an impressive impromptu beach party.

Janet reached out, and Callie accepted the gesture, forcing a harder grip as the agent's shake cut off her circulation. But Janet didn't let go. "Who are we looking for?" she asked.

"We have no clue," Callie replied.

"But this is a man who'll be trying to hide the fact he's taking pictures," she continued.

"Not sure it's a man," Callie replied again.

Janet gave their grip one more shake and dropped it. "I'll have a sign-in book at the door and a stack of my cards. Still need to think about the realty." She clicked her tongue. "Might even land a bit of business out of the deal."

Callie nodded. "And you'll keep this deal between us. That includes hiding it from your secretary, county administrator, even your therapist," Callie added. "The less who fathom why, the better."

Janet stiffened. "My therapist is an M-14, her office is the range, and she never repeats a word I say."

"Semper Fi," Callie replied.

Janet escorted the duo outside, giving a two-fingered salute to them as they descended the steps to the cruiser. Before Janet turned to the door, she hollered, "Keep your phone on, Ms. Morgan. I'll be in touch."

In the car, Seabrook buckled his belt then paused, both hands on the steering wheel. "How did that just happen?"

Still smiling, Callie let loose a laugh. "What? Getting her on board?"

"No," he said. "Getting her to like you." He stared back toward Beach Head's porch. "She barely gave you the time of day going in. Coming out, I was invisible, and you were her new best friend."

Callie hooked her own belt. "How about that?"

She hunted for the time on the car's dashboard. Eleven thirty. She wondered if Alex had gone to bed yet, then realized not a chance. Not with Sarah spending the night. Good.

She also pondered what MyOuttake fantasized over right now with the beach so busy. Didn't matter. He'd discard it tomorrow . . . as soon as he saw the tweets about the Sunday evening beach party celebrating Edisto in all its glory at Chelsea Morning.

Callie still didn't want to think of MyOuttake as the killer. Assuming the killer and tweeter were one and the same might cause her to make mistakes, focus too hard on one while the other waltzed in and took his prize.

The cruiser rolled past beach houses filled to capacity, bikini-clad girls strolling the sidewalks, potential beaus trailing behind. Callie turned to study a dark-headed twenty-something girl. Too young if they were correct about what the culprit preferred.

As solid and firm as she'd presented herself to Seabrook and Janet, she still held reservations. This shrewd stalker, killer, whatever, remained too many steps ahead of her. God knew he moved light years ahead of everyone else. And none of them could be everywhere at once . . . even in a place as small as Edisto Beach.

What if the party attracted all their attention, and he struck somewhere else?

Chapter 22

CALLIE RELAXED IN the front seat of Seabrook's police cruiser, feeling accomplished for a change. Catching Janet at home at eleven at night, then coaxing her into their plan made for a grand coup. Seabrook drove to Callie's house and put the car in park. The dashboard clock clicked to midnight.

She smiled. "We're on go. How about that?"

But he didn't return the joy. "Your plan makes me nervous."

"Edisto PD isn't a very proactive lot, are they?"

"It's Edisto, Callie."

She looked at him softly, to appease him. "You said Francis would be available, and you'll borrow a couple deputies to work the beach." They would study who gravitated to the target profile. From there they'd research the person, or persons, distilling their lives down to actual, tangible evidence. "It's only people-watching."

He turned off the engine, and she sensed a devil's advocate comment coming. "We can't all be there," he said. "With the swarm on this beach, I have no idea what'll go down elsewhere." He sighed. "Don't be surprised if I have to leave you. Hopefully not, but—"

"Don't overthink this," she said, but he sat stiffly, his mind obviously churning, his eyes meeting hers only when she spoke.

This effort represented an adlibbed hodge-podge, for sure, but they had no Plan B. Manpower was definitely its biggest weakness, but that manpower needed to be, well, manly.

His crow's feet squinted deeper. "Brea Jamison dropped dead in front of several dozen people. Plus, his online pranks are aimed at you. You fit the profile. He covertly takes pictures right under your nose."

"MyOuttake didn't kill Brea," she reminded him.

"He shadows you, taunts you. And at the same time we have an annual killer. Too many people know you're angling for him, them, whomever."

What a relief to have him on board. "I don't think so, Seabrook." She winked, to put her sudden apprehension to rest as well as his. His worry about her well-being touched her, but this wasn't about her. The bigger picture was their mission. To attract someone who'd been a ghost for six years. "But better he come after me than a civilian, wouldn't you say?" She took his hand.

He stared at her house, resituating their fingers so his thumb rubbed her knuckles, his discomfort all too obvious.

However, this sort of activity revved her, a nervous sort of adrenaline that sharpened her senses. She'd get little sleep tonight as she pondered whether to move her cameras and how to make the rounds during the event without appearing obvious. How much to tell Sophie. She counted her blessings that Jeb left with her mother.

"Callie," Seabrook started. "Crowds are hard to manage. Policing may be newer to me than you, but I'm no idiot."

She frowned, wondering where the heck these nerves sprang from. "Never said you were." Any other uniform would be jacked and primed, ready to play ball.

"If we back off, and another death occurs, not only have we given permission for that death, but your job is at stake, Seabrook. The media has unearthed this story. The whole state will wonder why you let it happen."

His fist holding her hand tapped on the seat.

"Look at me," she said. "You remember me the day I arrived on Edisto?"

"How can I not?" He nodded to his back seat, and Callie caught a bit of a twinkle in those blue-gray eyes. "Confined you in my squad car and took away your weapon," he said.

"How have I been since then?"

"Admittedly better." Then he looked down his nose. "Except for the fire."

"Of course the fire upset me. That's how my husband died." She clenched her teeth, suddenly pissed. "For God's sake, let me be human. I pulled myself together well in spite of it."

He nodded. "Yeah, got to admit that."

"Damn straight." She dug deep for another smile. "But let me tell you what does drive me mad."

Watching her, he waited.

"Doing nothing. This plan is me taking control, only like we explained to Janet, I need y'all take part. This is for those we care about, everyone we live with, everyone who visits this Garden of Eden we cherish tucked in St. Helena Sound overlooking the Atlantic Ocean. This guy is not disappearing on his own, Seabrook. I wish he would, but we can't wait and hope he does."

The tops of the palmettos bowed under a gust from the ocean, held the pose, then righted themselves. She leaned over to capture his gaze. "I killed the Russian with a broken bottle," she said. "I'll make sure there are lots of bottles at the party."

His chuckle turned to light laughter as he reached across the console and electronics that divided the seat between them. He hugged her tight, then laid a hard kiss on her mouth. "You're something, Callie Jean Morgan."

Yes, she was. Yet he seemed afraid to embrace the whole of her. The daring, savvy, methodical, crackerjack side of her. He wanted her experience some days and her femininity on others, but sometimes he appeared leery that the whole package might exceed his needs. Seabrook was a sweet man, his looks a delightful part of the deal, but when life got edgy, he retreated. She wished he wouldn't. Sometimes she preferred sharp edges.

After a few kisses to underline the first, Callie left the cruiser and climbed her stairs, waving as Seabrook left. High on the porch, breezes scattered her unkempt hair around her head, the short tresses stiff from the dried sweat from the day. Her finger caressed where Seabrook kissed, transferring some of his worry to her. But they acted now, or sat back and let fate happen. That's what she'd told him. That's what she had to believe herself.

But she didn't care how many times she experienced mortality, how callous she was supposed to be from seeing yet another set of eyes lose their soul, the shock never wore off. If anything, her history laid more guilt on her that she had more power to see death coming ... and more ability to do something about it. Yes, she hated death, but knew it better than anyone else out here. Thinking like a killer gave her power, way more than sitting idle and hoping the bad guy went away.

She turned to her door and tried it, ever vigilant someone entered during her absence. The lock held. Inserting her key, she entered, locked the door behind her, and blew out from the breath she'd held too long.

Keys dropped in the bowl on her credenza, she scanned her floorplan, stopping for a second longer where Papa Beach's son died two months earlier. In a day and a half, a killer might stand in this very spot. What would go through his mind? Because if she didn't have some idea as to how his brain functioned, all she did was feed the animal.

No, she mustn't think like that. This party was the next step in the right direction, and to raise her chances for success, she had to approach it positively. Shoes kicked off and slid under the barstools, she filled a glass and exited to the porch. The temperature had dropped to the upper eighties, the night muggy but not wet, both tolerable. Seabrook, check. Janet Wainwright, check. Propped in her favorite chair, habitually leaving the light off for security, Callie called and made her next connection.

"Hey, this is Callie Morgan. I'd like to request your assistance."

"First you love me, then you hate me. Now I'm an asset?" the girl replied.

"Granted, you've been a thorn in my side, Alex," Callie said. "But you have a valuable talent I'd love to borrow."

Alex sniggered. "Oh wow, how utterly selfish of you."

Though past most people's bedtimes, a woman as young as Alex usually stayed up late. Sarah spending the night under the Hanson roof probably gave the three women no lack of conversation. Miss EdistoToday didn't sound sleepy at all.

"You can't blame me for what MyOuttake posted," Alex said. "He's odd; I grant you that, but I have no control over his tweets."

"Well, I'm still asking."

Alex laughed. "You make it sound like I owe you a favor."

"Trust me, you do, but you'll like it."

Silence carried across the phone. "What is it?"

"Spread across your social media that there's a party at my house Sunday at five to celebrate Edisto's success this summer. Janet Wainwright's the sponsor, but the crowds rented any venues she'd normally use, so I volunteered the location."

"Hmmm," the girl replied.

Callie stood and strolled to the melted screen, scanning the grounds for wildlife that came out this time of night. She refused to remain locked in her house, and from where she stood, fourteen feet off the gravel and shell driveway, behind the dark screen mesh, someone would need a drone and lighting to snap her picture anyway. She thought best walking the sand, but that would be a careless move with her notoriety being inflamed.

She took another swallow from her glass. She'd promised herself one gin to slow down her brain. It had been a damn long day. "You know how Wainwright likes to collect names and solicit business," she said, fighting to consummate the deal with the blogger. "Janet is super eager to capitalize on this influx of people. Might even be press there. They sure bushwhacked me earlier today in case you missed my impromptu interview alongside the mayor."

"I saw it on the news," Alex said, sounding deflated.

"That story could've been yours," Callie said. "This time, however, I'm contacting you. Heck, come to the party. Tweet your head off. Just advertise it early, so people hear about it in time to make it."

Callie heard ice clinking in a glass as Alex sipped something. Then again. She was thinking. Callie didn't want her to think. She wanted the girl to act. Act fast. Maybe even start tonight. The beach played late on Friday nights. "Alex?"

"You're baiting MyOuttake, aren't you?" the girl replied.

"No, but now that you mention it . . ." Callie watched the Spanish moss on the oak next to her house swinging in the small gusts, one branch barely brushing the screen. "He'd see your tweets and redistribute them. Thanks, Alex! This last minute effort is nerve wracking. Janet's doing what she can, but knowing how she feels, I didn't expect her to be the one contacting you. My head is spinning with details."

"OMG, Callie, you are so full of bullshit!"

"What?"

Callie had told Janet to keep her mouth shut about the party's purpose. While she needed Alex's cooperation, the reporter spread news for a living, not accustomed to keeping it under her hat. Alex needed limited intel.

"You do too understand, but no matter," Alex said. "News is news, and you can't keep me away from this party now if you paid me. I want to see what you're into."

Callie slid back into her Adirondack chair, legs crossed, relieved yet somewhat ill at ease. Alex recognized instantly what was going down. Would the social be that obvious to a killer?

"Tell me this," Alex added. "How about I bring my grandmother? Or Sarah Rosewood?"

Callie stopped swinging her leg. Those two women were innocents, and her protective instincts stood at attention, enough to want them to stay home. But she refused to take Alex's bait and let the journalist ferret the party's purpose out of her. Callie stood and walked to the screen. "Of course they're invited."

"How about Jeb?"

"He's at his grandmother's in Middleton."

"How convenient," she drawled.

Callie set her drink on a plastic table and picked at a frayed edge of her screen. Her side porch faced Jungle Road where she pictured Alex looking back at her place.

"Callie," Alex said, with a hint of breathless irritation. "You forget I know what you've been investigating."

"I just want you to post—"

"Why is it always what you want?" Alex exclaimed.

"It's a favor. One that might benefit you as a journalist."

"So politely ask, damn it!"

Callie sat frozen, a little stung, trying to slow down and see herself in Alex's shoes. If only people would listen to her. She couldn't tell the world they baited a killer, much less admit to the beach he might be lurking. The news media treated it as a hoax, like the other island ghost stories. Best the Edisto jinx remain considered as such until Callie and Seabrook proved otherwise with an arrest.

"I'm asking you to provide the coverage before and during the event," Callie said, then added, "please."

"Hmmm. By the way, I freaked at that picture of Grant Jamison bleeding on the floor," Alex said. "I almost feel he's stalking me as well as you."

Of course the girl would think that. Callie had completely forgotten that Alex retreated to her grandmother's because of a misstep in Atlanta and still nursed a vulnerable side. Plus she was still so young.

"Just tweet then," Callie said, taking a protective stance. "That's your power anyway. You're quite proficient with those thumbs."

"Ha," Alex said. "That's practically an admission you have a plan. I may not have all the pieces, but I see there's a puzzle. Talk to me. Off the record."

Callie tried to mash the torn piece of screen flat, not responding.

"Fine. Guess I'll have to think about whether I cover your precious party, then," Alex said.

"I wish you would trust me on all this," Callie replied.

"Right back at you." Alex hung up.

Callie went to take another sip, only to find her glass empty. The chat had gone on longer than planned, ending more stupidly than expected. If she were betting, Callie would throw money down on Alex spreading the news. But she might as easily dig in stubbornly and refuse. Goodness knows there were enough other activities to consume her reporting this weekend.

Twelve thirty. Definitely too late to call Sophie, who'd be in bed so she could downward dog at dawn. Callie needed socialites at this party, and Sophie's social skills surpassed anyone's.

Callie started to sit and listen to the wildlife like she did most nights, to clear her mind of humanity. In spite of the beach population, the animals controlled the night. Deer strolled the streets. Raccoon tested trash cans, their tribble-like talk cute despite the damage they did to an unsecured receptacle.

The earlier hot breeze seemed to have found some other shore, and only the mugginess remained along with silence that allowed a distant roar of the surf. A noise lost in the busyness of the day.

But Callie wasn't tired. One drink hadn't slowed her down for bed as much as she'd hoped. Tomorrow would be grueling, a chaotic jumble of food prep, phone calls, deception and nerves.

How would she recognize the killer? Or MyOuttake? Someone who spoke to brunettes too long? A person who snapped too many pictures? Wickedly weird or charismatic? Would he approach a woman or eavesdrop on her conversations with others, hoping to catch her on the way home? Thank God Francis and Seabrook would be there, seeing what she might miss.

Or would they look as hard? Or take her interpretation of a suspect seriously?

Pulse unsettled, she inhaled, trying to force a yawn, but she couldn't find one in her.

No choice but to pour another half glass of Tanqueray, light on the ice.

CALLIE'S ALARM dragged her from a deep sleep at 7:00 a.m. The last tall drink had worked. She hit snooze and swore it cheated her of those extra ten minutes when it seemed to instantly go off again. She scrunched her eyes, then rubbed them hard, squinted, and kicked the coverlet off.

On her way to the shower, the long list of the previous day's events returned to her consciousness, each bringing her more alert. By the time she dried off, she practically had the day's game plan ready. Then dressed, she punched in Sophie's number.

Callie explained they would be preparing food, maybe making calls to inform people. Sophie had no yoga classes on Saturdays, and not fifteen minutes after hanging up, she arrived on Callie's doorstep at eight, way more chipper than a human should be.

Sophie whooshed inside and spun, walking backward as Callie closed the door and headed to the kitchen. Sophie danced in dressed in a yellow batik halter top, white sandals, and capris, her deep Italian tan accenting gold chains around her neck. How had she painted her nails?

"I said to dress down," Callie said. "I'll have to find you an apron. Want coffee before we start? Sweet tea? Toast?"

Sophie waved limp-wristed. "Honey, I ate like two hours ago. You go ahead, though. I know how you and morning don't get along." Scanning Callie, she squinched her eyes. "How many did you have last night?"

Callie poured her friend some tea and ignored the question. "Janet's delivering the food. She's having someone bring the beer and wine over this evening, but the rest of the day we spread the word." She returned to the pantry and pulled out cereal. No eggs this morning. She always craved milk the day after.

"Did Janet Wainwright really ask for us? Did she mention my name? I mean, I thought she hated me. Maybe she finally appreciates my allure at her parties." She pushed a placemat around the table. "Maybe she'd host one at *my* house sometime."

"You ought to ask her."

"Heard from Jeb?" Sophie asked, ever on top of the children. "Sprite's on the phone with him constantly."

"Briefly." Callie shoveled in a spoonful of flakes and talked between the crunching. "He needs to enjoy Mother a while longer."

Bent over the table, arms mashed beneath a set of firm bosoms, Sophie's mouth tightened. "Don't you blame that boy for being there when we sprung on you." She dropped her butt back in the chair. "I'd call your mother a bitch, but you share blood. She's a drama addict, and poor Jeb sat there, doing as told."

Callie inadvertently slurped, a drop dribbling down her chin. She grabbed a napkin from its seashell stand and dabbed. "Don't you think I know all that? But he's got to learn not to do everything she says, with that intervention a perfect example."

"But you exiled him."

"He chose to stay in Middleton, Sophie. Let him work it out. In the meantime, I have this party." She licked her spoon. "Can you get Rikki to help, too?"

Sophie eased back in her chair. "Why?"

"Her dinner tasted scrumptious. Surely she knows how to throw dishes together. I have no idea what Janet's having delivered, but we'll have to pull hors d'oeuvres, dips, and snacks together from whatever ingredients appear. Seems like a Rikki talent."

Sitting straight, Sophie's pixie hair danced at the jolt. "Like those cooking shows on the Food Network?"

Callie snickered. "Yeah, I guess Janet's the judge. What do you say?"

The playfulness left Sophie's eyes. "I say I don't like being played. Do you realize this is the first time I've come over since the fire?"

Callie stiffened. The accusation embarrassed her. "Sorry, I didn't mean to."

"Yeah, you did." Sophie stood, swooped up Callie's empty bowl, and glided to the sink, somehow washing dishes with her fingertips without wetting her gold bracelets and rings. "I'm no fool, honey." She turned from the sink, wiping her hands on a towel. "We both know you aren't one for social galas, and Janet's not your buddy. What's this last minute party for? And by the way, the first hint of a spirit in here, and I'm gone. They don't set fires at my house."

Callie stared at her waiting neighbor, mind churning for the appropriate subterfuge.

Sophie didn't know Grant confessed to killing his wife. Didn't need to. She held a minimal understanding about MyOuttake. She'd never be able to act normal tomorrow night if she knew, especially if anyone talked about the jinx. Her amateur sleuthing might tip off the wrong person.

Now what was Callie supposed to do?

"The mayor," she blurted.

Eyes wide, mouth open in an O, Sophie pecked the air repeatedly with her index finger. "Girl, I saw that on TV! Did he ask you to do this?" Then her expression morphed to cynicism. "I hope he's paying you. You're volunteering for the police, and then they want to use Chelsea Morning, too? That's not very nice."

Callie shrugged and rolled with the charade. "Hey, Seabrook asked, you know? Suddenly I'm in the middle of this high-powered deliberation for a party, and it's like my volunteer police job took on a new dimension. Janet's covering expenses, so . . . what?"

Sophie's head shook slowly. "That story's pure crap, Callie. This party is yours, and it hurts that you feel me too stupid to trust."

Fingertips kneading her temple, Callie weighed whether she needed Sophie badly enough to divulge the details, and while protecting her friend might be considered noble, omitting her from the inner circle felt turncoat. Sophie was right, but maybe Callie was, too? Which was the lesser evil?

And how much would Seabrook prefer remain confidential?

"I'm so disappointed," Sophie said, rising and pushing her chair back under the table. She continued to grip the back and stared down at her friend. "Hope you have fun, or accomplish whatever it is you're doing, but don't count on me. I'm out." Her eyes moistened. "I get enough of this from Rikki."

She left the kitchen and headed to the door.

Callie ran after her. "Sophie, don't be like this. I need you. I'm sorry."

Sophie turned back as she crossed the threshold. "Make sure you lock the door behind me."

Chapter 23

AT NINE IN THE morning, and for the fifth time, Callie searched her phone for Alex Hanson's morning social media posts. The girl flashed vendors, food, and skimpy bathing suits at the craft fair market on *EdistoToday*'s Twitter site. The same material appeared on her Facebook page. But Callie saw nothing about the event at Chelsea Morning. MyOuttake remained completely quiet.

Damn it! She threw a dish towel on the counter and tossed her phone on her table. She'd assumed Alex would jump at this opportunity, and therefore, so would MyOuttake. Now she worried she threw this event for naught. Had they all seen through her? She also began to worry that MyOuttake packed up and went home, which would mean another year to wait for their killer to take his vacation.

Last night she'd raked her mind raw with scenarios and preparations in how to spot this person. In doing so, she'd studied Twitter, learning the hashtag lingo. She'd set up her own account when this whole Twitter exchange started, claiming a name of her own. Maybe it was time to use it.

She had only ten followers, eight people who apparently followed anything Edisto-related, then Alex and MyOuttake. Maybe if she hashtagged #edistotoday, or added Alex's moniker on Twitter, she'd spread the news to a few people. She wasn't skilled at social media.

@EdistoCallie—Come to the Wainwright Realty party on Edisto on Jungle Road. @EdistoToday #edistotoday

Was she allowed to put *EdistoToday* in there twice? Whatever. She hit send. Watched. It disappeared down the line of tweets. Okay.

She sighed and set down the phone. Edisto may have missed its window. At least she liked to think of this effort as Edisto's and not all hers. Brea may have died near the middle or the end of the killer's two-week tour, throwing all their calculations off. And since Grant killed Brea, the killer might have decided to pass this year, claiming her death as part of his plan.

In her experience, however, Callie didn't see this guy so eager to bow to another man's assassination.

Assuming it was a guy.

She refocused on the work before her and opened the flaps to a box on her counter. Five boxes of food stuff had arrived from BI-LO, at Janet's direction. While the gesture reeked generous, Callie knew Janet expected the spread to be representative of the real estate agency.

Callie stared at shrimp, cheeses, so many cheeses, vegetables, crackers.

How was she supposed to do this by herself? She didn't own this many bowls.

And again, what if nobody knew the party existed? Who would get the news out?

She dug into the second box. Chips she could do. She held up a deli-wrapped package. Lobster. Other than dip it in butter and lemon, Callie had no idea what to do with this. She rummaged some more. No crab. Every native out here crabbed; visitors wanted crab.

Callie expected Janet to call before now to shout orders, direct the troops, probably ask what Callie intended to do with the overpriced lobster.

Reluctantly, Callie phoned the agency and waited, eying the wall of food, growing more irked. Her foot tapped the floor. *Wonderful.* Instead of setting up a sting, she cut up carrot sticks.

The receptionist answered on the second ring. "She asked not to be disturbed, Ms. Morgan."

"Of course she did," Callie said.

"Ma'am?"

Callie still felt sorry for that poor girl working Janet's phones. "I'm sorry you're caught in the middle here, but tell her it's me, please, and tell her I can march down there and interrupt, or she can answer the phone."

"Yes, ma'am."

She scratched the nape of her neck, disappointed and irritated. If Sophie hadn't ditched her, she'd be rocking the arrangements, able to keep herself revved and driven to catch their perp. Instead, she was elbow deep in cheese squares.

Janet picked up the line. "Ms. Morgan, is there a crisis?"

Callie stretched her neck and took a second. Her lack of help wasn't Janet's problem, though it sort of was if the party represented Wainwright Realty. "The food arrived. Thanks for providing it."

"I have a client sitting here."

"I'm one person. Do you happen to have anyone who might come help—"

"Ms. Morgan. Are you telling me you cannot accomplish your task?"

"That's exactly what I'm saying. I'm only one person."

"There are a lot of people on this island, my dear. Improvise. Adapt. Overcome." The agent hung up.

Well damn! Callie rested against the counter, resisting the urge to throw her phone in the marsh. What were her options now?

How about Beverly? Callie's mother would jump at the chance to orchestrate a party, probably hog-tie someone on her staff to come with her . . . and take over. Not only would Beverly butt heads with Janet, but Jeb would find out, and Callie didn't want him being here. Just in case.

Seabrook . . . no way, not with this beach crowd. Even if he'd wrangled up all his officers who were missing yesterday.

Ms. Hanson? Callie knew which side she'd have to take with Alex's sour mood.

Sarah? Callie huffed. Wow, how weird to call her father's mistress to put together finger foods? The Rosewood household had endured too much already. Best to leave her be.

Rubbing repeatedly across the back of a chair, she appraised her final option . . . Sophie. Excluding her neighbor from all the real purpose of the party came from a good place. She wanted to protect Sophie as well as protect the mission. How should Callie say, "Sorry, Sophie, but you'll talk too much?" Sophie's biggest asset was her love of people, which easily became her biggest flaw since she rarely culled her friends. She'd embrace Janet if given the chance.

Rehearsing an apology, still unsure how to bridge the need-to-know issue, Callie made the call. It went to voice mail.

"I need you, Sophie. Please come over. I'm sorry I upset you." Then having run out of atonements, she finished with, "Call me . . . please."

Well, the food wouldn't fix itself. She pulled her cutting board from the cabinet and emptied boxes, placing cold items in the refrigerator. As she lifted out the sixth bag of chips, she found a smaller box. The heavy weight slipped out of her fingers. Puzzled, she opened the top and found five hundred flyers for the party with a note. *Pass these out. You're welcome. Janet.*

Was this the sum and total of the island promotion effort she touted last night?

With that, Callie took a seat. Reality flooded in as did a degree of humiliation.

Janet took advantage of her. Callie had begged and pleaded, seeing herself strategic and a bit noble in drawing the citizenry of Edisto into a cooperative effort to solve this jinx. Seabrook would speak to the town administrator. The mayor might even make an appearance. Press wandered around the beach, primed.

A PR nirvana.

Callie brought a golden opportunity to Janet and beseeched her to participate while the Marine mentally hoo-rahed at her good fortune. Her agents would focus on acquiring rental deals while Callie served as Janet's ad hoc PR representative.

And geez, five hundred? She didn't want a tenth of that number in her place, but she figured most of them would get trashed. Janet probably knew more than she.

Nine thirty. Only so many hours left in the day. Callie snared an apron from a drawer. This affair would happen one way or another, and if Janet didn't like the quality of the results, screw her.

For two hours, she diced and concocted what she hoped were proper party snacks. Using a set of hardly-used knives Beverly gave her one Christmas made the work effortless, and she speeded up the process. She had to distribute those flyers while the crowd throbbed at its peak.

She jerked, halting her slap-dash dicing fury. No, no, no, no. Color bled into the moisture of the sliced onion quarter, the red fanning across the plate. Then the sting started, building. She found her nail tip gone on her middle finger and a deep gash across the tip. But the cut in her forefinger seemed to go to the bone.

Not again!

"Damn!" She yelled and threw the onion into the sink, watching it mingle with her blood as both slid down the drain under the water running wide out, like her frustration.

She did not have time for this!

Fifteen minutes later the bleeding diminished from the shallower wound, but the forefinger continued to ooze at a rate that made her nervous. The pain increased. She started dialing Seabrook, the only doc she knew, then decided against it. Her cooking cut didn't outweigh the madness and mayhem that covered Edisto.

Callie breathed deep when fifteen more minutes later, the flow finally slowed. Fingers shriveled and wrapped in a clean paper towel, she ran to the bedroom, yanked out her first aid kit, and bandaged the two wounds tight and thick. She quadrupled the gauze on the bad cut and taped it tighter, sensing that the nastier cut screamed stitches.

Now what, she thought, drudging to the kitchen. She wasn't incapacitated, but not far from it.

The setback seemed worthy of a small gin. One. A dose to settle her down, along with a moment to curb the impatience.

She poured one finger, then two, and before screwing the top back on, she decided to forego the tonic. If Jeb were here to help, she wouldn't be in such a state.

Then with glass to her lips, she stopped. Had she really used Jeb's own argument to justify what he deemed her bad habit? The argument where he said he postponed college because he needed to watch over her?

With a sigh, she funneled the rest of her drink back into the bottle before shoving it across the table. Tomorrow's setup had unnerved her more than she realized.

She thought she'd done well these last couple of months climbing out of that dark, private hole she dug for herself after Boston. Once a popular, savvy officer, respected by hundreds of people, today she found herself scrambling to make sense on how to communicate with the neighbors.

Deal, Callie. Elbow on the table, hand toward the ceiling to stifle blood flow, she scanned the room at all she'd done and had left to do. All this work for what might be for ten people unless she got those flyers distributed. She punched her phone to hunt for *EdistoToday* activity again. Still nothing.

The worse finger smarted. She lightly mashed the medical tape with her thumb, praying the bandage held. She couldn't get it wet, so now what?

"Oh good grief." A hopeful solution almost smacked her out of the chair. The Edisto Sleuth Society might have a serious purpose after all.

Or would she be using them, too? Like Sophie accused her of doing. Like she tried to do to Janet before Janet did it to her. Where did one draw the line between taking advantage and asking for help?

She searched for Frank's number from her phone's history, having long tossed his business card. For a fleeting moment, she wondered if she'd underestimated others in her short time on Edisto. Everybody she encountered wound up adversarial, for reasons she couldn't put her sore, cut up finger on.

But people were dying, and nobody seemed concerned. That drove her, which made her drive others. Was that so wrong? For goodness sake, she appeared to be the only person who recognized the danger.

Alone in her kitchen, beach traffic bustling outside her window, she realized her people skills fell woefully short without a badge. A lump formed in her throat, which irritated her more, and she rubbed an eye with the heel of her hurt palm. She called the ESS leader.

"Frank? This is Callie. I wondered if y'all were still around," she said, making herself smile, almost going for chipper.

"Yeah. Might be leaving tomorrow," he said. "Ava's sunburned. Most of the others are gone."

"Oh," she replied, disappointed.

"Why?" he asked with a bit of hope.

"I wanted to apologize for brushing you off yesterday. They had me running in different directions, and the mayor—"

"Hey, it's okay. You're the real deal. We were only trying to add some zing to our vacation and turned it into too much zeal."

"Well, I wish you wouldn't leave tomorrow," she started, trying to sound more social, hopefully not selfish. Sophie's words still stung. "Janet Wainwright is sponsoring another party, only this time at my house. With this herd of people on the island, nobody's available to help me throw it together. I have flyers to put out, food to fix . . ."

Frank's rowdy chuckle erupted through the phone. "Fix. I like that word you Southerners use."

Callie made herself chuckle. "We have lots of sayings, don't we?"

"So, that Brea lady's hardly cold and that real estate agent wants another shindig, huh? I heard that woman was a powerhouse," he said.

Bypassing the opportunity to denounce Janet, she cleared her throat. "I called to invite you but hoped maybe you'd help me spread the news. You know, like you did canvassing the area last time? Those people recognize you now. And call anyone you met at the last party. Janet's dumped a ton of food on me, and somebody's got to eat it. Beer and wine, too. It would be a good sendoff for the ESS."

"When is it?"

"Tomorrow at five."

After some low mumbles in the background, Frank said, "I think we can manage that."

"I have flyers if you want them," she added.

"Hey, Callie?"

"Yes, Frank."

"Thanks for keeping us in your loop. It means a lot."

She hung up, somewhat relieved and a bit confused. Not sure whether she did right with Frank or wrong with Sophie, she had to get over this emotional mess and set her head on straight for tomorrow night.

Someone rang the doorbell.

She scooted to the door, instinctively nursing her wounds against her, confused and not yet expecting Frank, Ava, or Terrance. Not recognizing the strange young man through the glass, she opened the door slowly.

"Callie Morgan?" he asked.

She glanced toward the stairs but saw no one behind him. "Who are you?"

"I'm with a Charleston news station. Thought I'd grab a quick interview with you about the recent deaths on Edisto, and the so-called voodoo business."

"It's called a jinx, and no thank you."

A cameraman sprang out, having flattened himself against the wall to her right. He aimed his lens in her direction.

Suddenly the reporter straightened as if in front of an audience. "Tell us how this jinx stayed silent so long, Ms. Morgan. What alerted you to this rash of murders?"

"Oh good gosh." She tried to shut the door, but the reporter nonchalantly slid his foot in the way.

Her gaze traveled down to the burgundy loafer, then up to his two-years-out-of-college eyes. "Do you want to keep that foot?" she asked, as if he were an arrogant perp on the street thinking about taking her on.

"Do you deny there are murders on Edisto?"

She maintained the glare. "Move the foot."

"Weren't you present at one of the deaths?"

Typical hardheaded reporter. "Hold on a minute," she said. "Give me a sec." She left the door resting on the man's shoe and ran to the kitchen. She raced back, opened the door wider, gesturing for him to move and let her out on the porch. "Here," she said and pushed a flyer at him. Another to the cameraman. "Cover that, and I'll answer your questions."

In the second he studied the flyer, she reentered the house and shut the door between them. For a second they stared at each other through the glass, his mouth open at her nerve. Then she turned and walked away, fuming at the audacity of journalists.

Television trumped Twitter. *Take that, Alex.*

She returned to her celery, the awkwardness cramping her fingers. She used a spatula to one-handedly move the tiny pieces to a bowl.

Someone rang the bell.

This time expecting Frank, Callie rushed to the hallway, but paused as she recognized the profile on the other side.

She opened the door.

Clad in denim capris, Birkenstocks, and a see-through beige tunic with a mauve tank underneath, Rikki looked down her nose from her six-foot altitude, eyebrow raised. "What are you up to, and why wasn't I called?"

"Who *did* call you?" Callie asked, stepping aside as Rikki made her way in.

"Frank somebody and his band of beach bums we saw at Janet's party," she replied. "They have a phone campaign going, but I already had a heads-up from Sophie. What did you do to your hand?"

Guess the ESS started with the people they'd met, and the group from Brea's event *had* formed somewhat of a bond. Callie reached the kitchen. "A knife attacked me."

Rikki picked up one of knives. "Quality. Let me guess, your mother?"

Callie shrugged.

"This isn't the knife you bloodied up, is it?"

Reaching over, Callie lifted the one from the sink to identify the culprit. But she stopped herself from what she really wanted to say. How Rikki liked to dominate, exactly like this, treating her friends like insubordinates, belittling with the razor-like acuity of these knives.

"Janet sent lobster," was all Callie could think to say with civility.

Rikki strolled around the kitchen, analyzing. "It's seafood. The average tourist won't care."

So she really came to help? "Thanks for coming," Callie replied then silently watched as the Amazon laid out the various bags, bottles, and deli items in some configuration clear only to her.

With foodstuffs placed into assorted piles, Rikki jotted a list on a notepad on the refrigerator. "Sophie's pissed."

"Yeah."

"Sophie told me how the party came to be, Callie. The mayor? Taking advantage of you? I don't buy it any more than she did. You're anything but a pushover." Rikki stacked the empty boxes inside each other and tried to carry them past Callie.

"I'll take those." Callie dropped them outside. She returned, finding Rikki reorganizing the refrigerator.

Callie held the door as it tried to shut. "Look at me," she said.

Rikki did, but in doing so, rose to her full height, forcing Callie to peer up see her face. Both let the refrigerator door close, removing the divide between them.

"You and I don't exactly understand each other," Callie began firmly, "so let's clear the air."

Rikki cocked her hip. "Agreed."

"Sophie's a friend."

Rikki scoffed through her nose. "She's been my friend for over a decade, versus your weeks. And you sure seem hell bent on crashing that relationship . . . not to mention your own."

Callie frowned. "What?"

"She adores you, but from what I've heard, she's also been a wreck since you appeared. You realize why I'm here?" Rikki asked. "It's because Sophie asked me to check on you. I'd do anything for her. You, however, have dragged her into shit she had no business being involved in." She rolled both wrists and aimed fingers at the floor as she swaggered side to side. "My coming here is to keep her from getting sucked into your crisis, whatever it is."

"I'm *keeping* her out of a crisis," Callie replied firmly.

"You entertain her ghost stories."

"You discount her beliefs."

This rally appeared never-ending, and drama was not on Callie's to-do list today. Plus a faceoff with Rikki would end badly with Callie losing her much-needed help. Sophie's accusation that Callie used people echoed again in her mind.

Rikki bent down. "You're up to something."

"For the better good of the beach," Callie replied, instinctively stretching her spine for height. "Leave if you like. I have a little over twenty-four hours to plan a party and don't have time to waste."

Reaching over for the last container of sour cream, Rikki opened the refrigerator door, set it on a shelf, and closed the fridge. "Why don't you like me?"

Oh good gracious. "Let's cut to the chase, Rikki. You treat Sophie like a child, laugh at her beliefs, and make her think less of herself. I've lifted her out of her doldrums twice after seeing you." Callie disliked how that sounded, but so be it.

The accusation unexpected, Rikki reared. "She's always seeking favor which makes her vulnerable. I keep her grounded."

Callie warned herself not to argue, but Rikki made Callie uncomfortable. In some way she wanted the woman to feel watched. "Sophie seeks favor, but you have a strange way of showing devotion. You border on psychological abuse. I work hard to protect her."

"I do, too."

The impasse stumped them both. Rikki's honesty was hard to read, but they didn't have the luxury of an afternoon to hammer this out. "We might have to agree to disagree, Rikki."

"Make sure nothing happens to her, you hear?"

"The same to you—"

Rikki pointed the knife to the table. "Sit. You're no good to me crippled. When I ask, tell me what you'd prefer me to do. Sophie told me to make this happen."

She had? When Sophie left, Callie assumed the yoga mistress burnt the bridge between Chelsea Morning and Hatha Heaven.

And was that a roundabout apology from Rikki? Curious, Callie sat as told, then a realization sank in.

With unexpected finesse, Sophie had turned on them both, pitting Callie and Rikki against each other to beat out their conflict, and to make each see how it stressed Sophie.

"You're just different, that's all," the Amazon said, her back to Callie as she rummaged through the utensil drawer. "Sophie talks about you all the time. Said we had a lot in common."

The way Rikki spoke her last words softened, seemingly lined with hurt. Jealousy? Rikki carried herself regally, as if she owned whatever ground she walked on, but maybe she wore a façade. She didn't seem quite the alpha personality anymore.

Finding the knife she needed, Rikki then opened every cabinet, taking inventory of her tools. Satisfied, she checked her phone, started to set it on the bar out of the way, then stopped. She raised the device as a sign toward Callie.

Callie grabbed her own. A few new pictures appeared from *EdistoToday*. The ocean. Sea oats. Some kids boogie-boarding along the water's edge. Nothing about the party.

There. Callie reserved reaction, but glanced up to see Rikki watching her.

MyOuttake posted a frontal pic of Chelsea Morning with a caption: *This is where the action happens tomorrow on Edisto.*

Chapter 24

"GO," RIKKI SAID, setting a bowl of Callie's fresh-made onion dip in the sink. She then opened cabinets until she found a new bowl. "Go do your thing. You'll drive *me* nuts sitting here watching you go nuts." She scowled at the sink. "Besides, mayonnaise doesn't make a dip, sweetheart, and it seems the only ingredient you use."

"I know how to cook," Callie said.

"I know better," Rikki replied.

Whatever, Callie thought. "Maybe I don't want to leave you alone."

Rikki put down the knife. "What, I'll ransack the house and steal your jewelry? Let's compare bank accounts and settle this right now."

Shaking her head in irritation, Callie rose from the table. "No, that's not what I meant."

Rikki waved toward the living room. "Then go do your thing."

The Amazon seemed comfortable making the kitchen hers, and Callie trusted Rikki as a chef, but the personal stuff stumped her. For instance, she strode in and offered help, in the name of Sophie. Was Rikki sincere or earning points to cash in later?

But Callie couldn't afford to be choosy. She rushed to her bedroom and donned cargo capris, a tank, and a gauzy long-sleeve shirt. Sneakers. She hesitated on whether to pocket her .38, then decided against it. She'd be surrounded by too many people.

Returning to the kitchen, she retrieved her phone and the box of flyers. At early afternoon, the crowd should be at its peak. "Thanks again, Rikki. I'll lock the door behind me."

"Yeah, I heard you're big on that."

Big sigh. "I guess I owe you."

"Yes, ma'am, you do," the Amazon replied, not looking up.

Callie would worry what that meant later. Checking for posts about the party and still finding none, Callie pocketed her phone. She walked the mile to the craft fair easily; a car wouldn't make it half the distance for the congestion.

Annually Edisto held several festivals and markets, parades, and cook-offs. They infused quaintness into the beach's personality while giving the vendors a financial shot in the arm. The right stars must've aligned with the proper planets, because the temperature remained only ninety, the breeze light and lazy, and the tide out as if to make more room for the extra bodies. The result: bathing attire on half the folks and wall-to-wall people at the fair. Everyone sweated and seemed happy doing it.

Gulls screamed overhead, zipping to and fro from the water to the large parking lot of vendors, giddy at so many pawns willing to feed the native wildlife. The mobile snow-cone shack threw out frigid sugary treats as fast as they shaved the ice, with customers ten deep. Kitchen tiles painted with sea creatures, hand-woven hammocks, sweet grass baskets, and watercolor landscapes filled canopied tents, their creators excited and personable at a throng so eager to spend.

Three tents let Callie leave a small stack of flyers. Today proved as perfect an August day as Callie could imagine for enticing people to a party, and her nerves dissipated a bit with each flyer she gave out. She tried not to think of the invitations as bait.

McConkeys poured iced tea from umbrella tables at the base of their restaurant's porch stairs. She gave out a few there. A bluegrass band played under a small tent. She wove in and out of the listeners, delivering invitations and moving on with the music too loud for them to ask questions.

An obnoxious guffaw caught Callie's attention as she exited the music. A striking, flat-bellied redhead in a string bikini and silk sarong sloshed some of her beer on her bare-chested beau sporting a straw fedora. She gave them one.

Rhonda Benson bumped into Callie, turned, and giggled loud. "Isn't this grand?"

"I guess so," Callie replied, bodies routing around her like water past a rock.

The chunky real estate agent with a fondness for silver and gold clothing resembled a past-her-prime Los Angeles society player. Her fondness for Callie traced to her doing business with Callie's parents and their rental, when Beverly fired Janet. Rhonda had considered Callie's father hot.

"Thanks to you, these Edisto people will make a killing selling their goodies," Rhonda said. "Your television interview did a job, didn't it?"

"I'm sure I didn't do all this." Shading her eyes in spite of her sunglasses, Callie tiptoed and scanned across the heads for a uniform, difficult to do from her five-foot-two level.

She started to give a flyer to a thin-haired senior in wraparound glasses about her height. An unwieldy broad-brimmed pool hat protected her from UV rays, a fat pink rose pinned to the band. Callie decided the paper would quickly find its way to a trash can.

Rhonda bent in close, lifting her sunglasses to read the flyer. "What do you have there?"

"Here," Callie said, peeling off about fifty. "Hand these out for me."

The agent twisted her head, a brow arched. "Are you crazy? These are for Janet."

Callie forgot to see Rhonda as Janet's competition. Before Rhonda asked why, Callie recycled the story that fell flat on Sophie. "Got roped into this by the mayor."

Rhonda tilted her head in a small pout. "Poor girl. Got to watch these allegiances out here. Some of them will bite you on the ass." Her head swiveled, searching. She seemed to settle on someone and wiggled her fingers, the silver nail polish glinting. "Got to go. Ta-ta."

Before long, passing flyers became second nature. She continued to hunt for Seabrook, to confirm if the county had loaned any of its deputies. At the same time she sought Frank or Terrance, maybe Ava's two-inch blonde ponytail and massive muumuu.

Two women approached. Callie extended a flyer and then withdrew when one took off her sunhat to readjust it, and brunette hair toppled out. The third time she'd caught herself profiling potential victims.

"What're you doing out here, Detective Morgan?"

Scouring through the masses, Callie hunted the source of the young female voice.

Alex hiked around people like they were trees in a forest. She pranced, adorable in cutoff jeans and a pink sports bra under a baggy navy tank top. A Carolina Panthers baseball cap shaded her eyes, her ponytail stuck out the hole. "How's it going?" she asked, then grinned at the flyers.

Callie read the smirk. "Janet gave them to me."

Alex moved closer to hear. "See my posts?" She leaned over to show, as if Callie owned no phone, but Callie paid no attention.

"I see no mention of a party, if that's what you mean," she said, reaching out with another flyer, then another as people strolled by.

Alex ignored the remark. "My numbers spiked. MyOuttake finally woke up."

"Wait. What?" Callie squinted, the sun reflecting off the phone.

Alex scrolled. "Oh my gosh, look at that," she whispered.

@MyOuttake—Edisto Detective Morgan and EdistoToday proving two heads are better than one.#edistotoday

The picture . . . the two of them, heads together, trying to talk in the noise.

Callie snapped to and scanned from the direction the picture might have been taken. Alex craned, too. Old, young, male, female, clean cut, hippie, redneck, the medley hid the culprit well. Any person with a smartphone possessed the potential to snap and slither away.

Another tweet appeared of a group of women taste-testing benne seed wafers. A woman fed her friend a French fry. Callie hunted for that view and missed it.

The pulse in her neck thrummed. "You have competition," Callie said, pushing her voice, trying not to show her worry.

"Yeah." Alex smiled. "It's weird doing battle with live tweets, but cool as long as he keeps mentioning *EdistoToday*. I'm toying with asking one of these Charleston reporters to interview me about it. What do you think?"

But Callie's attention wandered elsewhere, passing over the legion of tourists like a drone, skimming for the anomaly. He probably saw her now, overly attentive, vigilant, giving him a sense of control. But the fact was the more he posted, the better Callie followed him. Nothing a detective liked better than a trail, and MyOuttake had started to let his ego get the better of him.

As a detective, she lived for this sort of chase. The thrill of advance. The perp stalking her only brought him closer to her reach. His need to communicate fed her information.

She'd already noticed that every picture centered on women. At least one in each shot in her thirties, with dark hair. This guy *was* the killer. She felt it. MyOuttake had to be the Edisto jinx.

CALLIE RETURNED TO Chelsea Morning around seven to find the door locked. Once inside, she found a note from Rikki: *Remember, you owe me. I'll see you tomorrow night.*

Not only was the refrigerator exploding with covered dishes, but the refrigerator in the storage room almost overflowed its capacity, too.

"Impressive." Callie meant it, briefly wondering about her future indebted to Rikki Cavett.

Retrieving a fork, she peeked into the closest dishes on the refrigerator shelf, snooping for chicken salad, or . . . wait. Oh my goodness, seafood dip. She filled her fork. *Yum.* So that's what Rikki did with the lobster.

Images popped into her head of Brea writhing on the floor. She slapped the cover on the bowl. A woman died from something Callie ate without a second thought. She needed a warning sign for the guests. That story line wasn't happening again, particularly in her house.

A knock sounded. Callie slammed the refrigerator as if caught in the cookie jar. Using her finger to wipe the corners of her mouth, she ran to answer, halfway expecting Janet. Not recognizing the distorted face on the other side of the leaded glass, she stopped.

After half-sliding the credenza drawer open where her .38 lay hidden, she opened the door. "May I help you?"

A twenty-something man held out an Edisto T-shirt and a Sharpie pen. "Dude, I mean, ma'am, can I get your autograph? I can't be at the party." He turned around and spoke down the porch stairs. "Yeah, it's really her. I have a pen. Get up here."

Repositioning his ball cap, he tucked his chin down, embarrassed. "Saw you on the news." He held a flyer, then folded it and put it in his back pocket as it gained him admission. "Someone said you killed a guy, too. That's f—in cool." He turned around again. "Dude, get your ass up here."

She hung behind the threshold, cautious . . . then a sharp awareness rose in her. An idiotic awareness of how the flyers invited people just like this to set foot on her place. People awestruck about her biography and eager for free food.

Another man close in age in low-riding cargo shorts appeared with a road map. "Can she sign this?"

"Your names?" Callie asked, quickly taking his pen and paper.

"Porter," said one.

"Justin," said the other. "We came from Orangeburg on a whim. Never been to Edisto before. You need a McDonalds out here or something."

Callie scribbled a fabricated, illegible signature on the shirt then the map. "Y'all have a good day."

Porter actually tipped his ball cap. "Thanks, ma'am."

Then she shut the door and listened as the guys compared the two autographs and tromped down the stairs. Decent enough boys. But the next ones might not be so.

And tomorrow Chelsea Morning would welcome every inquisitive, bored, or cheap character on the beach, thanks to Janet's flyers and Callie's fervor.

She yanked out the vacuum to give the house a once-over, picturing where strangers would and wouldn't be allowed to wander. The floor not too dusty, the task went quickly. About the time she reached Jeb's bedroom, she heard pounding on her front door. She flipped off the vacuum expecting more autograph hounds.

"Callie Morgan?"

That voice sounded familiar.

"Yes?" she answered loud, still gripping the vacuum hose.

"It's Ben Rosewood. We need to talk right now."

"What about, Ben?" she asked loud, then worked her way to the credenza.

Never had Callie seen Sarah's husband demonstrate violence, but his words in the past showed potential. Sarah's tentative behavior likewise raised Callie's suspicion of how agitated this man might be.

He raised his voice. "Do you mind if we don't yell through a closed door?"

Now that she thought about it, she'd been opening doors to strangers all day. Why not Ben?

The .38 revolver rested in a small suede holster with a clip on the side. Callie slid it behind her, letting the clip fit onto her waistband. She cracked the door open and stood half behind it. "What is it?"

His face flushed, a whiff of alcohol carried to Callie's nose. "Leave my wife alone," he said. "You're not a real cop, so stay off my property."

Some adrenaline kicked in as Callie wondered if something went down at home. "Is Sarah okay?"

"Like it's a Cantrell's damn business," he growled.

She yearned to step in for Sarah, tell Ben his wife feared him, but how ridiculous was that? She craved to defend her father, too, but she had better sense. "Sarah's been through a lot, Ben."

His wavering posture confirmed he'd consumed a few. "Partially thanks to you and your bastard father." He grasped the doorframe as if about to come inside.

No way would she let him in. Not with his belligerence and her being alone. Callie retreated a step, assumed a stance, and reached around. "Back off, Ben."

The man frowned. "You're shittin' me. You'd actually shoot?"

Callie's fret for the wife magnified. "Back away and answer me, *now*. Is Sarah okay?"

"Of course. Why wouldn't she be?"

"Then get off my porch." She didn't want to tell him to go home. Sarah might have booted him out.

His equilibrium unstable, his foot slipped off the one-inch doormat, but he righted himself with the railing. Callie watched him make his way down the steps.

She locked the door and called Sarah.

"Are you at home? Safe?" Callie asked.

"I'm still at the Hansons'," she said. "I'm fine. Why?"

"Ben got in, and he's drunk. He left here on his way to your place. I worried—"

"Callie, I appreciate the concern, but he'd never hurt me. I need to get over there."

Callie heard a small quake in the tone. "Are you sure? You can call me, or 9-1-1, right?"

"I'm good. Thank you."

"Wait, before you go, how's Grant?"

"Oh, I'm sorry. I should've called. There's no bullet. It ripped his scalp badly but didn't enter his skull."

Callie paused. "That's good." She waited again for Sarah to bring around the fact Grant would be charged with murder. She'd already given Seabrook the recording and after the weekend, they'd prepare her signed statement witnessing the confession.

"Well, I need to go meet Ben, Callie."

"Yes, well, take care, Sarah."

Callie started to call Seabrook, but he hadn't the manpower for a domestic situation that hadn't happened. She was flummoxed how to . . . evolve with the Rosewoods.

But that problem merited another day for quandary, just not today. Or tomorrow.

After stowing the vacuum, she walked her house, noting where visitors would gather. She posed in a dozen different places, judging where she ought to station herself for the best vantage. Then she readjusted her five indoor cams a few inches here and there, totally relocating one since she planned to tastefully block her bedroom with a thin sofa table and lock Jeb's door.

She pulled the .38 loose from her waistband. With so many individuals arriving, her sidearm would go in her bedroom closet, the entry hall credenza no place for a gun. No risk wearing it, either, for safety and appearance's sake.

As she stood in the middle of her living room, gun in hand, Ben rushed back to mind. Just seeing she carried the weapon made him stand down. Before that, his engine revved to bully.

Poor Sarah. Marriages got rocky. Couples disagreed. But until Ben lashed out and injured Sarah, nobody would react. Like the party the next day. The killer could waltz in, scoop crab dip on his cracker, and pop open a beer, but what could Callie do until he took a crack at taking another life?

Chapter 25

SUNDAY ARRIVED dazzling and warm, breezes lively enough to remind tourists they cruised the beach, and hair-styling wasn't allowed. Callie swept the porches, hid her conch shell collection, and tucked framed photos in drawers, the what-ifs pinging in her brain about the party commencing at five. Nerves reminded her that while she swept, a killer prepped as well.

At least she hoped.

At three in the afternoon Janet called. "Did you manage the food, or did I waste my money?"

Phone to her ear, Callie stood damp in front of her bathroom mirror toweling off, not meaning to be this late getting dressed. "I would've called you if I hadn't."

"I'll be making an appearance," the old woman said.

Callie dropped the towel and rummaged through her underwear drawer. "As you should since it's presented as your party. Any idea when you'll arrive?"

"Does it matter?"

"No, Janet, I guess it doesn't, but I could use your help hostessing." Callie's scrutiny would be on the behaviors in attendance, scanning for those who obsessed with their cameras, matching Twitter posts to the potentials in the room.

Hunting for a killer.

But Janet hung up without a goodbye. Still holding her mascara wand, Callie dodged the instinct to roll her eyes. Janet's behavior was what it was, and in two hours, folks would arrive with expectations of a Wainwright Edisto function.

No wonder Janet and Callie's mother clashed. They shared too many traits in common, only with different delivery systems. Janet in hard-charging mode, with Beverly more of a slip-it-in-your-back style. Callie straightened at the thought. Good gracious, she prayed the event came and went without Beverly catching on. The idea of her mother making an appearance made her head hurt.

Her cut fingers hurt even more now. She grimaced removing the old gauze. The deeper one really needed stitches, but she already knew how to weather a scar. She popped three aspirin, slathered on ointment, and bandaged the two digits as minimally as possible. She threw Band-Aids on the palm abrasions from the trash can falling on her.

Clothing choice proved an issue, now that she thought about it. With a mini-smirk she pondered what Seabrook would like, then she thought sensibly and considered what she would wear that wouldn't impede her movement if she needed to react. Shoes especially important.

But she wanted to blend in, too.

She settled on natural, spinning off comfortable woven flats and worked from there. She yearned for her favorite peach-colored skirt of a loose cotton weave that flowed with a bohemian flair. But logic steered her to a linen-blend pair of beige slacks. To avoid her scar being a topic of conversation, she layered a see-through gauze tunic over a silk camisole. Loose, easy to move in, and with the long seashell necklace, she fit the setting. She turned in front of the mirror. Seabrook might even be pleased. Assuming that mattered anymore.

Neil Diamond's albums remained hidden in the entertainment center, the turntable in her closet. Instead, tunes played from her television where she'd found a beach channel.

She went to work setting out napkins, cups, and anything that wouldn't get too warm, too cool, or soggy in the humid air. Taped to the wall behind the table, she put a sign: *Do not eat if you have a seafood allergy.*

There. At a quarter to four, she flopped on the sofa, arms spread over the throw pillows, surveying all the work. Heck, she already felt spent. Laying her head back, she shut her eyes and listened to the ceiling fan whirr overhead, its hint of air movement settling over her as she willed her muscles to sag into the cushions.

She had some regrets. A cold case, an uncaught murderer, on her home turf. Eyes still closed, she slowly shook her head. She knew exactly what had drawn her into the jinx affair, and into this setup. The same magnetic pull that made her chase the Russian family and every other so-and-so who opted for crime, and for some damn reason, felt they possessed a God-given right to carry it out. Ignoring these lowlifes equated to letting your child play in traffic, thinking yours would never get hit. Eventually it hit close to home, making you rue not taking a stance sooner.

The auxiliary position scratched a small itch, but did she stop there? Seabrook would give her his job in a heartbeat. Edisto would be such an easy tour of duty.

She snorted, eyelids still shut.

The doorbell rang. Callie inhaled deeply and rose from her respite. Time to play ball.

The clock read only four, but Callie graciously welcomed the first couple inside. The woman wore shorts and an Edisto T-shirt, the man the same. "We're renting and were told this party was part of the package. We're not too early, are we?"

Ah, so Janet did spread some word. Callie showed them to the dining table and the bar. A huge Yeti cooler sat in the corner of the kitchen full of ice. "Sure, come help yourself to some food. The alcohol's there. The soft drinks beside it. There's the water."

Where was the Wainwright agent Janet vowed would man the door? Callie wouldn't call Janet . . . not to be hung up on again.

More knocks. More guests. By four thirty, Janet's assistant, the same agent from the Brea event, finally took over at the door after a mad dash to record everyone's name in her all-important sign-in book.

"I love the way this house is decorated," said the woman who arrived first, feeling particularly chummy with Callie since they'd had a chance to talk before guests appeared. "May I see the bedrooms and the second floor? How much is the rent?"

To keep her space within view of her cams, Callie blocked off the bedrooms. "I'm sorry, but this house isn't for rent this year. But Ms. Wainwright has a few floorplans almost like it, one that's even closer to the beachfront."

Totally fabricated, but Janet wouldn't deny it and would somehow make the tenant happy.

By the advertised five o'clock, thirty people draped across her furniture and welcomed themselves on her porches, and when Callie peered outside, she saw ten more strolling into her drive.

Come on, Francis. If Seabrook's too busy, at least you can show.

She extracted her phone from her pants pocket, another reason for the wardrobe selection.

@EdistoToday—The party has started at Chelsea Morning. Come see where everyone is on #edistotoday.

Now Alex tweets. Surely she wouldn't miss coming over.

Callie's pulse kicked in as the noise level rose. She committed every face to memory as she played hostess.

As hoped for, MyOuttake retweeted Alex's posts. Good, good. The beach was small enough for people to make last minute decisions to come. Add that to Janet's promo, whatever it amounted to, and the plan still had potential. He, or she, would want to be here, and a killer wouldn't be running loose amongst the masses. At least for a Sunday afternoon.

She scrolled through the secondary posts from people retweeting Alex's tweets. Then MyOuttake's new post lodged Callie's heart in her throat.

@MyOuttake—The jinx is alive and well, Ms. Morgan. Let's do this.#edistotoday

Her head snapped up. From her front porch vantage, she searched the approaching crowd. Nobody appeared like anyone she'd label as a killer, but that meant nothing. Everyone arrived with someone, no singles. In Boston she'd been taught by Stan, in his early days of mentoring her, that advanced surveillance saved time and possibly lives. In a critical setting, she learned to basically snapshot people. Appearing to relax against the railing, she memorized something about every face, cataloging their dress, hair, walk, who they came with.

Then Callie sidled to the agent standing guard. "Make sure everyone signs."

"Duh?" While the agent wasn't quite the sandpaper irritation of Janet, she obviously schooled at Janet's knee. Reliable only to the Marine.

Callie returned inside. One by one she made the rounds chatting, connecting, reminding herself of the personalities. Taking note of the brunettes. Four fit the profile, no, five.

Not counting her.

"May I get you anything?" she asked people first, then the all-important, "Where are you from?" and, "Have you been to Edisto before?" Not that the killer would tell the truth, but she might see the deception in their eyes.

Guests asked for her autograph more times than she liked and way more times they complimented her on her television appearance. Their attention stayed on her more intently than she expected.

"So you're a detective?"

"Have you killed anyone?"

"Is this jinx thing real?"

"What's it like being a cop on the beach. Cushy job, right?"

The crowd pushed in on her, the voices overwhelming the music. The lack of control threatening to overwhelm her. She needed Edisto PD backup. She checked her phone, now a glued fixture in her hand.

@MyOuttake—Am I there yet or not? #edistojinx #edistotoday

"I get it," shouted a twenty-something guy, raising his beer in one hand, his phone with the other. "It's a game! This whole thing has been an advertising stunt." He laughed. "That's awesome!"

"What's a game?" asked a lady nearby, appearing to be twice his age.

"The online Twitter posts about Edisto and this pretend jinx thing," the guy explained.

A young brunette girl almost thirty nodded in understanding. "Actually, that's pretty cool. So are there any rules? Who are we looking for?"

One of the guests snared Callie's arm, the one with the sore bandaged fingers. "What's the prize?"

"I'm not sure that's what's happening," Callie said, wincing when the woman's purse knocked her injured fingers. "Ask Janet Wainwright when she arrives. She's the sponsor."

The conversation level crescendoed, abuzz with the new excitement.

Callie hugged her sore hand to her waist after being hit for the third time. After six. Where was Seabrook?

"I bet this MyOuttake guy works for the real estate company, pretending to be one of us," yelled the young guy who started the wave of interest, now making himself home in her kitchen.

"A free week at the beach would be nice," shouted a man from across the living room.

"All right!" yelled someone else, and the remark seemed to take permanent form as people nodded in fevered acceptance.

A small alarm surged through Callie, not expecting anyone but she and MyOuttake to be involved in this test of observation. Instead, her guests fed the challenge, more of them following MyOuttake, a few responding with jokes and quips of their own. His followers numbered two hundred more since Friday's television interview.

She took note of the more dynamic instigators, wondering if her adversary had planted them or become one of them. She wondered about his strategy. MyOuttake could be anyone with a phone, which now meant about eighty percent of the room.

Alex walked in, signed the guest book, and paused in the hallway to snap a picture.

Callie meandered through people to reach her and gently put her good arm around the girl, whisking her off to the side. The journalist ogled her, surprised they'd jumped from adversaries to BFFs. Cornering Alex on the stairs leading to the spare bedroom, Callie glanced around to see if anyone noticed. Now a quasi-celebrity, her premature attempt to remain discreet had evaporated.

"Bet you love me now!" Alex grinned ear to ear. "Wow, my tweets worked. Pure delish!"

"Don't tell anyone who you are," Callie said under her breath. "They think this is a game, that you're in cahoots with Janet, and there's some golden ticket if someone identifies MyOuttake."

Alex's head dipped in disbelief, her mouth open. "Say what?"

Callie tilted her head toward the throng. "Scan the room. What are they doing?"

Alex studied the people, now wall-to-wall. She waved at a girl near the food table holding an empty bowl. "That woman wants more dip or something."

"Alex! The people. What are they all doing?"

"Reading their phones. I don't get it. What's wrong with that? Everyone seems to be enjoying themselves. And you might pull off a successful party. Janet ought to be thrilled at the rental potential."

The blogger wouldn't see anything wrong with the situation, but for Callie, everyone watching their phones meant no disparity amongst the guests. MyOuttake would blend in like spit in the ocean.

But Callie couldn't explain all that to Alex. "Oh, never mind," she said and ran toward the front door to find a quiet spot to call.

Damn it! Seabrook needed to be here now! Right friggin' now.

"We're out of two things over here," hollered the same hungry girl.

Stopping in the kitchen on her way to the door, Callie retrieved several filled bowls, ripped off their covers, and set them on the table. Thank God for Rikki.

Phone to her ear, she dashed outside. People stood in pockets in the drive under her house, along the steps, peering down on her and waving from the porch. Sixty or seventy in number. Remembering a spot behind the *pittosporum* bushes on the side of her drive, palmettos shading overhead and the wax myrtles from next door blocking the sun, she hid, dialed, and waited for Seabrook to answer.

The call went to voice mail.

She hit redial. Voice mail again.

She texted. *Where are you? It's crazy and I can't watch everybody.*

She picked a leaf off the tall shrubbery as she waited, bent it in her fingers, and dropped it into the mulch. Then another. Sweat formed on her upper lip, and she wiped it off. She flipped to Twitter.

Alex obviously continued her coverage from inside Chelsea Morning, broadcasting captions to pictures of the revelers. Either she had maneuvered to appear right under their noses, or the house filled thicker than a Hollywood after-Oscar bash.

A chill rippled through Callie in spite of the muggy heat as she caught the next post.

@MyOuttake—Where are you, Detective Morgan? I'm here and you're not. #edistotoday #edistojinx

But he added no picture. Could be a taunt. Or he indeed poised inside, which meant she didn't want him to leave.

@EdistoCallie—Or maybe I'm here and you're not. #edistotoday

The phone dinged. Seabrook finally answering.

Can't come. Can't send anyone.

Heaving a huge sigh, her arms fell to her sides. Son of a stinkin' bitch. She tried to call him again. Then again. Then again.

He answered, speaking low into his phone. "What, Callie? We've got an issue."

"What's wrong?" she asked, her core needing to understand what had become more important than their plan. Last night Seabrook expressed his nerves about the event, eager to help keep her and others safe. This wasn't like him.

"We got a call that a girl was abducted on Myrtle Street."

Oh geez. "Did she fit our victim description?"

"Why do you think I'm here and not there?"

This was so not right.

She heard voices in the call's background. Someone talking fast, upset. "Who witnessed the abduction?" she asked.

"Whoever called it into the station. They told Marie a black van pulled alongside the walking girl, some unseen person dragging her inside. Caller hung up without identification," he said. "Twenty minutes ago. I've got the rest of my men scattered, mainly near the entrance to the beach, hunting that van. The first house I knocked on happened to be where a girl of her description stays, but they don't know if she's missing or not. They thought she went to the beach."

The anonymous person called the station instead of 9-1-1? Marie told her at the station that only the residents knew to do that. The girl disappeared in broad daylight, on one of the busiest weekends of the year. No witness other than the source.

She wasn't buying it.

But Seabrook had to treat it like a legitimate abduction.

"I'd come help, Seabrook, but I've got to stay here. This ball is rolling. We don't need another crime happening under our noses."

"And I'm sorry about that, but—"

"Nothing you can do. Find the girl. But have you considered the intent of this alleged abduction?" she asked.

"The jinx. I know."

"No, Seabrook. To draw you away from here."

The pause was palpable. "Watch yourself, Callie. I'll get there when I can."

Chapter 26

CALLIE STARED awestruck at the marsh behind Chelsea Morning. Her phone said almost 7:00 p.m., and a shiver of isolation ran across her shoulder blades in spite of the heat and a hundred house guests. A breeze blew between the houses, playing with her tunic, rattling the palm fronds overhead, and a male painted bunting flew off, as if seeking a calmer place to hide. Callie might've enjoyed the uncommon sighting if a dozen worries weren't suffocating her. She'd enticed the jinx killer to her home only to possibly face him alone . . . basically inviting him to the shooting range to pick his target.

"Excuse me, are you Callie Morgan?"

Callie spun, her heart leaping at being discovered. The empty bowl girl jumped, her hands wrapped around a drink cup.

"Yes, I'm Callie. Everything okay upstairs?" She re-sorted her thoughts, ready to deflect another autograph hound. She needed to return to the party, where Chelsea Morning might more than ever be Ground Zero. Thank God this girl had strawberry-colored hair.

The girl shrugged one shoulder. "Sorry to interrupt, but there's an intimidating white-haired woman upstairs wanting you bad." She grimaced. "She's sorta scary the way she told me what to do."

Janet. Good. "Thanks. She can be that way." Then for some odd reason, Callie remembered Sophie's advice to make nice. "Are you having a good time?"

"Oh, yes, ma'am."

"Good, good."

They peered at each other in an awkward moment before Callie tipped her head in thanks and scampered back. In an afterthought, she gazed down the street, wondering whether Sarah went home to Ben. He stood on his porch, watching her.

Creepy.

But Janet awaited her presence inside. As Callie rounded the bottom of the stairs, she grabbed the railing. Voices called out behind her, and she stopped.

"The Edisto Sleuth Society has arrived," Frank bellowed from the walk, and Ava tittered from his shadow, wearing yet another muumuu, only with gold sandals this time, a glittered seashell glued to the top of each one. "And it looks like just in time," Frank added, holding up his phone to the whole crew. "Our online friend is in fine form already."

Callie hugged the husky insurance salesman with her good arm, happy to see an ally. "Thank goodness you're here. Can you tend bar?" She turned to Ava. "Can you watch the food? Everything's either in the kitchen or downstairs refrigerator."

Blushing at the intimacy, Frank cut a glance at his wife. "Sure, Callie, sure."

Amused at her husband's bumbling behavior, Ava laughed. "As long as I can sample."

Terrance slid around, beaming, smelling like fresh shampoo. "Sorry we're late. What can I do? Whoa, what happened to your fingers?"

Callie dropped her hand to her side. "The hazard of hors d'oeuvres. But you can work the room, Terrance. Make sure nothing breaks. And find me if you recognize anyone from the other party." She stopped short of saying who she hunted for, but all three knew.

Then she climbed the stairs and into the house. Clad in an orange silk sleeveless tunic and linen slacks, Rikki already held a drink right inside the door. She cut loose a hearty laugh to a cluster of women, raising a brow and her glass at Callie as she returned down the hallway to play host.

But she'd already been dethroned.

Janet stood in charge in the middle of the living room shaking hands, her red blazer vivid amongst the beachy colors. The mayor stood at her side doing the same, neat but informal in his Hawaiian shirt. Smartphones rose everywhere for photos.

And Sophie served the dignitaries drinks.

A sage green crocheted skirt hung off her hips, a jungle print camisole barely meeting the skirt, each movement flaunting her yoga abs and Italian complexion. Every man in the room had taken his eyes off his phone, and his date, in hope of seeing her bend over and stretch the knit stitches in that skirt.

"Ah, here's our detective now," the mayor said, sweeping his arm wide. A dozen cameras clicked and preserved the moment when he welcomed Callie to his side in a fatherly fashion. "A fine addition to our already extraordinary police force." He bent over and whispered in her ear, "Where's the chief?"

Callie whispered in return, "He texted that there's an issue on Myrtle. He'll be here when he can."

With his wide smile still intact, he spoke back through his teeth, "Well, I appreciate you representing him, Ms. Morgan. You make for a better photo shoot anyway."

A rousing surge of voices traveled the room. "He's here," someone said, waving his phone in the air. "He's really here."

Everyone gazed down at theirs or someone else's phone. There Callie was, shaking the mayor's hand, with comments following:

@MyOuttake—I'm in the company of Edisto's elite. Hopefully the seafood isn't a killer this time. #edistojinx

Callie's gut lurched. Her smile still pasted on, she tried to act nonchalant, at the same time studying the audience. The game appeared to be most definitely in full play.

The mayor was pulled aside, answering someone's question.

"Hey," Alex said, from Callie's left, a slight pout on her face. "He's not mentioning me anymore. Where's my *EdistoToday* hashtag? Dang, I really want to meet this guy."

From her other side, Janet gripped Callie's arm in a pinch. "Who is this moron? I don't need people to think the seafood is bad. Fix this." Then the Marine plastered on her smile again, nodding in exaggeration to something the mayor said.

A man's voice came from behind. "May I speak to you, Ms. Morgan?"

Callie spun to face the town administrator, wearing a white embroidered shirt she thought she recognized from the craft fair.

"I don't see what you're up to, but I don't like it," the administrator said. "You've disrupted our community ever since you arrived."

"Sir," Callie started, feeling this day slide through her fingers, sensing MyOuttake chuckling in the background. "You're more than welcome as a guest, as long as you don't disturb the other guests. But remember . . . this is my house."

"What!" the man exclaimed. "As the town's administrator, I've never—"

Callie's patience grew thin. "I said you're still welcome here."

"Whoa!" A roar rose again around the room, then laughter bounced off the ceiling.

The new posted picture caught Callie in a muddled expression, somewhere between sheepish and stunned, with Janet's body language asserting her power.

@MyOuttake—Turf war on Edisto? Maybe a cat fight? #edistojinx

Someone thrust the image before Janet. She stole a penetrating glance at Callie.

So Callie started typing.

@EdistoCallie—Listen to me.

No picture, no hashtag, no inciting slander. Simply a plea. And as she hit send, she watched the sea of faces, numbering about forty in the room, the rest crammed outside. The chatter settled as if all waited, listening on behalf of MyOuttake.

Like Act Three in a damn stage play.

Then Callie spoke in lieu of key-tapping, and all faces turned. "Whoever MyOuttake is, come on out. I'm eager to meet you. I owe you a bottle of bourbon, or whatever your favorite drink is, for helping make this party a rousing blowout affair!"

The room erupted in applause, MyOuttake's handle repeated by some in a rant.

Callie lifted her voice to be heard again. "And I'm sure the mayor and

Janet Wainwright are thankful to you as well. We're all here to celebrate Edisto Beach's summer success." She scanned the room. "Is he still here?"

Dozens twisted, turned, scoured the crowd.

"Aw, come on, Mr. MyOuttake, or Miss, whatever the case." She raised her arms. "Let us meet you and congratulate you on your creative entertainment. We owe you!"

Guests' heads swiveled, Callie watching each one, hunting for the fake in the mob. Nobody stood out. Nobody volunteered to be applauded.

"Well," she said. "Everybody keep your eyes open for this guy, and remember to have fun."

Claps scattered loosely around the room as she blended into the party.

No chance he'd come out, but Callie's five cameras would record faces, note reactions, and later Callie would sit down with Seabrook and study them.

MyOuttake had shown he was inside and enjoyed his ploy. She could, too.

Everyone returned to eating, drinking, and chatting. Then somewhere, in that corralled mass of people, MyOuttake decided to reply.

@MyOuttake—That was good, Detective. Change of plans now. #edistojinx

Callie checked her phone every five minutes, but the so-called change didn't appear. For almost an hour, he went quiet.

Dusk arrived as did a few more partiers. Janet left with the mayor, the pressure of MyOuttake's game resulting in the Marine promising that some lucky soul would win half off a week's rental, good through the calendar year. They only had to sign the guest book, leaving contact information, of course.

Nobody saw the town administrator exit.

Seabrook texted. *The girl is still missing. No van spotted. You okay?*

Callie responded. *Seems to have settled down but keep me posted. Don't feel good about this coincidence.*

Alex created posts of her own about how enjoyable the party rocked at Chelsea Morning and how Edisto's weather shined as flawless as she'd ever seen. Callie threw a look of gratitude, receiving a slight nod in return. Her tension eased as she started interpreting MyOuttake's change of plans to mean another day.

Smiling, thanking people for attending, she wandered the room, double checking the cams.

Crap. Two had been turned, one to face a pot of ivy, the other the side of a bookcase. Damn it! More smiling, more social niceties as she rounded the sofa. A cup half-filled with warm Coke blocked another camera, and she smoothly removed it. Someone smeared dip on the fourth. The fifth had simply been pushed to the rear of the entertainment center, making it drop off the shelf. It dangled, useless, out of view.

Son of a stinkin' bitch. How long had they been incapacitated, and how much or how little had they recorded? She couldn't reset them without drawing attention to the fact the guests had been taped.

"Something wrong?" a middle-aged man asked, a slight slur in his speech.

Callie snapped around, back turned to the incapacitated cam. "Um, someone lost their car keys. I was poking around places, hunting for them."

"No telling where they are in this mob." He took another swallow, eyes never leaving her.

"Yeah, more people than we estimated, but that's not a bad thing."

"Hmmm." He smiled, his glass at waist level, gaze on her breasts a little too long.

"I probably need to check on the food."

"Are you married?" His grin broadened. "I haven't seen you with a man and thought maybe you were on the market. You party, have a beach house, know the Edisto echelon. Not hard on the eyes, either." He slid forward, but she couldn't move against the entertainment center. His belly touched hers, and her nerves shot to attention. For a fleeting second, she pondered if this was MyOuttake, flaunting his *change of plans* strategy.

Rikki's arm suddenly draped across Callie's shoulder. "Maybe there's a reason there is no man, honey."

He took a moment to register the thought before his brows rose, and his shoulders drew back, the gut sucked in. "Sure. Listen, great party, you two." And he wandered into the happy horde, all too eager to disappear now.

"Thanks," Callie said.

"Don't mention it. You're too tiny, girl. Makes you appear vulnerable." She left, her six foot height easily scanning over the heads.

Rikki settled on another cluster of tourists, welcoming them. Callie'd noted how she worked the people, not staying with any group for long. Maybe her way of watching for MyOuttake. She sure wished she had Rikki's height.

But Rikki might have all this right working the people a few at a time. Rather than stalk the killer, they should protect the prey while observing behaviors.

Callie routed out Frank and Ava. "Act as hosts, if you don't mind. Mingle. Keep people occupied. Don't stick with one or two. Note anyone nervous or out of place."

Sophie came over. "What's wrong? I don't understand this texting thing. I'm antsy enough as it is to be here after the fire. Spirits hate this house, and they might not appreciate all the activity." She shivered. "I got tired of being mad. Anger is wrong and not my thing." She studied one face, then another. "I came to help, but . . ."

Exhaling, Callie draped an arm on Sophie's shoulder. "Can't explain everything to you right now. Please trust me about that." Then she hugged her friend, consoling . . . badly needing a hug herself.

The yoga instructor eyed Callie with doubt. "Maybe I need to go." She touched her chest. "My heart's beating so hard."

"Oh, Sophie." Callie's remorse only escalated her own jitters, and she felt a snippet of explanation necessary. "I'm sorry, but right now I'm worried the jinx guy is here."

With a gasp, Sophie covered her mouth.

"Don't," Callie said. "Don't let on. Can you stay? Keep the food going and the people entertained. That way I can do my thing and not get waylaid entertaining guests."

A girl squealed, and Sophie jumped.

"Can you do this?" Callie repeated.

Sophie nodded, turned her smile on like a switch, and went to the closest man to ask if he needed a refill.

Callie stood in the midst of all in disbelief, her own pulse rapid as well. What started as an effort to identify the culprit had turned into a prayer they would weather the party without MyOuttake getting squirrelly. At least the tweets had everyone watching for him, second guessing who attended the event. They even interrogated each other in jest.

Another swell filled the room. A picture appeared, taken from a corner of the living room, to capture as many people as possible.

@MyOuttake—So many brunettes to choose from. #edistojinx

Partiers laughed, some of the women touching their hair. One man reached across and flipped the bob of a nearby lady, who scrunched her nose and giggled in return.

Dear God, nobody took this seriously.

A woman stared at her from six feet away, measuring, and Callie realized her own angst might feed anyone else's. Maybe the nonchalance of the room was okay. Callie wasn't sure she wanted everyone to sense a criminal in the room. She knew crowds. Chaos and fear would cause a scene, or worse, offer camouflage for the jinx killer to perform amidst the mayhem. So instead she typed.

@EdistoCallie—I'm brunette. What's wrong with me? #edistojinx

She added a selfie of herself, seductive.

People laughed, drinking, enjoying the volley.

When she turned and found herself two arm's lengths from Rikki, she took in a breath. Rikki and Terrance were deep in a hug that said more than *Nice to meet you.*

"Um, hey," Callie said, waiting until they showed space between them rather than interrupt the moment.

The two unwrapped, both completely unabashed.

A creased formed between Terrance's eyes. "You're favoring your hand."

"Those cuts can hurt," Rikki said. "You ought to let Terrance look at it."

"No, thanks," Callie answered, impatient at the attention to something so trivial as her wound when brunettes were being stalked like rabbits in the woods. "Anyone odd jump out at you?" She wanted to check in with Seabrook, but he'd call. She'd settle for Francis. Any other cop-type.

Rikki glanced up from checking her phone. "No, but why'd you throw yourself out there like that?" She lowered her voice. "Sorry, girl, but that strategy screams stupid to me."

"Don't worry about that," Callie replied, more irritated, ever watching the people meandering past, sizing up brunettes, hunting for any oddball guy engrossed in his phone. "What you can worry about is Sophie. Would you speak to her when you get a minute? She's frightened to be here."

"The spirits?" Rikki asked, head tilted.

This wasn't the time or place for Rikki's skepticism or Callie's urge to rip into Rikki about it. "Yes, the spirits. But don't rub them in her face, you hear? She sees and hears them. Be the big girl here. She's scared."

"This woman communicates with ghosts?" Terrance asked, quite sincere.

"Sorry, Terrance, but yeah. She's very spiritual," Callie said, remembering he stood there, embarrassed he had to observe the small confrontation. "Hey, didn't realize you and Rikki were so . . . close."

Rikki gave Terrance a warm smile. "I knew him better than he knew me," she said. "His sister and I used to be close years ago when the two of them came here in the summers. He and I never met, but Tia talked about him all the time. She loved him to pieces."

The words *used to be close* kept Callie from delving further. But the details weren't her business, and she didn't want to hear an endless story of family history.

Rikki touched her glass to Terrance's. "After all these years, and seeing him here, I figured we were long overdue. We were sharing stories about her as well as discussing this Twitter war of yours." She leaned down. "You okay?"

Callie scanned for active ears around her. "Sort of operating on a loose plan B."

"Where's Seabrook?" Rikki asked.

"Yeah," Terrance added. "Thought you had a connection with the chief."

Callie shrugged. "He'll be here." The abduction didn't need to become the latest gossip. A girl's life might be at stake.

"Well, it's great we have you," Terrance said. "With your background, this guy won't try a thing here." He nudged her with a soft chuckle. "The Edisto Sleuth Society has you covered, too. Now tell me more about this spiritualist. I'm intrigued with that sort of thing."

"Well, I'm not a believer, but yeah, Sophie states she rolls with spirits all the time. You'd have to ask her about any details."

Rikki closed her phone. "The Twitter idiot sure got quiet. Maybe he left."

We can only hope, Callie thought. But she worried more about how he'd react if he left the party empty-handed.

Chapter 27

PEOPLE STILL STOOD wall-to-wall in Chelsea Morning, just not as compact as an hour before. Nine thirty, and the house's condition already screamed post-party, but in terms of festivities, Callie thought this one proved quite the accomplishment. Complete strangers continued to bond over the mystique of Edisto and its jinx. Too many people might know where Callie lived, but such a small beach didn't keep many addresses secret anyway.

Beside her, Rikki and Terrance chatted about food. Apparently, Terrance cooked as well. While Callie halfway listened, she kept an eye on the crowd, studying, wondering, her guard not willing to settle down.

Someone touched her shoulder. Callie turned, expecting another autograph request or an inquiry about an empty bowl of onion dip.

Her smile fell short. "Jeb?"

"Mom."

Her heart jumped. Her son was the last person she wanted here. Her mind needed to be one hundred percent on the case and not misguided by family concerns. He didn't need to be around a criminal. Or, as he would probably grouse, she hadn't time for his anti-law enforcement rant. "Thought you were at your grandmother's for a few days?" she asked.

Jeb and Sprite both had dressed nice for the affair, as if to partake of the festivities, but Jeb's stare bored a hole in Callie, representing more his purpose for attending. "Thought you weren't going to play cop anymore."

Rikki heard the boy's voice and glanced over, then sidled her and Terrance out of earshot. Sprite, however, paid no attention to Callie's stare that tried to suggest she go get a Coke.

"You promised," Jeb started. "How can I trust you?"

"What?" Callie asked. "Not sure I heard you. It's noisy in here." She tucked them against a wall, in strategic view of the front door and the living room, her eighteen-year-old son lecturing her like she was a five-year-old.

"Yeah, right, Mom. I hear you fine. I had to see you on television wearing a uniform to learn you'd gone to the dark side. I didn't even see the broadcast, but half of Middleton did, which means Grandma heard about it, which means she told me."

Sprite studied the people and spotted Sophie.

"We'll talk later." She patted Jeb's chest and left, but Jeb hugged her wake.

"Don't you think this is important enough—"

She whirled on him. "Absolutely not, Jeb. Not now. I'm the hostess, so I can't stand here and argue with you."

He scowled dark. "This isn't over."

She sucked in hard through her nose, wishing she could still spank the child. "No, young man, it's not."

Callie watched him weave through bodies. To return Jeb to being a teen and herself the parent, she needed to right that balance. But not this moment.

Sophie parted from Sprite and headed quickly for the door. Worried Sophie'd had enough of this so-called spirit-infested house, Callie barely reached her at the threshold. "What's wrong?"

"You're running out of food. Who stocks more booze than food, girl? That's begging for problems. Way too much dip and not enough veggies. I'm running down to BI-LO to grab a pint of crab dip and a few chips."

"Don't worry about it," Callie said, surprised at the missing stress that had racked the yoga teacher earlier. Sprite must have made the difference. "People ought to be leaving soon."

"Won't take a minute. Be right back," Sophie said, flitting silently down the stairs like her feet coasted on air.

Four revelers in their late thirties almost bounced into Callie as they decorated her steps, three of them feeling no pain. "Hey, great party, Callie. You do these all the time?"

"This is my first," she replied. "You're not driving, are you?"

The inebriated ones chuckled and rocked uncertainly, the sober one empathetic toward her host. "We're walking. Good job, though," the least drunk one said. "The Twitter activity stole the show. I assume they'll tweet the winner of the free vacation. Sorry we'll miss meeting that MyOuttake person."

Callie dipped in a partial bow, humored for the first time tonight. "You are quite welcome. Enjoy Edisto."

They stumbled and chortled down the steps.

Going on ten o'clock, the crowd receded by a quarter, the remainder still going strong. The tweeting had stopped, the attendees more sluggish in their movement, less crisp with their jokes, but still mellow without purpose to leave. Two of the ladies Callie would've labeled as targets were gone, and damn it, Seabrook's officers were supposed to be available to discretely follow them home. Instead, Callie helplessly watched them walk into the night with only a prayer that MyOuttake didn't feel spunky enough to snatch and grab.

Alex bumped into her and slung a caustic, "You tried to keep this story from me, didn't you? So I'd promote your oh-so-precious party!"

"Have no idea what you're talking about," Callie said, honestly clueless about the girl's sudden angst after they'd made nice.

The journalist's freckles weren't so cute mixed into a nasty glower. "Editor Jenkins texted me about the abduction. Nice try, traitor."

Callie remained stymied as Alex ran out without a glance. Just when she'd mended fences with the girl. She closed her eyelids for a brief time, centering herself. She was so ready for this night to be over. Out of habit, she glanced at the phone. The tweets had died, not unlike the party.

Heartburn gnawed at her insides. Her stomach grumbled, and she rested her sore hand over her midsection, realizing she'd forgotten to eat.

Yes, a long night. A long, uneventful night.

She was no closer to identifying this guy than before, with the party serving only to introduce him to potential prey. In hindsight, maybe not one of her better plans, and a stinging reminder she'd been out of the action for a while. An even stronger reminder she had no department behind her. Alone and guessing, with the fallout completely on her shoulders.

At least the mayor loved her.

Ten thirty rolled around.

Sophie never returned, which was fine. More food would've enticed people to stay longer.

Ava roamed the rooms, gathering empty cups and stuffing napkins in a trash bag. Frank aided a drunk individual to his feet before the sojourner made himself a bed on Callie's recliner. Jeb and Sprite picked through remnants on the food table.

Callie saw most of the merrymakers to the door one by one, and by eleven, the place emptied to about ten to include Rikki, Frank, and Ava. Jeb and Sprite had escaped, eager to enjoy an evening they considered still young.

The last three couples finally left.

Holding up a high-five, Rikki remarked, "Well done, my detective friend."

Fulfilling the slap, Callie sighed deeply. Her feet hurt, and she worried about collateral damage.

"Oh, Frankie, forget him." Ava kissed her husband's cheek and began carrying dishes to the kitchen. "He's bummed that his boyfriend disappeared on him."

"Who?" Callie asked.

"Terrance," Frank growled.

Rikki shook her head. "I hadn't finished talking to him, either, but no matter," Rikki said. "I'll go to his house tomorrow."

Frank slumped on one of the straight-back chairs used to manage the overflow. "Didn't want to help clean up, the bonehead. He always does that—disappears when there's work to do."

"Think about it this way, Frank," Callie said, fishing crackers from the cracks of her sofa cushions. "You're the last man standing of the Edisto Sleuth Society. Thanks for helping tonight. I really appreciate it. When are y'all headed home?"

"Tomorrow," he replied. "Not looking forward to that drive to Jersey."

Dumping several paper plates in Ava's garbage sack, Callie noticed Rikki moving slowly, collecting discarded paper items and crumbs, her expression almost melancholic.

Callie eased to her. "What's wrong?" she softly asked. Amazons weren't supposed to brood.

To Callie's surprise, Rikki returned an injured look. "I thought Terrance would stick around. Tia and I were very close." She seemed distant. "Seeing him brought it all back. She left so . . . suddenly."

"Left?" Callie asked, wiping dip off the arm of her sofa, suspecting the worse in the story.

Rikki's green eyes seemed to melt with the telling of the memory. "She hanged herself before I returned from Germany. I asked her to quit her damn teaching job and move to Edisto, with me."

Callie stopped scrubbing. "Oh wow." She rubbed the tall woman's back, stiffly at first, the mood so foreign on this woman. "I'm so sorry, Rikki."

"Yeah," she said, sniffling once. "I don't understand how the hell he can stay in that beach house after seeing her hang herself."

"Wait," Callie said. "She died there?"

The others froze at the death comment, listening.

Rikki nodded. "Underneath from a cross beam between pylons. Bushes and latticework hid her until Terrance arrived late that night. He traveled from New York, she from Florida, but he got stuck with an emergency at the hospital. They'd already come in June, after she finished school, but they decided to make a second trip that summer. As twins they were close, and she wanted his counsel."

"Twins?" Frank asked.

But Callie was puzzled. Why had such a horrendous tale been foreign to her after all her years on Edisto? Or why wasn't Paradise Lost, such an ironic name for Terrance's rental, considered haunted or crazy hard to rent? "My parents have owned our house since I was eight. That's only four blocks over." She crooked an open palm to the side. "I should know this."

"Y'all always came in the winter, rented Chelsea Morning out in the summer. And the owner repainted the place and changed the name to avoid the stigma. Used to be Laughing Gull."

Seabrook never mentioned this. Janet should have. The damn woman probably rented to the guy. Sophie'd made no mention either, but Callie never saw their paths cross, plus talking about the dead sometimes rattled Sophie's constitution. Callie turned to Frank. "He ever talk to you about this?"

"Good God, no." He continued to rest in his chair, wearing a stunned gaze. "We only know that he's been coming a year more than we have. Four, he said."

Her forehead creased, Rikki shook her head. "Not so. He and Tia came here every summer since they were kids."

Gripping the sofa, Callie replayed everything she'd heard of this person. A frosty trail of goose bumps climbed her arms and down her ribs. "How long ago did Tia die, Rikki?"

"Ten years, why?"

Terrance had gone out of his way to lie about how long he'd been coming to Edisto.

Callie put weight on the sofa, thinking. Recalling conversations, reactions, distractions. She stared at Rikki and asked the question she thought she already knew. "Is Terrance a doctor?"

"Yes," she said, her brow knitted. "I thought you knew that."

Callie didn't until this moment, after recalling Rikki's suggestion that Terrance examine her two cut fingers.

She yanked her phone out of her pants pocket. The son-of-a-bitch had danced under their noses the entire time. Another rash of goose bumps spread across her, partnered by an adrenaline to act . . . act now to find the man.

He'd been a constant throughout this search. The last to leave after Maddington's death. A piece of the crowd outside the fire, and a visitor the next day, ever eager to point out MyOuttake's in-your-face tweets. He knocked on her door, the only one anxious to apologize when she told the ESS to butt out. Oh so aiming to please, so he could be oh so present.

Most of all, he'd watched Brea Jamison die only three feet from his feet, violating his Hippocratic Oath, blatantly letting that pretty little thirty-five-year-old brunette choke to death.

She replayed the party. Brea would have made a convenient addition to his August jinx with no effort, no planning, no risk. Didn't completely fit the profile with her being married, and the party being in broad daylight, but maybe he recognized the opportunity with zero risk. He might've been scouting for number six when Brea literally fell across his path.

Was he elated? Or did that mess with his habit?

The attack on Grant felt out of place, though. That puzzle piece didn't fit at all.

But too many others did.

Callie's call to Seabrook went to voice mail. "Call me ASAP, Seabrook. I mean now!"

The others stood stupefied at her unexplained reaction. Ava reached for Frank, who wrapped her in a one-arm embrace. Rikki stared aghast.

"Damn it, call me, Seabrook!" Callie said through her teeth. She hung up to redial again.

Rikki moved slowly toward her. "Callie? What's wrong?"

But Callie wouldn't elaborate. She hadn't proven her theory, though she felt almost as sure of Terrance's guilt as her love of gin.

Too many people with too much information jeopardized things. They'd want to be involved, Frank in his ESS mode and Rikki's newly kindled friendship with Terrance. Callie's need-to-know gate dropped into place.

Footsteps echoed on the wood porch. Everyone turned as if expecting Terrance to walk in and apologize for not helping his friends, but Jeb opened the door. Sprite pushed past him. "Ms. Morgan? Have you seen my momma?"

Callie looked toward Rikki. "She left for the BI-LO, but I never saw her after that."

Everyone shook their heads.

"Is your mother's car at your house?" Callie asked, her nerves prickling.

Sprite's raven corkscrew curls shifted side to side, her eyes widening. "No, ma'am. She's not answering her phone, either. She always takes my calls." Her fingers twisted her see-through tulle covering the braless tank underneath, her repetitive worry ruining the fabric.

Ordinarily this would be when Rikki would blow off Sophie's

disappearance as flighty, a part of her friend's harem-scarem existence, but instead she remained frozen, absorbing events, uncertainty etched in her crow's feet. Then as if prodded, she lifted her phone. Callie followed suit. Rikki peered back with a hint of relief. "No tweets."

But Callie's blood ran icy at the words on her screen. There awaited a direct tweet, a personal message sent only to her, timed twenty-three minutes earlier.

@MyOuttake—The spirits accept one of their own tonight. BTW, great party Thanks for sharing your friend. #edistojinx

Shit . . . Sophie!
Callie dialed Sophie's number. Voice mail. She bolted to retrieve her purse and her newly returned Glock from her bedroom, Rikki running behind her. "Callie?"

"Not now, Rikki." Blindly digging keys out of her purse, Callie turned to Jeb. "You and Sprite stay here."

"Yes, ma'am," the boy said, understanding enough about his mother not to argue at this moment.

She ran to Frank. "What kind of car does Terrance drive?"

Frank paled. "An E-class Mercedes. Black."

She acknowledged his response with a jerk of her head and moved toward the door.

"Callie!" Rikki yelled. "You're scaring us."

"I'll explain later," Callie yelled over her shoulder and rushed the stairs two and three at a time. She rounded the corner to jump into her car. Only four blocks over, but minutes were valuable.

If she repeated the tweet to the others or explained the fear in her belly, they'd follow, and she had no time for amateur sleuths. Tires ripping gravel and shells, she reversed and sped onto Jungle Road, texting Seabrook to meet her at Paradise Lost . . . Terrance Mallory's rental.

Pompano Street wasn't a highly trafficked road, with a dead end facing west. Quiet and more secluded, even during peak season since more of the inhabitants there were year-round natives. Paradise Lost sat two doors from the dead end, close enough to the street to not warrant the extra address sign like Chelsea Morning. The ground level leading to the parking area under the house hid behind latticework across the front, the entrance oddly enough on the side. Four ancient unkempt palmettos, old lantana bushes at their base, dominated the front, a cluster of Indian Hawthorns lanky, blocking the front door and half the latticework. No wonder no one saw Tia's body hanging for hours ten years ago either if the owners tended the yard like this.

The name Paradise Lost suited the place way more than Laughing Gull.

The house design dated to the sixties and had been added onto, meaning no way to interpret what entrance led where, and which approach the most safe.

No lights shone. No car parked in the drive that Callie now blocked with hers only twenty feet from the stairs.

Callie's phone vibrated, muted enroute in case she hit the ground crouched and armed.

"Where are you?" she asked.

"Two blocks away," Seabrook said. "Before I ask what's going on, promise you won't tackle it on your own. Francis is right behind me, and we're almost there."

"I know who it is, Seabrook."

"You seriously picked him out at the party?"

She wished. God, how she wished she had. "No, he disappeared. Then so did Sophie. Then he sent me a damn message." A lump blocked her throat, causing her to cough to breathe. "He said *the spirits accept one of their own tonight.*"

"Might be the kidnapped girl, Callie . . . not Sophie," he said.

"He thanked me for sharing my friend, damn it!"

The blue light bounced off houses a block over, and Callie leaned her forehead in her palm, mashing the furrows between her brows.

"She's gone, nonetheless," she said. "Now that's two women missing, along with Terrance." She paused to get her voice under control, taking in a deep breath. "What more coincidence do you need, Seabrook?" Damn it, they hadn't needed crab dip. Why didn't she insist Sophie stay at the party? Her presence had triggered conversation, piqued interest, educated Terrance . . .

She slapped her steering wheel. Why the hell did she overlook Sophie, in spite of her frosty highlights? In spite of her mid-forties age? Sophie's yoga physique made any thirty-year-old envious, so Terrance would've considered her a prime target easily within the profile.

Callie assumed he'd come after her, or maybe some stranger, but Sophie never crossed her mind. How stupid was that?

The patrol car stopped beside hers, the front dipping at the sudden stop. Francis' vehicle slid in on the other side of Seabrook's. Callie exited her car, Glock in her grip. Her holster clipped to her pants, making her thank heaven she dodged wearing the thin skirt.

Her heart beat louder than the surroundings. Almost midnight. A new moon left the stars glittering to themselves on a cloudless night. Insects and birds alike had retreated and silenced so that the cops' footsteps crunched loud on the seashell drive as they reached her side. The tide muted as if the beach held its breath.

She recited the details before the two men had a chance to speak. "Terrance Mallory is white, in his forties, five-foot-nine, dark straight hair." She pointed sharply at Paradise Lost. "He rents this place for two weeks every August. Has been for ten years. Before that he rented in June going back God knows how long. Rikki's familiar with him."

"Rikki?" Seabrook interrupted, a deep frown creasing his face. "Is she involved in this?"

"No," Callie said, though she hadn't dissected that part yet. "But I'll swear on Daddy's grave that Terrance staged that abduction. You haven't found the girl, have you?"

"No, but her family is concerned now. No doubt, she's disappeared."

Callie studied the house, with no hint of activity inside, a search of the place calling her name all the same. "We need to start here, where Terrance lived. Where his sister died. Where somehow Terrance feels his life started, stopped, and fell apart."

"His sister?" Seabrook repeated.

She made a fist with her bandaged hand, the pain ignored. "Yes. I don't have the whole story yet but please, Seabrook, put your guys on finding Sophie, too. You know how important time is in these cases."

She gave the two officers Sophie's clothing description, the make of Terrance's car, the times they were last seen. Seabrook contacted officers with the information.

A thump sounded inside the house while he spoke, and Callie gripped his wrist. She mouthed for him to listen.

Glass crashed. The two uniforms readied on their side arms. Callie put her piece in both hands. Seabrook silently waved Francis toward the west side of the house, to cover the rear door. The acting police chief to the front stairs, Callie on his heels.

They'd just earned the right to bypass a search warrant.

Chapter 28

HER HEARING ACUTE, Callie noted the low-tide waves murmuring—her heart valves pushing blood to her arms, legs, her brain playing what-ifs like a silent talkie film. Salt with a hint of someone's leftover shrimp peelings filled her nose. The tiny muscles in her fingers tensed, taut around the Glock.

Callie hung behind Seabrook, watching for his direction, a controlled readiness heightening her senses yet her pulse a steady pace. "All three of us heard the thump and crash," she said. "Exigent circumstances. Go up and shoulder it, Seabrook."

"Not yet," he said.

An unlit Paradise Lost hunkered in the darkness, three houses from the nearest streetlight. Porch lights outlined a middle-aged couple and two teenagers next door, craning to see why cops were interested in Pompano Road. Seabrook waved at them to return inside. They scrambled, shutting off their light, retreating to continue their curious glances through window blinds. Then Seabrook began inching up the two dozen stairs leading to the front entrance, weapon drawn, slow enough to allow Francis to reach a similar place in the rear.

Dampness fell over them, half briny water, half summer heat. They hadn't been in it long, but suspense had both of them sweating. Callie risked a quick moment to shoulder wipe a drip from her temple.

Terrance might be inside or not. He might have drowned the girl for all they knew. But they had to start here. The noise inside had beckoned.

He'd shown no sign of threat until now. She'd even learned to like the guy. But she realized what she knew wasn't the real Terrance Mallory. He'd cloistered his persona to slide into Callie's world and fit appropriately.

This made him unpredictable. But then any killer was unpredictable. A switch tripped in their psyche. A switch that enabled these sorts to make sick choices with rational calm.

His Twitter handle, for instance. MyOuttake. She mistook his online presence for a rival reporter what seemed like ages ago. The name meant news bite, and he used it to become newsworthy, the center of attention without being seen. He juggled some issue he could not solve, an itch he could not scratch. Deep inside he needed to be caught, and this Twitter business served as the crumbs he laid out for someone to find him. Before now no one sought him out. Nobody validated his crimes. Until Callie.

But that didn't mean he'd be caught easily or without danger.

Seabrook tried the knob. Locked. Waving Callie to ease aside, he held his firearm at the ready and banged the door with his fist. "Edisto Police. Open the door."

Poised, muscles taut and primed, Callie listened hard. Nothing. "Do it, Seabrook."

His six foot plus mass needed minimal effort to force their way in, the wood frame aged from weather coming off the beach for many seasons. Seabrook entered first, sweeping, Callie covering his flank, the two canvassing a generic living room of pressboard end tables, jute rugs, and a Naugahyde couch. Lamps filled with shells. A fifty-year-old mounted barracuda hung faded on a white-washed paneled wall.

Callie flipped on the lights and covered their backs as Seabrook let Francis inside. The lanky officer remained at the rear side of the house as Seabrook returned to Callie to examine the bedrooms.

"Here she is," Seabrook hollered, flipped a light switch, and ran into the first bedroom.

Callie rushed behind him, anxious to see which *she* he meant.

It wasn't Sophie.

About thirty, the woman lay sprawled on the pale oak floor, hands and ankles bound with duct tape, her fingers clinging to the shade of a busted glass lamp. Her toenails were painted a bright coral. She wore low-riding baby blue shorts and a paisley bathing suit top. Soft, irregular moans escaped her throat.

Holstering his weapon, Seabrook dropped to a knee and pulled out his pocket knife to release the bindings. Then he checked her pulse, examined her eyes. "Pupils are dilated. She's been drugged." He keyed his mic, a shared frequency for all the Edisto emergency services. "Send an ambulance to 21A Pompano Road. We have a thirty-year-old female unconscious, possibly drugged, substance unknown."

"On the way, Mike," came the reply.

Feet thundered up the steps. Callie left Seabrook examining the girl and walked to the living room end of the hallway where Francis had already positioned to meet the trespasser, not comfortable at all with the tension from the tight, edgy expression on his face.

Rikki entered the room, breathless. "Did you find Sophie? She's still not answering her phone."

Francis grunted with relief and walked past Rikki to the front porch. "Hey, I'm going to get the crime scene tape. Keep her out of there," he hollered over his shoulder.

Callie blocked Rikki from coming further than the middle of the living room, Rikki's midsection pushing against Callie's palm. "No, we didn't find Sophie."

"Crime scene tape? What about Terrance?" Rikki asked.

Callie sensed Rikki still tried to see Terrance as one of the good guys, the brother of a girl Callie assumed Rikki dated years ago.

"We haven't found him yet." Callie tried to ease her toward the exit. "Go home, and I'll call when anything develops."

The woman used her size this time, refusing to budge. "You don't even care, do you? About either of them."

Callie bit her tongue, craving to scold Rikki for the childish rivalry for Sophie's attention and her ignorance of Terrance's probable involvement. The woman was smart enough to put two and two together by now. "I do care, but you can't be here. It's a crime scene." Callie swallowed. Her own fear threatened to eke through. Sophie was her friend, too, and no telling where she was right now. While this unconscious girl required their attention, no denying the fact she delayed them finding Sophie.

Disco flashing off buildings, the ambulance's light flashed through the front window.

"Wait," Rikki said, nervous again. "Who's in there?"

Callie opened the door as the medics reached the landing. They went to the bedroom, as she directed, Rikki attempting to follow. Callie stepped in her path. "Get your butt home, Rikki!"

Outside, voices spoke, then escalated to an argument. Francis stood guard outside against a new intruder who asked a hundred questions.

Alex.

She peered around Francis and caught sight of Callie. "How did you beat me here? Is the kidnapped girl here? Did the same guy take her?"

Nobody answered, Callie almost ready to ask Francis for his cuffs if either woman pushed any harder. During a crisis, she held little patience for the nosy, even less for the press. She envisioned Rikki shoved against the wall. Alex likewise against the door. Arms fastened together behind their backs to keep them out of everyone's hair.

"Have you heard they took Sophie Bianchi?" Rikki asked, approaching the reporter.

"Wait. I know her." Alex extracted her phone and snapped a shot.

"Don't tell her a thing," Callie told Rikki, but when she turned, Alex was already speaking into her phone, recording where she was and what was going down . . . though she didn't understand squat about Sophie's disappearance.

Callie shoved Rikki toward Francis. "Watch her." Then she strode over and yanked the device from Alex's grip. She turned it off and escorted the girl by the elbow to the corner of the porch.

Alex reached for her phone, missing when Callie pocketed it. "Hey," Alex said. "You can't—"

"Shut up and listen." Her fingers wrapping around Alex's arm, Callie reined her closer, putting little distance between her mouth and the reporter's ear. "I'll give you an exclusive on all of this, but on my terms."

"You can't—"

Callie instinctively reached around for cuffs she hadn't worn in two years. "Francis, throw me your cuffs."

He did so in a smooth toss. Callie caught them and dangled them inches from Alex's nose. "Or I can have you escorted to the Colleton County jail and give you zilch."

Her eyes wide, Alex exclaimed, "Okay, chill, damn!"

If Callie confiscated the phone, Alex would find some other way to report, only with a vengeance, so Callie let her shrug off the grip.

"What terms?" Alex said, mouth pursed over a temper-fueled stare.

"Report only what I authorize until I cut you loose to do otherwise."

Her brows came together, untrusting. "That's pretty damn open-ended. For how long?"

"Until we find her. Alive or dead."

The reporter fought not to appear eager. "We're talking Sophie, right?"

"Yes. The other girl is here. Drugged, but we think she's all right."

"You found the girl?" Alex inhaled, excited, containing her thrill in landing the front row seat. A pretentious veil of professionalism fell into place. "So why the ambulance?"

"To make *sure* she is okay. We're not doctors."

"How do I trust you're good for your word?"

"I just gave you confidential information that she was drugged. What else screams trust?" Callie replied, tiring of this banter.

A flash of Sophie whirled in her mind, happy, giggling, the effervescent image driving Callie to move on to find her friend. She leaned in closer, her jaw tight. "Do you want to kill Sophie? One wrong Tweet, one misstep, one sarcastic or over-the-top spin to highlight your reporting just might snuff out her life."

Alex's gaze shifted to the other end of the porch. People hung out on their porches, too, from all sides of Paradise Lost. More lights flashed on. Many watched the two of them, and Alex clearly noticed.

Callie pushed. "You believe your reporting cost a teenager her life in Atlanta, right?"

The slight jerk in Alex's mouth told Callie enough.

"Then do as I say so we don't repeat that story here," she said. "You'll have the story before anyone else. But if you cost my friend her life, I'll come at you, little girl. I live on Edisto now. And as cliché as it sounds, I know where you live. We can be friends, or we can be adversaries, but even if you hate me, do not give this guy the satisfaction of your attention."

Their stares connected.

"Fine," Alex said.

Callie returned the phone. Then she tried Sophie again, to no avail.

Rattling on wheels, the gurney readied to leave, Seabrook behind them. The girl seemed asleep. No injuries, no blood.

Seabrook stopped on the porch and directed Francis to accompany them to the hospital and notify the family enroute. Then he keyed his mic again. He asked somebody to check the traffic cam leading off the beach on Highway 174. Ordered officers to initiate their searches.

"Mike? This is LaRoche," came a voice over his mic.

"Go ahead, LaRoche."

"We found Sophie Bianchi's car in the BI-LO parking lot. Looks like it's been here at least a couple hours. Nothing in it I can see. Want me to force the trunk?"

"Be there in three minutes. Stand by." Seabrook turned to Callie. "I've got to call SLED and Colleton Sheriff's Department about all this. What are these two doing here?" he asked once he keyed off, spoken as if he'd been Callie's boss for years.

"Rikki's leaving after I ask her a few questions," she replied.

"And Alex—"

"What questions?" Rikki asked, Alex prepping for thumb action on her phone.

Rikki eyed Seabrook, seeking confirmation whether she had to oblige.

He nodded. "Do as she asks, Rikki."

"Rikki," Callie started calmly, to settle the moment. "We think Terrance took Sophie."

"What? I don't understand. I—"

"Wait a second. Answer my questions. It's easier this way."

The woman gave her a jerky nod, but mumbled, "I should've seen. Are you sure?"

"Not your fault," Callie said, recalling the hug between Terrance and Rikki at the party. Remembering how Rikki ceased working the crowd once she connected with him. "Slow down and tell me what you and Terrance talked about. Anything. Doesn't matter what it is."

"I mentioned Tia and introduced myself. He remembered me. I apologized that we hadn't consoled each other when she died."

Alex sighed impatiently, and Callie held up a finger, shushing her. "What else, Rikki?"

"We talked about Tia a long time. How she loved teaching. How she didn't get an associate principal position she wanted badly thanks to some witch of a teacher that worked with her. I'd told her to quit that thankless job, but she enjoyed the students. She taught at a private school for girls and loved it. I kept trying to get her to move to the beach, for good."

"Did you discuss Sophie?" Callie asked, trying to bring Rikki around. At a quarter to one, Sophie had to be a basket case . . . or pissed that no one noticed her gone before now. Callie preferred thinking the latter.

Blinking her eyes at what she felt obvious, Rikki replied, "Yes, he said Sophie was hot. Every man says she's hot. I didn't pay any attention to that."

So Terrance took note of her early on in the party.

"You and I spoke of spirits right in front of him, remember?" Rikki said as if Callie should shoulder some of the blame.

"I remember," Callie said. "He showed interest. What about after I left you two?"

The self-assurance Rikki usually carried abandoned her. "I said she talked to spirits, believed in ghosts, like those of her daddy and her aunt. She told Brea to cross over."

Yeah, Callie remembered that, too.

"I actually tried to explain her feelings." Rikki's worry made her seem smaller. "Mainly because you kicked my ass for not giving her the benefit of the doubt. So I took her side . . . telling him how I respected her belief. He . . . seemed interested . . . oh my God. Did he bait me?" She breathed shallower, faster, gripping her tunic, crinkling the silk. "Did I do this to her?" Tears welled. "Oh no, I did," she whispered.

"No, you didn't do this, Rikki. Go to Sophie's house," Callie said, looking past the woman to Seabrook, who gave her a subtle nod. "Sprite needs you. Those kids don't need to be left alone. And Sophie might call Sprite or Zeus. An adult needs to be there if she does so we can come get her."

The logic convinced Rikki. "Okay. Call me, though. Please keep me updated."

"Will do."

Then as Rikki left, Callie spun on Alex. "Do not Tweet a damn bit of that. Not yet, you hear?"

"I'm supposed to twiddle my thumbs?" She bobbed her head toward Rikki. "After hearing that?"

"No," Callie said. "You're coming with me."

But she had no idea where to start. Seabrook had patiently stood by as she handled these two, but he should leave and join the hunt per his town's contingency plan, coordinate with SLED, coordinate Colleton and Charleston County's deputies since the island crossed two county lines. They held no assurance Terrance wouldn't leave the beach. They operated per a system Callie wasn't a part of.

She took her phone from her pocket, now a permanent fixture. She opened Twitter and typed, Seabrook's eyes narrowing.

@EdistoCallie—Where are you?

Not only to Terrance in a direct post, but across the Twittersphere, Callie gambled he'd prefer the broader audience.

"What are you doing?" Seabrook asked.

"I'm reaching out," she said. "Baiting."

"Well, I don't have time to weigh the merits of your method, but call if it works." He moved awkwardly to her and drew her into a hug. "Call me every hour on the hour, you hear?"

"Okay."

He kissed the top of her head and left.

Callie resisted the urge to duck. The affection felt so out of place amidst others' damage.

"Nice," Alex said, studying the picture she took of the intimate gesture.

"Don't let me see that anywhere," Callie said, then noticed replies to her tweet. Even in the middle of the night, three tweets appeared, promising a diverse array of romantic and alcoholic rewards if Callie came to their place. Crazy how these people flaunted where they lived to strangers.

Not unlike Callie's house party.

This online exchange was madness, but she had no choice but to use MyOuttake's communication of choice. He'd be watching for posts, restless for validation, hungry for anybody to recognize him for snaring the August victim nobody knew about yet.

Callie suspected he felt robbed with Brea. He received temporary credit for her death and probably entrenched himself in the ESS to watch the fallout. But between Callie's refusal to accept Brea as the year's token and the Edisto Sleuth Society's hankering to break the case open, he'd probably concluded a true victim was in order. As if he owed the beach its anniversary episode. This year, however, he'd become addicted to the little prods not only from Alex, but also the public, the press, eventually Callie. Why else had he play-acted?

He didn't quite know what to do with this jinx reputation bestowed upon him, but he quickly learned to enjoy the world watching his show. He'd never had notoriety before. Nobody believed he existed before.

Callie's fingers hovered over the letters, phrases jumping like fleas around her brain. Words were easy, punching his buttons no contest.

The issue was whether an online debate would make him hurt Sophie . . . so he could blame it on Callie . . . and stake his true sixth claim.

Chapter 29

AT ONE IN THE morning, the prying eyes in neighboring houses quickly lost interest, and silence fell equally as fast. The last to leave Paradise Lost, Callie and Alex sat in the front seat of Callie's Escape. But while the world seemed silent, her insides churned, her head harboring an intense racket as she measured options.

"Post this on Twitter on behalf of *EdistoToday*," Callie said. "*An exquisite weekend for the Edisto Beach craft fair. Visitors galore. Weather from heaven. And no sign of the #edistojinx.*" She let Alex concentrate on her typing a second. "Can you fit a picture link on there? Of the market or something?"

Alex's fingers danced over the tiny keyboard. "Give or take a word. There. Sent. Now what?"

Callie started the car. "We drive to places Sophie frequents. There's a slim chance she's not kidnapped—"

"Or killed," Alex added.

"Thanks for that." Lips pressed, Callie almost wished Rikki had come instead. "What I tried to say is that if she's free, she might be afraid to lead him to her house."

"He grabbed her from her house," Alex said rapidly, not feeling the late hour at all.

"She went to BI-LO for more dip. Her car is there. His car is gone. He nabbed her from BI-LO."

"Oh, yeah."

Tapping her steering wheel, Callie moved down Jungle Road slowly, too slowly, searching side streets, studying cars, resisting a compulsion to floor it . . . with no place to rush to. She phoned Sophie's number again. Nothing.

Late night, and the night critters were in bed, breezes gone. Headlights appeared in her rearview mirror about a block behind, but otherwise everyone had found a place to be for the night.

Think, Callie. Damn it! Collect your thoughts. Make a plan. You had a damn plan with the party. Come up with one now, when it really matters.

What were Terrance's haunts? Nobody knew. Frank just met the guy. Rikki, too. He'd become so friendly yet remained a stranger and suckered them all in. Crazy part was he'd probably been coming to Edisto as long as any of them.

If you don't know Terrance's favorite places, think about Sophie's.

Sophie taught yoga at 8:00 a.m. in the small waterside bar of the old Pavilion while Finn's prepped for lunch. Might as well start there. On her way to the old building and its short pier, Callie drove into the BI-LO parking lot, strikingly empty after the dancing, shopping throng of the weekend. Only a few cars remained, belonging to the skeleton crew that kept the grocery store open 24/7.

A patrol car idled alongside Sophie's vintage powder blue Mercedes convertible, dew coating the windows an indicator of how long the infamous car sat cold. Then the cruiser left.

Callie reached the car Sophie loved so much and rolled down her window, pulse thumping, ultra-aware her friend disappeared here. The flat tire told her everything she needed to know about how the abduction took place, how Terrance set it up and pretended to be of assistance.

"Wow," Alex whispered. "You think they checked for her in the trunk?"

"Shut up, Alex," Callie said. The parking lot was too public. Wide open and viewable from too many places.

Plus, the police would've checked.

She proceeded to Highway 174, gunned it to the right, and slid into Finn's. Fighting to toss aside Alex's vision of Sophie crammed against a spare tire, Callie scrambled out and ran around the place, checking doors and peering in windows, Alex remarkably efficient doing the same around the other side, eventually moving to the water. Nothing on the dock . . . or under it. They remained silent after each call, listening. They repeatedly assured Sophie it was safe to come out.

A car slowed, the streetlamp at the wrong angle to show the driver. When Callie tried to study it, the driver sped on.

The two women returned to the car, the pitch of the hour wrapping around them such that their tiny phone screens reflected light against their faces like a campfire. Alex gasped. Callie rubbed her face, the message only escalating her feeling of ineptness.

@MyOuttake—The weekend wasn't exquisite for everyone. #edistojinx lives. Someone else won't. Choke on that @EdistoCallie. #edistotoday

Oh dear God, she did choke on all this. She baited him to attend the party, but sensed somewhere along the last few hours, she'd been the one hooked in return.

Callie looked south down the beach. A flashlight appeared barely visible in the distance. Most likely one uniform wandering the sand, hunting. She wanted to be out there, but would Terrance revert to his original MO of drowning? Intuition told her no. So what next?

Should she respond to Terrance? He'd called her out using @EdistoCallie, assuring his post went directly to her as well as to *EdistoToday* and Alex's followers. How would he react to her replies? What were his triggers?

Finally, she opened Twitter and typed:

@EdistoCallie—Help me understand. Help me find my friend. #edistojinx

They stood waiting for a response for five minutes, but the only replies came from other followers offering to help Callie understand, offering to be her new friend, joking about what a cool charade had spun off the party game. MyOuttake had shared his adventure with the world before, but now he seemed preoccupied. Which scared Callie to pieces.

Callie started the engine and drove to the parking lot exit, debating whether to remain in the town of Edisto Beach to her left or venture across the marsh to the bigger Edisto Island on her right. Terrance knew that the Edisto PD sought him in town, their jurisdiction and the locale of all the other deaths, so why stay there? But he'd never ventured off the beach before; why change his habit?

She turned left more so to make a move than justify any choice and trolled Palmetto Boulevard. Sophie adored Whaley's. As good a place as any to go to next.

"We have no idea what we're doing, do we?" Alex said softly.

"No, we don't," Callie said, staring down streets, hunting for the black car, no easy feat in the moonless night where any color other than white fit the bill, on a beach where too many people drove dark-colored luxury rides.

Pressure built in her temples, and she shook her head with a huge inhale. She groped for clues that weren't there while Sophie probably wondered why her friend with all the famous detective skills hadn't found her.

Headlights turned from Matilda Street to trail behind them. The vehicle hung back, in no hurry. Not unusual for a vacation beach, but as Callie altered her speed, so did the driver.

After four blocks, Callie grasped a small LED Maglite from her console. Then foot slammed to the brake, she threw the gear into park, and slung her door open in the middle of Palmetto, shining the beam into the driver's eyes.

"Get out of the vehicle," she yelled, motioning with the light. "And show me your hands."

The long, lanky frame unfolded out of a mid-sized white Lexus. "I'm not staying home when I can search for Sophie," Rikki yelled.

Callie stomped the asphalt, closing the distance between them. "Then why the hell are you following me?" Callie shot her arm out, fingers splayed. "Go, go find her. I don't care what you do." Then she remembered Rikki's words from Terrance's house. "I do care, Rikki," she said, lowering the Maglite. "But time matters so much here, and you'll get in the way." Rikki following her seemed a complete waste of time anyway. So where to turn next?

She sighed and faced where she could see the rollers hitting the sand. This man seemed more a creature of opportunity than careful planning. That made him all the more difficult to stalk. Dissecting him had amounted to nothing more than acknowledging his desire to take out brunettes.

She looked up. "Rikki, why dark-headed women of a certain age?"

Shrugging, Rikki shook her head. "I only met him tonight, remember?"

"No, don't discount yourself," Callie said. "When did his sister die?"

"Ten years ago."

"So this is a key anniversary," Callie mumbled more to herself than the others. Whether Terrance realized it or not, this year he seemed more deceptive, in her opinion. But her presence might have nudged him in that direction, too.

"Describe Tia," Callie continued.

Rikki's gaze went distant. "Dark and short like her brother," she started. "Gentle with a laugh so pleasant to hear. Never loud." She quietly laughed once. "She hated her toes, thought they were too stumpy, so she wore close-toed shoes all the time. And skirts. No pants. Liked the material wrapping around her legs in the breeze."

Callie asked low, "But what made her hang herself?"

The trace of joy on Rikki's face melted. "She wanted the vice-principal's position at that girl's school, and another department head wanted it, too." Rikki's face twisted. "The other woman spread rumors about Tia being gay . . . and liking teenage girls."

Callie thought she saw tears, but Rikki didn't brush them off. Instead, she covered her face for a moment, then rubbed her eyes, running her hands down to stop on her chest. "She was fired." She dropped her head back and stared into the night sky. "She called Terrance. They'd already been down in June, but he wanted to bring her here to tend to her. She obviously had no obligations for the upcoming school year, and he was successful enough in his practice to set his own agenda." She settled her gaze on Callie. "But an emergency delayed his departure, and when he arrived at nine that night, she'd already . . . hanged herself. The coroner said she died only an hour earlier, around eight."

That explained the victims dying at night. "You couldn't stop her, Rikki."

The woman teared again. "I asked her to give me one more day to finish some business." She swallowed her tears. "I should have been there."

While horribly tragic, the story only explained Terrance's addiction to August. While losing his twin initiated a shift in Terrance's behavior, none of this explained the origin of the jinx. Or why four years lapsed between Tia's death and the first murder. Or did they?

Callie felt the presence more than saw it and remembered Alex. Callie spun and got in the girl's face. "None of this until I tell you, remember? It puts Sophie at risk."

Alex wilted against Rikki's car. "You made your point." Then she said softly, "Callie?"

"What?"

"Um, we're standing in the middle of the road."

"Are we blocking traffic, Alex?"

"No. Guess not."

Funny, but standing in the center of Palmetto had empowered Callie, as if to fly in the face of rules. That's exactly where her head needed to be—outside plain, common schools of thought. Outside the *Edislow* speed of reacting instead of proactively seizing control.

She knew a lot more about Terrance thanks to Rikki, but not enough. She knew Sophie, but none of that knowledge seemed to matter. Something had to click. Some word, behavior, habit, or desire. Her breaths came quicker, shallower, heart pumping.

No anxiety attacks. No. She didn't do those anymore.

"Callie?" Alex asked.

"Give me a second," she replied, resting her butt on the Lexus, counting, breathing. Hearing the ocean inhale as it drew the water back from land and then exhale, the small whitecaps barely visible in the night. A focus on the lazy tide. Cleansing breaths.

No storms expected. Only a still summer night broken by the whisper of the surf.

Again, deep breaths. She needed to give her thoughts a chance to slow and gel.

Ever since Callie brought her son to the beach, Sophie had tried to hammer her yoga beliefs into the former-detective's head, telling her to chill, breathe, reach inward. Callie had interpreted that mentality as weak, an excuse not to confront the world head-on and label the things that were black as black and the things that were white as white. Grays caused confusion.

But there, in the middle of the road, as those around her slept, and Sophie's life dangled over a precipice someplace, Callie heard her yoga friend's voice.

When we change our thoughts and expand our inner vision, we change our circumstances. Our conscious awareness focuses on physical reality. Attempt change there first. By creating a mental vision of the changes we want to make, we shift our belief system to more closely fit with a reality we want. Our circumstances will change for the better.

Her vision was one of Sophie home safe. Her physical reality didn't exactly cooperate with that vision. Maybe Sophie's belief system made more sense. "Rikki?"

"Yes?" she replied. Both Alex and Rikki had patiently watched Callie, waiting, worried.

"Where's spirit central around here?"

"What?"

Callie waggled her bandaged fingers, trying to rush Rikki's understanding. "Where do people think ghosts hang out on the island? A place where star-crossed lovers died, or Civil War soldiers can't rest. You remember these tales. I heard them on the telecast Friday night. The news story that drove everybody here for the craft fair."

Rikki nodded her understanding before Callie finished talking. "Edingsville Beach is one of them. That's where the ghost bride waits for her fiancé to return. He died in a hurricane, and she walks the sand, sometimes is seen in the water, but that's only during storms."

That one didn't seem to fit, but this was good. This was proactive. "Okay, where else?"

"Brick House. Jenkins land. A woman named Amelia was shot by her ex-lover on her wedding day, but that one hasn't been seen since the house burned down. No real place to hide."

Alex tapped Callie's back.

"What, Alex?" Callie said, glaring with irritation over her shoulder.

"Julia Legare," she said. "It's in the Presbyterian Church cemetery, amongst all the other ghosts. I know you know it."

Indeed Callie did. The mausoleum where the young girl was buried alive and refused to let the tomb be sealed. The graveyard Papa Beach took her to at age ten, probably the most negative experience she recalled with Papa, before he died. The Legare tomb sat behind the graveyard, barely visible from Highway 174. A few daring tourists had seen and photographed the wisp of a spirit that remained in that tiny brick structure. Callie had no love lost for the place.

"Stay there," Callie ordered and ran to her car. As the other two remained in the middle of the road, she parked the Escape on the curb and trotted to the women. "You drive, Rikki."

"What about me?" Alex asked, her facial expression defying being left behind.

"Get in the back," Callie ordered, still wanting a grip on the reporter and her all-too-quick trigger fingers. It made sense that Terrance would match Sophie to the Legare tomb and its active supernatural reputation. Whether Callie was correct was left to be seen.

She bet it scared Sophie out of her mind.

"The church?" Rikki asked as she turned the Lexus around to head out onto 174.

"The church," Callie said, adrenaline infusing her system.

Seabrook would scoff at her deduction, a plan derived from talk of cemeteries and ghosts. The main reason she hadn't called him at two. It was ten past. He'd texted on the hour, but she didn't respond. She typed, *Still looking. Call when you hear anything.* He texted back with a thumbs up sign.

She had an hour before he'd worry again. A lot would hopefully happen in that hour . . . If she was wrong, Seabrook wouldn't have wasted time on Callie's silly theory.

However, if Callie was right, with a big IF accenting that thought, Terrance snatched Sophie for one of two purposes: To speak to his sister, or to off his victim at a place that matched her style. Stupid, but she couldn't make herself discard the idea for something more solid. A man who took a vacation to pick out a girl to kill wasn't solid to begin with. Guilt or vengeance, one or the other drove this guy. Either way, he desired to return to where his sister hanged herself and live there two weeks. What did that annual gesture represent other than a need to be closer to Tia? So why not her ghost?

What better way to connect with spirits but through someone who experienced them every night? What better place than where souls thrived as if perched at afterlife's portal.

Yeah, Seabrook and every other sane human being would consider her deduction far-fetched, but Callie easily envisioned Terrance depicting Sophie as a medium able to tap him into the nether world and conjure his twin sister's spirit.

"Hurry, Rikki."

Edisto would have its next jinx death when Sophie couldn't connect the call.

Another message appeared.

@MyOuttake—She's with the spirits now. #edistojinx

Chapter 30

THE AIR CONDITIONING ran on high, chilling the car's interior enough to send a rough shiver down Callie's spine as she gasped at the tweet.

She's with the spirits now.

"What is it?" Rikki cried as she peered over, the Lexus veering to the road's edge.

Alex had already read the post. "Oh my God. What do we do now?"

Ignorant to the facts, Rikki sped up, the Lexus hugging the deserted road. "No, don't tell me. I might not get us there in one piece."

Callie gripped her armrest as acceleration threw her against her seat. She glanced at the speedometer. Eighty-five on a two-lane road where massive four-foot live oaks could stop a full-sized semi-tractor trailer rig. Like they did her father. "Rikki, if you don't slow down, you'll kill us. That does Sophie no good whatsoever."

Rikki kept whispering, "Don't tell me. Don't tell me."

Holding down panic, Callie turned in her seat. "Slow down, I said. Stop freaking. This is what he wants."

MyOuttake already proved he relished nuance and deception. The hint in his post had rammed Callie's heart into her throat, but she repeated her own words to herself, *This is what he wants.* Until she saw a body, Callie refused to believe Sophie dead, but the tweets had changed. They were dark, and their infrequency meant Terrance must be preoccupied . . . probably with Sophie. Hopefully Sophie used her pain-in-the-butt-side to fight and stay alive. Losing someone close to Callie . . . again . . . no, she wasn't willing to cope with that. She would not go home to tell two kids their mother died before Callie reached her.

She dialed Seabrook, bumping into her window as Rikki took a curve.

"Where are you?" he answered.

"He's tweeting me," she said. "Did you see?"

His breath came loud over the phone. "Yes. What do you think?"

"We're on our way to the Presbyterian Church on 174."

"Fill me in why."

Two miles from the church, Callie covered the phone. "Slow down, Rikki. Drive normal and roll past the church first. Let's see if his car's there."

"Callie? What's going on?" Seabrook said louder.

"Listen to me," she said, "before you discount my theory."

"Talk."

"The messages mentioned spirits twice. At the party, Terrance expressed a big interest in the fact Sophie claimed to have spiritual connections. He talked at great length to Rikki about it after he spoke about it with me. His twin sister committed suicide at his beach house ten years ago, before you worked here. He's a doctor, and maybe not being able to save her screwed with his head."

He didn't respond.

"Or he killed her, too," she added.

"Jesus!"

Even before she said it aloud, she knew it sounded strange. "He might want to use Sophie to reach out to his dead sister."

"What?"

"Hold on."

Rikki slowed to the speed limit and passed the tall white clapboard church with its four thick, white columns.

Callie peered through the inky night, scouring for a silhouette of the Mercedes. Nothing in the parking area, wait. A glint of something in the shadows on the west side. A car, but she missed the make and model. Too many shadows. They moved too fast. She let Rikki drive on for a half mile then motioned for her to park on the edge of the road.

"Seabrook?" Callie asked.

"Yeah. I can do the math, but this makes him crazier than ever. We need to wait for SLED. They're en route."

"Sorry, not happening, Mike."

Sophie'd waited long enough thanks to nobody noticing her gone. It had been at least four hours since she disappeared. Callie shut her eyes and pushed emotions aside.

By now, Sophie might easily be dead. Waiting for the state's law enforcement team to arrive only increased those odds.

"I'm checking out the church," she said, to right herself. "And if he's not there, I'll head to Steamboat Landing. I don't believe Brick House is worth the effort, but—"

"You're hunting ghosts?"

Of course he'd know all the tales. As an Edisto Seabrook, he had the history all the way back to plantation days.

"I'll meet you at the church," he said. "Give me twenty minutes."

"We're in a white Lexus." She hung up.

But she damn sure wouldn't wait twenty minutes.

Terrance ached for his sister, and for some perverted reason, killed women who resembled her. That part didn't make a lick of sense, but then, depraved minds never made sense to anyone but themselves.

What if he did kill Tia? But if he repeated killing her via his victims, why hadn't he hanged them, too?

The Lexus idled, Rikki staring ahead, grips at ten and two on the wheel, her long braid draped over her shoulder almost into her lap. Alex kept her focus on her phone, both women stiff, neither quite ready to face what lay ahead.

"Turn around, Rikki," Callie said. "Drive almost to the church and park on the left, under that thick stand of trees. I'll walk to the cemetery."

Rikki made a three-point turn and headed back, lights off.

Callie cursed the choice to bring the white vehicle, an oversight on her part. She quickly picked a spot hidden from the church, a little over a hundred yards from the vicinity of the hidden vehicle. Rikki excelled nesting it amongst some oaks and behind somebody's ten-foot azaleas not far from a fence row. A soldier following orders to the T.

A car was indeed parked near the west wall of the structure, quite obscure. Maybe the Mercedes. A location easily missed from the direction they first came.

But he was there. Callie felt it. All those Boston cases teaching her that her gut didn't lie. In the sanctuary, in the cemetery, maybe amongst the trees, he was here. Because if he wasn't, Callie had to start hunting for a body.

Thank goodness for one of Sophie's new moon nights. While a full moon would've made the hunt easier, a moonless sky gave her cover. Unfortunately it covered him, too.

Callie pined a nanosecond for her friend, realizing Sophie had missed burning her black candle on this night, making good-luck wishes for all her friends.

Pivoting around to see both the ladies, Callie spoke firm but composed, her voice even and low. "Y'all pay attention."

Alex nodded in slow motion. Rikki listened.

"Alex? You stay here. Watch for the police." She reached over and tapped the girl's phone with her fingernail. "That screen is going to shine like a flashlight out here. You're safer if you leave it off."

The girl's eyes narrowed, then eased as the logic set in. She clicked off the cell.

Callie touched the driver's arm. "Rikki? I'm giving you a choice."

The Amazon's detached stare evaporated. "A choice?"

"Yes. You can sit here with Alex, or you can come with me."

"Hey, why can't I—" Alex started, but Callie cut her off with a look, before returning to Rikki.

"You know Terrance better than anyone," Callie said gently.

"I just met him," Rikki replied.

"But you understand his history, knew his sister. You might be able to talk to him."

Rikki's long fingers rubbed across her eyes, swiping down to stop on her neck. She gazed into the floor, thinking.

"I'll be there," Callie murmured. "I'll take him down if need be, but if we can talk him out of this situation, it's best for everyone. I'd wait for SLED, but I'm afraid . . ."

"Let's go." Rikki opened her door and had the awareness to ease it silently closed.

"Alex?" Callie said. "You might climb into the front seat, just in case."

"In case what?" she asked, but Callie already exited the Lexus. "Wait. What about the keys?" Then, "Oh" when she saw them hanging in the ignition.

Together the two women left the hiding place, into the shadows of more oaks until they hunkered at the corner of a short, three-slatted, three-foot fence marking a house forty yards to the left of the sanctuary. The perfect model black Mercedes hugged the church.

Validation Terrance was MyOuttake.

Darkness favored them there, but a streetlight illuminated the eastern part in front of the cemetery, not far from the walk that led to the mausoleum.

Where was Terrance? Where were they supposed to hunt first?

"There, that way." Callie pushed past Rikki, snaring her silk top. They stooped and took the front steps, flattening against the backs of two tall, grooved columns.

For a large woman, Rikki did stealth well. "What now?"

Callie eased over and tried the church doors, not surprised at the aroma of her own sweat when she moved. Fear.

The doors were locked. No lights inside. She slipped next to Rikki behind the same column. "Which side has more cover? Have you been here before?"

"Who hasn't been here?" she whispered.

Callie hadn't, at least since Papa Beach tried to bring her here at age ten. She'd been raised Episcopalian, not Presbyterian, to adhere to her mother's social needs. But she hadn't set foot in any church since her infant daughter died from SIDS three years ago. Blind from the night and ignorant of the territory, she needed the Amazon's guidance more than ever.

This wasn't about Terrance. This was purely about finding Sophie and escaping without injury.

"That one," Rikki breathed, nodding toward the east, the cemetery. "More shrubs. More fencing. More tombstones."

Callie peered out, trying to see, and snapped back behind the column. "Okay. You stay here."

"Thought you wanted me to talk to Terrance?" Her frown seemed laced with pain. "I built myself up for this."

"Honey," Callie said, gripping Rikki's forearm, "you still might, but you aren't armed. Here you're safe. I'll call when it's time for you to do your thing."

The frown eased, and Rikki nodded. "Gotcha."

She liked Rikki more and more. The woman had smarts and paid attention to reason. But Callie couldn't afford for her to tag along as this lackadaisical plan tried to gain traction. An unarmed partner equated to liability. They didn't provide cover and had to be protected.

Callie wanted every neuron in her brain honed in on finding Sophie.

Brushing fingers over the Glock in her waistband, for nothing other than to lessen the impotency building in her gut, Callie sucked in a lungful of the wet air and scooted in the direction Rikki stated.

Rounding the corner, still hugging the building, she welcomed the five-foot azaleas. Sweat dripped in her eyes already. She'd kill for a breeze. Not only for the relief, but for the extra cover. Wind meant leaves rustling, tree limbs rubbing, the plump eight-foot tendrils of Spanish moss dancing, enabling her to move without being so easily sighted. Right now any movement would prompt the dimmest of wits to notice her.

She questioned whether to inch down along the church walls or cross the path into the graveyard. Easing her head up she studied how far the shrubs went and how dense. She ran around a set of steps and hid again amongst the greenery. An identical set of stairs near the rear of the church, then darkness beyond, maybe thirty, forty feet between her and that darkness.

Her breaths sounded loud in her own ears. She slowed them, turned them shallow, listening for anything that would define Sophie. Her voice, a moan, a cry, the clinking of her bracelets. She swallowed the lump in her throat. Nothing.

Then she analyzed the graveyard. Ancient tombstones of a wide array of design and size spread out past a grassy ten-foot walkway. She remembered the huge tall spire that served as a landmark, commemorating a family lost at sea. Blending into the blackness toward the Legare mausoleum at the very back of the cemetery, wrought iron surrounded clusters of markers. Square-shaped family plots. Townsends, Popes, Mikells, Whaleys, McConkeys, Edings, and yes, Seabrooks. She couldn't read the stones. Didn't have to. Any Edisto resident recognized the families who'd defined this island. If Seabrook went to church, she'd expect him to go here.

Funny how she didn't know if he did.

Too much time ticked by.

Lacy in design and centuries old, the fencing seemed worthless for cover. Plus the enclosed family plots and irregular tombstone placement meant constant stumbling. Nix that.

Come on, Callie.

Only one or two no-see-ums had buzzed around her head when she hid behind the column with Rikki, but with her now immobile in the bushes, overshadowed by Spanish moss, they labeled her dinner en masse. Afraid to wave, she blew softly, dying to fan them off. They nipped and buzzed, ducked in her ears, her nose.

Focus. Sophie had already dealt with this place for hours, atop her fear.

After pushing through and around bushes to the rear corner, within sight of the tomb and a wall of black trees behind it, she knelt. As her two compatriots had become so fond of saying, *Now what?*

A flashlight came on, and she flinched about the time she heard the voice . . . from within the Legare mausoleum fifty feet away. "You're a damn fraud!"

"No, no," Sophie said, meek and terror-filled, her little voice traveling in the silent night. "I can do this. But that light in my face ruins it."

"Liar," Terrance said.

Her voice quivered. "And you have a gun aimed at me."

God help her, but Callie'd pegged him right. And she so wish she hadn't.

Sophie sounded petrified.

Terrance's small flashlight seemed no bigger than one a doctor would use, but when it flashed across the opening, it revealed enough to show that he'd somehow removed wooden bars from the tomb's entrance. They tilted askew, splintered, most likely kicked in. It used to be open all the time until too many tourists appeared too often and too eager to experience the mythical ghost inside. The legend of Julia Legare, a girl being interred while in a coma, only to rise and attempt to claw her way out, intrigued the curious.

Callie's blood chilled. Sophie's sensitivities to such things had to be unraveling her sanity. But as much as Sophie bragged about her spiritual beliefs, her experience didn't run this deep. She damn sure didn't have ghosts at her beck and call.

And Terrance had just figured that out.

Sweat trickled down Callie's spine, the gun biting into her lower back, reminding her it was time to deal with MyOuttake. She filled her hands with her weapon and started to rise, ignoring the damp pants wrinkled and sticking to the backs of her legs.

"Leave me alone," Sophie pleaded. "Let me rest a moment. Give me ten minutes. That's all. Then I'll try again."

"Five," Terrance answered. "I won't be far."

The light jumped then exited the tomb first, held tight in Terrance's grip. His body language reeked hostile with jerky, angry movements, a Mr. Hyde to the Dr. Jekyll she'd experienced with the Edisto Sleuth Society.

He moved a few yards in Callie's direction and stopped. His gaze swept across where she hunched.

She held her breath.

His attention, however, returned to the tomb, glued to the entrance as Sophie half sang, half mumbled, giving the role her best effort. Putting the gun in his pocket, he turned off the flashlight. Soon a flame rose, then went out, the end of his cigarette glowing red in the nothingness. Then he froze, the only movement being his cigarette arm. His intense study of the tomb's entrance showed how acutely he needed Tia to walk out and greet him.

Callie tensed her leg muscles, at the ready, recognizing an opportunity.

She raised her weapon.

"Terrance!"

What the heck? Callie backed down, leaning in tighter, her crouch only two feet high.

Terrance threw down the cigarette. His flashlight flicked on, the beam resting on Rikki.

Chapter 31

RIKKI WALKED OUT from the shadows of the other side of the church. She kept walking, the flashlight accenting her approach like an actor to the front of the stage. She didn't stop until she stood between Terrance and Callie.

What the hell was she doing?

Callie sank behind the branches as Terrance crisscrossed the beam around him.

"Don't you think I would've reached Tia if it were possible?" Rikki asked him.

Terrance stood agape, the .22 lowered at his side.

"You left me at the party, Terrance," she continued and backstepped toward the direction from whence she came. "For so many years I've cried for Tia . . . I see you at the party. Then you just"—she shrugged—"disappear. What was that about? Don't you recall how much she meant to me? How much I meant to her?"

She eased toward the car, distancing herself from Callie, and if Terrance followed, opening the walk for Callie to reach the mausoleum.

"You weren't there when she died," he said, not pleased.

"Neither were you," Rikki replied, like a strong, frank friend. No fear in sight. "And that means we understand each other's pain, doesn't it? It eats you up. I was in Germany when she called, telling me how she lost her job because of her sexuality. How that whore of a teacher there painted those lies, saying Tia abused young girls. I delayed a day. One day!"

"I took another patient," he said, his words heavy with emotion. "I left her alone too long."

"We both did."

Rikki had reached the corner of the church. Then she burst into tears. Terrance seemed stymied what to do.

"But I don't understand, Terrance. Why are you killing women like Tia? Why are you tarnishing her memory?" A deep sob fell out of her.

"No, no, that's not it." He cried as well, so pitiful and so opposite from the personality who'd just threatened to kill Sophie.

"Then why?" Rikki asked.

Callie scurried toward the tomb, grateful for the grass walkway to mute her steps. At the entrance, she hugged the rose-colored cement wall and hid on the shrubbery-draped side of the structure, praying snakes or lizards weren't startled out of their sleep. Sophie sang and chanted. She couldn't see Callie, and Callie couldn't see her. She didn't want to startle Sophie and ruin the risk Rikki took.

Terrance cleared his throat. Callie stiffened in case he glanced behind him.

"What?" Rikki asked, the whimper heartbreaking. "Tell me, Terrance, please. When I realized who you were, I assumed you were killing Tia over and over, and that stabbed me in the heart."

The flashlight suddenly shined against the church wall as Terrance embraced Rikki. "I'm so sorry," he cried.

Fear snaked across Callie's shoulders. The man's roller-coaster emotions clearly indicated how detached he was from his sanity. And to think this man treated patients.

"That bitch stole Tia's life," he said again. "Tia's life at that school. And took the principal's job earmarked for my sister."

"She enjoyed teaching those girls," Rikki added, sniffling.

He swiped at his face. "Well, that slut died."

Rikki gasped, and Callie almost did, too.

"Of cancer," he continued. "Four years later. She took my sister's job, reputation, and hope. Ruined her entire life then got cancer and died. I . . . she . . . it wasn't right! It wasn't fair!"

"What wasn't fair, Terrance?"

He'd quit crying, outrage sliding in. "That woman returned from the dead every time I came to the beach, inserting herself into those women, taunting me, walking past as if I didn't know, but I knew. She knew I knew."

Callie's mouth fell open. Tia's nemesis became Terrance's trigger. His meek personality had denied him that vengeance for four years. The cancer, however, propelled his internal conflict to take action. In a deranged, distorted logic, Terrance took out his agony on other women he thought were that woman, reincarnated.

The singing continued low inside the brick structure, the words gibberish as Sophie desperately adlibbed, as if stopping would end her life.

"Keep singing," Callie whispered.

Sophie tripped over her words and then continued a lilting chant. Callie hoped that meant she understood.

She glanced toward Terrance. Gone!

Where was Rikki?

Crap!

Without the assurance of Terrance's whereabouts, Callie slipped inside the tomb, the dusty, stale odor filling her nose. Stifling. Thick. But bless her heart, Sophie kept singing.

"It's me," Callie whispered, hearing her to the right, pulse rushing. No telling how long Rikki could keep Terrance occupied, and she jeopardized her neck even trying. "You're doing great, Sophie." Callie groped the walls, getting her bearing, defining the seven foot width, maybe eight in depth, and a sloping, rough textured ceiling she touched when reaching up on her toes. "Can you stand?"

But Sophie didn't stand.

Callie knelt, and by pure sense of feel, found Sophie's legs, the complete blackness hindering her speed.

"Remove your shackles, release your hands and feet," Sophie sang. "Free yourself and come to me."

Good job, Sophie!

Callie's adrenaline pumped. Her friend's positive outlook on the world remained intact. She hadn't crumbled. With Sophie's mental shape, they had a chance to slip out.

But the good feeling dissipated when Callie felt duct tape. She'd brought no knife, unable to see well enough to find a sharp piece of anything. Frantically, she searched Sophie's ankles for the raw seam of the tape.

Pressure built in her chest as seconds spun past. She went to the wrists instead. Again duct tape. An edge! She picked at it with fingernails then unwound with care, fighting hard not to make it rip and reveal her presence.

A light flashed on, then off. She whipped around. The light flashed again, piercing her eyes this time, blinding. Instinct took over, and she dropped and rolled.

Sophie screamed.

The kick glanced off Callie's hip. Her momentum stopped abruptly against the wall, her head smacking at the stop. Though stunned, she held onto her Glock and swung it around.

The light flashed again. She instinctively flinched then went to roll again, but Terrance calculated properly this time. His kick connected with her midsection. Her lungs whooshed as a sharp jolt of pain shot through her ribs. Her gun flew off into the darkness.

"Callie!" Sophie cried.

Her brain's instinct pushing her to breathe instead of shoot the bad guy, Callie fought for control and for breaths that wouldn't come. The Lowcountry moisture seemed to smother her.

And in the midst of suffocating, in one single micro-second, she worried what happened to Rikki.

Then everything brightened in a dull way and remained that way as Terrance left the light on. The scattered, tiny flashlight beam sank into the rough surface to make the room slightly visible in dark grays.

Though the gig was up, Sophie mumbled her singing again at the presence of her captor, the words quivery and more of a hum. But God help her, she wasn't stopping until someone ordered her to. And for some reason, Terrance allowed her to continue.

"Where's Rikki?" Callie managed to croak, her left arm shielding her middle in case of another blow. With the other, she lifted herself to a seated position against the wall where three Legare headstones hung, representing the bodies below them.

"Sleeping," he said harshly, as he drew out his .22.

Jesus, what did that mean? But she had to keep him talking. "Why, Terrance?" she asked. Her gun lay a yard from him, too far from her.

There they were. Sophie bound and propped against the back wall, Callie injured, leaning against the left, Terrance on guard at the entrance. In the middle of the floor lay a coffin-length stone pad an inch high. At the head of it rested a formed stone resembling a pillow, probably where people kneeled or placed memorials. Too cramped to avoid a bullet from an itchy trigger finger.

"Terrance, let me help," she said. "Your pain has to be a heavy burden after so many years."

But he shook his head. Then a soft smile tried to crease the corners of his lips. One that told Callie he teetered between worlds.

Her heart jumped when she remembered she resembled the other women, even more so than Sophie. Terrance was a slight man, but Callie was smaller, and injured. She might not fend him off.

"The best vacation I've had since Tia died," he said, lips mashed into a grin. The playful Terrance who knocked on doors for the ESS. "I wish you'd moved here sooner."

Frankly, Callie did, too. Papa Beach might not have been murdered. Maybe one or more of the dead women would still be alive. Life at Edisto might have been what it was supposed to be, eventless, a retreat from a harsher world everybody wanted to escape from.

Definitely not this.

"So we're good, right?" she asked, reaching for a connection, regardless how incredible.

"No, I need to be able to return, Callie. If you're here, I can't. Nobody's come this close before. Hell, nobody's ever suspected before. You're an exceptional woman."

Like Callie hadn't spoken to nary a soul? Like Seabrook didn't know?

Seabrook. He had to be close.

Her Glock lay at Terrance's feet.

He waved the .22 like a toy, an animated extension of his hand.

"What are you going to do, shoot me?" Callie asked. "That's a little daring. Your methods are usually more distant, less personal."

Sophie's eyes widened. Callie tried not to look at her, to keep the attention on herself. Each second brought Seabrook closer and kept Terrance's mind occupied.

"Like Grant, for instance," she continued. "There he sat, in a chair, half-drunk after his wife's death, and you miss." She rolled her eyes and wondered if Terrance could tell. "With that gun, too, if I'm not wrong."

He stared down at the weapon and lifted it a bit higher.

Callie saw a man not comfortable with a firearm and a chance to drag this out until Seabrook arrived.

"It's obvious you're not used to shooting people," Callie said, the facts piecemealing together slowly. "Maybe that's why the women died so many other ways. You never found the correct way to get even with the woman who ruined Tia's life, did you, Terrance? No method seemed to blast that bitch completely to hell, did it? She wouldn't stay dead."

"No," he said softly. His shoulders weren't braced any more, his voice no longer emboldened. The man who wanted to drink mimosas with the Edisto Sleuth Society and enjoy being an amateur gumshoe on Callie's front porch. He seemed to retreat into himself, digesting memories. "You'd think a doctor would get it right, wouldn't you?"

What else could Callie say? She struggled to keep him engaged. "Grant meant nothing to you, not that he was a particularly nice guy. He killed his wife, in case you hadn't heard. Or is that why you shot him?"

Terrance adopted a puzzled expression and waved his gun again. "I love how you think things through then lay them out there, Detective. Frank and I talked at great length about Brea Jamison's death and who did it. He said the boyfriend. I said the husband. Of course I think I saw him slip something into her drink. I would even testify to that effect. Doctors make credible witnesses."

"Not after you shot him, Terrance."

He scrunched his mouth, then his nose. "Not my original intention. But when everyone credited his wife's death on the jinx, and it appeared he might get away with it . . . I mean, she didn't fit! Brea seemed a genuinely decent person. No sign of the bitch who liked women more like my Tia. But if I didn't take action, that would mean the damn whore would've won this summer. Maybe become more powerful. You see? I had to keep, like you said, *blowing her back to hell.*" He gave a heavy snort, then shook his head again. "No, just wasn't right. Besides, her husband was an ill sort." He studied his .22. "I really thought I aimed properly. As a doctor, you'd think I would . . . and . . ."

He quit talking. His stare seemed to disappear into the front corner, to his right, directly in front of Sophie. Off went his light.

Callie tensed for a move, recalling exactly where her weapon lay. She eased forward on her hands and knees, pain piercing her middle.

Terrance swung his gun around as he turned on the light, nuzzling the shaking barrel against Callie's forehead. "How'd you do that?"

Sophie's eyes stretched wide as silver dollars, but not at Terrance. She seemed horrified at the room's corner, too.

"How'd I do what?" Callie asked, queasy from the acute stab in her side, petrified at the feel of the metal on her skin.

His stare returned to the corner. "Tia?"

Chapter 32

TOO PRIMED FOR a chance to shrink from his aim and not willing to fall into his psycho world, Callie didn't follow his gaze to whatever had Terrance mesmerized. His hand shimmied. A low moan climbed hoarse and scared from his throat.

She fought to control her own shake. If she timed it right, she could dip, snare her weapon, and fire toward his head.

Warbling sounds of fright came from Sophie, but Callie remained fixed on her purpose. Pulse thrummed in her ears. She steadied the weight on each knee, her palms, poised, sweat dripping, reaching slowly . . . pushing aside the pain.

Pressure rose in her ears, like a tornado on the brink of landing, the compressing kind of sensation every Lowcountry native knew. The air grew thick, weighing on her chest hard, then harder. Hair rose on the nape of her neck. She couldn't breathe.

Terrance bolted out the door.

Darkness cloaked the room.

Callie snatched her weapon.

"Callie?"

She crawled over to Sophie, wincing, panting, hearing Sophie huffing as well. Fumbling with the tape again, Callie managed to rip the loose end and free her friend's wrists.

"Oh my God, did you see it, Callie?"

"Hold on a minute."

"No, did you see the smoke?"

She had to free Sophie. Terrance would return any moment, only this time less willing to chat.

She ventured to the doorway and groped around the entrance until she found a long cement screw that had held the bars in place. She crawled back inside, raked the screw threads over the tape constricting Sophie's ankles and cut her loose. She rested a moment, her Glock in her lap.

Seabrook appeared, his Glock drawn.

"Where's Terrance?" Callie asked. "You didn't see him?"

"No, for God's sake, what happened?" Frustration coated his face, like he'd gotten it all wrong.

"He parked on the west side of the church." She fast waved at him to leave. "Go. You might still see him."

Seabrook dashed off, his running footsteps immediately gone from detection with the moist ground dampening the noise.

They heard him before they saw him, speaking into his mic as he returned. He clicked off.

"He's gone," he said. "I called it in. We must have two dozen people out there hunting him now."

Damn it! She had Terrance. She almost had him. "Here, help Sophie." She stood with effort. "I can't."

He assisted Sophie through the entrance, the yoga instructor still unsteady. Then he returned for Callie. She cried out as he tried to wrap arms around her. "Don't. I think Terrance cracked a rib."

Letting her hoist herself holding onto his arm, he said, "There's not a soul around."

She dug nails into his arm. "Not even Rikki?"

"No. Why would she—"

"Rikki?" Sophie cried. "Did Terrance hurt Rikki?"

But Callie's feet had already dug into the grass, trotting best she could muster past the acting police chief. She rounded the Seabrook family plots with a limp, across the back of the church, then cut left to where the Mercedes had parked. Nothing. Gone. Her heart beat like a hummingbird's. No sign of Rikki whatsoever.

Callie's phone vibrated in her pocket. "Did you see him, Alex?" She stood in the man's tire tracks, her fist clenched with no target to pound. "Did you see which way he turned?"

"See, hell," the reporter shouted over tires humming in the distance. "I'm on his damn bumper. Now what?"

"Which direction are you headed?"

"Toward the big bridge," she yelled.

"Seabrook!" Callie shouted, about the time he rounded the corner. "Alex is on his friggin' ass." Her breaths came labored, exhales tortuous. "In the Lexus. They're almost to the bridge."

Instead of jumping into some sort of action, he calmly reached for his mic.

"Seabrook!" she exclaimed.

He relayed the information to authorities on the other end. "Thanks, Seabrook out."

"Your car," she said. "Get Sophie. Let's—"

"Sophie's in my car. Callie. Let's go put you in the car with her. We've got to get you to a doctor."

"But—"

He gingerly touched her shoulders. "There's only one road off this island, and I've had county deputies blocking it since Sophie disappeared. He's as good as caught. You can call off your blogger." He held the next words for a second. "You cannot be the entire police force. You should've waited."

She'd heard that before. From Stan. And it had done her in after John died, forcing her to leave Boston.

But this time she saved Sophie.

"What about Rikki?" Her stomach tightened. The stress, the late night hour, and the injury were about to make her hurl. "Terrance brought her this way. There wasn't time to do much with a . . ." She started to say body, but didn't. She had no proof Rikki was dead. She'd heard no gunshot, and Rikki was so much taller than Terrance. He only said she was sleeping. That meant anything. She might be anywhere. "Fan out. Look for her."

"I'll do it. You quit moving. You don't play with broken ribs. Go to Sophie and sit. She might need you."

Seabrook radioed deputies to be on the lookout for Rikki in the Mercedes. "I'll call if we find her here," he said and signed off.

Sophie scurried to them, too wired to sit, too upset over Rikki's disappearance to wait in a car. "Callie, why was she here? She had no business coming after this guy," she said, her movements antsy, eyes wide and frantic.

"Sophie, please help him hunt for her. She might be hiding, or unconscious, still around here."

Sophie immediately began pawing through bushes, not realizing she couldn't see two feet in front of her until Seabrook placed a Maglite in her hand to help. The two of them scoured every azalea and tombstone on the property to no avail. There were two streetlights between where the Lexus had been parked and the mausoleum, their light easily sucked into the dense darkness so common on the rural island.

The minister in the house next door woke and asked why people clowned around his church at three in the morning.

The preacher joined in the search still in his robe, but they completed canvassing the area in minutes. Terrance hadn't the time or constitution to carry Rikki far, which still led them to believe she had to be in the car.

Callie felt herself wilt as she settled into the cruiser. Sophie stooped and peered inside the vehicle, glancing down periodically to pick dead leaves out of her crocheted skirt.

Seabrook got in. "Your ribs require attention this island doesn't have. The minister's taking Sophie home."

Sophie's multi-ringed fingers brushed Callie's shoulder. "Thank you doesn't seem to say enough, Callie. What did I do before you came to Edisto?"

That drew a faint smile from Callie. "You did perfectly fine, Sophie. You'll always do fine."

"The ghost saved us," her friend continued.

Callie closed her eyes, too tired and sore to respond to that comment.

"I wished she'd saved Rikki," Sophie added.

Rikki. Callie couldn't help thinking the worst.

Sophie teased some debris out of her hair. "I take it you didn't see the spirit."

Exhaustion owned every cell of Callie's body. "No, I didn't."

"Well, count your blessings, girl, because Terrance sure did. He turned ten shades of pale. I'm bringing flowers to that mausoleum tomorrow. And I'm bringing Rikki with me."

"We need to go, Sophie," Seabrook said, starting the engine.

Callie was too tired to marvel at Sophie's wishful thinking, using her positive outlook to make reality what she wanted it to be. And Callie wished Rikki were here right now, to launch a crack at Sophie about the experience, blaming gasses or fear or some sort of guru trance—anything but a spirit.

Sophie would probably appreciate hearing that snide remark, too.

They drove off the property and headed toward the bridge, the only way to Charleston. Callie rested her head against the window. Why had she let Rikki come? She'd bought them time, thrown Terrance off, but at what cost?

Seabrook's hand gently covered her wrist.

Her phone vibrated. "Alex?"

"They stopped me, Callie. I tried to catch him."

"You did what you could, Alex." Callie started to sigh and grunted at the pain. "Did they stop him? Do you see Rikki?"

"What do mean Rikki?" she asked. "They wouldn't let me go any further to see, but I'm guessing they got him. He wasn't that far ahead." She repeated herself. "What about Rikki?"

"We haven't been able to find her. Did you see her in Terrance's car?"

"No, but Callie, if you don't mind, I'm staying."

The first time the girl had asked Callie's okay on anything. "That's fine," Callie said and hung up. Ever the journalist, Alex probably wanted pictures, conversations, and the chance to record a blow-by-blow of whatever she scraped from the outskirts of the apprehension, but not so cold she wasn't concerned about Rikki. Nice girl.

Callie yearned to be in Alex's shoes right now.

Adrenaline ebbed as twitches traveled her arms and legs. She never guessed Rikki to be the casualty in all this. The six-foot fifty-year-old blonde couldn't be more opposite from the profile.

The McKinley Washington, Jr. Bridge carried cars across the Dawho River to the big Edisto Island. Seven miles or so from the church. Thirteen miles from the beach. Blue lights shone from a half mile away as Seabrook's cruiser approached the overpass. Charleston County, Colleton County, and three Edisto PD cars speckled the gloom in flashing color.

Callie craned her neck. "There!" she pointed, spotting the Mercedes. "Seabrook, pull over."

"There are enough people here," he said, though he scanned the sea of uniforms as well. "We need to get you to—"

"Rikki! They have her on the ground. Stop, Mike. Please stop."

They eased by, the deputies manning the traffic directing them through the road block. Callie tried to twist in her seat, but the pain prevented it. So she moved the rearview mirror, adjusting, hunting for the right angle. "Turn around."

"No," Seabrook said firmly. "We can't do a thing to help."

"I don't want to help. I want to see Rikki!" She thought she'd care more about nailing the Edisto jinx, but right now she only wanted to hear Rikki's sarcasm.

Seabrook continued across the bridge, taking the car to eighty, the Dawho River winding beneath them, but Callie couldn't see for the tears filling her eyes.

"But I made her come with me tonight."

Chapter 33

SEABROOK UPDATED her around five thirty in the morning as she waited for x-rays. They took Terrance into custody with little incident, which almost disappointed her. In her book, he deserved more of what came along with fighting off law enforcement.

Then Seabrook told her about Rikki. She wasn't dead, but that's all he knew.

A simple nondisplaced rib fracture they called Callie's injury. Nothing simple about how she earned it, she thought. And it didn't feel simple while they did all their poking, prodding, and head shaking. Callie left the hospital with a bottle of souped-up ibuprofen and a warning to be careful for a few weeks. Bruises decorated her from head to hip. It was past eleven before Seabrook crossed the bridge back to Edisto, Callie dozing in the passenger seat.

She slept fitful, chasing someone she could not see, darting unseen objects, hunting for Rikki. Snatches of naps. Her mind still wrapped too tightly around the night's events. Cracking her eyelids once, she recognized Highway 17, her cheeks moist from dream tears, then what seemed like seconds later, she saw the Dawho River, and a sense of peace settled her a bit.

"Callie? Wake up. You're home."

She opened puffy lids, grateful for sunglasses protecting her gritty eyes.

"I'll get you out," he said.

"No, I got it . . . unh," she moaned as she tried to push open her door, the ride having allowed stiffness literally to settle in her bones.

"I said I got it," he complained, holding out his arm to help her stand. "They would've kept you overnight if not for me promising to watch over you. That includes listening to what I say. About your health, anyway. Heaven knows any other advice to you falls on deaf ears."

She studied the rising stairs at Chelsea Morning. Then over to the right at the burnt shell of Papa Beach's home. Amazing how no pink slips fluttered on that house.

With effort and a slow one step, pause, one step, pause pace, they went to the porch. Then as she reached for the knob, the door opened.

"Mom!" Jeb reached his long arms around his mother. But as she stiffened, readying for the pain, Seabrook, Sophie, and Beverly yelled, "No!" pushing and dragging him back, red-faced.

Friends and family crammed Callie's entry hall, and even Officer Francis stood off to the side in civilian clothes, a shy smile on his face. He tipped his narrow head as she caught a glimpse of him. A comrade now. That warmed her heart.

One person, however, would've rocked her day, regardless of her exhaustion. But the towering head was missing from the crowd.

Callie eased through people, each gingerly touching or kissing her. The place showed no sign of the party that served as the catalyst for all this, her home spotless. She owed some angels her thanks. Fatigue began to hang on her, and she decided if she had to entertain guests, she would do it seated in the living room.

After passing Alex and Ms. Hanson, Sprite and Zeus, she reached the end of the hall and turned to find her sofa . . . and halted.

The Amazon got up from a chair.

"You'd see me over everybody's heads if I stood," she said. Tears sprang to her eyes. "I wanted to surprise . . . God, I'm so glad you're okay."

A cry escaped from Callie as her legs almost collapsed. "Oh, Rikki, I'm so sorry."

Rikki covered the distance to Callie in two long steps. Callie wrapped her arms around Rikki's waist, the woman gingerly hugging the detective to her chest. "Shhh, I'm fine," she said.

"You were so ridiculously brave." Callie held her at arm's length.

"Nothing compared to you, hon," Rikki replied. "You saved Sophie."

"No," Callie said, serious, grasping the woman's arms hard. She shook them. "*We* saved Sophie." She studied Rikki's face. "How are you? I still can't imagine how he—"

"Good thing I'm twice the size of Sophie. Terrance zapped a needle in me with something in it meant for her. It came out of nowhere, I tell you, so it must've been on him. I won't lie, I thought for that quick second I was done. Then the next thing I found myself in an ambulance. Missed out on the whole ordeal. Other than a headache and a few bruises from the struggling, bumbling way the stupid asswipe must've creased and folded me into his trunk . . ." She thrust out one of her long legs to show purple and blue on her calf and twisted to flaunt similar on the side of her arm. "That's only the ones I can show in front of children. The docs assured me my insides weren't damaged or anything from the stuff in that needle. He probably had plans to stick it to Sophie and . . . whatever."

A swoosh of a broom skirt appeared front and center to the moment, then inserted herself between the two women, an arm around each one. "Oh good heaven, Rikki, I'm standing right here," Sophie exclaimed. "I already saged this house before y'all got here, but now I've got to do it again. And isn't anyone worried how I fared? I almost died!"

"No, you didn't," Rikki said. "We almost died so you wouldn't."

"Still, I had to endure it longer. I"—she rested fingertips on her chest—"was subjected to fear longer than you were."

The room laughed. Callie whispered in her ear, "I'll kick myself every day for forever. It never should've happened." She kissed her friend on the cheek. "I'm so sorry. Are you really okay? I mean, really?"

"We can cry together later," Sophie whispered, then winked for the room. "Tried to tell you I'm tougher and smarter than everyone gives me credit for. I'd have escaped on my own."

Callie sniggered and turned to the group. "Sit, grab a seat. It hurts too much to look up at everyone. Who cleaned my house?"

Different people gestured at each other. Basically, everyone who hadn't chased Terrance.

Guests and family hustled to the sofa, recliner, bar chairs, the younger ones on pillows on the floor. Beverly snared the spot next to Callie like they were playing musical chairs and the tune stopped. She reached over and brushed down Callie's back, her touch gentle and light.

Callie turned at the gesture to see her mother's eyes filled to flowing. "I'm fine, Mother."

Beverly sniffled, chin out, blinking the weakness away. "You should call me next time something like this happens."

The chuckle bubbled to the surface before she had the good sense not to laugh, and Callie hugged her arms into her ribs at the pain.

"Oh, baby," her mother started.

Callie hadn't heard her mother call her that since before college.

"Mom," she said, using the less formal name for her mother that *she* hadn't used since before college. "Now why would I call you for something like this? And let's hope there's not a next time."

"Well, hero or not, I'm still on the fence about you and law enforcement," Jeb spouted from across the room. Sprite draped against him on the floor pillows, her brother Zeus propped on one hand beside her.

Seabrook had been quiet until then. "On the fence?" He scoffed. "I may not have known you long, son, but you haven't fence-straddled one moment since I met you. Don't think too many of us haven't heard you fuss how you feel about your mother and a uniform. Well, I've got news for you. She's pretty damn good at the job. I think most of Edisto is beginning to appreciate their luck in having her here."

Zeus stood in a dramatic fanfare, his mane of dark hair dancing to his delivery, arms stretched wide. "I, for one, am damn glad your mom's a cop, Jeb. My dear mother might be the community witch, but she's mine, and your mom made sure she came home."

Awwws made a circle around the room.

He bowed, and Sophie shook her head, pride splashed all over her face.

Alex bragged about Callie's cool head under pressure. Ms. Hanson mentioned Callie's diligence. The small gathering then turned a welcome home into a toasting party, without the booze. Callie tried to sit against the too-soft sofa cushions to better situate and endure the round robin remarks, stiffening her shoulders and shifting when no position seemed to work.

Seabrook apparently noticed. "Y'all, I think she needs about twenty-four hours of sleep, starting immediately."

She smiled weakly. "He's right. I'm about to drop dead right in front of you."

Her guests gasped and tsked at her choice of words before laughing to shrug off the reference.

Guests headed to the foyer, each congratulating Rikki, Sophie, and her until finally Beverly took over shooing everyone through the door. Callie didn't have the heart to send her mother home to Middleton. Jeb told Sprite he needed to remain home that evening. The last two family members she had, and tonight they wished to cherish that fact.

Seabrook left a lingering kiss on her lips, a deeper affection in his eyes. "Call me when you're awake. We'll go eat." He trailed fingers down her jawline, then leaned in. "Don't care what time it is." He gave her a last peck on the cheek. "I've got to learn to stop underestimating you. I keep getting it so wrong."

Rikki and Sophie remained next to Callie. "I'll leave you ladies for a minute," Beverly said. She strutted toward the kitchen, capturing Jeb by the arm. "Sweetheart, I can manage things here if you want to spend time with your friends," she said.

"I'm not sure about that, Grandma." The two voices lessened as their conversation continued around the corner.

"So," Callie said, analyzing her friends. "Why the convenient moment alone?"

Sophie teared. "To thank you, Callie. You were amazing. You risked yourself for me, and I can't fathom how to repay you."

Unable to think of what to say, Callie gave her a whisper of a hug. "You don't owe me anything. I dragged you into this."

"Indeed you did," she said in her trademark sarcasm, then cracked the facade with a smile.

Callie sensed a bittersweet moment in Rikki's awkward stance, her unsure motions, but wrote it all off to emotion, little sleep on all their parts, and Rikki's attempt to cope. "I'm sure you two are as tired as I—"

"I'm leaving Edisto," Rikki spouted.

Sophie laid her head against Rikki's arm and embraced her waist. With no surprise in her expression, Callie surmised she'd already heard.

But Callie didn't ask Rikki why. She suspected Tia had been a heavy burden on Rikki's mind for a decade. She connected with Terrance at the party, in what she interpreted as somewhat of a homecoming, and misjudged him to where she almost lost her life.

"It's not like I'm selling my condo or anything," she said. "It's already listed for rent, a long-term annual lease preferably, not a week-to-week tourist rental. I need some distance from the island."

"Has anyone ever done that before? I mean, leaving Edisto is like opting to abandon the Garden of Eden." Then Callie quit kidding. "I'm sorry to hear that. You're a decent woman, Rikki. A real asset around here."

"Yeah, well, I have my place in Germany, too. Friends there." She hunched her shoulders with a sigh and dropped them. "Seems the right thing to do. It's not because of you, though."

That sounded more like the normal Rikki—finishing a sentence with a jab. "No, it's that mixed blood of yours," Callie said. "Keeps you confused. Go on, do your German thing. But your Lowcountry blood will call you back like a siren, my friend."

"Yeah," she said. "Maybe. Look how you bounced around before planting your feet, Miss Boston Detective."

Yeah was right. In spite of every event on this beach that should have scarred her life and sent her packing, Callie considered Edisto home.

The only thing that could make it any more perfect would be John.

Chapter 34

THE POSTMAN ARRIVED as Callie reached the door. She read the return address and delayed another few minutes to open the envelope. She had dressed early with an hour to kill. Not like they would hold the specially scheduled four o'clock meeting without her.

Dearest Callie,

> *We are both distressed and pleased to hear the update of events on Edisto. Resultantly, the Edisto Sleuth Society has been abolished. We have lost so many nights' sleep over how we fraternized with Terrance Mallory. Perhaps we did a good thing introducing him to you, though, as you ended his spree. Regardless, we are not letting that man keep us from the enchantment of Edisto Beach. We're relieved your wounds were easily healed, and while we wish the jinx had been a myth, we're happy its reign is over. We'll see you next August. The mimosas and dinner are on us.*

—Frank and Ava

The message added yet another bright spot to her day, a day that already seemed completely devoted to going her way. She folded the note and tucked it in her pocket then checked her watch, a gift from Rikki. Good for her word, Rikki packed and left three days after Callie's homecoming and hadn't been heard from since. That had been four weeks ago. Her Amazon friend needed the distance and the time to heal.

Callie'd done a little healing of her own. While a deep breath reminded her of the rib, it didn't shoot to her core like it once did. The Charleston doctor told her what Seabrook already had . . . like any bone fracture, healing averaged about six weeks. Ibuprofen became her friend, and jogging would continue to suffer for a few weeks more.

She drove her Escape into the government complex parking lot on Murray Street, where Seabrook had first asked her out, and she'd turned him down. Vehicles packed the lot, but they'd reserved a place for her. Such attention seemed surreal.

With a controlled inhale, she reached to open her car door, then stopped and breathed again, not quite ready to enter. These people felt accolades in order for her. Between the tweets, Sophie's grapevine, and the police department, and then the special edition paper from Jenkins who sang her praises to the moon and back, everyone not only knew about Terrance, but also about the Russian. A few, however, still touted she brought the Russian upon herself.

But the jinx had been all theirs. Not a one of them questioning the deaths for six years, choosing to be ignorant to the clues.

Boston would've thrown an award at her, too. A medal, even. She wouldn't deny Edisto their right to do the same. She learned long ago that awards were often a way to assuage guilt and face the future with hope that lessons were learned.

She left her vehicle, and as she beeped it locked someone called, "Hey, Ms. Morgan." She waved, not quite sure of the name of the gentleman who had no problem recognizing her. She reached the building and opened the door for an older lady. "Thanks so much, Ms. Morgan." Residents called her Ms. Morgan everywhere she went. BI-LO, Whaleys, McConkey's. She liked Callie better. Hopefully, that would change over time, of which she hoped to have much of at the beach.

At the entry to the town council's meeting room, not much larger than Stan's office at the Boston PD, she hesitated in the hall.

"Callie?" Seabrook asked from behind her.

"Yeah," she said, straightening her slacks, checking her belt, analyzing her shoes one more time.

"I think they're waiting for the guest of honor. You haven't changed your mind, have you?"

"No, I've made peace with all that's happened. It's a big step, though." She scanned his smiling blue eyes. "This doesn't bother you? I mean, you've been a part of this force for years."

He shook his head, his laugh lines endearing. "I think all this is what the doctor has ordered for quite some time. Doesn't bother me in any way whatsoever."

With a heave of a sigh, she dipped her head and said, "Then let's do this."

She walked in, and the mass of attendees parted to let her to the front. She passed Sophie and Sprite, the former announcing no spirits since her night with Terrance. Some believed her, others didn't. She was fine with that. Zeus even attended, having wrapped his day on the water, his fully licensed fishing charter business reinstated without question once Callie made the news and then mentioned the discrepancy to the right people.

At the front, Beverly, as mayor of Middleton, sat nearest to the mayor of Edisto, who beamed almost as wide as Callie's mother, his coat and tie replacing the Hawaiian shirts he was renowned for. He claimed full responsibility for hiring Callie to start with.

Minus the smile everyone else in the room wore, the town administrator hung back from the mayor. Callie pledged to make nice with that particular man, like she'd eventually win over Marie. All three of them stood as strong advocates for Edisto Beach, and Callie hoped to connect via that commonality.

As if she'd orchestrated the entire affair, Janet nodded crisply, a sign of approval. They weren't buds but they understood each other better. Callie wanted to, but didn't, ask the Marine how much guilt weighed her down after having rented to two murderers. No doubt she'd spout hard lines about business dealings, but Callie cut her some slack. Without Janet coming on board to throw the party that outted Terrance, none of today might have happened.

Callie even dismissed the notes on her door, the personal note on her car, the one given to Sophie. But pursuing the blame game would only serve to undermine the fragile repairs started with Janet and the town administrator, either certainly capable of the deeds, neither needing the embarrassment. And if either Grant or Terrance penned those threats, well, nothing gained in forcing their admission.

The Rosewoods were nowhere to be seen. Not even a call from Sarah, which made Callie both worry and wonder, yet understand the shame and pain of all that had happened to their family. Grant was in custody, and Callie would be following that case for a while as a major witness. She felt ninety percent sure he'd trashed her yard and messed with her trash can, as if that compared to his murder charge. Ben wouldn't have shown period.

Alex stood to the right with her cameraman. After the arrest, after her role in the tweeting charade that drew Terrance in, she'd declined freelance offers from papers up and down the sea island coastal area and accepted a television offer in Charleston. She hinted of writing a book, no longer needing to shadow Callie to research and break her own stories.

"Welcome to friends and family of Callie Jean Morgan and acquaintances from near and far," the mayor began. "We are thrilled to hold this special meeting to honor Ms. Morgan. But frankly, I think the honor is ours."

The white-headed mayor continued with some humble pontification and thank-yous to almost each person present. Callie remained at attention but let her gaze wander over the forty or so individuals crammed in the small space. And it touched her. Her heart thumped a bit harder as she recalled coming to this beach broken and lost, and in spite of the trauma that littered her path, she'd grown . . . both as a person and as an Edisto islander. These were her people.

Three people were missing. Unfortunately, they'd always be missing, and her heart would never cease to ache in their absence.

Her husband had never doubted her, John ever the cheerleader. Memories of fishing with her daddy, or Captain, as she called him. Callie Scallywag as he called her. Swinging her too-short-feet under Papa Beach's kitchen table, having peanut butter cookies and hot chocolate with her childhood mentor, surged at her, too, raising a choke in her throat. Only now did she comprehend how long ago her Edisto heritage began thanks much to those men.

But as she caught Beverly's face, her mother's delight aglow behind the makeup and under her straw-colored hat, Callie wondered if Beverly knew what handing her that deed to Chelsea Morning would do to heal her daughter. While they harbored a less-than-normal mother-daughter relationship, every once in a while Beverly surprised her. Suddenly she sensed her mother got it right this time. And, of course, she'd remind Callie of it relentlessly from this moment forward.

"Now, by the power invested to me by the people of Edisto Beach and the state of South Carolina," and the mayor paused, a brow raised, "sounds like a wedding, doesn't it?"

The audience burst into laughter.

"Well, it is a union of sorts. Anyway, as the mayor of Edisto, I officially endow Ms. Morgan with the title of Police Chief of Edisto Beach, South Carolina." He reached out, and his fingers waved to someone in the crowd. "Come on up here, young man."

From the mesh of folks, Jeb appeared to stand before his mother. Callie repeated her oath after the mayor, then with moist eyes, Jeb accepted the insignia and reached down to pin them on his mother's collar points.

He took a few seconds longer than he must've expected, and he tried not to frown as the pins challenged him. Callie, however, cherished the delay, enjoying watching her young man accept who she was. Today, anyway.

She stood firm and held her breath, because to breathe would raise emotion. Returning to law enforcement ... accepting this level of responsibility . . . This formality restored her.

It no longer hurt to live.

On this date, she officially embraced her identity, no longer denying what she loved to do. She had returned to the living, and gracious, to have Jeb accept her, and stand beside her, pinning this new life back on her, ranked close to perfection for all she could ever ask for.

The razor-creased, right-out-of-the-wrapper dark blue uniform fit her like a custom made glove, the utility belt her size, the billed hat just right. The stance at attention. Damn, it had been too long.

Jeb finally consummated his task, and with relief and a flash of embarrassment, he moved beside his grandmother, who, like the rest of the room, stood in ovation, recognizing their first woman police chief.

Zeus let out a whistle. Seabrook clapped with gusto, giving her a wink. Francis did a thumbs up then a salute. Beverly hugged her daughter then slid over to grab photo-ops with the mayor and town administrator, Alex making sure of the coverage.

Alex took a second to ask Callie, "Seen my tweets? You're all over them."

But Callie shook her head. "I'll pass." She hadn't looked at tweets since she tossed them to and fro to Terrance. Didn't plan to, either. Not for a very long time.

Callie shook hands until hers ached, though her right palm had healed from the trash can incident. The finger cut deeply in her kitchen, however, had been stitched when they x-rayed her ribs. Another scar added to the collection.

Disbursing to the fire station, attendees addressed the catered fixins from Po Pigs Bo-B-Q laid out on folding tables. The oath of office hadn't taken fifteen minutes, but nobody rushed pork barbecue, so six thirty came and went before the attendees disbanded.

Once the mayor and assorted dignitaries left, the fire chief approached

Callie and Seabrook. "Congratulations, Chief. New chief, rather," he said, acknowledging Seabrook's brief tenure in the job. "Didn't want to interrupt your swearing-in festivities but thought you'd like to know that we declared the Henry Beechum fire an electrical issue. You hadn't asked, and with all that's happened, I can understand."

"Wait, you're kidding me," she said, surprised. She assumed Terrance set the blaze then he, like any arsonist, had watched from the sidelines. That night he'd remained on the opposite side of the street until most of the fire department left.

"No," the chief said. "That house had to be sixty or seventy years old, and he'd upgraded nothing as well as performed some extracurricular wiring of his own."

The house had never changed in Callie's mind, but she attributed that to a child's happy memories. It had been a safe haven when her parents were busy with politics, or when, as she learned later, her father visited his paramour.

"Imagine that." Seabrook grinned. "Guess Terrance wasn't the total menace we thought."

"Right," she said. "He was only a serial killer, not a murderer *and* an arsonist. My bad."

Firemen and admin assistants dismantled the tables and filled trash cans, the leftovers conveniently disappearing into the fire station's kitchen refrigerator.

Seabrook walked Callie to her car. "I'd take you to a celebratory dinner, but seems we just did that."

"I enjoyed it, too. Paper plates and all." They walked a few more yards. The day whirled in her head. "I still can't believe this, Mike."

"Yes, you can. You were meant to wear a badge. You just got lost for a couple of years." He gave her a one-arm hug, then released her abruptly. "Oh, sorry, didn't mean to fraternize with the boss already."

"That'll take some getting used to."

"Fraternizing or being my boss?"

"Yes and yes. What do you think the mayor would think?" They reached her Escape.

Seabrook pursed his mouth and leaned on the car. "He'd be all right, but you also serve at the pleasure of the town council, too. But I can help you with that."

She didn't need to indoctrinate her administration with a scandal though Edisto ran pretty loose. "Maybe we need to cool it for a while," she said, thinking of the grizzly town administrator.

Seabrook playacted a frown, glancing side to side. "Or I might slip into your place after dark." Then he busted out laughing. "Trust me, it won't matter. Everyone's into each other's business out here anyway. Chill, Callie. Go into this job expecting to enjoy it. Today you became a force on this beach, as if you weren't before. Only now you have the weight of the badge behind it, like you always picked at me about. So, hey, Chief. What do you think?"

"Let me take a rain check tonight," she said and patted his sleeve. "I'm looking forward to my porch, some Neil Diamond, and a cold drink.

His expression turned serious. "Drink?"

"Coke, beer, geez, Seabrook, give me some credit. There's not a drop of gin in the house. The minute I got the word I had the job, I gave it to Sophie." She had indeed, but while she still thumbed her nose at having a problem, she knew the job held her to a higher standard. This time she needed to quit. For image's sake, anyway.

"Call if you change your mind." He gave her a peck and left.

She exited the parking lot and drove down Murray Street to Palmetto Boulevard, turned left, and parked alongside the street at Access Nine to the water.

September meant the tourist season receded, but not quite yet into the more dormant winter. She changed shoes in the car, from dress to black sneakers, having thought about this moment since she got up this morning. Then sunglasses on and billed cap affixed smartly, looking every bit the law enforcement official she'd just become, she strolled to the sand and walked southwest, the sparse number of tourists probably thinking she canvassed the beach.

The warm temperature drew sweat around her hairline in spite of the breeze, but not too hot to enjoy the stroll. Nothing would ruin this stroll.

A senior couple passed her headed the other direction, both taking a hard stare at the woman cop in uniform. "Something wrong, Officer?" asked the man.

"No, sir," she replied. "I'm off for the day, just enjoying the evening before heading home."

"That's nice," the woman replied, smiling. "We appreciate what you do for us."

Callie smiled, realizing a cop might hear more thanks than criticisms on Edisto, a place where people vacation and retire to find better quality of life. An entirely different lifestyle than Boston. "May I ask a favor of you?"

"Sure," the man answered.

She slid out her phone. "Would you take my picture? I want to send it to an old friend of mine who didn't realize I worked in heaven."

After some counseling on how to use a smartphone, the gentleman nailed two good shots. Then Callie shook their hands and wished them a wonderful holiday.

Making her way to a pier, she sat on a post near the twelfth access as she sent one of the pics. Once it rang sent, she placed a call, her heart pounding and crazy proud at the same time.

"Well, look at you, Chicklet," Stan answered. "I'm forwarding this to the department. So, how'd it go?"

She laughed. "Stan, I'm about to bust."

She'd waited until after the ceremony to share a conversation with her old boss, even though it risked catching him at home. He and his wife had recently reconciled, to give their marriage another go. She saw Callie as a potential weakness for her husband.

She had a right to think so.

Stan gave one of his *he-he-he* laughs, the bass sounding so James Earl Jones. "You came around. You just needed time." Then he sobered. "Wish I could've been there for you."

"Me, too," she said, watching a line of pelicans coast over her head.

The sea ebbed and flowed, foam leaving trails for terns to play with as they hunted for minute snacks. Tiny shells tumbled and floated, then settled down in new places as the water swirled and retreated.

"John would've been insanely happy for you," Stan added after the moment's silence.

"Yeah, he would." Then she remembered her manners. "How's Misty?"

"Let's keep this about you," he replied. "It's your day. A new chapter, I think. An important one. You going out to celebrate? Have a drink with your subordinate?" He chuckled again. "Messing with you, Chicklet. It's not like they can transfer him to a different department."

She smiled at the extreme difference between Boston's police department and Edisto's. "We don't do departments. We do it all."

The use of *we* tumbled out naturally.

"So, how're you celebrating your big moment, Chief?"

Rays from the setting sun over her right shoulder reflected tangerine and pink off clouds hugging the water's horizon. Not that long ago she dodged this time of day, the memory of John's demise coinciding too harshly with it. She placed a hand on her chest. Not a flutter. Instead, she sensed him closer. This place, this time, this dying light . . . she imagined his arm around her.

"I think I'll celebrate my big moment right here with John a while, Stan."

The End

About the Author

C. Hope Clark holds a fascination with the mystery genre and is author of The Carolina Slade Mystery Series as well as the Edisto Beach Series, both set in her home state of South Carolina. In her previous federal life, she performed administrative investigations and married the agent she met on a bribery investigation. She enjoys nothing more than editing her books on the back porch with him, overlooking the lake with bourbons in hand. She can be found either on the banks of Lake Murray or Edisto Beach with one or two dachshunds in her lap. Hope is also editor of the award-winning Fundsfor Writers.com. Find out more about her at <u>chopeclark.com</u>

Made in the USA
Columbia, SC
14 January 2021